WHEN IN DOUBT . . . RUN.

When the bolt on the front door snapped, I almost jumped out of my skin. The door flew open and I heard someone stumble into my gear, knocking the bucket over as heavy footsteps moved through the entryway. I turned, heart pounding, but it was just Dragan, back early. He stepped into the living room as the door swung shut back behind him with a thud.

"Hey," I said, switching off the TV. He didn't answer. He was still dressed in his military uniform, his pistol still strapped to his hip. His eyes were wide.

"D?"

Something was wrong. His cropped salt-and-pepper hair was spiky with sweat and grease, and the lines in his face looked deeper than usual. He was pale, and the rims of his lower eyelids were the color of a bruise.

"Sam," he said distantly. "Get your things."

THE
BURN ZONE

JAMES K. DECKER

A ROC BOOK

ROC
Published by New American Library, a division of
Penguin Group (USA) Inc., 375 Hudson Street,
New York, New York 10014, USA
Penguin Group (Canada), 90 Eglinton Avenue East, Suite 700, Toronto,
Ontario M4P 2Y3, Canada (a division of Pearson Penguin Canada Inc.)
Penguin Books Ltd., 80 Strand, London WC2R 0RL, England
Penguin Ireland, 25 St. Stephen's Green, Dublin 2,
Ireland (a division of Penguin Books Ltd.)
Penguin Group (Australia), 707 Collins Street, Melbourne, Victoria 3008,
Australia (a division of Pearson Australia Group Pty. Ltd.)
Penguin Books India Pvt. Ltd., 11 Community Centre, Panchsheel Park,
New Delhi–110 017, India
Penguin Group (NZ), 67 Apollo Drive, Rosedale, Auckland 0632,
New Zealand (a division of Pearson New Zealand Ltd.)
Penguin Books, Rosebank Office Park, 181 Jan Smuts Avenue,
Parktown North 2193, South Africa
Penguin China, B7 Jiaming Center, 27 East Third Ring Road North,
Chaoyang District, Beijing 100020, China

Penguin Books Ltd., Registered Offices:
80 Strand, London WC2R 0RL, England

First published by Roc, an imprint of New American Library,
a division of Penguin Group (USA) Inc.

First Printing, February 2013
10 9 8 7 6 5 4 3 2 1

 REGISTERED TRADEMARK — MARCA REGISTRADA

Printed in the United States of America

PUBLISHER'S NOTE
This is a work of fiction. Names, characters, places, and incidents either are the
product of the author's imagination or are used fictitiously, and any resemblance
to actual persons, living or dead, business establishments, events, or locales is
entirely coincidental.
    The publisher does not have any control over and does not assume any respon-
sibility for author or third-party Web sites or their content.

ALWAYS LEARNING   **PEARSON**

For Mom and Dad

Acknowledgments

Big thanks to Jessica Wade for all of her hard work and support, as well as to Brad Brownson, Jesse Feldman, Rosanne Romanello, Jodi Rosoff, and all of the other fine folks at Roc for helping me put this novel together and make it the best it could be. I would also like to thank artist Dave Seeley and art director Patrick Kang for such a terrific cover—I couldn't have hoped for a better one. Thanks also to my agent, Ginger Clark, who has helped me in more ways than I can count and whom I am very lucky to have in my corner. Thanks to Dana Kaye for her fantastic publicity work, and also to Richard Kadrey, Robert J. Sawyer and Mira Grant for taking time out of their busy schedules to read and blurb the book for me. On a technical note, thanks to Karin Hsieh for all of the assistance with things Mandarin, and of course, thanks to my wife, Kim, for putting up with the hours and hours of writing.

Chapter One

The elevator rattled its way up toward my floor as I leaned back, eyes closed, only half-aware of the world around me. The bitter aftertaste of Zen oil lingered on my tongue, and while it still had me pleasantly disconnected my thoughts buzzed around in circles beneath the haze. I felt like I should be upset, or afraid ... like I should be freaking out or something, but I wasn't any of those things. I didn't know how to feel anymore, about anything.

"To anyone receiving this transmission ..."

The voice, a foreign man speaking butchered Mandarin, sounded distant, rising through a faint static whine from over the ad box maybe? Somewhere nearby.

"... the race you call the haan are not ..." More static. *"... this is not a dream. ..."*

I snorted as the elevator jostled me out of my trance, and shook my head to clear it. I rubbed my eyes, and as I took a wobbly step forward I saw the ad box screen mounted inside the door flicker to display a panel of cool electric gray.

"Xiao-Xing?" a female voice asked, issuing from the speaker underneath. When I didn't answer, it tried again. "Sam?"

"Not now," I said, chewing my lip.

"Sorry, but elevators cost money, you know. I have two names on record matching your ID. Which do you prefer?"

"Sam, I guess." The box screen flickered, updating info. "Was that you talking, before?"

"Sorry?"

"Something about a transmission? The haan? I thought I heard something."

"It wasn't me. Since you have a moment, though, I would like to talk to you about—"

"Do you have any news?" I asked it. "About the bombing? Do you know anything?"

The A.I. paused, then tried another tack.

"Would you like to be sexy?" it asked.

I laughed a little at that, a giggle that sounded a little more unhinged the longer it went on.

"I am sexy," I breathed.

"Well, maybe," the A.I. responded, sounding a bit skeptical.

The screen dissolved the standby gray, and splashed the Sultrex logo while saxophone music began to pipe softly through.

"Look, do you know anything about the bomb?" I asked again.

"No, Sam," it said, "but I do know this; as you're probably aware, given your calorie allotment, it is impossible for you to naturally develop the kinds of curves all women want and all men desire, but why be a victim of circumstances beyond your control?"

The elevator shook to a stop, and I hoisted my gear as the screen displayed two images of me. On the left, under the word *before*, was a shot it had taken of me when I first got on, standing there with my gear and covered in sweat. On the right, under the word *after*, was the exact same shot manipulated so that in place of my more-or-less flat chest was a big set of computer-generated tits.

They strained against the material of my tank top, while a drop of sweat did a slow roll down into the crevice between them. I laughed again, a little.

"Nice touch."

"It came out of the latest eye-tracking study," the A.I. admitted.

"Uh-huh."

"For a very reasonable fee, you could be one of the most desirable young women in Hangfei—"

"Who says I'm not?"

"More people than you might think."

"I gotta go."

"Don't forget, there is a scheduled demolition along the Impact rim tonight," it said. "Curfew will be in—"

The A.I. was still yammering as the elevator door squealed open and carried the screen away with it into the wall. I stepped out under the buzzing overhead in the hallway and dug into one pocket to find my last loose cigarillo, bent but not broken. I stuck it in the corner of my mouth and crunched down on the end with my teeth as I cracked my back. With the heat wave, washing windows up on Ginzho Tower was brutal, and a day of squeegeeing biocide and smog resin off hot glass had left my brain cooked. The cool air felt like water trickling down over my burned face, chest, and shoulders.

As I started down the hall, I crooked my neck, a motor cortex key that brought up the 3i front end. The braided lanyard from my wet drive implant brushed my shoulder as the holographic display appeared in front of my face with its candy pink neon borders, and immediately social taps from friends, notifications, and ads sprinkled into the foreground. The word cloud that formed in the corner of one eye was ugly, full of variations on bomb, suicide, attack, and dead. That last one flashed on headline tickers, the feeds a fever of rising death counts while laying bets on what horrible thing might come next. I glanced left to screen out the static, and most of the little icons scattered. I tapped friends back to let them know I was okay, and then tuned out the tide of chatter as I headed down the hall toward home.

The other apartment doors were all showing red locks, and I clomped past them, searching my pockets for a light. When I turned the corner I heard my surrogate haan, Tānchi, crying, and his low, shuddering keen snapped me out of it a little as it carried down the hallway. Already I could sense him, a faint haze of anxiety, fear, and hunger—always hunger.

I sent him a single ping and immediately the wailing stopped. His mood turned on a dime, and the cluster of haan brain-band mites tingled deep in my forehead as he reached out to make contact. Requests started trickling in and getting rejected by the 3i's junk call filter as he picked at any and every open socket, trying to say hi. When I got a little closer the mites locked in fully on his signals and he was there, like a tickle at the edges of my mind. An excited signal spiked through and nicked my visual cortex, causing two ghostly scaleflies, their single compound eyes flashing, to jitter through the air in front of me along with a brief, flickering image of a surrogate formula bottle that quickly faded.

"Mommy's home," I singsonged around the cigarillo.

He heard me and I felt a surge, a happy bubbling that always made me smile no matter how bad my day had been.

It faltered as I approached the front door, though. I could see the spray paint from down the hall. Tānchi was my third surrogate so far since we moved here, and I'd thought the people in our building were starting to get used to it. As I got closer I could make out the sloppy squiggles of hanzi that had dribbled before drying.

They eat—we starve.

I abandoned the cigarillo, tucking it behind one ear

and spitting out a fleck of tobacco. My mood soured, and pulled me from Tānchi's happy little wave, but I tried to shake it off. It was just paint. I didn't want to get Tānchi upset with a bunch of bad bleed-back, and it wasn't like there wasn't any truth to it. With the world population at just under fifteen billion, food scarcity was a problem even before the haan showed up. Even our country had been affected, and now there was no getting around the fact that the haan took the majority of the food we produced just to survive. The gamble would pay off in the long run, or so they said, but it was easy to forget how much they did for us when you went to bed hungry every night like some lost worlder.

I took a deep breath and let it out slow. It wasn't worth scaring Tānchi over. It wasn't a bomb, say, or something even worse. It was just paint.

I used my badge to trigger the lock and then pushed open the door, feeling the anticipation rise from the direction of the junkyard crib across the room where a single scalefly buzzed in a lazy circle around a hanging mobile. It lit down on the edge of the crib's backboard, scraping its wings together as it used its hooklike forelegs to preen its stinging proboscis and its black marble eye. The shadows of Tānchi's spindly, delicate little webbed fingers danced on the wall next to it.

I put down my washer rigging, along with the bucket of squeegees and glass cleaner, next to the worn counter where a tin pot sat still dirty on the hot plate. Even in the dark I could see the clutter that had built up. Dirty clothes were draped over the sofa and chairs, and pretty much every counter and tabletop had hit capacity. I had some major cleaning to do.

Ling hobbled out from the kitchen, peering up at me from under heavy, wrinkled eyelids and looking tired. She noticed the spray paint on the door as it swung shut, and put one hand over her mouth.

"It's okay," I told her. "It's no big deal."

"I didn't even hear—"

"It's okay, Ling, really." I glanced back. "I bet you anything it was that little Heng shit. Punk's going to end up in jail for sure. Everything go okay?"

She nodded and wrinkled her nose. "I fed it at the times you said. I entered the log too, like you said."

I peered through the bars of the crib, the worry an unconscious habit. Ling noticed and added, "I know they're delicate. I was careful."

"Sorry, I know. Thanks for doing it."

"They're so ugly." She frowned, the wrinkles in her face deepening. "Do you need the stipend that bad? Doesn't your father take care of you?"

"Guardian," I corrected. She waved a bony hand at me. "We both work. What do you want?"

She looked at me critically.

"You're twenty now," she said. "Why are you still here anyway? You should be on your own."

"I was on my own until I was twelve. Cut me some slack."

"You're not twelve anymore. You're a woman now." She shook out a cigarette of her pack, staining the end pink as she held it between her lips.

"Yeah, I know."

"Find a man," she said, lighting the smoke and sucking down a small gray cloud. "Get on the list to have a real baby, not one of those."

My face flushed, making the sunburn flare up. I reminded myself that Ling didn't know.

"Why don't you like them?" I said, nodding over at the crib.

"They don't belong here."

"Well, they're stranded, Ling. It's not like they have a choice. Besides, we're better off now, aren't we?"

She waved her hand again, dismissive. Ling was old,

and probably didn't care much about brain band, jump-space gates, or graviton tech. I thought she would have at least cared about the defense shield the haan were building for us, but maybe she didn't care much about that either. It was a big-ticket item for me. When the first pieces started going up in six months, I'd feel a lot better.

Ling watched Tānchi paw at the air, the scalefly buzzing in a circle above him, and sighed. "We shouldn't let them breed."

"They have to have some or they'll die out."

"Let them die out. Governor Hwong should put a stop to it. He would never agree to this."

"He did, though."

She frowned again. She wouldn't criticize Governor Hwong—her loyalty to him was too ingrained—but a look of betrayal flashed in her eyes. No one was sure exactly why the haan wanted the human-haan surrogate program, or exactly why Hwong agreed to it. Some thought the haan were controlling him. Others thought the haan had made the flow of tech and the promise of the defense screen dependent on it. There were a million theories as to why the haan would put their fragile young in our brutish hands, but if nothing else it was a good show of how little a threat they really were. They were immune to all disease and most toxins, but their bodies broke all too easily. Wherever they came from, it was a gentler world than ours.

"They know how hard they make it, Ling," I said. "They hate how hard they make it. They'd leave if they could."

"Your father should put a stop to it," Ling said. I almost corrected her again, but didn't bother. "How is he anyway?"

"Okay, I guess. He's on patrol in Měnggǔ Province and I haven't heard from him in a while. He's been kind of blowing me off."

"Maybe he found a girl there," Ling joked.

"He wouldn't—" I started, meaning to say that Dragan wouldn't hook up with a Pan-Slav when of course, he was Pan-Slav himself, or used to be. "He doesn't have a girl," I snipped instead, and Ling smiled. "They've probably got him off dodging bullets, or . . ."

I stopped myself before I went down that road again. I didn't like to think about him over there. The foreign buildup to the south and offshore was bad, but the Pan-Slav border territories, especially the Měnggǔ and Hasakesitan provinces, were the worst. The Pan-Slav Emirates were falling apart, and they were looking across the border at us like we were the last floating straw to grab on to. All kinds of weapons, even nukes and biological stuff, had been split up by new borders, and the pieces were getting grabbed up by desperate, starving lunatics with Dragan right there in the thick of it.

"Your father is brave," Ling said. "He is there to keep us safe, to keep you safe."

"Once it's up we should just wipe them out," I muttered. "We could do it then. Six months to start, another year to build, and then we should just . . . wipe them all out."

"It's not so simple."

"Well, not easy like Měnggǔ or Hasakesitan, but once the shield's active, what's to stop us?"

"Those territories were spent," she said. "Without the tech to make the space valuable, it was barren and their people were dying. They had to let us take it. This is different."

"I know," I said. "I'm sorry, Ling. I'll just be glad when he's back in Hangfei. He should be in tomorrow night."

"Good."

"Look, thanks for covering, really. I know you don't get it, but I need this gig."

I fished a short stack of coin along with a crumpled

paper bill from my pocket, and put the coins in her hand, curling her knobby fingers around them.

"You're a good girl," she said.

"Thanks." I smoothed out the red bill and held it out so she could see. "Got any shine back in your place?"

She grinned, pinching the cigarette in her lips, and reached into the pocket of her knit shawl. She drew out a glass pint bottle filled with crystal clear liquid and handed it to me. As I took it, she plucked the bill from between my fingers.

"Thanks again," I said. "He'll settle down once I feed him. You have a good night, Ling."

She patted my cheek, and her smile faded a little.

"They are a mistake," she said, nodding toward the crib.

She hobbled past me, then out the front door and back down the hall toward her apartment. When the door closed, Tānchi keened again, and I saw him fidget behind the crib's bars.

"Hey, sweetie."

I scratched my head and remembered the smoke tucked behind my ear. I found my lighter in the bottom of one pocket and sparked it up, dragging until the crackling fibers formed a cherry. I sucked in a lungful and felt the nicotine-tetraz blend begin to calm the gnawing in my belly, at least a little. I blew the smoke out through my nose and felt the kid relax a little. Not because of the chems—they didn't have any effect on him—but because the mite connection worked both ways and so when my brain chilled, his did a little too.

It meant he sensed when something was wrong too, though, and I could feel anxiety pricking in his mind as I approached the crib. His big, flat, ember orange eyes glowed in the shadows, looking up at me as I leaned over and planted a kiss on the cool, glassy surface of his forehead.

"It's okay," I told him. I wasn't sure he believed me, but then, I wasn't sure I believed me either. One bombing had shocked me. Two had worried me. After that . . . I wondered if this was going to pass for normal now, if it would just keep getting worse. Were the days leading up to that first attack the last normal ones any of us would have and we just didn't know it? Was this really just the beginning?

Tānchi's eyes stared up at me, more anxiety bubbling up over our connection.

"Sorry."

I reached down and carefully picked him up out of the crib still in his swaddle of blankets, then cradled him in my arms and let him reach up to paw my face.

"Don't listen to Ling," I told him. "You're very cute."

Tānchi farted sour air out of his feeding vent and I laughed to myself. I carried him across the room and took the second-to-last surrogate ration from the satchel hanging next to the fridge where the display said there was one human ration left—scalefly, of course. The fact that the haan pests were edible was supposed to be the one consolation for getting stuck with them, but considering how they tasted, it wasn't much of a consolation to me.

Taste aside, my stomach felt hollow, but I didn't want Dragan to come back to nothing at all. They'd send him home with a fresh ration punch sheet, but they always backdated them and the punches wouldn't be redeemable until the next day. I took another puff off the cigarillo and then went back to plop down on the couch in front of the TV. My reflection looked bony in the windowed wall behind it, a pale ghost in front of the city lights beyond where streams of air traffic painted lines in the night sky.

The canister's black haan certificate overlapped the human one, both stickers askew above the Shiliuyuán logo. The round authorization stamp, basically a haan signature, was orange this time around instead of red like it had been since my first surrogate at thirteen. The symbol was different too, I'd noticed. Under that were my surrogate ID number and the name SAM Shao. Tānchi began reaching for the canister as I found the remote.

SAM. Dragan tagged me with the nickname after a detail with an American expat—it stood for Surface to Air Missile, and was also a Western name. He said it fit me because I left everywhere I went looking like a bomb went off. Now practically every A.I. in Hangfei used it.

Guardian. I thought about how quick I'd been to correct Ling. True, Dragan wasn't my real father, but I still felt guilty for saying it. It wasn't like I was any great prize. There was a reason meat farmers grabbed people like me—when they chopped us into scrapcake and sold us on the black market, no one cared. When Dragan broke me and the others out of there, I wasn't anything to take home—a used-up twelve-year-old train wreck who kept a knife under her pillow and had panic attacks—but that's what he did. He took me home. He never judged me, or pitied me. Why couldn't I call him my father?

Tānchi pawed my face, the ghost image of his bottle appearing and then fading as a throb of hunger seeped in through the mites. It ached, making my own stomach feel even hollower, but beneath it was that constant warm thread that bonded us, and I smiled. Ling thought she was helping with her prodding about a family, but I'd lost that option a long time ago. Haan were the only children that would ever truly be mine, and I was okay with that.

"Sorry," I told him. "Long day."

I cracked the seal on the top of the bottle, and felt it warm in my hand as I pulled out the rubber tube. At the sound, two little hands with their five delicate fingers reached out of the cocoon of blankets and began to grope at the air in front of his face, which was the color and texture of smoked crystal. The wrinkled gray mass of brains that lurked behind his bulbous forehead shifted eagerly, the second, smaller one drawing up beneath it and shuddering in the dark fluid there. Behind his honeycomb lattice of ribs, his tiny heart beat a steady samba at the thought of gorging. With my free hand, I used my phone to enter the feeding time into the online worksheet.

Once I got the confirmation, I pointed the business end of the bottle toward his wide, contoured face, making a spaceship noise in the back of my throat as he chattered happily.

"Coming in," I said, moving the bottle closer. "Beginning docking sequence . . ."

When the tube touched his glassy lips, his mouth and chin dissolved into cool smoke. As the tube was sucked down into the tiny cloud to coil inside his belly, his hands grabbed hold of the bottle and I heard a greedy sigh.

"Easy there," I said.

My stomach growled as I watched the haan child eat, and I took another drag on the smoke to compensate. Swaddled in his blankets, he clutched the silver canister to his little chest in a death grip, consuming calories at a rate that still amazed me every time I saw it. The cylinder, a variant on haan inversion tech, contained liters even though it fit neatly in my palm. Calorie-wise, that one bottle alone could easily feed me and Dragan for a week if it weren't for the fact that, despite being processed from feedlot stores, haan formula would rupture a human's intestines inside of a minute.

The scalefly landed on the canister's bottom, and I waved it away as I put one foot up on the coffee table next to a cluster of shot glasses packed with chewed, lipstick-kissed butts and flipped on the TV.

The channels were full of bomb news. I'd thought I

wanted to know, like it would help somehow, but the barrage of video footage, blood, bones, and black smoke turned me off. I couldn't watch it, not right now.

". . . explosives were smuggled in via a one-man skiff and then carried across the tidal flats to avoid detection at the Hangfei gates," a reporter rapped out as I flicked past. On the next channel, the headline CYBER ATTACK hovered over another talking head. A crawl at the bottom of the screen showed the current food index for the different feedlots. Most stayed steady while one, feedlot five, had gone up another tick. That was eighty-three point one percent in total now being sent directly to the haan.

". . . suspect that the mysterious signal, first noticed a month ago buried in the time server feed, may be part of an ongoing cyber-terrorism attack whose purpose is not yet known. All attempts to block the signal have so far failed, as have all attempts to decipher—"

I flipped again.

"The bombing took the lives of sixty-three people, and completely destroyed the largest ration distribution center in the borough—"

Flip.

". . . how long before a conventional bombing turns to something far worse such as nuclear, or even biological? We need to strike first or . . ."

The camera zoomed in on the ocean's horizon where the ever-present fleet of foreign ships sat like a city skyline, the sky above it streaked with jet contrails.

I punched in the code for my friend Vamp's site and jumped away to Channel X, replacing the stream of reality with a welcome splash of electric glitz.

He'd changed his site backdrop to a new fan pic, a tall, whip-thin black girl in a two-piece that didn't leave much to the imagination. She had a big Afro and lip gloss and made the signature X sign with her index fingers. At the bottom of the screen, the countdown to the Fangwenzhe

Festival ticked off the remaining thirty or so hours second by second.

I glanced down as Tānchi's little body shuddered with pleasure, and smiled. After a minute the last of the gelatin disappeared and he squeezed the canister one last time before stretching, shivering, and then going limp in a fit of post-gorging bliss. He groped with one little hand and when I reached down he gripped my index finger. The tube slithered back into the bottle, and his face turned solid again, lit by the mellow orange glow from his big, lidless eyes. When the twin trios of pinprick pupils found me, I felt a low rush of exhausted happiness. Then his digestion kicked into overdrive and he passed out.

As he snoozed, I cruised to Channel X's main page where a map of the city displayed the blue specks of active users like scattered stars. Under that he'd posted a countdown to the haan's Phase Five tech, which was due to be released to us in six months, along with a copy of the catalogue. We'd get the Escher Field, second-generation rations, limited freestanding gate portals, and of course, the defense shield.

One of the little pink hearts throbbed in the corner of the 3i window where a tap from Vamp let me know he'd posted the music cracks I'd been after. I pulled the files down to my phone and rang him up.

"Hey, Sam," he said. "You get my post?"

"Yeah, thanks. Nice backdrop."

"I thought you'd like it."

"That your new girlfriend?"

"She wishes. She's the lucky winner."

I rolled my eyes. "Tell me you're not still doing that."

"Jealous?"

"Hey, I just feel bad for her," I said.

"It's for a good cause."

"What, the 'you getting laid foundation'?"

"In my heart, Sam. That's where that hurts."

"Upkeep for your pirate site and spying on security doesn't count as a good cause," I said, a smile creeping over my face. "You just like to date your fan mail."

"Fame is a blessing, but also a curse, I'm sorry to say. Besides, how else would you have met me and then subsequently gotten both of us banned from the Joy Coffee Bar for life?"

"That was your fault."

Normally he would have kept ribbing me. Our infamous contest date, which also got us kicked out of the skate park, was usually ripe territory, so when he didn't respond my smile began to fade. I knew what he was going to ask next.

"You see the bombing from where you were?"

"No," I said, "but I heard it."

"Did you see the blast site on the—"

"I don't want to talk about it right now, okay?"

"Sure. Okay." He got quiet for a minute. "You getting psyched for the festival?"

"Totally. I need it this year." I paused. "Can we do something fun tomorrow?"

"Like what?"

"I don't know. Something fun. Here, though. I've got the kid. Is that okay?"

He didn't let on, but I knew haan babies creeped Vamp out a little. He hesitated a little, so I pushed.

"I just want to forget all this, you know? Just for a while."

"No, I know," he said. "You got it."

"You don't have plans?"

"Nope, I'm all yours."

My smile came back.

"Dragan's back tomorrow, right?"

"Yeah, but not until late."

"You must be relieved."

"Yeah."

"How's he holding up over there?"

"I don't know ... he's been kind of blowing me off."

"He probably scored some primo Pan-Slav tail."

"He did not," I said. My hackles went up, but just then the floor vibrated, and outside a soft rumble began to swell. Through the plate-glass window, I saw a distant light flash above the clouds and I looked off toward the skyline for the source. At first I thought it was another bomb, but it wasn't. Past the colorful sprawl of neon lights, flashing ads, and coursing air and street traffic, off where the electric pulse trickled and faded to black at the rim, one of the dark towers there had begun a slow-motion fall. I could see it silhouetted against the faint blue light of the dome behind it as crews chipped away at the urban ruins that still surrounded the Impact site.

Right, the demolition. The ad box had tried to remind me. They were doing more demo tonight, and right in our backyard this time. Any drug cookers and meat farmers they shook out would come running right into our little warren of Tùzi-wō, with security right behind them.

"Perfect," I muttered, hoisting myself off the couch and carrying Tānchi over to the window.

The rumble swelled above the shaking of the air conditioner as hundreds of stories' worth of concrete and glass collapsed into a growing black cloud that billowed out in front of the blue force field and the towering hulk of the haan ship behind it.

Over thirty years they'd been here now. A stray graviton eddy on the platform of what used to be Shiliuyuán Station was about all the warning anyone got that they were coming, or so the story went. Then a quarter million people were gone in the blink of an eye, the haan's force field dome growing around their ship while the rubble still smoldered. They hid then, safe behind that field, until they could convince us that what happened was an accident and not an attack. I understood the haan better than most, I thought, but even so I had to wonder when I looked at that field what promise they could possibly have made that kept us from retaliating when people still screamed for it even now.

I'd never know. It was all classified, and it all happened before my time. Even Dragan was just a kid, drinking vodka or whatever eleven-year-olds did over in the Pan-Slav Emirates. Whatever they'd promised, it wasn't anything they'd given us so far—the food was payment for that. Not the defense shield. Something else. Something better.

We will save you. It's all they would say.

"You're inside, right?" Vamp asked.

"Yeah, but I have to go back out."

"You're nuts. The sweep's going to be up your ass in like an hour."

"I know, but I'm out of meds."

"Are you kidding me?"

"Don't start."

"I'm not starting, I'm just saying a little Zen oil here and there is one thing, but—"

"That's starting."

"I'm just saying there's a reason all that shit got legalized. They want to keep everyone fuzzy. Don't play into it."

"I want to be fuzzy," I said. "I need to be fuzzy. When I'm not fuzzy I . . ."

I didn't know how to put it. When Vamp and I met, I'd already been living with Dragan for a couple of years. He didn't know what things were like before that, the things that happened to me and the things I'd done.

"What do you want me to say?" I said instead. "I'm a mess."

"It's okay," he said. "I get it."

He didn't, though. He thought he did, but he didn't, and I didn't want him to.

"It's not narcs anyway," I said as a warble snuck into my voice. "These are legit meds. I don't sleep without them, Vamp. I—"

"It's okay. Sam, I know."

The bundle of blankets had begun to get really warm as Tānchi slipped deeper into his food coma. I could feel his rising body heat against my chest and neck as I looked out the window to where the distant dust cloud formed a column, rising high into the night sky. If I was going to go, I had to get out there and back before the sweep, and before Tānchi's last feeding.

I realized then that I really didn't have very much time at all, and if I didn't make it I was going to be in for a long night.

"I have to go," I said.

"What about the kid?"

"I'll bring him with me. It's just down the block. I'll be careful."

"Okay, get going. Run the new eyebot build, though. We're tracking the sweep live, and the more nodes the better."

"I'll be back in before they get this far."

"Just run it. You never know."

I lowered Tānchi back into his crib and tucked the blankets around him, then crossed to the balcony door and slid it open. The concrete floor outside vibrated under my feet as the racket rolled across the city like thunder. A blue arc of electricity snapped up from the expanding cloud and flashed over the rim, a huge, electric tentacle that touched the bubble of light in the distance. A bright, hexagonal mesh pulsed around the strike point, lighting up the northern face of the looming ship. White-hot flakes tumbled down the side of the force field as the glow faded, and the blanket of clouds above formed a huge, lazy whirlpool over the dome's peak.

"Damn it," I whispered. The streets were buzzing—I could hear it from fifty stories up. A lockdown would shut the markets down early. They'd be a madhouse right up until the point they had to scatter.

I looked back through the balcony doorway. Should I really take him with me out there? Or would he be okay until I got back?

"Vamp, I gotta go."

I turned away from the crumbling bit of skyline and headed back in, canned air chilling the sweat on the back of my neck.

"Run the app."

"I will. Bye."

I hung up and stood there for a minute, not sure what to do first. It might be safer to leave Tānchi, but it was also against the law. I crossed back to the crib and reached down to get him ready to go out.

When the bolt on the front door snapped, I almost jumped out of my skin. The door flew open and I heard someone stumble into my gear, knocking the bucket over as heavy footsteps moved through the entryway. I turned, heart pounding, but it was just Dragan, back early. He stepped into the living room as the door swung shut back behind him with a thud.

"Hey," I said, switching off the TV. He didn't answer. He was still dressed in his military uniform, his pistol still strapped to his hip. His eyes were wide.

"D?"

Something was wrong. His cropped salt-and-pepper hair was spiky with sweat and grease, and the lines in his face looked deeper than usual. He was pale, making the wire-thin scar on his cheek stand out raw red, and the rims of his lower eyelids were the color of a bruise.

"Sam," he said distantly. "Get your things."

"What?"

He didn't answer. He just stepped farther into the room, a kind of slow shuffle, and I noticed something, a stain of some kind, spattered on the front of his uniform.

"Is that blood?" I asked. He still wouldn't look at me. He was just staring straight ahead like he didn't know where he was, or who I was.

"What's the matter? You're freaking me out."

"Is there any food left?" he asked.

"One ration."

He nodded. "Get it."

"Didn't they pay you a new ration sheet?"

"It's gone," he said distantly.

"What?"

"It's gone. Get the ration."

I crossed over to him, and when I touched his arm he flinched.

"D, you're scaring the shit out of me."

"Sorry," he said, and for just a second whatever else it was that was on his mind shifted to the background. For just a second, he looked at me the way he had that day he found me, and still did whenever he stopped thinking about himself and there was only me.

"It's okay," I said. "I'm okay."

My voice had turned hoarse all of a sudden, and my face began to get hot. Something was wrong. Really wrong.

I saw the security part of him tick off that I wasn't in any immediate trouble, and then his eyes drifted over the apartment. For just a second, irritation flared up on his face, but it died just as quick, even as he spoke.

"What the hell did you do to this place?" His voice sounded far off, though, his words forgotten as soon as he said them. He wiped his face with his hand and stared out the big window, off toward the force field dome and the ship on the other side.

"Dragan . . ."

"She's dead," he whispered. There were tears in his eyes.

"Who?" I asked, but he just shook his head.

"We're leaving. Now."

"What?"

"Now," he said. "Take only what you need."

"We can't just leave, D. What's wrong with you?"

"Listen," he said, raising his voice. "Take just what you need and—"

Tānchi squawked from the other side of the room, and at the sound Dragan's eyes went wide. He stepped back, crashing into the wet bar and knocking glasses down to shatter on the floor. He turned to the crib, and I saw his hand move toward his gun.

"Dragan!"

He eased his hand back down, still not taking his eyes off the kid.

"Now," he said. "We're leaving here in five minutes."

His boots crunched through the broken glass as he crossed to the doorway and down the hall to his bedroom. I went to Tānchi and stroked his cheek, humming softly until the mewling stopped. His slack limbs twitched as he metabolized, still warm to the touch, but when he looked up at me from the crib, his flame orange eyes were alert. His growing fear seeped through the mites, like a spastic electric current that sent jolts through my forehead.

"It's okay," I told him. Dragan came tromping back into the living room, and I saw he had a second gun in his hand, which he slipped into his belt just behind the first.

"Leave it," he said.

"What . . . Tānchi?"

"Leave it."

"Dragan, we can't just leave him here. If he doesn't get fed he could die—"

"Don't argue with me, Sam!"

The front door's knob turned, and the door thumped as the bolt kept it from opening. Dragan spun around and drew his pistol as something pounded against the other side, hard.

"Dragan . . ."

"They tracked me," he said to himself.

A loud boom shook the apartment and sent an avalanche of paper trash sliding off the kitchen counter. A second crash came as the front door's bolt tore loose from the jamb and it blew open in a shower of splinters and drywall powder. Tānchi screamed as Dragan grabbed my wrist and pulled me close, hissing into my ear.

"When I say run, you run," he said. I nodded. "If you don't hear from me in an hour, I've arranged a transport out of the country to Duongroi. Go to Central Transport and—"

"Duongroi? D, why?"

"Please, Sam, just—"

He stopped short as several figures came tromping through the doorway.

"Nobody move," a woman's voice said from behind him.

Dragan put his hand on my cheek.

"You're going to hear some things about me," he said. "Don't believe them. I love you like you were my own flesh and blood, Sam. Remember that."

A lump rose in my throat as two men and a woman, all dressed in black body armor, came marching into the room with us through a haze of dust. Their scaly, formfitting combat suits hummed, creating static that made my hair stand on end, and their faces were shielded by light disruptors, giving their hooded heads the look of empty black eggshells.

Dragan turned, standing between us and facing them. He aimed the pistol, but before he could get a shot off, the closest soldier lashed out in a blur and clamped down on his wrist. Dragan fired twice, the bullets thudding into the far wall before the suit whined and I heard the crack of bone. He grunted, and the gun clunked down onto the floor between them. The goon stomped on it and kicked it back behind him with his boot.

Still pinned, Dragan reached back with his free hand and drew the second pistol he'd tucked in his belt. He plowed into the guy who had his wrist, and fired two shots into his side while the other soldiers piled on.

"Now!" he yelled. "Sam, Go!"

Across the room I could see the front door hanging from one twisted hinge, offering a clear path to the hallway outside.

"Go!"

The two men held Dragan while the woman stepped in. A round red stamp stood out on her armor's right shoulder plate, marking her as the ranking soldier. She took two steps toward Dragan, and as he struggled against the men she fired the heel of her boot into his chest. His eyes bugged, and his face turned purple as blood coughed from his mouth and his legs dropped out from under him.

I looked to the open doorway again and then back at Dragan, bouncing between decisions like an ignition that wouldn't quite catch. Fear cut deeper and deeper through the Zen fog until my brain felt like a fuse inside was threatening to trip.

Do something.

Spotting Ling's bottle of shine on the floor in front of the wet bar snapped me out of it. I snatched it up and stormed toward the woman, wielding the bottle like a club. She looked over just as I swung the bottle into the blur that covered her face. The glass broke, splashing liquor, and several scaleflies buzzed away from her shoulder plates as she staggered back. I whipped the jagged neck around, spraying alcohol and blood as I slashed at her again.

Dragan spat and managed to suck in a breath. He ripped one arm free from the guy behind him and then turned and delivered a vicious head butt. His forehead disappeared into the dispersion field and I heard a solid crunch. When the soldier fell back, blood squirted from out of the blur.

"Control them!" the woman barked.

One of the soldiers unclipped a graviton emitter from his belt and aimed it at Dragan. A low hum made the furniture vibrate as the field washed over him and he staggered, legs folding underneath him. The hum went up in pitch, and Dragan fell to his knees, struggling to keep his head lifted.

I dropped the bottle neck and took the knife out of my pocket, flicking the blade out as I made a beeline for the guy holding Dragan with no idea what I would do when I got there. I used the little blade to scrape stubborn residue off windows; it would never penetrate combat armor. . . .

The guy used the emitter to drag Dragan toward him, ready to hit him once he was in range, and I stabbed the point of the knife through the seam at his knee. It didn't go all the way in, but enough to make the guy yell and spin around. When he did, the emitter's field moved off Dragan and sucked the end table next to him across the room. It crashed against the wall as he reached down and jerked the knife out.

"You little—"

Dragan was back on his feet and hammered the guy in the face with one fist. He had reached back to hit him again when an armored fist closed around my arm and jerked me away.

"Stop," the woman said.

Dragan stopped in midswing, his eyes going wide as

she put her other hand over my throat and squeezed, just a little.

"She doesn't know anything," Dragan gasped. "Just let her go . . . please."

She stepped toward him and I followed desperately, toes barely touching the floor.

"Get his wet drive," she ordered. Two of the soldiers held Dragan, one of them pushing his head down until his chin touched his chest while the other parted the spiky hair at the base of his skull.

"It's not there," he said. "He ditched it."

"Search him. Find the twistkey."

One of the soldiers stood back and aimed a scanner, running it down the length of his body. I caught a glimpse of bones and soft tissue moving across the screen, along with buttons and equipment standing out in sharp relief.

"He doesn't have it," the soldier said. "Just the standard-issue security override." The hand squeezed my neck a little harder.

"Where did you take him?" she asked, her voice an electronically altered crackle. Dragan looked around the room at the soldiers.

"Is this how it is?" he asked them. "You're going to just turn on one of your own?"

"Watch your mouth, traitor," one of them said.

"Don't talk to him," she said. She turned back to Dragan. "I'm going to ask you one more time. Where did you take Alexei Drugov?"

Dragan shook his head, a single bead of sweat dropping from his stubbly chin.

"That place was destroyed," Dragan rasped. "How can it—"

She clamped her black, scaly glove down on my neck hard then, and I gasped. I tried to squirm free, but the combat suit gave her incredible strength.

"Tell me where you took him," she said, the armor making a low whine as she slowly tightened her grip.

"Don't let her do this," Dragan said to the other soldiers. My throat felt the size of a straw as I gasped air in. "You know me. This isn't—"

She lifted me up until my toes brushed the floor and I choked. Grabbing at her wrist to hold myself up, I tried to pull in another breath but couldn't. I struggled, trying to peel her fingers back, and felt a flood of emotion surge through the mites as suddenly as a shock of cold water to the face ... anger, hatred, and disgust bled through my brain like chemical poison. Underneath it all hunger simmered, a desperate, driving hunger that made my stomach clench into a painful knot. It wasn't coming from Tānchi. The signal was a million times stronger. It was coming from her.

She's a haan, I thought, staring down into the empty hood created by the dispersion mask. The thought buzzed in my head.... *But they're so delicate. How can she ...*

The room seemed to get darker as I struggled to stay on my tiptoes. As dark clouds bloomed in front of me, I saw a fat scalefly come crawling down the length of her arm, then out of sight below my chin. A sound like water rushed in my ears as the world around me began to fade.

"Wait," I heard Dragan say. Through the slits of my eyes I found his face, and when I did I barely recognized him. I'd seen what he could do the day he found me and in the days since, but now the fierceness and strength that I'd always associated with him were stripped away. There was only fear in his eyes, just raw fear. Not for himself, but for me. I'd broken him.

"I'll tell you," he said again. The room seemed to be tilting, and he sounded far away.

I glanced right, swiping the 3i icons away in a streak of hot pink hearts and neon that left trails across the blurry backdrop of our ruined apartment. My friend list scrolled up until I spotted Dragan's name and grabbed it. When I tapped him, he'd already begun to move, and I saw metal flash as the knife at his belt came free from its scabbard.

love u 2.

"I'm sorry, Sam," I heard him say.

The knife came down in an arc as he launched toward us, and the blade struck the soldier next to him. The soldier staggered back while groping for the blade's handle, now jammed into the meat between his shoulder and neck. He struck the wall and left a streak of blood as he slid to the floor.

Dragan seized on the 3i connection, his desperate reply stopping almost as soon as it started.

Forgive me—

The other soldier crashed his plated fist down on the back of Dragan's head, and his 3i connection dropped as he went down like a stone. He wasn't moving, but the soldier knelt over him and hit him again.

"Don't kill him, you idiot!" the woman shouted.

He hit Dragan again, casting dots of blood across the wall next to him, and my feet came up off the floor as Red-stamp stormed across the room, colliding with the coffee table and shattering the glass top. Before I could even get my bearings, she'd swung me around in a complete circle and then hurled me away. The room tilted, receding as I flew through the air.

My back hit something hard enough to force the air out of my mouth and nose in a spray of snot and spit. Then the surface behind me gave away with an earsplitting crash.

Everything slowed down, and I saw a million sparkles fly away from me as I passed through the cloud of glass. Shards and chunks spun end over end through glittering powder as the living room curtains rushed out after me on a wave of cool, canned air. For just a second, it formed a faint, smoky fog as the hot, humid night breeze outside washed over me.

The balcony rail passed underneath me as the inside of the apartment fell away. Back through the broken window I could see Dragan lying crumpled and still. My momentum slowed and I fell back, staring up through the sparkling glass bits as the stars wheeled by in the night sky above. Then I plummeted away from the balcony, and the windows of hundreds of apartments whipped past in a blur while my clothes billowed and snapped around me.

Hot summer air roared in my ears as I narrowly missed the huge metal frame of a building sign and neon lights began to streak past in a stream of liquid color. Fifty stories below, past the crisscrossing streams of air-cars, the lights of the street were quickly rushing up to meet me. I screamed over the racket of graviton engines and honking horns.

Something tugged at me from behind, and my skin suddenly began to tingle. The tug grew stronger, and the rushing wind let up until the traffic sounds swallowed it. I'd begun to fall more slowly somehow, like I was connected to an invisible elastic band that had stretched taut.

The graviton emitter, I thought. *One of them . . .*

Hanging facedown, I dangled in midair sixty stories above the street, the tingle from the field increasing even as I felt it begin to lose its grip. I was too far away, and I was too heavy. Any second now, I'd fall again and this time nothing would be able to stop me.

Below, something flashed. A white point of light appeared, and then a second later the lanes of speeding air traffic directly below me were blotted out by a floating patch of empty space. A thin, bright white outline surrounded it in a perfect hexagon while the inside resolved into a view of an alley that appeared to float in midair.

What the fu—

The tether holding me snapped and I plunged, arms and legs pedaling, into the opening. All at once the city around me disappeared and all sense of movement stopped. For a minute, there was no up or down, no frame of reference at all. I just hung in limbo, like I'd been frozen in time.

My ears popped and then just as quickly as I'd gone into the hole, I'd come out again, still screaming, as I tumbled out the mouth of an alley and skidded a few feet before crashing into the side of a parked car. When I looked up, I saw a crowd of people who were standing under a streetlight look over in surprise.

What the hell?

I stood up, gasping as I took stock of myself. Stinging scratches crisscrossed my face, shoulders, and arms, and one palm burned with road rash, but that was it. I was alive, back on the street just outside our apartment building.

Spinning around, I looked down the sidewalk behind me. A stream of people there had stopped to look back, wondering what was happening. I did a complete turn and saw nothing but staring faces looking down at the girl who'd just appeared out of thin air.

Across the street, a scrawny boy sat on the neon fiberglass bug shell of an airbike he'd just started, gaping at me. I looked back up the sheer building face toward our apartment, too high above to pick out.

A gate, I thought. Someone gated me down safely. Was it one of the soldiers? The haan hadn't shared free-floating gate tech with us yet, but there was no way she had done it—it had to have been one of them.

Something tinkled onto the pavement, and then bits of glass began to rain down onto the sidewalk and street as the falling debris caught up with me. I shielded my head, ducking under an awning as someone hollered. A loud pop echoed down the street as a metal rod trailing one of our living room curtains speared through the windshield of a parked car in an explosion of glass dust.

"Shit!" someone yelled as the car's alarm began to whistle. The wind blew the torn curtain like a flag, and as the last of the glass skittered and spun away, I snapped out of it.

Dragan.

I pushed away from the concrete wall and crossed the street to where the kid sat stunned on his airbike.

"Hey, are you okay?" he asked.

"I need your bike," I said.

"What? No way, kid—"

"I need your bike!"

I snatched a shard of broken glass from the smaller pieces littering the sidewalk and felt the edge bite into the crooks of my fingers. I slashed at him with it, spraying drops of blood across his shirt as he ducked back. He tried to slide off the bike and lost his balance, tumbling down onto his butt. Before he could get back up, I threw the glass at him and straddled the still-warm seat.

"Hey!"

I cranked the throttle and then opened up the graviton emitters. The street beneath me lurched away on a rush of wind, and horns blared as I cut through the layers of traffic above. In seconds the cursing kid dwindled to the size of an ant, and then was lost altogether beneath the rows of streaking headlights.

Shit. . . .

I pulled back on the stick as our building's neon sign rushed back in reverse, spinning as I tried to steady the bike. I cut too quickly and the undercarriage swung up toward the sky. I clamped my thighs down against the sides as my stomach flipped in weightlessness.

"Shit, shit, shit. . . ."

The building face sheared past as I completed the

loop and wrestled the machine back under control. Wind rushed over me as I picked up speed. I spotted our balcony, where a single curtain still fluttered, and closed in.

When I cleared the railing I leaned forward and crouched below the windshield. The bike accelerated and the nose went straight back through the hole in the glass where I'd gone out. The remains of the window exploded into the living room as the bottom of the bike tore through the carpet and ripped into the floor underneath. Through the racket, I could hear Tānchi screaming bloody murder.

The undercarriage caught on something and the bike jerked to a stop, throwing me off the seat and over the broken edge of the windshield. I tumbled through the air, then rolled across the carpet and slammed into the opposite wall.

Pain shot through one leg as I pushed myself back up onto my feet. The soldiers were gone. I didn't see anyone else except Tānchi.

"Dragan!" I yelled. No one answered.

Tānchi continued to scream as I looked frantically around the room.

"Dragan?" I lurched down the hall, but he wasn't in any of the other rooms either.

Limping back, my shoes kicking through broken glass, I approached the spot where he'd struggled with the soldiers. There were boot scuffs left behind in the debris, heading back the way they'd come. I knelt down, my body shaking from the adrenaline, and I realized I was alone. Amid the wreckage, glittery specks of glass powder drifted slowly up from the floor in a stray graviton riptide. They twinkled, twirling in slow motion like the specks inside a snow globe. He was gone.

The only father I'd ever known was gone.

Chapter Two

I stepped through the wreckage of our apartment in a daze, the humid breeze blowing in through the shattered window and out through the broken front door, which still hung from one stubborn hinge. Tānchi's wails pounded through my head as I went to the crib, my shoes crunching through broken glass.

"Shh," I whispered, kissing his forehead. "It's okay. Calm down...."

He was so fragile. His little bones were like spun glass beneath his skin. It was a miracle he hadn't been crushed during the attack or my airbike stunt afterward. The gate end point in the alley was probably how they'd left the building anyway; what had I even been thinking? I could have just waited there and ...

And what?

"Shh, Tānchi."

I clenched my fists and tried to calm down. Tānchi's presence vibrated, anxious as he felt around in my head. He sensed danger, but relaxed a little at the sound of my voice.

Outside, I heard a siren chirp and when I turned I saw a streak of blue flash among the streams of traffic. Even if the soldiers didn't come back, it would only be a matter of time before the place was crawling with security. I had to get out of there, and fast, or a detention center might be the least of my worries.

"Shh . . ." I stroked Tānchi's cheek. "It's okay. I'll be right back."

"I love you like you were my own flesh and blood, Sam."

My throat burned and I cleared it, blinking back tears as I stepped away from the crib. I spotted my knife, the tip still red with blood, and wiped it on my pant leg before folding the blade in and dropping it in my pocket. Lying on the floor two steps away from it was a shiny black object, like a little electronic corkscrew. Dragan's security twistkey.

I picked up the key, turning it over in my fingers. Twistkeys were used to alter gate destinations. All the soldiers carried coded keys that let them override the street gates.

"Search him. Find the twistkey."

"He doesn't have it. Just the standard issue."

The soldiers had been looking for one, but not this one. I stuck it in my pocket and crossed to the broken window that looked out over the city. The remaining curtain billowed in the warm wind as I passed into the kitchen and took the last ration from the fridge, then grabbed the surrogate ration kit and slung it over my shoulder.

As I moved down the hall, I saw both bedrooms had been tossed. The door to the safe had been cut off and propped against Dragan's desk. Inside I could see a gun and some other stuff they'd left behind.

I grabbed my backpack from the floor next to my bed and stuffed the ration into it before heading back to the safe. Inside I found a palm pistol with a scope, a stunner, and a baton. I wrapped them in a towel and stuffed them in the backpack. Underneath the weapons sat an emergency ration sheet and Dragan's spare security badge. I put the badge in my wallet next to mine and took the sheet, revealing a strip of three pill tabs underneath. They were clear blue, with sparkly speckles inside. I flipped the strip over so I could see the foil backing, and used the 3i to run a search on the text there.

The first few links that popped up were for something called seritoxedrine or "blue shard," a military-issue battle drug. I stuffed it in my pocket along with the ration sheet. I pulled an intact pint of shine from the wet bar's wreckage and dropped that in too, then shouldered the pack and went back for Tānchi.

"Come on," I told him, taking his swaddle out of the crib and cradling carefully him in my arms. "Come on, we have to go."

I ran with him, and fled into the city. By the time I stopped to think, I was deep in Tùzi-wō under a canopy of flashing signs, pushing through the street market against a tide of shoppers and sellers looking to beat the sweep. I hadn't stopped long enough to even think about where I should go, or what I should do when I got there. I just pushed my way, shell-shocked, through the haze of human funk while doing my best to shelter Tānchi from it.

Off to my left a vendor yelled something at the neon displays that loomed over the street above his kiosk, shaking his fist at a buglike haan construct that was dancing across the support frame. It stopped and swiveled its head toward him, sending a red laser bar flickering across his face.

"Go ahead and report me!" the man shouted, and threw his shoe. The construct jumped in surprise and gated away, vanishing as the sneaker arced and then flopped into the street.

Ahead, a stand displayed the ghoulish faces of festival masks staring from beneath a canopy of floating cellophane lanterns. Stacked up around them were fireworks and gaudy souvenir snow globes made to look like the haan force field dome with the ship inside, complete with the ring of wired balls, the government's failsafe graviton lenses that surrounded it. The kid working the register there had a girl in his lap and his fingers stuffed down the back of her low-riding shorts. He opened one eye and broke his lip-lock to watch me go by while her hand worked rhythmically at his crotch. He stared as we passed. Everybody stared. A bloodstained girl hobbling down the middle of the sidewalk, a screaming haan child clutched to her chest.

The foot traffic parted grudgingly in front of me while the kid bawled himself hoarse. On some level it registered, but the cries sounded like they were coming from underwater. Everything did. It wasn't until his little hands grabbed fistfuls of my shirt that his fear cut through the fog. I touched the side of his face with my fingers, and the smooth skin felt hot.

"It's okay," I said. "You're okay. I've got you."

Keeping stride, I hoisted the kid to one arm so I could adjust the surrogate kit's strap. For the first time, I noticed the eyes around me weren't just staring at me, but at the rations I carried. Greedy, desperate eyes followed us, and broke off only when they saw the black Shili-uyuán stamp on the side of the canister.

Dragan's in trouble. The thought bounced around in my head like a fly inside a jar. *I have to help him. I have to do something.*

I made myself stop and catch my breath. There were plenty of cops around looking to clear out the square before the sweep made its way here, but they wouldn't help me. Soldiers had attacked us and everyone knew what the pecking order was. Hangfei had been under martial law since before I was born, and the local cops had zero clout with the military. Telling them would be the same as announcing that I was still alive, and where

I was. I tried to tune out the chaos around me and think. I needed help. I needed someone who had some clout, who I could also trust.

Kang.

Jake Kang worked security, but he was an expat like Dragan and they went way back. His lawyer wife had even helped clear the paperwork through when Dragan made my adoption legal. If there was anyone in security I could trust, it would be him.

Ahead, scaffolding had been set up over the sidewalk and covered in sheets of plastic. A row of black-and-red posters sporting Military Governor Hwong's profile were plastered at sidewalk level, urging citizens to join the United Defense Force. I stopped next to one of them and dug out my phone, then thumbed in Kang's contact.

"Hello?" a woman's voice answered—Kang's wife, Lijuan. She sounded like she'd been asleep.

"Um, hi," I said, raising my voice over the street noise. "I'm looking for Jake Kang?"

"Jake isn't here right now," she said. "Who's calling?"

"Do you know when he'll be back?"

"Who is this?"

I paused for a minute. She sounded mad.

"I'm sorry," I said. "I'm sorry to call so late. . . . I just . . ."

"Xiao-Xing?" she asked. She sounded surprised, but she remembered my name. I smiled, tears beginning to brim over.

"Yeah," I sniffed. "Yeah, it's me."

"Hey . . ." Her voice softened immediately. "Hey, what's wrong?"

"I don't know. I think I'm in trouble."

"Where's Dragan?"

I looked up and down the street nervously.

"Lijuan, they took him." An uncomfortable pause stretched out on the other end of the line.

"Who took him?" she asked finally. She sounded more awake now, and I heard her sit up in bed. "What's going on?"

"I don't know. . . . I wanted to ask Jake if he knew anything."

"He'll help any way he can, but what makes you think he would know something? What's going on?"

"They were military," I said. "Soldiers took him."

I heard more movement in the background as walls of people trudged past me on either side. I stuck near a streetlamp pole, hooking one arm around it while I listened to her shuffle out of bed on the other end of the line.

"I'm sorry," she said. "Jake's out on assignment."

"Is he on the security sweep?"

"No . . . he's on some special assignment. After that he's off duty for a while, but he sprang a trip to Duongroi on me, and we leave tomorrow." She paused, listening. "Xiao-Xing, it sounds like you're on the street. You need to get inside, right now."

"Right." I nodded, rubbing my eyes. "I know." If I got caught up in the sweep, I'd get hauled in for sure.

On the 3i, I brought up Vamp's eyebot map, where people throughout the city were feeding in information through the client app whenever it spotted a soldier. The blob of sightings inched in my general direction, spreading down sidewalks and through alleyways.

"I'm sorry," I told her. "I shouldn't have dumped this on you."

Past the floating, colored window I made passing eye contact with a wandering vendor selling festival gear. I looked away too late, and the old woman started over.

"No," Lijuan said. "Jake gave me an emergency number. I'll try and contact him. Was Dragan actually arrested?"

"I don't know. I think he was."

"Do you know where they took him? What detention center?"

"No."

"Did they say anything that you think might help? Anything I should tell Jake that might be important?"

I thought about telling her about the haan that had been with them, but something made me stop just short of doing it. The haan didn't fit. Even with combat armor their bodies could never handle that kind of stress, but I'd felt her through the mite cluster; I was sure of it. There'd been a flood of anger and hate, along with an undercurrent of sadistic pleasure. She'd been hidden under the armor and behind a dispersion mask. Was it possible?

"Sam?"

"They . . ." I tried to remember as the old woman approached with a wrinkled smile. She held up a papery jiangshi ghost mask with green, iridescent eyes.

"Handmade," she said. I smiled politely, shifting the phone to my other ear.

". . . where did you take Alexei Drugov?"

"They were looking for someone," I said.

"Who?"

"A Pan-Slav. Someone called Alexei Drugov?"

"Jiangshi," the old woman said.

"Not now."

The old woman poked me in the tit with a bony finger, and I swatted her hand away. "This one's perfect for you," she said. "What do you say? Half price."

"Hang on," Lijuan said. I heard faint typing on the other end of the line.

"They'll be twice the price at the Fangwenzhe Festival," the old woman explained, holding out the mask. She tugged at my pant leg. I looked past her and saw the spinning shadow and burning incense of a gonzo shrine.

"I know," I told her. "I don't have any money." I held out my empty hand. "No money."

"What?" Lijuan asked.

"Not you."

"Sam, get off the street," she said. "Keep your phone handy. Jake will get back to you."

"Do you know why they took him?"

"Not yet. Just get inside and lie low for now. Don't talk to the cops, the military, or anyone in private security until you hear from Jake."

"Okay."

"We'll get this straightened out. Hang in there."

"I will. And thanks."

"No need. You'll hear from us soon. Bye."

The line cut as the old woman with the festival mask held it out toward me again.

"Look, I told you, I don't have any—"

The weight on my shoulder suddenly disappeared as the ration kit's strap sprang loose. Before I even knew what happened, the kit was torn from my side and the two ends of the severed strap whipped away, trailing behind a boy who had it tucked under one arm.

"Hey!"

He darted into the crowd, and in seconds I'd lost him. I turned back to the old woman and found that she'd disappeared too. The crone had set me up.

"You little shit!" I yelled after the kid. "I hope it kills you!"

Heads turned toward me, but lost interest just as fast. Way off in the distance, a blue arc flashed in the sky between two buildings while another distant rumble began to swell.

A hot breeze cut through the summer air, smelling like B.O., car exhaust, and scalefly repellent. I hugged Tānchi to my chest, feeling his warm weight in my arms, and for the first time it occurred to me that I couldn't keep him, not anymore. Even if the kit hadn't been stolen, our place had been destroyed. I couldn't go back there. I had to hunker down and I couldn't just keep Tānchi out on the street with me. It was too dangerous for him.

Security blues flashed down the street over the thick lanes of traffic, and through the layers of street signs above me I spotted a couple of security vehicles as they floated past. One of them shined a cone of light down onto the sidewalk as it went, sweeping it around as it turned between two buildings. Eyebot called it out, highlighting the ship in white outline, then noting the license plate ID, make, and GPS coordinates.

Do they already know I'm still alive? Are they looking for me?

I had to go. I spotted a gate hub across the lanes of traffic about two blocks ahead and made my way over to it. At the queue, I split off from the flow of foot traffic and headed for the rightmost gate, the one leading to the haan settlement of Shangzho. Unlike at the others, there was no crowd waiting to go through and the scanner flickered out of sleep mode when I approached the thin metal frame. On the other side I could make out a long, reinforced brick wall topped with rings of razor wire. Over the wall, low in the night sky, star Fangwenzhe glowed like a second, smaller moon.

In spite of his anxiety, Tānchi had fallen back into his food-induced sleep, warm and limp inside the blankets. I held him to my chest as I strode up to the gate, whispering into his ear.

"One . . . two . . ."

A strange feeling of limbo gripped me when I stepped through the portal, and then a beat later space and gravity returned as my foot came down on a sidewalk across town.

"... three!"

A klaxon made me jump as a red light flashed from behind. I turned around and saw a holographic panel flicker on, a grainy translucent display with instructions in six different languages. It wanted me to pay the balance for the trip. Back toward the wall, heads were beginning to turn as I swiped my cash card and headed toward the settlement entrance.

Razor wire sat spiraled along the pitted, spray-painted wall that separated the fourth colony from the rest of Hangfei, until it reached a guard station where two armed human soldiers stood. There were others there, people lined up in loose groups eyeing the wall sullenly from a makeshift camp of bedrolls and sleeping bags scattered on the pavement just outside the security zone. Faces watched me as I approached, lit by the steady glow of an electric lantern. I could make out their handmade signs that were propped up halfheartedly, with slogans like THEY EAT: WE STARVE and 0%, a reference to the food index. One old man with a scraggly beard and hollow cheeks held one that just said SIPS. Starving In Plain Sight.

A short distance away from the protesters, a group of Fangwenzhe worshipper gonzos had set up shop. There were five of them, three men and two women, all on their knees with their eyes closed and hands clasped, facing the brick wall. A shrine had been set up there next to a poster of their leader, Gohan Sòng, the tips of incense sticks glowing cherry red in the breeze and a cheap plastic apple spinning in midair a few inches above them. Behind it, someone had spray-painted their catchphrase in colorful hanzi: ONLY HE CAN MOVE THE STARS.

All of their eyes followed me as I broke through the line and approached the guard station. The eyebot app painted the two guards when I got closer, and I saw some data go scribbling across the bottom of the 3i's pink win-

dow as it identified their faces. One of the guards, a tall
guy with bronze skin and oily hair, looked up as I fumbled for my ID. His name was Gang Sun. I cradled the
kid in one arm and held the badge where he could see.

"What's this?" Sun asked. The other guard, a broad-
shouldered guy with a buzz cut who eyebot identified as
Shen Liao, chuckled to himself.

"I need to get inside please."

"Does this look like the mall? Go home."

"Visitors are allowed inside."

"During specified hours," he said, "with a written permit. They're locked down for tonight anyway. There's a
security sweep about to start, in case you hadn't heard.
Go home, and come back in the morning with a permit."

I fished out Dragan's spare badge I'd found in the safe
and showed it to them. "My guardian is military. We're
part of the surrogate program," I told them.

His eyes glanced from the badge, down at the kid.
"Then take it to Shiliuyuán."

"I'll never get there and back before curfew. It's an
emergency." He frowned. "Look, my ration kit got stolen, no thanks to you guys, and he can't go a whole night
without—"

"You really Dragan's kid?" Liao chimed in. His partner shot him a dark look.

"You know him?"

"Where is he during all this?"

"On assignment. I'm alone and I need help." Liao
frowned again, like he thought he might be making a
mistake, but he sighed.

"Let's see your papers."

Sun rolled his eyes. "For shit's sake . . . ," he muttered,
but Liao waved him down.

"I don't have them on me," I said. "Look, I can't take
care of the kid anymore. Shangzho has a surrogate center, right? I'll just drop him off there."

"You need your papers at least," he said, shaking his head.

"Okay," I said. I bluffed, holding Tānchi out toward him. "I'll just leave him here with you while I go back—"

"No, no, no," he said, holding up his hands like I'd just handed him a dirty diaper.

"Then can you take him in?"

"We can't leave our posts. It's a security lockdown."

I waited, holding the kid while they glanced at each other and Sun shook his head. After a minute, though, Liao sighed again.

"You're killing me, kid."

He reached through the guard station window and scribbled something on a little pad of tickets. He thumped his palm down on the flat red button next to the pad, and the main gate opened a few feet, trailing what looked like a length of toilet paper in the breeze.

"Here's a temporary pass," he said, holding the ticket out along with my ID. "Go to the center, drop it off, then come right back."

"Thanks."

He blocked me with one arm when I tried to pass. "Backpack stays here."

"But I—"

"No buts."

I didn't want to leave it with them, but I didn't have much of a choice, it looked like. I dropped it just inside the guard station doorway, and he lowered his arm.

"Thank Dragan next time you see him. You got thirty minutes, but leave time to get home before curfew."

"What happens after thirty minutes?"

"Then your temporary pass expires," Sun said. "You're officially in violation of border security."

"Then what?"

"They eat you, I think."

I snatched the ID and ticket back and slipped through

before they changed their minds. The two chuckled, and one of the protesters yelled something unintelligible after me in a hoarse voice.

Racist assholes.

The gate clanged shut, leaving me alone inside.

Chapter Three

I'd seen three of the settlements from the outside, small chunks of the city given to the haan when they began to outgrow the ship, but I'd never actually been inside any of them. The other ten were outside Tùzi-wō, but Shangzho, while not the first, had over time become the largest and the most well known in Hangfei.

People come here all the time, I told myself. *It's no big deal.*

They came during the day, though. As I made my way across the empty, stone-paved plaza, the whole place looked and felt abandoned. Part of it was the darkness—haan almost never used visible light, so the only real light to see by came from whatever bled over from the surrounding city, the moon, and the pale glow of Fangwenzhe. Shangzho sat like a dark hole in a sparkling sea, but at ground level it was downright eerie.

Up ahead I could make out the ornate entryway of what used to be a school, with a deserted playground carved out in front of it where the occasional scalefly flitted from shadow to shadow. A lopsided carousel and a rusting swing set cast shadows across the stones, and when I looked closer I could make out the names of children etched on their surfaces. A tourist sign hung from a metal arch in front of the whole thing, where calligraphy characters spelled out PEACE BRICKS.

It marked the spot where, back before I was even born, the first haan to die on Earth lost his life. Five construction workers beat him with lengths of rebar while he'd clung to those carousel bars, and onlookers cheered. They shattered his bones like glass until his corpse disappeared, gated back to the ship. He never even lifted a finger to fight back. Maybe he couldn't. He might have been unconscious after the first couple of blows. At least, I hoped he had been.

The names on the peace bricks, put there by the schoolkids who had sat by helplessly, were old and worn now. My footsteps echoed softly as I crossed over them, the only sound except for the street noises back on the other side of the wall. Particles of grit rose lazily from up from between the pavers here and there, floating up through the ambient light like rain in reverse as a graviton eddy coursed through.

"Look," I whispered to Tānchi. "Look where we are." His eyes were fully lit now, looking curiously into the darkness up ahead. I heard a low note twang overhead and looked up to see a little haan construct, its purpose unknown, creep along a taut power line. Tānchi's gaze followed it until it disappeared down an alleyway.

The buildings that loomed around the square were human built, but without any trace of smog stain or biocide residue anywhere. No trash littered the ground, and no graffiti marked the walls. Every window had been glossed over black, and some kind of smooth honeycomb scales covered just about every vertical surface. Above, through the framework of unlit signs and currents of swarming scaleflies, I could make out irregular clusters of shadows that hung from the building faces like big urban barnacles.

I couldn't see any haan, but they were there. A haze

of signal bled through the mite cluster constantly, pooling in the back of my mind. There were too many to pinpoint any one specific feeling or intention, just a constant tide of brain stew that was as palpable as the summer heat.

I pulled up the Shangzho map on my phone and pushed it around with my fingertip until I found the surrogate center. I plotted a route and then hopped onto the glassy surface of a moving walkway. Once I had my footing, it picked up speed, and the building faces on either side of the street began to streak past as it carried me into the darkness.

As a humid breeze coursed over me, I sat down on the conveyor and held Tānchi to my chest while empty outdoor cafés, bars, and shop fronts flowed past us. I cracked my neck and let out a deep breath, then watched myself in a street-length window as we sailed past. The scratches that crisscrossed my skin looked black, and I could make out pale skin peeking through holes in my shirt. A mixture of half scabs and wet blood covered my face and neck like war paint. I followed it with my eyes, staring back at myself as the belt turned away, and caught a flicker of red light from somewhere up above, behind me.

I turned around and looked up to see a pair of flame red eyes staring down from the face of the building across the street. They were coming from one of the barnacle shadows that hung there. As I watched, several more pairs of eyes lit up around it, and in the resulting glow I saw that the shapes were actually haan. They were sitting on the layer of hexagonal scales as if they'd been glued there, staring down at me.

Graviton plating. They sat in groups, some twenty stories above. More and more of the eyes were lighting up, a mixture of reds, oranges, and yellows. There were hundreds of them up there, all watching me.

The first call came in on my 3i then, and the display

popped up of its own accord as one of them pried open a channel. Before I knew it, dozens of them had begun to hammer the connection, and the junk call buffer overflowed. I cricked my neck to stow the 3i window, but it just popped up again.

"Enough, guys," I said, but my voice sounded a little unsure. Several shadows moved along the walls of the buildings to either side, and I heard footsteps from the darkness of the side streets there. A few seconds later an empathic spike shot through the mite cluster, and I felt a pang of hunger. The intensity of it made my stomach clench, and it grew as the eyes followed me down the walkway. All the while, a mass of invisible feelers probed the 3i for a crack they could sneak into.

"Enough!" I shouted.

The hunger signals grew stronger as my phone buzzed in my pocket. One of them had given up on the 3i and found the cell connection. I dug it out and my hands shook as I switched it off. I told myself I would be okay, but as a wave of firelit eyes surged in my direction, I felt fear prick in my chest.

What happens then?

They eat you. . . .

I stood up and began to take long strides down the walkway in spite of the pain in my leg. One at a time the haan weren't exactly intimidating, but when the streets and building faces all began to crawl with movement, my fear edged toward panic. The kid picked up on it and squirmed in my arms.

Wait.

The word appeared in the 3i window in front of me as one of them somehow managed to sneak its way in. More of them had started to worm their way through, and unlike the kid's curious probes, these were pushy and insistent.

"It's okay," I whispered. I shut the 3i down but

couldn't do anything about the mite cluster. The hollow ache in the pit of my stomach had turned my legs weak.

They're hungrier than we are, I thought. *They take so much . . . eighty percent of all consumable calories from the combined feedlots . . . how can they still be so hungry?*

The surrogate center loomed up ahead and I picked up the pace. When I got closer to it, I noticed that the eyes around me began to thin out until, by the time the pinprick scanners at the gate flashed black-light blue, they were gone.

I hopped off the walkway. The front entrance, a thick glass partition so clear and clean I hadn't even realized it was there, slid silently on its track to let me through. I glanced back once and saw the smattering of staring eyes in the distance wink out one by one.

"It's okay," I whispered in Tānchi's ear, hugging him to my chest. I felt him relax a little as he held me back.

Inside the building a long, empty corridor stretched off into darkness where there were no signs in any language. Not sure where to go, I started down, the squeak of my damp rubber soles echoing ahead and behind. The air turned cooler, and I'd passed several closed doors on either side when something flickered in the dark up ahead. Electronic black-lit eyes stared down at me, and a knobby metal ball dropped down on a mechanical stalk that trailed a web of hair-thin wires. The array of electronic sensors focused on me, and the ball emitted something between a chirp and an electronic fart, but my attention had turned to the shadows beyond it.

Whoa.

Past the eye, the walls had been stripped down to their I-beams. The tiled floor had been peeled away to form a yawning, circular hole underneath the steel framework.

What the hell is that?

The hole dropped down into blackness, ringed by what looked like giant spines or bristles. A low rush of air rumbled from its mouth, and the kid clucked happily, pawing at the air toward it as the shape inside his head shuddered.

I had stepped past the eye to get a better look when I felt a hitch and the view in front of me changed. I'd passed headlong through an unseen gate and stumbled into a dark, low-ceilinged room somewhere else. I heard scurrying overhead and looked up as a series of soft white lights flickered on to let me see. Tiny little servos, biogel blobs with wiry mechanical legs, streamed across ordered clusters of wire above me.

With a jolt, I spun around but saw only a honeycomb-scaled wall behind me. I turned around again and found myself facing a semicircular guard station on the other side of the room, where a uniformed male haan stood.

His wide-set eyes glowed brilliant orange, his skin glistening in the low light. Through the forehead of his handsome mannequin-like face, I could make out the grublike curls of his two brains, and the clusters of cilia that tethered them to other half-seen nodules in there with them. The little brain began to quiver, and when I glanced down at Tānchi I saw the smaller shape inside his head stir in response.

"Excuse me," I said, breaking the silence. One of the haan's eyes turned to me, the pupils making a quick revolution. His suit draped from his broad shoulders, folded around him like leathery wings as he stared.

"I need to—"

"Wait," the haan said, the voice box at his throat flickering as the smooth, synthesized voice issued from it. A scalefly buzzed out from the folds of his suit.

"But I—"

"No further information is required of you at this time," he said.

"Stop cutting me off," I said evenly. "Don't you want to know why I'm here?"

"No."

I opened my mouth to say something else, but closed it again. Sometimes haan were like that. I adjusted Tānchi's weight in my arms and tried to keep from swaying as I waited.

"I'm fine, by the way," I said. "Thanks for asking."

He just stood there, unmoving, even when the air next to him began to crackle and the wall shimmered and warped. A moment later, a pinprick of light dilated out until it formed a hexagon that stretched from floor to ceiling, and through it, I could see a second haan.

This one was female, and it struck me as weird to see two haan females in one day. She was smaller and lither than the males, with slender limbs and a pair of translucent breasts that rested to either side of her pulsing heart. I wondered if they dispensed the same speckled goo found in the surrogate rations.

She made a low, fast clicking sound as she leaned closer to me. Her neck was long and thin, and her glassy face was delicate and pretty. Her eyes were the color of fire, surrounded by a cornea of hot blue. When she entered the room, I felt a surge of excitement from the male.

"Um, hello?" I said. She stared at me, then gestured for me to approach, to step through the gate. I looked to the guard, then back to her. She gestured again, her thin fingers beckoning me.

I stepped through. When my foot came down on the other side, I found myself in another small chamber, this one round, with some kind of console to my right.

"The guards signaled that you were coming," she said, voice box flickering as her deep, sultry voice issued out of it. "I'm sorry to have made you wait, but I wanted to meet with you personally."

I stepped toward her, really unsteady now. The events of the night had begun to catch up with me.

"Sam Shao," she said without consulting any sort of computer or tablet.

"That's me."

The silence stretched out, and the warm glow of her eyes seemed to bob and drift in front of me as her brains fluttered behind her forehead like swimming krill.

"I ..." The room seemed to spin a little. The tank of adrenaline that had fueled me so far was running dry. "I need to return the child."

"I know."

"Something happened," I said. "The place where I'm staying ... some people broke in. They grabbed Dragan—"

I stopped short as she moved closer, seeming to grow in size as her eyes turned more focused and intense. The dark pinpricks of her pupils were like sunspots in the flame of her eyes.

"I will take the child."

"He wasn't hurt," I said.

"I know."

"I kept his feeding schedule," I told her. "He'll be okay for another four hours or so."

"I know."

"It's just ... my guardian is missing and our apartment is wrecked. Someone stole the ration kit from me ... I don't have any money or any place to stay. He'll have to go to someone else."

"I will take the child."

She reached out, opening her hands. I adjusted the blankets around Tānchi and carefully handed him to her. As I did, I felt a pang from him that made my breath catch. Fear and a sudden shocked hurt poured through as if to say, of all things, he would never have expected this.

You're sending me away? his eyes seemed to say. He reached out for me with his little hands. *Why? What did I do?*

"Sorry, kiddo," I said. I felt a lump in my throat I didn't expect.

"Do you want to say good-bye?" the female asked softly.

I nodded. "Yes . . . thank you."

She waited, holding Tānchi out while I leaned in close.

"I'm sorry," I whispered in his ear. "I really am, but you'll be better off with someone else now."

I always got a little sad when I gave them up. The mite links made for a deep bond that happened fast, and moving on always hurt a little, but this time was worse. Our time had been cut short. On top of everything else, I realized I really didn't want to lose him too.

Maybe I can take him back. Get more rations and keep him on. I can find a motel that will take us both, and . . .

I didn't have much money, though, and anyway I had to find Dragan. I just couldn't worry about a surrogate right now.

"I'm really sorry," I said in his ear. I gave his cheek one last stroke.

I looked up at the female and nodded. Tānchi watched me over her shoulder, still hurt and confused, as she carried him to the empty station. She opened a smooth metal hatch there and then placed Tānchi inside. He looked back at me, and I gave him a little wave. He raised one little hand and waved back before she shut the door again with a vacuum thump. A low rumble came from the wall, making the floor vibrate slightly as she tapped at a virtual keyboard in the air in front of it.

"Where are you send—" I had started to ask when the mites went dark and the connection broke.

"Back," she said.

"Back wh—"

"Your transaction is complete."

She handed me a black strip of paper with a series of haan stamps on it, which I realized was a receipt. I sighed, not sure if I should laugh or cry. I stuffed the receipt in my pocket and ran my hand through a sweaty lock of hair.

"Look," I said, "I need help, okay?"

The haan stared, not speaking.

"Soldiers took my guardian," I continued, the words coming on their own. "They tried to kill me. I can't—"

"Thank you for your service," she said. "Your transaction is complete."

I leaned a little closer, lowering my voice. "One of them was a haan." She didn't answer, but the shapes in her head writhed a little in their fluid bath. She watched me, the rigid contours of her glassy face not moving. Whoever she was, she was good at controlling the mites. I couldn't feel at all what she might be thinking. "She was pretending to be a human—"

Light flickered behind me, and the hairs on the back of my neck stood up. I didn't have to turn around to see that the gate had opened again. She was giving me the boot.

"You guys are so far beyond us," I said, looking at the floor and shaking my head. "I know you could help me. I know you could. If you wanted to you could—"

"Your tra—"

"I know." I turned, a little wobbly on my feet, and wiped a pink mixture of sweat and blood from my forehead. "Thanks for the help." I put air quotes around the last word, but she didn't seem to pick up on the gesture.

I turned around and found myself looking through a gate in the wall, back into the room I'd come from. With nothing else to do or say, I stepped through.

She followed me, which I hadn't expected. On the other side I watched her as she reached up to grip a metal, many-eyed orb nestled up in a ceiling niche. Her long fingers rotated it so that the eyes stared up into darkness.

"What are you—"

A second gate crackled into existence on the other side of the room, and through it I could see the city street outside the settlement. The protesters and worshippers were still there, and they perked up at the sudden appearance of the portal.

"Leave now," she said.

"Fine."

I stepped through, back into the humid night air. On the other side, I turned back in time to see her approach the haan guard who first greeted me. She placed one hand on his shoulder, and I heard a muted slither followed by a crunch. As the gate fizzled out of existence, I heard the distorted splash of water and, for just a second, it looked like the draping material of the guard's suit collapsed to the floor.

Then the portal vanished, leaving me to stare at the brick wall. The protesters who were gathered at the perimeter looked at me with contempt, while the gonzo worshippers looked at me with awe. To my right, the guards at the station looked up from whatever they were doing long enough for one of them to laugh at me.

"How'd it go?" Sun asked.

I gave him the finger, but he just laughed and tossed my backpack over to me.

"Go on, get home before someone sees you out."

I shouldered the pack and headed back the way I'd come. When I passed the protesters, one of them muttered at me.

"Haan fucker."

"Excuse me?"

I couldn't see who said it, but a small group of the men were scowling, their ugly faces lit by the glow of the electric lamp.

"Race traitor," one spat.

"Race traitor?" The fatigue had me punchy. "For real?"

"When they take over—"

"There's not enough of them to take over even if they wanted to," I snapped back, "so can the 'invader' bullshit. They gave us gate tech, force field and brain band tech, better rations, clean water, and free energy. The only bad thing they gave us was scaleflies, and even those at least you can eat."

"The Impact," the guy said, raising his voice. "Was that bad enough for you?" He threw a half-empty can at me and I swatted it away.

"That was an accident," I said, raising my own voice. "It sucked, but—"

"A quarter of a million people died!"

"An accident, ass-wipe! It was an accident! They've been trying to make up for it ever since, but it's never enough, is it?"

"They'll take over one day," the guy said. "You'll see."

"What are you afraid they'll do if that happens? Clean the place? The sweep's in less than an hour. I hope you all get arrested!"

I pointed at the lamp they were huddled around.

"The batteries in that thing are haan tech, you know," I said. The oldest man turned as I passed by him, and stared up at me from the hollows of his eyes.

"Fuck you," he wheezed.

Chapter Four

Rain had begun to fall hard and the security sweep was in full swing by the time I got back to my neighborhood. Vamp's app displayed a cloud of orange markers moving toward Tùzi-wō, the 3i's holomap laid over sheets of drizzle and the throngs of people hustling through street fog to get somewhere dry. If I zoomed in to the map, I could actually see the individual units strobe slowly down the streets as they were seen, lost, then seen again, and twice it warned me to take an alternate route to avoid them. It was the first time, I think, that I realized Vamp's project was probably going to get him into real trouble.

As I slipped through knots of people on my way toward the market, I pulled up my chat contacts. I was about to tap Vamp's heart to tell him what had happened when I saw the stack of messages from him in the 3i tray. He already knew.

I thought about messaging him back but wanted to get off the street first. Security hadn't reached my block in force yet, but groups of local cops were out, rain pelting off their helmets and black ponchos while they watched the vendors all trying to pack up and leave at the same time. As they broke down kiosks they made last-minute sales under clusters of umbrellas, some with the cops themselves. I moved under a shop front awning with a crowd of others, nestling into a gap next to a rattling rain gutter to get the lay of the place. Red and blue lights flashed through the haze of neon from in front of my apartment building a couple of blocks away. A bunch of cops were out front waiting to see if the nut who crashed the airbike would show, and I could see an aircar hovering up near our ruined balcony, its lights flashing off the building's glass face. Going back there wasn't an option.

I skirted across the street and made my way down the block to the Nan Hai Hotel where Vamp and I sometimes got a room with friends if we wanted to cut loose a little and Dragan was home. It was a shit-box, and I really didn't want to spend the money, but I needed a place to clean up and sleeping in a crash tube wasn't going to cut it.

When I headed inside, a small crowd of people were in the lobby, dripping rainwater as they watched a TV mounted on the wall. It showed the wreckage from inside our apartment, reflected police lights flashing in time with the ones outside the hotel window. I recognized the remains of the smashed wet bar, where police were standing and pointing toward the battered airbike. The camera panned down and zoomed in on a few shell casings that were circled with chalk.

"One?"

I looked over at the woman sitting at the check-in counter. She'd checked me in before but didn't show any sign she recognized me. Her stringy hair was streaked with gray, and her leathery lips were pinched around a thin black cigarette.

"Yeah," I said, approaching the counter.

"Hourly or nightly?"

"One night."

"I got two singles up on forty, no AC and no TV."

"Shower?"

She nodded. "Sixty yuan."

"I'll take it."

She swiped my card and pushed it back to me along with the room badge.

"What the hell happened to you?" she asked, like she'd noticed the scrapes and bruises for the first time.

"Long story."

"I'll bet."

I took the card and badge and made my way to the elevator lobby.

The A.I. yammered at me as I rode it up. Something about lip injections, I think; I wasn't listening. My clothes were wet and uncomfortable, and the chemicals in the rainwater made every scrape and cut itch. When the elevator finally stopped and the doors opened, I trudged down the hall feeling tired, beaten, and very alone.

The hotel room offered little more than a dingy closet with a single twin bed and an end table with a plastic lamp. It had its own toilet, though, and the tiny bathroom had a standing shower stall, as promised.

As the door latched behind me, I tossed my pack on the bed and peeled off my tank top. It was stained with blood and there were some holes in it, but it was going to have to do for now because I hadn't thought to grab another one before I left the apartment. I kicked off my shoes and wiggled out of my pants, then hung the clothes on the curtain rod to try and dry them out a little, stopping for a minute to look out at the streets below. I could see my apartment down the street, where another police aircar cruised down from the sky lane to join the others on the ground.

What am I going to do?

I didn't have a good answer to that at the moment. I just stared through the sheets of rain that washed down over the window, and watched the lights stream by until my stomach growled and I remembered the ration. There was no point saving it now.

I unzipped the pack and found that the guards hadn't looked inside, or if they had, they didn't confiscate anything. One piece of good luck anyway. I grabbed the ration and carried it into the bathroom, where I turned the shower dial to a single rinse. The pipes thumped in the wall, and while the water tank filled I pulled the plastic wrapper off the ration and ate the dry crunchy puck while sitting on the toilet.

As the food made its way down to my belly, the pounding in my head eased somewhat, but it didn't do much to stop the empty ache. I felt a tickle on my cheek and wiped my eyes. Once they started, the tears wouldn't seem to stop. They'd beaten him so bad. He was knocked out, facedown, and bleeding, but they'd just kept beating him. How could they do that?

"I love you like you were my own flesh and blood...."

Dragan never said stuff like that. He just didn't. He pushed. He teased. He yelled sometimes, and swore. He didn't tell people he loved them, not even when he did.

It had taken me so long to trust him. The thought chafed in my mind as I chewed bitter scalefly that was supposed to be his. I'd spent too long waiting for the other shoe to drop, for him to beat me, or touch me like so many other men had done or tried to do. It felt like time wasted now, and I realized that I was starting to get scared, really scared, that I'd never see him again.

I swallowed the last of the cake. What would I do without him? Ling kept saying I should be going off on my own, that most people my age couldn't wait to get out of the house. She acted like it wasn't normal not to have any plans to leave, but the truth was I just wasn't ready to go. I didn't want to go. I wanted things to stay the way they were. I just wanted to hang out, bitch about work, and go to Fangwenzhe Festival with him instead of using it as a place to pickpocket. Even when he got on my case, there was a small part of me that kind of liked it. It made me feel like I was his real kid. What was I going to do if—

The tank thumped and the hiss of water ended in a muted dribble. I climbed in and stood under the shower-head, rubbing alcohol gel over my bare skin even when the cuts lit up like fire. The slice from when I'd picked up the glass shard burned so bad it made my nose run as I wiped my hands off in my hair, then turned the faucet and let the liter of hot water dribble down over me. I rinsed the cleanser away as best I could and scrubbed the funk out of my hair until the last drops patted down on top of my head. Then I leaned against the wall for a while, looking down my flat chest at the ridges of my ribs and feeling dizzy.

When I stepped back out into the hotel room naked, I saw an arc of blue lightning flash over the top of the skyline through the mist outside. Way off, another building lit up and began to fall as fat drops splashed off the window. I kept the light off and grabbed the bottle of shine from my backpack. I cracked it and took a big gulp, then let out a long breath and crooked my neck to reactivate the 3i feed.

Vamp, it's me.

Sam, are you okay?

Yeah.

I took another swig off the bottle, and fished the pistol out of the backpack.

You're all over the news.

I know. I'm okay.

Where are you?

Someplace safe. Don't worry.

Don't worry?

I headed over to the window and sat on the sill with my head against the glass, peering through the rain toward my apartment building. I pointed the gun up toward our balcony, then squinted through the scope, trying to frame it.

They took Dragan, I said.

He paused, his heart icon beating several times before answering, *I know. Did you hear what they're saying?*

No. What who's saying?

The feeds are already buzzing. Word is he got picked up for smuggling some kind of weapon into Hangfei. Something bad.

I clenched my jaw. *That's bullshit.*

I'm just telling you, that's what they're saying.

What do they mean "weapon"? Like a bomb or something?

No one knows. It sounds like it's worse than that.

It's bullshit.

I know.

You better know.

I found the edge of the shattered glass through the scope and followed it to our balcony, where one of the curtains flapped in the open air like an ugly flag. There were lights on inside, and I could make out movement.

Where are you? I'll come over.

You can't, security's got Tùzi-wō locked down. I'm going to hole up for tonight and lie low. I'll message you tomorrow once things have cooled down a little. Another pause.

Okay.

I wanted to tell him what happened, to tell someone what happened, but they might actually be scanning the feeds for keywords and I didn't want to risk it. Not until I was ready to put some distance between me and Tùzi-wō.

I put a call in to Kang. I can trust him. Hopefully he'll get back to me soon.

Isn't he with security? What if he just comes after you instead?

He doesn't know where I am. I know it's not perfect, but I need info, Vamp. I need to know something, anything.

Okay, I get it.

Dragan isn't a traitor.

I know.

Peering through the pistol's scope, I adjusted the zoom until I could see past the mangled railing and through the hole the airbike had left. Something moved inside again, and I spotted a shadow cast on one wall as whoever was there stepped in front of the light. It was someone big, someone tall, but there was something weird about him, like he had a sheet draped over him.

"What in hell?" I said under my breath. The shape moved, and seemed to come apart as a series of ropy silhouettes undulated slowly across the drywall.

I blinked and rubbed my eye, but when I looked again the shadow was just the shadow of a man wearing a helmet and poncho. I sighed, lowering the pistol before tossing it on the bed. All the adrenaline had burned through whatever meds were left in my system, and all I had in hand was the shine. It was going to be a long night.

Can you come tomorrow? Once things have cooled off? I asked him.

You got it.

Thunder rolled as I took another swallow from the bottle. It burned going down, but it helped keep my hands steady. I took another one and leaned against the window. Below, clusters of rain-slick, helmeted heads moved down the street through an alternating blue and red strobe while the whoop of a siren occasionally drifted up. I brought up the eyebot again and watched the orange markers move in time with the officers on the street.

The eyebot works really well, I sent. *Are the security guys tracked by people who are running the app, watching from windows?*

Mostly. Some are on the street. If you're watching now then your feed is part of the model.

You realize they're going to crack down on this, right? Hwong isn't going to like people being able to track any officer or soldier who . . .

I perked up a little suddenly, wiping breath fog from the window. As the helmeted heads moved, so did the markers.

What?

Does this thing keep a log?

You mean like a history of troop movements? The users can't access it, but yeah, I store it so we can see how operations like this play out.

How many people are running it?

Actively running it, I'm not sure. Downloads are in the tens of thousands, though.

Then could I use it to track Dragan maybe?

Someone has to see the guys who took him. He's wherever he's going by now.

Not track where he is now. I want to know where he was between the time he came back to Hangfei and the time he got to the apartment.

The app only tags security, though. A person only gets painted if he's fitted with a security transponder.

Dragan was still kitted when he came home.

Vamp thought about that for a minute. *Okay, yeah. He'd get picked up for sure then.*

Can you find him?

Problem is, with the sweep and now the mess at your place, he'd be like a needle in a haystack.

Can you do it?

He wasn't part of the sweep, so he might have been out of the main jumble. I don't know if I can pick him out of the general noise of regular patrols, but I'll see what I can do.

Thanks. See you tomorrow?

Tomorrow. Be careful, Sam.

I logged off and took another swig from the bottle. Good guys like Vamp didn't come along every day.

He was kind of famous online, but that wasn't why I liked him. I mean, I used to think he was cool, and when I kicked in a yuan to his pet project I was psyched when my name actually got picked. I wasn't his first contest date, but he was my first real date ever, which was kind of funny because it was a complete disaster on almost every level.

I smiled, remembering it. Afterward I really didn't expect to ever hear from him again, but he wouldn't leave me alone until I let him apologize and try again. Our second date wasn't really a date, but that was when we clicked for some reason. He became the first real friend I ever made, and we'd been close since.

I sighed and stared up at the ceiling. I forget when I first noticed the change, but now his voice dropped when he talked to me, and his eyes had started to linger. He sat closer to me these days, and smiled more. I wasn't sure what to do about it. I mean, it wasn't like I totally couldn't see myself with him, but I didn't want to ruin things, and it seemed like moving either way could do that now. I'd been avoiding the whole thing so far, but it had gotten worse and now he was too ready to go out on a limb for me. I was going to have to deal with it sooner or later.

Not tonight, though. Tonight I didn't have the strength left to think about anything. In the morning I'd figure out what to do next. Until then, I just wanted to get numb. Fuzzy wasn't going to cut it. I wanted to be numb enough to sleep through the night.

With half the bottle gone I got pretty close, but I still didn't get my wish.

Chapter Five

"I'll help you, but first you have to help me. . . ."

Sleep came, but it was a fitful sleep full of sweat, jitters, and bad dreams. It dredged up murky clouds of half-remembered voices and faces. Memories of being woken by gunshots and groping fingers.

"Touch me. . . ."

In my dreams I smelled human waste, engine smoke, and cooking meat that made me salivate even though I knew it was the flesh of men. A low rumble filled the air, and a faint hiss bubbled up over it while a child sobbed from a few feet away. I shifted on the slick concrete floor to try and wake my leg up, and winced as my back pressed against the grimy wall. My throat was so dry it ached, and when I turned my head toward the water bottle hanging next to me, the hand's length of cable connecting my nylon collar to the eye screw above pulled taut. The edges dug into the raw chaff around my neck as I licked the ball bearing at the end of the bottle's metal tube, careful not to let any of the warm, foul-tasting water dribble away. Through the wire mesh basket that held it in place, I could see there was only a tiny amount left.

The men were back. I could hear their footsteps as they came closer, and then the squeal of a rusted bolt being turned.

"No!"

The child, a boy, screamed suddenly and pulled at his collar as the heavy metal door groaned open across the room. We'd been brought in together, he and I. He'd been in a blind panic ever since, quiet only when he slept, or when they finally got fed up and shocked him into unconsciousness.

I didn't bother to try and shush him. It didn't work. When I looked in his eyes, I could see he'd gone over the edge. He was next now, the row of collars next to his dangling bloody from their hooks. They'd hung the last woman to bleed out earlier, and the drips had finally stopped maybe ten minutes before. Two figures came through the door, indistinct shapes in the haze of steam. They clomped across the wet concrete floor as the door slammed shut behind them.

"No!" the boy shrieked. "Please no! Please!"

The two dark-skinned, tattooed men approached the woman who was still hanging by her ankles over the trough. One of them guided her over to the platform of butcher block, while the other worked the controls. Her head thumped on the wooden surface as the winch began to lower her.

"Please! I want to go home!"

"Gonzo, please tell me he's next," one of the men muttered.

"He's next."

He unhooked the cable from around the woman's bony, broken ankles and moved it off to the side. His partner grabbed a heavy apron and slipped it over his head, then yanked a machete out of the block.

"Don't!" the boy cried.

"Shut it," the man with the machete said. "You don't, you get the prod again. Get me?"

The boy went quiet, but he was clenching and unclenching his fists frantically, eyes bugging from hollow sockets. He slid across the wall behind him, away from the men until the collar tugged at his bloodied neck and he almost knocked over the shallow, shit-stained bucket next to him. The man cursed as he went back to join his partner, who had spread out the dead woman's arms and legs. They'd chop her up next, like they did the others.

That's going to be me. The thought used to send me into a panic, as bad as the boy's, but now it just crawled around in my brain like an ugly certainty. That was going to be me. They'd do the boy, and then they'd do me. They'd winch me up and cut my throat, then leave to go have a cigarette while I dangled.

My empty stomach turned, bile threatening to creep up on me. I swallowed hard and squeezed my fists until the nails cut into my palms. I was shaking, shivering even in the heat, and I couldn't stop.

"Don't watch," the old man said from my right. I didn't look over at him, but I could sense him there, head lolled against the taut cable. I reached down behind me with one hand and found the length of wire I'd managed to work off the water bottle's mesh basket. I poked the point I'd sharpened with one finger. It seemed puny next to the blades the butchers used.

The man with the machete looked down at the woman, and his eyes lingered on her breasts. He reached down with his free hand, and cupped one, giving it an experimental squeeze.

"Kind of a shame, huh?" the second man said, shaking out a cigarillo and sticking it in his mouth.

"They're real," the first one said.

"Well," the second one said with a yellow-toothed grin as he sparked his lighter, "the taste is in the fat."

"Why do you watch?" the old man rasped. I didn't answer. I poked my finger with the wire again, the jab of pain waking me up a little. I might be able to surprise them, but I felt so dizzy now I could barely hold my head up. I told myself one of them would have to reach down to unfasten the collar. If I went for the eye . . .

The old man opened his mouth to speak again, but he froze, like he was on TV and someone paused him. His image flickered.

". . . receiving this transmission, listen carefully," a voice said, Mandarin with a heavy Western accent. *"What you are experiencing is not a dream. You're—"*

The old man flickered again, and the strange voice cut out. The butchers laughed, one of them spreading the dead woman's arm out across the block while the other got into position. He hoisted the machete, and then everything froze again.

". . . attempting to reach you . . . if anyone can . . ."

The voice crackled out again. Everything jumped forward a few seconds, and the sounds and smells all returned as the man brought the machete down hard on the woman's shoulder.

I jerked awake and crashed into the wall behind me as I scrambled back. In the seconds it took to register that I was back in the hotel, and that it was just a dream, I'd retreated from the mattress and stumbled on all fours into the corner of the room. My body was covered in sweat that made the cuts sting, and my breath came in fast, shallow hitches.

A dream. Just a dream. Calm down. Dim sunlight shone in through the window. It was day. It was just a dream.

I hadn't had it in a while, but it had been waiting. It had been just waiting for me to miss a dose or two, to sleep too lightly, so it could seep in and take me back to that place. Why hadn't I . . . ?

The events of the night before were still tangled in cobwebs, and for a few seconds I listened for the sound of Dragan in the shower or Tānchi keening from the crib before I realized where I was.

I wiped drool from the side of my mouth and tried to blink the dryness out of my eyes. I'd passed out the night before, and the bottle lay capped on its side on the end table next to the lamp. One of the 3i's chat windows blurred off in the corner, where a string of text still sat.

Sam, forgive me, I couldn't— I jerked upright as I realized the message was from Dragan. I seized on the chat window and dragged it to the foreground, firing off text as fast as I could manage.

Dragan, where are you? Are you okay? He didn't answer.

Dragan?

His contact icon was gray. The message had been sent hours ago and I'd missed it, although it looked like he hadn't managed to even finish a sentence before he got cut off.

Forgive me, I couldn't . . . what? I stared at the text, trying to make something out of it, but I couldn't. It couldn't tell me what happened to him, only that he was alive. Or he had been, a couple of hours ago. It couldn't tell me where they'd taken him.

Or could it? I pulled up the message details, fingers crossed, and smiled when I saw a location tag was included. At the time Dragan sent the message, he was in . . .

Shiliuyuán Station.

My smile shifted to a frown. That didn't make any sense. There wasn't any Shiliuyuán Station, not anymore. It was destroyed in the Impact. Did it mean the location where the station used to be? Had she taken him to the ship?

On the tray underneath it, another message indicator flashed. That one was from Vamp, sent maybe an hour or so before Dragan's message.

Still pulling the eyebot data but got you something else. Check your phone.

I rubbed my eyes, making the holodisplay warp as I pawed around for my cell phone. He'd sent me a mail with a single link to somewhere on one of the Channel X servers, and when I touched it, a long string of text appeared. I squinted, head pounding, as I tried to focus on the scrolling characters.

It took me a second to realize what I was looking at, but when I did, a weak smile spread over my face.

"Holy shit, you're the best," I said under my breath. They were messages from Dragan's e-mail account. Vamp had managed to hack into Dragan's security e-mail and pull copies of the messages that had been sitting in his in-box. There were only a few, but accessing them like that was enough to get him in huge trouble, never mind posting and distributing them. Add to that Dragan was flagged as a violent dissident. . . .

Vamp? There was a slight pause.

Yeah.

Vamp, you have to take that down right away.

I will. Make a copy.

Thank you. Thank you so much.

Where are you?

I can't believe you would do that for me.

He paused again, a little longer that time. *Where are you? I need to tell you something.*

That place we sometimes stay. You know where I mean?

Yeah.

What do you need to tell me?

In person.

Ring me when you're here. I'll come down.

See you soon.

I thumbed through the e-mail entries, excitement mingling queasily in my stomach with the remains of scalefly and too much shine. The first mail on the list, the last one he'd received, was from some guy named Eng with no subject. I opened it up and found just a few sentences:

Passage clear to Duongroi. Meet me at my place in the Pink Bull, Hǎiyáng-Gāodù, to pick up passports. Bring payment, and come alone.

I checked the date. He'd received the message the morning before, after he'd arrived in Hangfei maybe, or shortly before. He hadn't responded, but he'd read it.

Passports. My heart sank a little as doubt tried to worm its way in. Dragan had a passport, so why would he need new ones? Why would he need to get them from some guy in Hǎiyáng-Gāodù, instead of through security, and why was he so hot to sneak over to Duongroi?

There's a reason, I thought. *You don't know what's going on. He had a reason.*

"Hǎiyáng-Gāodù," I said to myself. Did he know this guy Eng? I'd never heard him mention him.

I rustled through my knapsack and found a few cigarillos in a squished pack. I pulled one out with my teeth as I tapped in a quick search for the Pink Bull—it was a hotel. Dragan must have gone there before coming home maybe, or maybe this guy Eng was still there waiting for him. I lit the smoke and took a deep drag, a small nicotine rush kicking in as I blew it out through my nose.

Eng.

I sifted through the other e-mails. Most of the ones below it had to do with work. The one right below Eng's had the subject line *RE: Alexei Drugov.* I opened that one.

The brass is shutting this one down. From this point on, any and all information regarding the Drugov family has been marked classified. Drop it, Shao.

The rest of the thread had been redacted. The ones below it suggested he and a team of others were investigating abductions in a place called Lobnya, in the Pan-Slav border territories. Most of it was just requests for supplies or personnel, along with status reports that were encrypted so I couldn't read them. A couple looked like they were between him and someone else, though, some civilian. There were two mingled in with the rest to someone named Innuya Drugov. They were in Pan-Slav gibberish, but the Web translator was able to decipher it for me. The first said just:

> *Please, Dragan, tell me something. Is he alive? Is my son alive?*
>
> *I found him. He's alive. Stand by.*
>
> *Thank you, Dragan. I owe you my life.*

The last one read:

> *Innuya, read this carefully and do exactly as it says. If this works we'll have a very limited window to get him into Hangfei, so you have to be ready when I say. Gather a single pack containing only what you can't leave behind. You will never return. I know this is hard. Be strong. I love you.*

My eyes lingered on the end of the message.
I love you.
Before I knew it, my face flushed and I started chewing the inside of my lower lip. He did have a girl there. The son of a bitch really had hooked up with someone, some Pan-Slav, and her Pan-Slav kid.
Alexei Drugov.
I glared at the name. I felt stupid being jealous, but I was, and I couldn't help it. Was this why my messages had gone unanswered? Did he have some kind of second family over there or something?

"I'm going to ask you one more time, where did you take Alexei Drugov?"

That was the name the woman soldier, the haan in disguise, had used during the raid. They were looking for him ... but why?

... the feeds are already buzzing. Word is he got picked up for smuggling some kind of weapon into Hangfei. Something bad.

Possibilities, all the worst possibilities that had been floated across the news channels for the past months started firing off in my head. Could it be true? Had one of them finally snuck something over here that was a million times worse than just a roadside bomb?

And had Dragan helped them?

If this works we'll have a very limited window to get him into Hangfei, so you have to be ready when I say.

I shook my head, taking another drag off the cigarillo.

"It's not true," I croaked. Dragan would never attack his own country. It had to be the kid, or his mother, and if Dragan really did sneak them into Hangfei, there was no way he could have known about it. He wouldn't do that. There was no way in the world Dragan would do that—

A knock came at the door, and I jumped so bad that I dropped the phone down onto the bed next to me. I took a step back and froze.

Who knew I was here? Just Vamp, and there's no way he got to the hotel that fast.

I didn't say anything. I didn't even breathe, I just stood there, completely still, as the knock came again.

"Sam Shao?" a voice called softly. It was a man's voice, but I didn't recognize it.

I started looking around for some other way out, but there was nowhere else to go. When the knock came a third time, I pulled the curtain shut and tiptoed over to the end table in the dim light.

I'd just picked up the pistol when I heard the low crackle come from the direction of the door, and whipped around to see a point of bright white light floating there just inside it. Immediately it expanded into a hexagonal portal, a haan gate, and through it I could see the hallway on the other side of the door where a dark shape stood. I saw two pink lights and a mellow green glow that flashed near his throat as he spoke.

"Oh, you are here."

I stumbled back, pointing the gun in front of me, as the figure stepped through the gate and into the room. I squeezed the gun's grip like Dragan had shown me, and a thumbnail-sized display appeared floating next to the chamber. The magazine was full, with twenty rounds total.

"Don't move," I said, trying to keep my voice even. The gun was shaking, and I tried to steady it with my other hand. "You move and I'll . . ."

My voice piddled out as I saw the pink lights were actually large, glowing eyes. At the same time, a signal came through the mite cluster like an arrow driven straight through my forehead. It surprised me, and I sucked in a breath, but it didn't hurt or anything. It was just the opposite. The signal sought out some feel-good part of my brain, and I felt happy all of a sudden, like an old friend I'd thought was gone had stepped through the door. Relief and the joy of his being back, the comfort of being in his arms kind of washed over me even though I knew it was all just in my head.

"You're a haan," I said.

"Yes."

His voice was a calm tenor, quiet but confident. The flashing light, I realized, was the flicker from his voice box.

My eyelids drooped, and a loopy smile grew on my face as the gun lowered a few inches. The tingling in my head was branching out, nudging other pleasure centers until I felt a little numb.

"I am not a threat to you," he said, taking a step closer as the gate collapsed behind him. "You don't need your weapon." He had his hands held up by his head so that I could see them, black material draping from his arms.

What with my hunger, my fear, my hangover, and his diddling through the mites, I had trouble keeping the gun from drifting. I'd never fired one before, and it must have been obvious, but I wasn't ready to put it down just yet. I kept it pointed in his general direction while he waited to see what I would do.

I flipped on the light. My first impression of him was his eyes, which were an unusual sunset pink. My second impression was that he was short for a haan, not being very much taller than me. My third impression was, as strange as it was, that I knew him.

His face was haan-handsome, in that way that made you think of a doll or mannequin. They looked like masks, formed into something almost humanlike, except for the fact that they didn't conceal anything and were breakable as ceramic. His brains rippled calmly around the edges behind his large eyes, and I could see the dark shadow of his feeding orifice behind his molded lips. His clothes showed off long, lean muscle underneath without being too flashy and he held himself with the confidence and balance of a gymnast or martial artist. The suit he wore was sharp, crisp, and a flawless fit.

My fourth impression was that I'd never dressed after my shower the night before, and was still stark naked.

"Do you always just gate into people's private rooms?" I asked.

"No."

His presence in my head trickled through to another part of my brain, maybe on purpose and maybe not, and my face flushed. As I looked into the intense pink of his eyes, the twin ribbed crescents inside his skull shifted. Two smaller masses on either side pulled back, the network of veins around them engorging slightly above his brow. In spite of myself, I was getting turned on.

"All right," I said, trying to ignore the sudden pang below my waist. "That's enough. Out of my head."

He retreated immediately.

"Those are for surrogate bonding," I said. My lips felt warm when I licked them. "They're not for you."

"I understand."

"Who are you? Are you armed?"

"My name is Nix."

"Are you armed?"

"No." He stayed motionless, with his hands still up. I kept the gun on him as I approached.

"Open your jacket," I said. He did, spreading the material apart so I could see.

"What's that in the pocket?"

"My tablet."

"Let's see it."

He reached into his coat and removed a slim metallic device whose screen appeared as a mirrored, metal surface. It was an Escher Field tablet. The screen was a small gate field that led to a larger storage area.

"How do I know you don't have a gun or something in there?" I asked. He swiped the screen casually with one finger, and the metallic screen crackled, then disappeared. He handed the tablet to me.

I took it, and looked inside. Through the field I could see a gap of impossible space above a series of hexagonal compartments. Each one was several inches deep and big enough to reach into. All of them were empty.

When I put my hand in front of the screen, the field expanded and jumped forward a little. I smiled as I swiped across it with one finger, and the compartments on the other side scrolled past. Some were full, but I didn't get a good look before I stopped the sweep and tried to back-track.

"Pretty slick," I said, admiring the gadget. Come Phase Five, I was getting one for sure.

"Thank you," he said. "Though I think you would not like it if I held you at gunpoint and searched through your things."

"I think you would not like it if I gated into your room without asking." I collapsed the field and held the device up between my thumb and fingers. "No one asked you to come here."

"That is false." I tossed him the tablet, and he caught it. He stowed the device back in his coat, then lowered his hands by his sides.

"What's that supposed to mean?" I asked.

"You came to Shangzho last night," he said.

"So?"

"You made a strange claim. Then you indicated you needed help."

Right. With everything else, I'd forgotten about that.

"And they sent you?"

"Yes."

I struggled to remember what I'd said and what, if anything, I knew about haan interactions with human security. "Does security know you're here?"

"My capacity here is not official."

"So they don't know?"

"They do not."

I thought about it, still not sure this was a good idea. I didn't like the way he'd tracked me down like that. He'd known right where I was, and if he could find me, so could someone else.

"I think I might be okay," I said carefully. "Just . . . forget I said anything."

"Forget?"

"Security took him. . . . You don't have any pull with that. I don't need your help."

His voice box clicked, then began to flicker as a different voice, my voice, came out of it.

"Look, I need help, okay?" I heard myself say. *"Soldiers took my guardian. They tried to kill me. I can't— "* It clicked again, like static, and my voice continued. *"I know you could help me. I know you could. If you wanted to you could— "*

"Look, I wasn't thinking straight last night. I don't think you can really do anything about this," I said, talking over my own voice. He clicked again.

"One of them was a haan," I heard myself whisper. *"She was pretending to be a human— "*

I started to say something back, but stopped. His pupils rotated as he watched me.

"She sent you?" I asked him. "The female from Shangzho last night?"

"Yes."

"Why you? Who are you?"

"I was obtained from the axial hive in Shangzho to look into this incident."

"What, at random?"

"Not exactly. Do you— "

"Who was she? The one who took my surrogate?"

"Her name is Ava," he said. "She is transitioning to become the new haan female."

"Yeah, well, she's got the rack for it."

"What made you think one of your attackers was haan?" he said, ignoring me. "What did she look like?"

"She wore military combat armor," I said. "Her face was covered by a dispersion mask. She looked human. But I picked her up," I said, tapping my forehead. "Strong. She was haan."

"You're certain?"

"Yes."

"And you are certain this haan was female?"

"Yeah." I rubbed my forehead, gun still pointing at the floor, and sighed. "Okay. You're already in. Have a seat if you want."

"No, thank you."

He entered the room, then extended his hand and I shook it. The skin of his hand felt smooth and cool against my palm.

"I am Nix," he said.

"I'm Sam."

"I know."

He took his hand back and looked around the room, pupils revolving as he turned his head robotically. He followed the stuff scattered across the floor until he found my feet, then followed all the way up until he finally met my eye again. "You are naked."

"I see they sent over their top investigator," I said, tossing the gun down onto the mattress and turning around to grab my clothes off the curtain rod.

"What caused the lacerations?" he asked.

"I got thrown out a window." His brains twitched, like he wasn't sure if I was serious. "No, really, look . . . you can see it from here."

He stepped closer and followed my finger to the shattered glass hole in the side of my apartment complex. By the light of day it looked even worse, and my stomach dropped a little when I followed the path I'd fallen. It was a long, long drop.

"The haan threw me."

"The female haan tried to kill you?"

"Yeah."

"I do not think a haan would have the strength to throw even a small human with such force."

"She had on combat armor." I held the smoke between my teeth as I slipped one leg into my pants, squinting as smoke burned one eye. "Look, if you asked me yesterday I wouldn't have bought it either."

I pulled my pants up and cinched the belt. They were still a little damp, but wearable. The same went for the tank top. I pulled it down over my head and snapped the waist tight to my hard stomach and smoothed the material down over my ribs. "So, are you here to help me or what?"

"Help you?"

"Find Dragan. Find my guardian. The haan and the other soldiers took him last night. Are you here to help me find him?"

"No."

I frowned, picking up the stunner and pistol and stuffing one in each front pocket. "Then no offense, Nix, but why are you here?"

"I was obtained to investigate the potential involvement of a haan in the attack."

I shook my head. "Well, you'll never get in there now, not until security's done going over it, and probably not until they manage to pull the airbike out of our living room."

"I don't need to. If you'll allow, I can gather what I need from you."

"Me?"

"If you'll allow."

I was picking up something, an anxious hum through the surrogate cluster. Something was bothering the haan, something he was trying to keep to himself but wasn't quite able to.

"I'll make you a deal," I said. "How about I let you do whatever you're looking to do and you help me find Dragan?"

The anxious feeling grew worse as he looked into my eyes with his iridescent pink ones.

"Yes," he said.

"So you agree to help me?"

"Yes."

Nix moved in front of me and leaned closer, until I could feel the warmth of his face against my neck. After a moment he reached into his tablet and drew some kind of electronic wand from out of the field. Sprouting from the tip of it was a set of metal prongs, two thin ones coiled around a central, thicker one. He held it between two spindly fingers as he drew in air, and then something under his clothes made that rattle again as he vented it.

"What's that?" I asked him.

"A congenital defect sometimes causes an internal scraping of —"

"No, the wand."

"It will take the sample I need." I looked uneasily at the device as he moved it closer to me. The prongs were wickedly sharp.

"Will it hurt?"

He stepped closer, and I felt another weird surge through the surrogate cluster. A wave of unhappiness, and uncertainty mixed with a strange longing . . . a sense of familiarity, as if someone he thought he'd lost was returned to him after a long absence.

"Nix, do I know you?"

He shook his head, moving the prongs closer to my chest. "I was born in the axial hive."

I peered down at the wand, feeling like I wanted to back away. "Wait, will it hurt or not?"

He held the wand frozen in front of me, so close that whatever energy it gave off made the skin beneath it tingle. Through the jumble of strange feelings pouring in over the link between us, I felt a sudden pulse of deep, abject misery.

"Hey, are you okay?" I asked him.

The current of signals stopped. He moved the wand away from me and stowed it back inside his tablet.

"Yes," he said, "and no, it won't hurt."

"You sure about that?"

"Yes. I've already taken the sample."

"Oh," I said, but he was lying. I didn't get haan completely—no one did—but somehow I was sure that what he'd just said was a lie. I'd just missed something, something important, but I didn't know what.

"This will help," he said.

"Will it help with the fact that you're a big, fat liar?"

His rigid face offered no expression I could read as he fell quiet. For a second I thought he'd gone into some kind of trance or something when I noticed a lot of little movements through the smoked glass of his skull. They settled down, and the sunset pink of his eyes flickered once.

"Your guardian's security transponder is no longer active in Hangfei," he said.

"What?"

"Each of your security personnel is fitted with a transponder used for identification purposes. Your legal guardian, Specialist Dragan Shao, cannot currently be located in Hangfei."

"You're saying he's not in the city anymore?" That didn't make any sense.

"Maybe. His transponder may also inactive, or someplace where the signal cannot be reached."

"Oh." I dropped the pack back down on the bed.

"That's all I can say."

"Are you . . . supposed to know that?"

"I have to go."

The sudden shift had left me off balance, and a little angry. My head was pounding again.

"Fine," I said. "Great. Go."

He paused for a minute, then turned and crossed back around the bed. I followed him as he stepped back toward the hotel room door.

"Look, will you just tell me what's going on?" I asked him.

"No."

He stopped at the door and turned back to me. He extended his hand, and I shook it again.

"Wait," I said. "Before you go."

"What?"

"The haan female . . . Ava."

"She is transitioning to become the new haan female."

"Whatever. Will you see her again?"

"Yes."

"Can you ask her for me about Tānchi?"

"Who?"

"Sorry," I said. "The kid I dropped off last night. My surrogate."

He nodded. "Ask her what?"

"I was wondering if there's any chance I can finish the imprint with him," I said. "Once this gets straightened out."

He paused, and there was more subtle shifting from inside his skull. "You have already failed to complete the imprint."

"I know, but—"

"Failure to complete an imprint disqualifies you from further surrogate service."

My mouth dropped. As he turned to leave, I grabbed his sleeve and stopped him in spite of the fact that doing so could, under the current laws, be interpreted as an assault against a haan.

"Wait," I sputtered. "This wasn't my fault."

"I know."

"He could have starved if I didn't bring him back. I did the right thing!"

He looked down at my fistful of his suit, and I took my hand away.

"Failure to complete an imprint disqualifies you from further surrogate service."

"But—"

"Thank you for your time. Good-bye."

"Wait," I said, squirming past to block him. I held my hands up between us, and he stopped. "Just wait a minute, please."

It hadn't occurred to me until right then, not really, just how much I'd come to depend on being a surrogate. Not just because of the extra money or rations, and not just to earn my keep with Dragan. Taking care of the little ones was one of the few bright spots I had, one of the few things that really, truly made me feel good. Now, just like that, not only had I lost Dragan but I was going to lose that too.

"This has to be a special case," I said. "I'm a good surrogate."

"I don't—"

"Just ask her."

"I—"

"Just say you'll ask her!"

He paused, his body tense, before relenting.

"Your assigned foster has already been sent back," he said.

"Where did you send him?"

"Back."

"Back wh—"

"Your transaction is complete."

"Wait," I said, almost grabbing his sleeve again. An awful feeling was sinking into my stomach. "Back where? What does that mean?"

I knew, though. On some level, I knew. I remembered waving to him as Ava closed the hopper door, and the low vibration that went through the floor afterward. It had reminded me of a garbage disposal.

"All haan young must be imprinted," he said. "No exceptions. I'm sorry. I thought you knew."

I couldn't say anything. A lump grew in my throat, and I felt tears in my eyes, but I couldn't speak.

I killed him. It was all I could think. I'd talked those guards into letting me inside. I trekked all the way across town in the middle of a security sweep, just so I could send him to his death when I could have just gotten a new kit in the morning.

"Are you okay?" Nix asked.

"Go," I said, my voice thick and hoarse.

"If I—"

"Go!" I snapped, a fleck of spit landing on the shoulder of his coat. It was all catching up with me finally. I clamped my hands down over my head like it was an eggshell I was trying to hold together. My stomach was full of bile, and the pressure building up behind my eyes was horrible. The shine had been a mistake. I put one hand on the wall to steady myself, using the back of the other to wipe my eyes.

"These are your government's rules," I heard Nix say.

"You guys are so cute when you're little," I said. "What happens?"

Nix just stared at me, unblinking. "We grow up."

I pressed my palms to my eyes and watched spastic, electric spots swim in the darkness behind my eyelids.

"I suggest you do the same." He stepped through the gate and it closed, leaving me alone.

Chapter Six

I stormed back to the bed and grabbed my pack so violently that stuff came spilling out of it. A tube of lipstick and an empty glass perfume bottle bounced onto the floor while the stun gun clattered across the end table and almost broke the lamp.

"Damn it. . . ."

I grabbed the stun gun and tossed it back into the pack, then snatched the stuff back up from off the floor. When I stuffed the tube of lipstick in my pants pocket, a piece of paper crunched and I pulled out a black slip of paper covered in several haan stamps. It was the receipt they'd given me for Tānchi.

Tears welled up in my eyes as I crumpled it and threw it in the trash. I went to drop the bottle in the pack too when something rattled inside. I held it up where I could see, and found a stray tetraz tablet stashed inside that I'd forgotten about.

"Oh, thank Gonzo."

I shook it into my palm and popped it in my mouth, crushing the bitter pill piece between my back teeth, then using a swallow of shine to wash it down.

Tears welled up again, and I forced them back. I couldn't think about Tānchi right now. On top of everything else, it would push me over the edge. I had to focus on what I could fix.

I'm downstairs. The message appeared in the chat window. It was Vamp.

Sam?

I'm on my way. Meet me out back.

I tossed the gun in the pack, zipped it up, then headed out and took the elevator back down to the ground floor. I signed out at the desk, then crossed the lobby and made my way down through the first-floor hallway to the exit that went out into the rear lot. It was already hot outside, and the humidity hit me like a wave when I pushed open the warm metal door. Vehicles streamed by in a line past the mouth of the alley, where colorful graffiti covered the sweaty brick face. A miasma hung over the little pocket of blacktop and metal outside the door that smelled like chemical fumes and smoke. I didn't see any blues flashing out on the street anymore. The way was clear, for now.

Vamp leaned against the wall by the stairs, his white tank top plastered to his wiry but chiseled brown body. His thumbs danced over the screen of his phone, the muscles in his forearms causing his ornate jiangshi tattoo to ripple. Most of Vamp was tattooed, all of it expensive, detailed work I never got tired of looking at. Braided lanyards, one black, one white, dangled from the wet drives embedded behind each ear, swaying in the gentle breeze. When he saw me, his eyes widened.

Something clunked behind me and I spun around to see a chunk of rust fall from the fire escape above. It pinged off the wall and skittered off into a drift of city grit that had collected in a shallow pavement sink. I shielded my face against the glare from the hotel's mirrored face, but I didn't see anything. High above, the sleek shadow of an airship cruised past.

"Sam, are you okay?"

"Huh?" I turned back toward him. "Yeah."

A scowl formed on his face, and anger flashed in his eyes. "No, you're not. What the hell did they do to you?"

"I'm okay."

He put his phone away and reached out, angling my face so he could see the other side. I squirmed away.

"The soldiers did this?" His voice had turned serious. I nodded, leaving it at that for now. He'd gone into protective mode, which sometimes felt like an inconvenience, but not now. Right now it made me feel a little better, but I needed him to focus.

"Vamp, I need help. I need to find out where they took Dragan, and how I'm going to get him back."

"Sam . . ." He looked uncomfortable.

"First thing is we need to find out what detention center they took him to so we can—"

"Sam," he said again, squeezing my arm gently.

"What?"

"I have bad news," he said.

"What?"

He shook his head. "It's about Dragan."

My heart began to drop before he managed to get the words out. I'd never seen a look like that on Vamp's face before, and as he struggled with how he was going to say what he had to say next, I realized what that was going to be.

"Don't," I said. My legs went shaky.

"Because of the weapons trafficking charge—"

"He wouldn't do that."

"I know, I'm just saying . . . when you get flagged a dissident, they can treat you a lot different. He resisted, and during the fight—"

"No," I said, holding up one hand. "It's a mistake."

"It's on the feed already," he said. "Sam, I'm sorry. I'm really sorry. They shot him—"

"Shut up!"

My throat knotted, and I felt like I was going to bawl,

but it never came. It just stayed there, stuck in my throat like a bitter chunk of scalefly I couldn't swallow. I couldn't speak. Even the sounds of the city, the vehicles and the blanket of anonymous conversation, started to sound far away.

"Sam, are you okay?" He went to take my arm again, but I pulled away. The ground felt like it had begun to move. It was true that he had resisted. The last thing I saw as I went out the window was him fighting the soldiers. By the time I got back up there, he was gone.

"Sam?"

"There was no blood," I said.

"Huh?"

"When I went back, there was no blood."

Vamp just pressed his lips together while looking so sorry it made me sick. He knew it didn't prove anything, and I knew it too.

"He messaged me," I said. "Late last night, he messaged me on the 3i. He's alive."

Or he was.

Vamp didn't say it. He was thinking it, but he didn't say it.

"Do you have any idea what he was up to?" Vamp asked carefully. "His e-mails made it sound like he'd gotten mixed up in something."

I shook my head.

Passage clear to Duongroi. Meet me at my place in the Pink Bull, Hăiyáng-Gāodù, to pick up passports. Bring payment, and come alone.

"Eng," I said softly.

The name started to pulse in my brain like a fire alarm klaxon. Whoever he was, he was one of the last people to see Dragan before . . .

I couldn't finish the thought.

He's not dead. He messaged me. They have him, somewhere.

"Sam?"

"Did you get the eyebot logs?" I asked, my voice rough.

"Yeah, but—"

"Send them to me."

"Sam—"

"Just do it. Please."

He nodded.

"I have to go."

"Go where?"

"There's someone I have to go see."

"I'm coming with you."

"Vamp, no, I'm sorry."

"Sam, I'm coming with you."

Before he could push any further, I broke away and sprinted to the mouth of the alley.

"Sam, wait!"

I stopped and turned back, just for a minute. "Don't follow me! Look . . . I'll call you in an hour."

"You're going to get pinched. They're not coming out with it officially, but the buzz is the weapon they're looking for is still here in the city. Security is through the roof, Sam."

"I know. Wait for me?"

He didn't answer, but he'd wait. Once I was around the corner, I lost myself in the crowd and kept one eye on the main drag. When I saw a taxi approach, I darted out into the street from between two parked cars and tires chirped as the cabbie laid on his horn. Before he could squeeze by, I opened the back door and jumped in, slamming it behind me. A pair of tired-looking eyes in a wrinkled brown face glared back at me from the rearview mirror. I peeked out the window and saw a couple of cops waiting outside the apartment go back to talking.

"Hey," the cabbie said while someone leaned on his

horn behind us. "What's the—" He stopped when I held up the cash card where he could see.

"The gate hub to Hǎiyáng-Gāodù," I said. "Hurry."

He shrugged, rolling the car forward just as the line behind us started trying to sneak around on his left. He picked up speed, closing the gap ahead and then breaking with about an inch to spare between his grille and the guy in front's back bumper.

"What's in Hǎiyáng-Gāodù?" the cabbie asked over his shoulder as I thumbed in the hotel name and pulled up the exact address.

"The Pink Bull."

He raised his heavy eyebrows. "You a hooker?"

"Just drive the car."

He shrugged again as we passed a couple more security guys standing on the corner. I rode low in the seat, watching the people and buildings cruise past, and risked a glance out the back window once we were past them. Neither of them bothered to look up. When we hit the tunnel I sat up again and put my forehead to the window next to me, feeling more alone than I'd ever felt in my life.

I couldn't believe it was true. I wouldn't believe it was true until I saw it for myself, but I couldn't bring myself to check the news feeds. I didn't want to know for sure, not yet. I wanted to hold on to uncertainty, or even denial if that's all it was, just a little longer.

My stomach felt hollow again, clenching and unclenching like an anxious fist. I slid one hand into my side pocket to make sure I still had the ration sheet, and felt its rough edge under my fingertips. It had a full five punches left. I leaned back to nurse my throbbing head, turning my face into the cool current dribbling out of the cab's vent. The streets were already thick with people, and they got thicker the farther on we went. By the time I could see the Heights off in the distance, the sidewalks were swarmed, bodies brushing the side of the cab as we passed. Through the front windshield, all I saw were chains of cars and an uneven blanket of bobbing black-haired heads sprinkled with the occasional shiny smoke-gray dome as the road sloped down and away. Arms waved in the air as people crowded around the rows of street kiosks, buying and selling. They were like a huge, surging organism with a steady, babbling voice that rose over the distant sound of the surf beyond. Even through the vent a wet, salty musk had started to simmer under the street smells.

"Don't bother pulling up," I said. "Here is fine." The cabbie rolled to a stop and shut off the meter. I handed my cash card through the partition and grimaced a little when I saw how much it was.

He swiped it and took a tip without asking. The machine spat out a receipt and he tore it off before handing both back.

"Thanks."

I stepped out into the sweltering heat, feeling the breath of hot methanol exhaust against my leg as the engine rumbled and he pulled away from the blue-gray cloud.

I joined the throng of people queued up in front of the hub, and even through the gate I could see the Pink Bull sign: a half pinwheel of turquoise arched over a blazing pink bull with a phallus the size of an airbike's sidecar.

I pushed my way into the current, following a chiseled guy with a zebra-pattered bandana that held down a nest of home-perm frizz. When it was my turn to go through, I sensed something behind me, something moving toward me, and a shot of adrenaline made my skin prickle. Before I could turn and see who or what it was, though, my momentum carried me through the gate and I stepped into the bustle of downtown Hăiyáng-Gāodù.

The exit gate had brought me right up to the corner of the hotel where that obnoxious plastic dong pointed down at me from above like Gonzo's pink fist.

The funky surf smell was a lot stronger there, and the humid sea breeze carried with it the chemical stink from the offshore feedlots. Down at the far end of the street, I could see through to the muck gray expanse of the tidal flats and mountains of waste salt. Way off in the distance an irregular, speckled dark cloud hung low to the ocean surface—scaleflies, swarming their way down the coast where most would get harvested, and the rest sprayed.

A little pink heart blinked on in the corner of my eye as a friend request came in on the 3i.

NIX.

My face got hot at the sight of his name.

Denied.

I approached the hotel, weaving between the tricked-out cars and rowdy pedestrians that filled the street. A lot of festival masks and costumes were already on display, and splashes of red dye were fanned out across the blacktop. The party was already starting, and the odd firecracker popped here and there over the din.

The outside of the hotel was wall-to-wall people, but no one paid me too much mind as I squeezed through to the front door and into the lobby. I passed through a cloud of smoke, cologne, and perfume and made my way to the front desk.

"Can I help you?"

The hotel clerk sat behind a faintly rippling force field, eyes staring up over a pair of bodega-rack purple sunglasses. A little fan sitting on the desktop next to him didn't quite dry the sweat on his bronze skin.

"Yeah, I need to get into a room," I said.

"You need a room?"

"No, I'm visiting someone."

He turned the handset on the desk around deliberately with one finger. "So call him and have him ring you up."

"It's a surprise," I told him.

He didn't smile. "You working?"

"Sure."

"Then call up."

"It's a s—"

"Nobody likes surprises, kid."

People around us had started to take notice, and a couple of tall guys with gold chains around their necks laughed. I leaned in closer, until my nose tingled from the force field.

"Look, he knows me."

"Then have him let you in."

Appealing to him wasn't going to work; I could see it in his eyes. He didn't know what my problem was, and he didn't care, not even a little.

"What's it going to take for you to give me a room key and let me up?"

He shrugged. "What do you got?"

"I've got some credit."

"Five hundred."

"What?"

"You heard me." He was serious. I didn't have anything close to that.

"That's too much," I said.

"Then beat it."

"I can't."

He stared at me a few seconds longer, and then his heavy brow came back up just a hair. He leaned across the desk and lowered his voice.

"You think I'm stupid?" he asked. "I can see what you got in your pockets, right down to the panties you're not wearing."

The ration sheet. He had some kind of scanner aimed at me, and he'd seen the ration sheet. Wherever the emitter was, the angle must not have let him see into the backpack, at least, not yet.

"I'll give you two punches," I told him.

"Three."

"Two, plus fifty yuan. That's my final offer."

He sucked his teeth for a minute before a faint smile crept across his thick lips. "What's the name?"

"Eng, 423."

He sighed, reaching under the desk and fishing out a key card. He held it between his fingers.

"The tickets," he said.

I fished out the sheet and tore off two tickets. I passed them under the field, where he made them disappear. I swiveled the desk reader around and touched my card to the scanner, then punched in the amount. The LCD flickered green, and I snatched the key from his fingers.

"Watch your ass. Like I said, people around here—"

"Don't like surprises. Got it."

The two guys with the chains were still watching as I backed away, keeping me between the backpack and the front desk until I could turn and push back through the crowd to the elevator. The one on the left opened and a tired-looking woman with red hair stepped out. Fishnet stockings clung to her wiry legs, disappearing up under a miniskirt that barely cleared her crotch. She gave me a knowing glance as I passed her and stepped into the cramped car with a cloud of perfume fumes thick enough to catch fire. I tapped the contact for the fourth floor with one knuckle and held my breath as the car rattled its way up.

"Sam?" a voice said from the ad box speaker in the door.

"Not now."

"If you want to opt out, you can present your card to the—"

"Look, I don't want any plastic surgery, okay?"

"I hear that," the door said, "but the question is, can you afford not to have any? I'm just a virtual construct, but even I can spot at least fifteen correctable imperfections and that's just your face."

"I don't care."

"Maybe not, but it matters. Believe me, it matters. If you don't care about your appearance, then how—"

The car stopped and I slammed the button to open the doors with my palm. As soon as they parted enough for me to sneak through, I was out of there.

"BeauVisage!" the elevator called behind me, hammering my 3i with contact info as I stalked away. "The company is BeauVisage! They can fix you!"

The hallway upstairs didn't smell much better. I passed a few more guys in the hallway, but nobody bothered me as I turned the corner and found the door marked 423.

I waited until the coast was clear, then slid the key card through the slot and waited for the click. The second I heard it, I slipped through and shut the door behind me.

The room was dark except for slits of light that shone in through the closed window blinds on the far side of the room. The air stank of heavy cologne mixed with something else, something edible that hung just underneath it.

The room was empty, and the bed still made. On one nightstand I could see a cell phone, so he hadn't gone far, but it looked like I had the place to myself at least for a little while. I looked around and saw a pill sheet with six double-cross tabs still in the blisters on the nightstand next to a woman's handbag. Wherever he was, he wasn't alone.

I tore one of the pill tabs off, and as I slipped it in my pocket I looked back and saw light coming from under the bathroom door. I hadn't even thought to check the bathroom.

Holding my breath, I crossed past the closet and back

toward the closed door. I shouldered off the backpack
and unzipped it, taking out the stun gun before knocking
three times.

"Eng?"

No one answered. I opened the door and peeked inside. The overhead light had been left on in there, one of
the two exposed tubes faded to a soft gray, and I could
see little bottles of man products lined up along the back
of the sink along with a stick of women's deodorant.

As I stepped into the room, I smelled the food smell
again and my stomach growled. There was food here, or
there had been, and not just ration packs either. The
smell came from real meat. Street meat.

I'd lived in a hotel room on the Row for a year before
I got grabbed and eventually rescued, and I'd worked
cleaning rooms for the old super, Wei, for most of it. I
knew where to stash stuff. I lifted the porcelain back of
the toilet off with a hollow scrape and laid it against the
wall next to the sink. Sure enough, a little metal cooler
sat just under the surface of the chemical soup there. I
pulled it out warm and dripping, then laid it down in the
shower basin and popped the latches.

Inside were more pill sheets, passports, forged ration
sheets, and a handwritten order list he'd crossed some
names off from. I quickly scanned down the column of
names, until one of them caught my eye near the bottom:

Shao, Dragan (sec).

Like a lot of the others, his name was crossed off,
maybe indicating he'd already picked up the passports.
He had been here.

I thumbed past the stacks of paper and found the edge
of a plastic bag with my finger. There were six vacuum-
sealed packets in there. Each was filled with cubes of
meat, each topped with a square of browned, fatty skin,
all suspended in a stew of stock, spices, and rendered fat.
Each was labeled with a handwritten sticker.

Scrapcake. Human meat.

"Fucking creep . . ."

I didn't even think before I used my pocketknife to slit open the first bag, and then squeezed the glop into the toilet bowl. When I'd pressed out the last of it, I stopped myself a second before unconsciously sucking the grease off my thumb. The smell was intoxicating, making my stomach growl, and making me hate myself for not being able to help it.

I dumped them all, and dropped the empty bags in the trash. One cube floated on top, the edge of someone's tattoo still visible on the attached skin, and I had one hand on the chain when I noticed something else in the toilet's basin. There was another bag in there that had been tucked under the cooler. It didn't have food or drugs in it, though. It was tightly wrapped around some kind of little cylinder.

I reached in and pulled out the bag, unraveling it and then shaking it dry. Down in the bottom was a little white plastic cylinder with a tiny, hair-thin plug on one end. It was a wet drive. What had the soldiers said? *"Get his wet drive."* They had been looking for Dragan's.

I broke the bag's seal and carefully removed the drive. It was Dragan's; I was sure of it. He'd come here before going back to the apartment, and he left it here, just in case.

The lock at the front door clicked as someone fed a key card into it. I wrapped the drive in a sheet of toilet paper, then stuffed it in my pocket just as the hotel room door opened and a gaunt, middle-aged man, Eng, no doubt, stepped in carrying a small plastic shopping bag in one hand.

He spotted me immediately, and his free hand reached into his jacket before he got a good look at me. Once he did he relaxed a little, his watery eyes peering down at me from under the brim of a panama hat. He stepped under the air conditioner vent, and the current blew down his unbuttoned neckline, inflating the silk and flashing a patch of sinewy chest and greasy black hair.

"Jesus, you want to get shot or something?" He looked at me more carefully, and grinned a little. "What happened to you? Cut yourself shaving?"

"I—"

"Look, I'll cut you a break. Put back whatever you took and beat it before I cut out your—"

"Are you Eng?"

His eyes narrowed a little. "Who wants to know?" He looked toward the bedroom. "Where's Kala ..."

His voice trailed off as his eyes went to the floor and saw all of his contraband spread out there. Color crept into his face, a vein beginning to bulge in his neck as he looked down into the toilet bowl.

"Don't you fucking dare—" he started, and I flushed it.

He dropped the bag in the hallway and shoved past me to drop down on his knees in front of the toilet. His hands were poised over the meat gray swirl like he meant to go in after it, but he was already too late.

"You stupid little cun—" He turned to me, his ugly face twisted in fury.

"That was twenty thousand yuan you just flushed," he growled, standing and glaring down at me. I backed out of the bathroom, and he followed.

"You owe me," he said, "big-time."

I reached into my backpack and pulled out the gun, sticking it out in front of me. He stopped short, his chest only a few inches from the shaking barrel.

"Whoa," he said, holding his hands up in front of him. "Hey, take it easy, kid."

"A man named Dragan Shao contacted you," I said.

"That name doesn't sound fam—"

"His name is on your list!"

He glanced back toward the rug, where the passports and the rest of it sat.

"So maybe he did," he said. "What's it to you?"

"Why?"

I felt a warm trickle down one cheek and wiped it away with one hand while I kept the gun on him.

"He wanted fake passports," he said, "and passage to Duongroi for four."

"Four?"

"Himself, two women, and a kid."

"Who was with him when he came?"

"Nobody. He was alone."

"Why did he want to get to Duongroi?"

"He didn't say, and I didn't ask."

"Why did he leave his wet drive with you?"

"For safekeeping, in case he got pinched before he got back." His face changed then, as something clicked. "Wait a minute, I know who you are."

Another tear ran down my cheek and I wiped it away.

"You're the girl," he said. "I made your passport."

I put both hands on the grip of the pistol to hold it steady while I aimed at his chest.

"How did they know?" I asked.

"How did who know what?"

"Dragan was still deployed. He snuck back early. How did they know he'd be home?"

Eng didn't answer.

"He left here, and by the time he got home, they'd already caught up with him. How did they know?"

He still didn't say anything, but I could see it in his eyes. More tears came, blurring my vision and making my throat burn.

"There was a reward, wasn't there? When he came you checked the security feed, and saw they were offering—"

"I don't turn clients in for money, or rations."

"I should kill you," I said. "They came to our apartment, and they . . . they . . ."

I had my finger on the trigger, and I wanted to pull it, but I couldn't. I couldn't do it. The gun wavered as I lowered it a little.

"I should kill you," I said again.

Eng lashed out and grabbed my wrist. I struggled, but he was a lot stronger than me and he forced the gun away. Once he was in the clear, he didn't try and hit me or anything. He just took the pistol from my hand and tossed it down onto the bed next to him.

"Quit crying," he said. When I looked up at him, I saw his face and neck were flushed. His gruff face looked sheepish and guilty.

"He trusted you," I said.

"Yeah, well, I didn't know he was a Pan-Slav agent. What was I supposed to do? This doesn't exactly help me, you know."

"He didn't do what they said."

"Sure, kid. Okay." He wiped his brow and sighed. "Look, it's all over the feed—whatever he brought back with him is still out there, and the rumor is it's something bad this time, something biological. I'm on the first transport to Duongroi until this blows over. If you're smart, you'll come with me."

"Come with you?"

"I still got your passport and ticket. I'll take you, if you want."

"You've got to be out of your mind."

He shrugged.

"Suit yourself," he said. "The wet drive stays with me, though."

"I'm taking it."

"No way, it's too valuable. Besides, you want those people coming after you next?"

"I said I'm taking it. . . ."

I sensed her before I saw her. The mite cluster lit up suddenly and sent an ugly vibe deep into my head. The intensity of it triggered an adrenaline surge, anger and aggression building up in response.

Eng frowned. "What the fuck is wrong with you?"

Something moved behind him, up near the ceiling. Something big that had somehow remained hidden even while I'd passed through the room just moments before. His face changed as he watched my attention turn away from him, instincts warning him that there was trouble before I even knew what I was seeing.

He turned in time to see a female form decked out in full combat armor unfold from the shadows of the corner ceiling behind him, a few feet from the open window behind her. Her long legs swung down and she dropped with a thud and then lashed out and clamped one gloved hand down on his throat.

"What the fu—" he managed before the armor whined and his voice was cut off. She swung him around, then let go, shoving him back against the closet door so hard that a framed picture above the bed dropped to the floor. When she stepped into the light, I could see the red stamp on the armor's shoulder plate.

Eng didn't hesitate as he pulled open the closet door and reached inside, hauling a shotgun out from where he'd had it propped. His eyes flashed surprise for just a second when he spotted a woman who was sitting on the floor there, pressed back into the hanging shirts and pants with a zombielike stare stuck on her bruised and battered face.

He swung the shotgun around and fired at Red-stamp almost point-blank, the boom thumping through my chest as my face caught a blast of heat and burned powder smell. Red-stamp staggered, but the armor absorbed the pellets and she swung back around to clamp her fist down around the barrel, pushing it away as he fired again.

The wall next to her exploded in a shower of wood

splinters and drywall powder, and that seemed to wake the girl stuck in the closet. Her eyes snapped fully open and she backed farther into the hanging clothes, pushing with her feet.

Red-stamp wrenched the gun out of Eng's hands and threw it away behind her as she closed in on him again and grabbed his wrist. When they moved out from in front of the closet, I caught the woman's attention and reached out one hand to her.

"Come on," I hissed.

She kept her eyes on the two struggling outside the door as she stumbled out. A blond wig had slipped halfway off to reveal a black pixie cut underneath, and mascara had run down both cheeks. She wore a fake leather mini and a half shirt that was a size too small, sporting a silvery iron-on decal that said FUN GIRL.

"Hand over the wet drive," Red-stamp said, moving the empty shell of her hidden face close to his while he struggled futilely to twist out of her grip.

"Fuck you," he grunted.

She squeezed and I heard the bone crack. Eng's mouth dropped open and his eyes bulged as his hand jutted off at an odd angle. She stifled his scream by grabbing his throat with her other hand.

"One more word," she said in a low voice, "and I'll eat you right here. Alive."

Fun Girl lunged toward me, her stiff legs giving out at the halfway point and causing her to fall forward into my arms. While the struggle continued by the doorway, she began to sob.

"You're okay," I said in her ear, pulling her back away from the other two. "Take it easy."

I heard another crack of bone and Eng gasped, his face dark. He didn't dare speak again, but his bulging eyes moved toward me and stared as he raised one shaking finger to point.

Red-stamp let go of his wrist, then shoved him back against the wall with a crash that knocked a picture frame down onto the floor. She grabbed his head in both her hands and wrenched it around with a meaty pop that left his chin pointing down at the small of his back.

Fun Girl shrieked as his arms fell to his sides like deadweight and he crumpled to the floor. Red-Stamp turned toward us, and her head cocked barely little as she focused on me. A low buzz whined as a big scalefly flew around her head like a halo, then lit down on her chest plate.

"You," she said. "You're alive."

There wasn't any time to think. As she closed the distance I reached into my backpack and pulled out the stun gun, fumbling the business end around just as she reached to grab me. Electric blue light flashed as the prongs snapped and she jerked back, crashing into the wall.

She recovered almost right away and came at me again, so I cranked the voltage up to maximum and jabbed her ribs a second time.

The bang sounded like a gunshot, and I actually saw light flash under the combat armor as she flew back into the wall again, this time hard enough to crack it. An end table collapsed under her as she fell, then went facedown onto the floor in front of me. Her scaly, gloved hand groped for me feebly and then went still.

I scrambled over and heaved her onto her back. I patted her down, looking for anything that might be useful, anything that might tell me who she was.

"What are you doing?" Fun Girl mumbled woozily. "Is she dead?"

"I don't know," I said. "Just take off. Get going."

A little dark shape flitted toward me and I slapped down hard on the side of my neck as a sharp pain jabbed it.

"Ow!"

I looked at my hand and saw the mangled body of a scalefly, its hooked forelegs broken and plaque-colored guts poking out of its cracked body.

"Stupid thing . . ."

The word fizzled out as a strange sensation overcame me. It started like a bad head rush, but three heartbeats later it was if I'd just OD'd on Zen oil. Darkness rushed in like the cold black of the ocean bottom, and my legs buckled. I felt myself fall, crashing into a table and knocking over the lamp there. It shattered, sounding far away.

A signal surged through the mites and caused a flicker in the darkness. It flashed brighter and then an image formed around me all at once like a waking dream that shunted out everything else. In an instant I was somewhere else, and everything I saw had a ghostly, washed-out quality to it. I was in a room that had partly collapsed, where steam drifted from sheared pipes that stuck from a ruined wall. My field of view turned, and I realized that I could see through the concrete rubble to where the pipes extended into blackness. The tiled floor was buckled and covered with a film of greasy black powder, but I could spot movement underneath, blobs of heat and the tiny skeletons of several small creatures. An array of computer consoles stood on the edge of a huge hole in the middle of the floor, thick bundles of wire trailing down into the pit. I could see flickers and pulses of light as power and data traveled along the wires.

It's coming from her, I realized. *The haan. It's a dream, or a memory.* I'd get the occasional flash from a surrogate, a stray image here and there that were sometimes strung together, but nothing like this. It felt completely real.

She moved to the edge of the hole and looked down into what looked like the mouth of a huge fluke, but as I stared I realized that the inward-pointing teeth were actually rings of beds bolted around the inner wall of the pit. Lying motionless in each bed was a person. They appeared as skeletons surrounded by the phantom gauze of soft tissue. I could see their hearts pulsing behind rows of ribs, and their brains resting behind their translucent skulls. Specks, tiny electric impulses darted through, making the brains appear to shift behind the staring white orbs of their unblinking eyes.

We look a little like haan to them. The thought popped into my head as I watched them through her eyes. She leaned forward to peer down on one of the men, and when she did I saw a bulbous shape on his chest come into focus. It looked like a huge, fat tick perched there, legs spread around it and its swollen abdomen sticking up in the air. Its insides were throbbing, and she watched as little blobs of fluid traveled through a tube that connected it to its host. It wasn't sucking blood out, though. The little pulses were traveling in the other direction, into the man.

She turned her gaze to the others. Everyone there had one of the strange constructs sitting on them, pulsing, and inside the bodies below them was something else. Something else was in there, something moving, but I didn't get a good look before she moved away.

She crossed to some kind of console, electric impulses coursing through its guts, and opened a panel there to reveal rows of glass jars sealed at both ends with swarms of little specks buzzing around inside. What looked like two long tentacles moved into view, placing a new one at the end of the bottom row, while scaleflies flitted past, and crawled down the length of each wormlike appendage, crawling in and out of deep, black pores . . .

The images snapped away, and I found myself back on the hotel floor surrounded by broken plastic and fluorescent bulb powder. Red-stamp sat up on the floor as I shook my head, trying to shake it off so I could shock her again, but before I could she swatted the stun gun out of my hand. I hadn't even seen her move.

"You should have run," she said.

I backed away, waving at Fun Girl. "Go!"

Another fly flew over and landed right on her face, causing her to wipe at it with both hands as Red-stamp thumped one hand down onto my chest and shoved me back like a rag doll. I crashed into the wall, and then fell down hard onto my butt. She rose one foot over my right leg, and I managed to roll away just as I heard the suit's pneumatic pop. Her heel crashed down onto the floor where my knee had been a second before, crunching through the wood beneath the carpet.

Fun Girl tried to skirt past to the door but hesitated at the last minute. Red-stamp ripped her foot from the hole and turned to face me again as I grabbed the girl's bloodied wrist and pulled her away, back toward the window.

"Come on!"

I climbed up over the air-conditioning unit and stuck one leg out the window, looking back at Fun Girl, who shook her head. Behind her, Red-stamp was closing in fast.

I slipped out onto the narrow ledge outside, then reached back in and held my hand out. "You can do it. Hurry up!"

She grabbed the window ledge and began to pull herself out as I scrambled back to give her room.

"I can't," she whispered, her voice shaking.

"Just keep your eyes on me," I told her. Down below, people on the street were starting to look up. She got her other leg through the window and kicked off her high-heel shoe as she pressed herself against the outside of the window. Someone shouted below us as the shoe fell.

"Hurry," I said. "Come on—"

"I can't—"

The blinds were yanked down in a clatter of metal and plastic. Fun Girl cringed as a scaly, black-gloved hand reached through the window and grabbed one of her wrists.

She screamed. I reached out to try and steady her when the glass between us shattered as an armored fist punched through. It grabbed her throat and squeezed until her face turned dark and veins bulged at each temple. Before I could do anything else, she was hauled back through the window in a shower of glass.

Shit . . . shit, shit, shit . . .

I looked down at the street four stories below as an airbike flitted by underneath me, and my stomach dropped. On the other side of the street, people at the windows were beginning to gawk and point. One guy pointed to the back corner of the hotel a few windows down from where I was. There was a fire escape there.

Red-stamp's head appeared through the hole in the window, looking down the ledge after me. Keeping my chest to the brick wall, I stood up and started a quick shuffle until I was close enough to lunge for the metal railing of the fire escape.

When I did, my foot slipped off the ledge and my fists slid down the slick metal bars until I was dangling. Back toward the hotel window, I heard glass crunch as Red-stamp stepped through after me.

I swung my legs up until the soles of my sneakers touched the grate, and I felt something slide out of one of my pockets. Hanging upside down, I watched Dragan's collapsible baton fall end over end and then clatter off a parked car below. A few people looked up as I managed to scramble over the railing and then start down the stairs.

"Hey!" someone yelled.

At the bottom I slid down the ladder and landed hard on my feet down below. A bunch of drunks who'd been whooping it up before the festival backed away. One pointed up toward the window, a bottle wrapped in a paper bag clutched in his dirty hand.

When I looked up, I saw she'd reached the fire escape and her heavy boots thudded down onto the landing. She looked down through the grate at me from the empty shell of the dispersion field. She began to climb down after me, and I made a break for the nearest gate.

As I ran, I stumbled past a lone gonzo who knelt before a chintzy shrine set up next to a rusted rain gutter. She stopped praying long enough to turn and watch me go.

"Only He can move the stars," she called as I clipped a pile of water warped cardboard, lurching out of the alley and into the moving crowd.

Chapter Seven

19:41:43 BC

A cough of static crackled through an amplifier as I scanned the street ahead, trying to see through the crowd to the intersection's gate hub. I couldn't make out where the haan soldier was exactly, but I knew I needed to get lost, and quick.

"A gold sheet to the person who stops this girl!" Red-stamp's voice boomed over the amp.

I glanced back, and saw an image floating in the air above the heads of the crowd. It was my face, scratches and all, looking wide-eyed and scared. Information streamed across the holographic screen below it, giving my name, physical description, and ID. Above it was the word WANTED, and as I backed away I saw the word CANNIBAL scroll past underneath it.

"Got her!" a man behind me yelled. A hand grabbed my elbow, and then the street erupted around me.

Someone swung a fist over my head and struck the man who'd grabbed me, hitting him square in the throat. His grip loosened and I tugged free as the man who'd thrown the punch made a grab for me. Everyone tried to move in on me at once, and in seconds the whole street was a tangle of surging bodies, fists, knees, and flying elbows.

Someone grabbed my backpack and pulled while

someone else got their fingers hooked in the waist of my pants. I slipped and went down onto the sidewalk, crossing my arms over my face as the tangle of people clashed above me. Whoever had my waistband dragged me across the blacktop, and I reached in my pocket for the stun gun. I managed to dig it out and jabbed the prongs into his hand with a loud pop that made him let go.

A woman fell down near me, feet stomping over and around her as people reached down to grab at me. I zapped the closest one and he jerked back, taking two more with him as he fell. In the small break, I scrambled between a pair of legs and slammed into the side of a building at the edge of the crowd. Keeping my head down so they couldn't see my face, I slipped behind a metal trash bin and squeezed through to the other side. Traffic was stopped, bodies clustered in around the honking vehicles as uniformed officers tried to get them under control.

In the chaos, I made a run for the intersection. People had started to pile up to find out what the riot was all about, and I squirmed my way through the human wall toward the gate behind them. As I came out the other side, I felt my phone buzz in my pocket.

There was no time to answer it. An electronic sign mounted on the building across the street flickered, and an image of my face appeared as I plowed headlong into a woman carrying an armload of shopping bags. Something smashed as she fell back onto the pavement and I spun off into the side of a boxcar idling at the curb.

"Hey!"

"Sorry!"

My phone buzzed again as I pushed off the truck and stumbled toward the gate, falling as I passed through. For a second, everything stopped and I hung in weightless space. The hiccup passed and I continued my fall, landing on the sidewalk on the other side. The sounds of the riot turned distant, coming from somewhere several blocks away off to my left. Back through the portal I saw people being shoved aside as Red-stamp stormed after me. Behind her, high up above the crowd in the street, two aircars had appeared with their emergency lights flashing.

Immediately the gate buzzed, an angry red light twitching on to demand payment. The crowd clustered around the gate watched as I jumped back to my feet then cut the line and bolted through the gate directly next to it with no idea where it went.

The next time my feet touched the ground, I was somewhere uptown. Once the gate klaxon stopped, I couldn't even hear the riot anymore, though I could hear faint sirens in the distance. Red-stamp had been right behind me, though. My little double-back wouldn't fool her long, not with every gate I used squawking about the skipped fare.

I looked around as the people coming through behind me shoved their way past. Ahead, the queue waiting for the direction to change were eyeing me, wondering if I'd still be blocking the way when they got the okay to head in.

I reached into my pocket and found Dragan's twist-key. I didn't know what destinations it was programmed with, but neither did Red-stamp. When the light changed and the last of the people moving through behind me had passed, I turned and jammed the key into the socket on the gate's frame. I twisted it, and the view on the other side changed. It was now looking into some kind of garage or hangar. Two military men in jumpsuits looked up suddenly, frowning as I twisted the key again.

"Hey!" someone called from behind me. The crowd was starting to grumble.

I turned the key three more times before I spotted a sign for the metro on the other side. I jerked the twistkey out of the socket and stuffed it back in my pocket.

"Sorry!" I called, and jumped through.

On the other side, I turned back and saw the men and women in the crowd glaring after me. One was trying to flag down a cop, but in less than forty seconds the gate would revert to its original setup and I'd be long gone.

I took the first metro tunnel entrance I spotted. Slipping by a clot of people, I vaulted over the pitted metal rail and down onto the gum-spotted concrete steps below.

I jumped the turnstile just as a businessman in the row next to me presented his pass to the scanner. An alarm went off and when I looked back I saw a security guard headed my way, a scowl on his ruddy face.

"Hey!" he barked.

I scooted through the crowd on the other side of the turnstiles and ran until I spotted a platform where a train sat with its doors open. I slipped in and headed toward the back of the car, past rows of commuters. There, I leaned forward as best I could with my hands on my knees to try and catch my breath. My legs felt ready to buckle.

My forehead tingled, like a gentle tug at my sleeve, and I looked down to see a male haan looking up at me from his seat with his big yellow eyes. He stood and made a graceful gesture toward the empty chair.

"Oh," I said. "You don't have to—"

"I know," he said, the light on his voice box fluttering. He gestured again, and I felt another tingle, a cool, soothing calm.

"Thank you," I said, giving his arm a gentle squeeze and then plopping down in the seat. When I looked back through the window, I saw the guard staring back at me from the top of the stairs. He looked angry, but he didn't bother to follow. He must not have gotten word about the bounty, at least, not yet.

The haan stood in front of me with his back turned,

holding the bar and letting the material of his suit form a makeshift privacy curtain for me. I tried to stop shaking, but my whole body just didn't want to stop, even when I hugged my ribs and squeezed. I made myself take a deep breath, and let it out slowly.

"You're okay," I said to myself. I'd lost her. I was safe, for now.

A bell chimed, and out on the platform a voice began to rattle something off over the loudspeaker. I remembered the pill tab I'd nicked from Eng's hotel and dug it out of my pocket. I pushed the double cross into my mouth and crunched down on the chalky pill, grinding it into a bitter paste.

"You're okay," I told myself again.

The little pink heart appeared in the corner of my eye again. Another friend request from Nix, this time with a message:

I spoke with Ava. You can stay in the program.

I sighed, feeling annoyed and relieved at the same time. The pill acted superfast, and my jitters were already smoothing out.

Accepted.

He appeared on my list and I sent a quick reply.

Thank you, Nix. Very, very much.

We need to meet—

No time to chat, though.

I signed off as the doors slid shut, and the intercom chimed followed by an unintelligible stream of babble. Sucking the last of the pill grit from my teeth, I swallowed, watching out the train window as the buildings peeled away to reveal the expanse of tidal flats and blue-green ocean beyond. Off in the distance I could see waves crash against the platform housing the desalination derricks, steel-frame pyramids around pumps that sucked up seawater twenty-four-seven.

Six hexagonal shadows appeared in the sky in a tight

formation, and a low sonic boom sounded as the ships rocketed past the shoreline toward the foreign fleets in the distance. Foreign jets scrambled in response, rising off the carrier like little scaleflies, but our guys wouldn't start anything. It was just a message, a reminder that with the haan tech on our side their ships were powerless against ours.

The opiate synth kicked in for real, slowing my heart as it eased me toward a mellow pharmaceutical calm. The adrenaline throttled back, and the alarm bells in my head grew muted as I watched the world pass through the window.

My phone buzzed again, three quick pulses that said I had a message. I reached into my pocket and felt a wad of toilet tissue with my fingertips as I grabbed the phone and checked the screen. It was a text message, from Kang.

Don't call this number. I'll try you again in ten.

"Damn it," I muttered.

I slipped the phone back into my pocket and grabbed the wad of toilet tissue, then coaxed it apart to reveal the wet drive nestled inside.

"Gonzo, Dragan. What did you do?" I whispered.

I pinched the lanyard that dangled from behind my ear, and a little notification popped up on the 3i's display as I pulled my drive out. I unclipped it from the lanyard and swapped in Dragan's, then reached back and nestled it into the port.

Initializing . . .

Some music files got pulled into my library, and two new contacts were read and added to my 3i list as the drive was scanned.

Alexei Drugov.

Innuya Drugov.

I knew those names. Innuya was the Pan-Slav woman he'd been e-mailing right before he went AWOL, and

Alexei was her son, the one the soldiers were looking for. The status icon for each of them was gray.

"He wanted fake passports and passage to Duongroi for four . . . himself, two women, and a kid."

Himself, Innuya, Alexei . . . and me. According to Eng, Dragan was alone when he stopped at the hotel, so he had to have dropped them off somewhere beforehand. If it was true and one of them really did smuggle something back with them, they might still have it.

I checked the drive's contents. Other than the stray cached stuff, Dragan had wiped it except for one file, some kind of video file. I dragged it down to the tray's media player and dropped it in.

When the player window first popped up, it was mostly dark. Shadows shifted at the edges, like the frame was moving.

"This is Specialist Dragan Shao." His voice was tinny in my ear through the 3i's audio tap. *"I am making this recording in the event I am captured or killed. If anyone finds this message, it is critical that you deliver it to Military Governor Jianguo Hwong immediately. Do not hand it over to security, only to him."*

A flashlight snapped on, lighting the way ahead of him. He was in a dimly lit corridor, water-stained cinder block scrolling past at the right edge of the screen as the view jostled a little in spite of the image stabilizers. He stopped, and turned to look down at a woman in tattered clothes. She was obviously Pan-Slav, with round eyes and thick eyebrows.

Scaleflies buzzed back and forth through the flashlight beam as he turned back and moved quickly toward a dim light at the far end of the hall. They weren't in the PSE; the graffiti was a mishmash of hanzi, so they had to be back in–country, but wherever they were, it looked like no one had been there in years.

"I have evidence that a major attack is under way," he

said quietly as he hurried on. *"The attack involves an engineered bioweapon that violates international law, designed to wipe out human life on a massive scale."*

"Dragan," a woman's voice whispered on the audio tap. *"Gde zhe my? Chto takoe jeto mesto?"*

The screen flickered as he looked back at the Pan-Slav again. Her eyes were wide, and terrified.

"Dvigat'sja, dvigat'sja . . . ," he hissed. His hand moved into frame, gesturing for her to follow, and then the scene reeled as he turned and began to move again. As he did, I saw a sign on the wall, just for a moment, before he passed it. An arrow pointed in the direction he was moving, next to the words SHILIUYUÁN STATION— PLATFORM N.

"Shiliuyuán," I said under my breath. That was the old metro station where the haan ship was now. It was destroyed in the Impact.

"The delivery system for this weapon is the haan scale-fly," Dragan said. *"The specifics are encoded in this file along with the names I've been able to dig up, but just know that carrier flies have been engineered with a genetic fuse that shortens the life span of each generation until they die out. Given their very predictable reproductive cycles and migration patterns, it's possible to chart the zone where they will be active within fairly rigid boundaries. During that time, they and their offspring will spread the bioweapon to every human living inside what has been termed the Burn Zone."*

The scene moved through an underground metro station, the concrete platform cracked to expose jutting rebar. Off to his left a train was visible, crushed in a collapsed tunnel.

"If these projections are true," he said, *"the Burn Zone will cover over ten million square kilometers . . . big enough to wipe out an entire continent."*

A window blinked on in his field of view, showing a

map in glowing white vectors. Their location was marked, and a little ways away to the north another marker pulsed. He was tracking something.

The scene moved faster as Dragan ducked through a doorway at the opposite end of the platform and followed a string of battery-powered emergency lights to the end of a hallway where an exposed stairwell was half-covered in rubble.

Dragan followed the flashlight beam down into darkness. At the bottom of the stairs, Dragan pushed open another door and I caught a glimpse of hanzi, stenciled onto the rusted metal:

DEEPWELL BIOT—The woman behind him gasped as the flashlight beam settled on a young boy, maybe ten years old, with the same Pan-Slav features as the woman. He was sitting on the floor, leaning back against the cinder block wall behind him while some kind of black membrane held him stuck in place. His eyes were closed.

Dragan moved toward him and immediately used a knife to cut through the sticky stuff, which peeled and shrank away. The boy twitched, and his eyes opened.

"Shh," Dragan warned. The boy's eyes widened, but he nodded.

Dragan took his hand and guided him to the woman before moving through another doorway off to their left and then quickly through a large, dark room on the other side where beds were lined up in rows. I caught glimpses of people lying on some of them as he sprinted toward a dimly lit doorway on the far side of the room. On the other side, I could see shadows moving.

"Kto tam?" the woman whispered. Dragan shushed her, then responded, whispering even lower, "Ja ne znaju."

I dug up the Web translator and kicked it off, causing pinyin to pop up onto the feed.

The view stopped at the edge of the rusted doorframe

and he peeked carefully around the corner. As it panned, it showed the tiles cracked and broken around the edge of a black hole that had consumed almost the entire floor.

Across the chasm, the camera caught movement through an open double doorway on the opposite side of the room as a metal cart of equipment moved into view there. Just before Dragan moved to duck behind something, I saw the figure pushing the cart, blazing red eyes leaving trails of light in the shadows.

It's a haan.

Once the way was clear, he moved farther into the room, tilting to look down over the edge of the huge hole.

Starting about six feet down, a ring of beds were fixed by their steel-frame headboards around the interior, pointing in like a ring of teeth in the mouth of a giant fluke. My lips parted as I stared.

I've seen this. . . .

Lying in each bed was a single person, men and women of all different ages. All of them had a black rubber mask pulled tight over their eyes, with clusters of white wires trailing from electrodes stuck to their sunbronzed foreheads. The only thing that was different was that where Red-stamp had seen those strange constructs sitting on each of them, they weren't there in the video. The people all looked asleep, or comatose.

Beneath the ring of beds was another, and another, and another, going down deeper and deeper into the hole until they were lost in blackness.

What in the world . . . ?

Dragan moved farther and farther into the room, leaning forward and looking down to better see into the pit of beds. A swatch of red jumped out from the edge of the frame as the frame moved, and another bed moved into view.

My stomach sank, and I swallowed around a dry

throat. The bed had a body covered with a sheet like the others, but the sheet had been pulled away and was drenched in blood. The body underneath was that of a young man with his mouth unhinged to reveal blood-stained teeth while he stared, blind, into his rubber mask. There was a ragged hole bored into his gut, big enough to reach into. Instinctively I turned my face away, but the 3i window followed as the pan continued.

The next four rows of beds were all the same. Men, women, girls, and boys all lay dead with their bellies bored out, ribs jutting up over huge black pores torn in the sunken, stretched skin. Some had more than one hole. One had a third, gaping over a collapsed pit in his right thigh.

The camera moved, focusing on the lit face of a console that fanned out at the edge of the pit. An image of the fluke mouth, each ring of beds called out, traveled down the left side of the main screen. It focused on the information displayed next to each bed, printed out in varying shades of faint, deep purple, rows and rows of haan symbols that I couldn't decipher.

Suddenly something moved in front of the camera, blotting out the scene, and I jumped in the train seat. The frame reeled and I saw Dragan lift a pistol into frame as he backed away, signaling for the woman to run. The door to the room with the bodies in it opened the rest of the way.

"Go!" he shouted.

The frame turned and became chaotic. I saw Dragan grab someone from the closest bed on the top ring of the fluke mouth, a little girl with scrawny arms and legs. Tubes and electrode wires stretched taut, then broke free as he dragged her from the sweaty sheets and hauled her up into his arms.

"Run!" he yelled. The woman ran, hauling the boy along after her. She pushed open a door and went

through, tracing her route back the way she'd come when at the junction she stopped, unsure. She started to go one way, and then Dragan grabbed her wrist and pulled her in the opposite direction. As the camera swept by the hallway they'd come from, I saw the door at the opposite end bang open, where saucer-shaped eyes glowed in the dark like embers.

The image began moving so wildly I couldn't make anything out. At some point the flashlight came back on, the beam flashing in and out of frame. He was running, looking back over his shoulder down the abandoned corridor as he went.

He turned back just in time to see the woman stop short in front of him, like she'd snagged at the end of an invisible leash. The boy stumbled forward, falling onto the floor as his hand slipped from hers. She screamed as something I couldn't see yanked her off her feet and she soared through the air back past Dragan.

His eyes followed her as she went crashing down onto the dirty-tiled floor farther down the hall. He had started back when a looming shape rose behind the woman, and her shirt was suddenly ripped open to reveal the bare skin underneath.

"Dragan!" she screamed. *"Pomogite mne! Pozhalujsta pomogite mne!"*

The Pan-Slav words turned into a shriek that made my blood run cold as her pant legs began to deflate, the legs inside them dissolving away into nothing.

Help me, the Web translator printed. *Please, help me.*

Dragan's gun moved into frame, but before he could fire the boy moved past him and he stopped to quickly grab his shirt from behind, dragging him back as he wailed.

"Mama!"

The woman's sneakers flopped over at odd angles as her waistband relaxed and then wrinkled. Her belly and ribs began to disappear, emptying her chest cavity. She pawed weakly in front of her for a second, and then something slammed down on top of her like an invisible sledgehammer. I saw an explosion of blood . . . the torn edge of her severed wrist, and beyond that, the remains of half her head scattered along after it.

The view spun around again as Dragan turned, picked up the little girl, and ran, dragging Alexei along after him. He took them toward a door at the far end of the hall, then shoved it open.

For a long stretch, I couldn't make anything out at all, and then they were in a room, facing a bare concrete wall. In front of it was the empty doorframe of an inactive gate.

Dragan jammed a twistkey into the gate's socket, but not his military-issued one. This one was made of polished blue metal, and when he turned it the gate field flickered open.

The view jostled around then, sweeping across brick face and blacktop. He was back outside, in the open air. The streets were paved and filled with traffic. Neon light flashed the length of the strip along either side, and I saw a row of vendor kiosks lining the sidewalk. A couple of them had stands set up with hanging jiangshi masks and red street dye.

He's here, in Hangfei.

Dragan started speaking to the boy rapid-fire in Pan-Slav tongue, while the 3i's translation spat out beneath the feed.

"Alexei," Dragan said. He looked down at the boy's ashen face. His eyes were swimming, like he was about to lose it. *"Alexei, listen to me. I'm going to take you someplace safe. Do you trust me?"*

Alexei didn't answer. Dragan shook him, gently. *"Alexei, do you trust me?"*

The boy made eye contact and nodded, slowly.

"I'm giving you this," Dragan said. He handed him the metallic blue twistkey, the one that accessed wherever it was they'd just come from. Alexei reached out and Dragan slipped the elastic band around his arm so that it dangled near his elbow. *"Keep it safe for me. I'm going to take you someplace safe. Then I have to take care of a few things, but I'll be back for you. I will find help for you. I promise I'll be back for you—"*

The feed cut out, and the screen went black. I shut down the player and turned to stare out the window.

Suddenly I felt a jab of pain deep down in my gut that bent me over in my seat. Sweat broke out on my forehead, and I clutched at the area just over my crotch, but it was over as fast as it started.

What the hell was that?

I hooked my thumb in the waistline of my pants and pulled so I could see all the way down. There was no mark, or bruise or anything. Just the purplish symmetrical spay scars that had been there since puberty.

"You're okay," I told myself, letting the waistband snap back. I glanced over and saw the guy sitting next to me still staring down at my crotch wistfully.

"Show's over," I said. He looked away.

The maglev plunged back into the city and a wall of buildings began streaking past outside the window. With a huff of air, it turned black as we dove into a tunnel. Lights along the tunnel wall began to whip past, forming an electric blue streak.

I felt myself pulled forward by inertia as the train decelerated quickly. Outside the window the wall of the tunnel huffed away and lights from the platform streamed in. A row of waiting commuters began whipping past, slowing as the train approached the platform. We came to a stop, and the doors opened.

Where was I? I looked around and spotted a sign for

Zhenzhuhe Terminal. I was in the Central Hub. Another good place to get lost.

The haan who'd been standing in front of me stepped back to let me go ahead of him. I stood up, still shaky, and pushed into the line of bodies, following them as they shuffled toward the doors and onto the platform. When I looked back to wave to the haan, his back was turned and he was moving toward the opposite end of the car. I caught the reflection of his eyes in the window and something else, a movement I couldn't explain. Something writhed, out of sync with the figure next to it.

"Move it, sister," the guy behind me muttered.

I rubbed my eyes and left the train.

Chapter Eight

I made my way across the station, following a stream of foot traffic over one of the glass skyways. Below us, rows of people glided along the system of moving walkways in every direction, while free-roaming mobs bustled through the open central space. I took the first set of stairs down onto the floor and stepped out into a blanket roar of conversation that echoed under the station's huge dome. Being in the midst of the crowd relaxed me a little. I was invisible there, just one of the faceless thousands.

I used the 3i to look up the best route to the Row, which I'd decided would be my next stop. As I followed the color-coded path it laid over the station in front of me, Vamp's heart popped up in the corner of my eye to let me know he'd left a message.

What happened to "an hour"? Check your mail. Turn chat back on.

I hopped a moving walkway and people brushed past me while I leaned on the rail to check my phone. There was a message in my in-bin from Vamp, with a stack of eyebot logs attached.

It's not complete yet, but I found Dragan's ID last night. Let me know what you want to do.

"Score."

I opened the file and it expanded to show a section of

the satellite map. Vamp had isolated two trails, partial routes where Dragan's transponder ID had been spotted. One of them started at our apartment where he'd been seen going in. It only went back a few blocks before it lost track of him, but it looked like he'd come from somewhere downtown. The second trail started at the Pink Bull Hotel, then headed east several blocks before going cold.

He was using the jump gates, I thought. He could have been spotted somewhere else along his route, and Vamp just hadn't zeroed in on it yet. It wasn't much, but it was something. It was a start.

You're the best, Vamp, I sent. *Find him, please. I'm sending you something. You have to keep it quiet, though.*

I packaged up the recording from Dragan's wet drive and sent it to Vamp along with a message:

Do not show this to anyone else. I'm heading to Wei's hotel in the Row to lie low. Meet me there. We'll talk then.

Check. I'm on my way.

"*. . . transport A13 to Hǎiyáng-Gāodù is now boarding at gate fifteen,*" a voice chimed over the intercom, chatter leaking in from the jump port terminal. "*Transport D45 is now queued for passage through gate nine from Zhen-zhuhe to Tùzi-wō. Transport B74 to Duongroi is now boarding at gate twenty-seven. . . .*"

My phone buzzed in my hand as a call came through. It was Kang.

"Mr. Kang, I'm sorry I missed your call. I was—"

"It's okay, I heard. They're gunning for you, Sam."

"I noticed." Two teenagers muscled by, one of them clipping me with the duffel bag slung over his shoulder.

"Watch it, ass!" I called after him.

"What?" Kang asked.

"Not you. Sorry."

"Look, you're not going to like what I have to tell you," he said.

"He's not dead," I said. "He—"

"I know," Kang said quickly.

"Because he—"

"He's not dead, Sam. They still need him. He's alive, at least for now."

I realized then that, in spite of what I'd been saying, there was part of me that was pretty sure I'd lost him. Relief welled up, and I blurted out a sharp laugh.

"Oh, thank God," I whispered, putting one hand over my mouth.

"Sam, it's still not good," Kang said soberly. "They beat him bad, and word is he still hasn't come to. Even if he does wake up, he's facing a treason charge. There's a good chance he could be executed."

"He's not a traitor." Someone on the walkway glanced over at me. "Just . . . tell me, is there any chance he'll be okay? How bad is it?"

"Bad, but he's alive. That's a start. I'm going to see what I can do, okay?"

"Thank you," I said. I let the relief bubble up a little more, and a smile broke over my face. "Mr. Kang, thank you, thank you so much. . . ."

"Don't thank me," he said. "Just drop this now. You're already in it up to your neck."

"That's why I can't drop it."

"Sam, you have to. I'm going to see about getting this bullshit cannibalism bounty shut down, so in the meantime just lie low. Let me look into this, and don't get any more involved than you already are."

"I can't just—"

"What would really help is if I could give them the boy and the woman he brought over. If I had them, it would go a long way."

I opened my mouth to tell Kang about the lead from the eyebot logs, but I couldn't really share that with him without getting Vamp in serious trouble and it didn't really give anything to go on yet anyway. I knew from Dragan's wet drive recording that Innuya was dead and Alexei was in Hangfei, but I couldn't tell him that without explaining how I knew.

"If anyone finds this message, it is critical that you deliver it to Military Governor Jianguo Hwong immediately. Do not hand it over to security, only to him."

Kang paused on the other end of the line. "Do you know something, Sam?"

"No."

"Are you sure?"

"I'm sure," I said. "Believe me, I'll tell you if I do."

He paused again, but let it go. "When you land somewhere, don't tell anyone else where you are. Call me and I'll come meet you."

I nodded. "Fine. Okay."

"Promise me."

"I promise."

He hung up, and I put the phone away.

Dragan was alive. It sounded like things were far from over, but he was still alive and so there was still hope. If I could just—

I staggered as another sharp pain dug deep into my gut. A man plowed into me and I had to grab the rail to keep from bowling us both over.

"Hey!" someone barked from back behind me.

"Move it," the man said, pushing past me as I tried to stand upright again and another sharp pain bent me back over. I held on to the moving rail with one hand as I felt a drop of sweat roll down my face. Another body pushed past me, and then another as my legs threatened to give out underneath me.

Something was wrong. Something was really wrong. Up ahead I saw a spot to jump off the walkway, and when it came I took it. I shoved my way out of the crowd, leaving behind a wake of angry curses.

"Watch it, bitch!" someone spat after me, but I barely heard him. I scanned the rows of tunnel shops and kiosks across the slow-moving current of people ahead until I spotted a sign for a public restroom. Forcing myself to stand up straight, I made a beeline for it.

At the entrance I veered left toward the women's room. I pushed open the door and blundered down the narrow row of toilet stalls along the left-hand wall and sinks with steri-gel dispensers along the right. A few women stood in front of the mirrors primping, and their eyes followed me as I made for the closest open stall door. Once inside I pushed it shut and latched it, plopping down on top of the toilet with my pants still up.

"You're okay," I told myself, sweat trickling down my face and neck. "You're okay. . . ."

I was starting to wonder if maybe it wasn't the double cross I'd taken from Eng. Was it laced with something maybe? Or maybe the scalefly ration was bad, or—

"The delivery system for this weapon is the haan scalefly. . . ."

I'd been bitten by one of the scaleflies that had been hovering around the haan soldier in Eng's hotel room. Could I be sick? It sounded like the weapon hadn't been released yet, but something happened back there. The vision I'd had happened right after it bit me. . . . The pain stopped, leaving behind a phantom ache that lasted several seconds before my brain registered the relief. My stomach unclenched, and the sick feeling went away. The sweat cooled and began to dry on my face, and I used a fistful of toilet paper to dab it dry.

"What's wrong with me?" I whispered, my voice reverberating louder than I intended in the cramped room.

"Are you okay?" one of the women at the sinks asked.

"I'm fine," I said. "Thanks."

Through the crack I could see her, a woman in a business suit with neat, sculpted hair and pretty, angular features. Her eyes watched back from the mirror, trying to make me out through the narrow gap of the stall door.

I leaned back and noticed a chat notification flashing in the 3i's tray. I locked on to the icon and flicked my eyes upward, popping the window out in front of me.

Кто-то есть?

I didn't recognize the weird characters, and figured some foreign spam had tricked the junk filter. I was just about to delete and block it when I spotted the contact name.

Alexei Drugov.

"Shit," I whispered. His icon had turned pink, the little heart beating. The little shit was alive.

Пожалуйста, ответьте мне.

Alexei, I can't understand you. Where are you?

A pause, then:

Я вас не понимаю. Вы можете написать, поэтому я могу понять?

Alexei, hang on. Let me get a translator.

The icon went gray.

"Damn it."

I found a translator link and piped the conversation through to see what he'd said.

Is someone there?

Please, answer me.

I don't understand you. Can you write so I can understand?

Wherever Dragan had ditched him, he was still there, then. His mother was dead, but he was somewhere in Hangfei. Where?

I pulled up the message details, and checked the location.

Out of Range.

"Screw you, out of range," I whispered. How could he be out of range? Everything pointed to him being somewhere right in the city. It didn't make sense.

"Sam?" a voice asked. I jumped a little as the screen flickered on the stall door a few inches from my face.

"Huh?"

"That's some nice ink work," the A.I. said.

Crunchy, driving music began to pipe through the speaker at a low volume as a stylized logo appeared in front of me.

"Oh, come on. . . ."

"No, really. It's nice work."

I held out my right arm and made a muscle, flashing the bond bands there: Dragan, then Vamp. "Thanks."

"Are the wrist ticks for each successful surrogate imprint?"

Not many people knew what those were for. The bot was pretty good, but I wasn't in the mood.

"Are you okay?" it asked when I didn't answer.

"Yeah," I said. "Great."

"I'm glad to hear it," it said. "You know what else is great?"

"No."

The music swelled and the screen did a slow pan across the shoulders and back of a guy with some of the best ink work I'd ever seen.

"Actually that's not half bad," I said, wiping my brow.

"I know, right? When I tell you about the deals we have going on—"

The restroom door slammed against the wall, and the woman jumped, dropping a mascara brush down into the sink. She turned to her right, her eyes widening as the door groaned shut again.

"Quiet," I told the A.I.

"But you haven't heard about the deals yet—"

The screen flashed and the images were replaced by a security lockdown warning as boots clomped across the restroom floor outside.

"Security," a woman's voice barked. "Everyone out."

I leaned closer to the door crack and peered through. I could make out the women by the sinks as they packed up their things and hustled out. One of the stall doors opened and a toilet flushed. A few seconds later, another one opened.

I stood up and pushed open the stall door. When I stepped out into the bathroom, I saw a woman in full security gear standing there, one hand resting on the butt of the pistol strapped to her hip as she watched the stragglers scurry away. I started to leave with the crowd, but she put one hand on my chest and stopped me.

"Not you," she said.

Shit.

When the others were gone, she went down the row of stalls, pushing open each door. When she was sure they were all empty, she stalked back to the restroom door and slapped a security boot on it.

"What's the problem?" I asked her.

She crossed back to me, then drew her pistol and pointed it at my face. A stamp-sized image of me appeared next to the grip. It flashed red, and the woman smiled.

"I knew I recognized you," she said. "End of the road, cannibal."

The bounty. The guard was looking to collect.

"Listen," I told her. "It's not true."

"Shut up."

"I'm not a—"

"I said shut it, you little skeeze." Outside the door, someone started working the handle, shaking it when it wouldn't open. The guard shouted back over her shoulder, "Security lockdown! Can't you read?"

"Please," I said. "Look, I can pay you."

A fraction of the hardness went out of her eyes. "I'm listening."

"I have ration punches," I said. "I'll give them to you."

"Unless it's a gold sheet's worth, try again."

"A credit chit," I said, wishing I'd grabbed the stack of paper money from Eng's hotel room. The guard made a face. "I can get money. Please, you have to let me go."

"Look," she said. "You ask me, the charge is trumped. You can't afford scrapcake and you're too small to be a meat farmer. The thing is, though, I don't care. They're offering a good bounty for you. So either at least match it or let's go."

I stood, my hands still out toward her in appeal, and struggled to think. What else did I have or could I promise that this woman would want? If I tried to offer the stun gun or the drugs, she'd just take them as a matter of course, and if I tried to zap her she'd shoot me for sure.

"Please," I said.

She shook her head. "Sorry. That just isn't the way it works." She waved for me to come over to her, and reached down for one of the zip ties on her belt. "Come on. Turn around and put your hands behind your head."

"My father needs me. Please."

"Now."

Something crackled softly and as I felt the hair on the back of my neck stand up, the guard turned alert.

"What the hell is that?"

The air warped behind her, like ripples coming off heated blacktop. A bright point of white light appeared, and expanded to a large hexagon that blotted out the room behind it. At almost the same time, a figure stepped through from out of the shadows on the other side. As soon as he was through, the gate collapsed again.

I jumped back in surprise, one hand going to my mouth as almost at the same moment I realized I actually recognized the figure. It was a male haan, clad in a draping black suit that looked like wings as he spread his arms apart. His softly glowing pink eyes peered at the guard as he opened his long-fingered hands and began to reach around on either side like he meant to embrace her.

She sensed him and whipped around, jamming the barrel of her pistol into his gut as his arms enveloped her in a ruffle of cloth.

"Nix, don't!"

I gasped as the gun went off, but the report sounded dull and muted, like a distant boom of thunder. I stepped back, shocked, and waited for him to collapse onto the floor while the guard stared with wide eyes.

Nix didn't collapse. Instead, the guard went limp and I thought maybe she'd taken the bullet herself when the flattened slug fell onto the tiles between them, then spun to a stop. Her arm dropped to her side and the gun fell from her fingers, clattering to the floor. Nix held her, her cheek pressed to his chest right over the mass of his heart, which pulsed behind the honeycomb lattice of his rib cage. Her eyes went dreamy, lids drooping. Her cheeks flushed, and her lips turned a little darker as she slipped her other arm around his neck for support. As he lowered her to the floor, her eyes squeezed shut in what might have been pleasure and she convulsed suddenly. As she continued to twitch, the strength seemed to go out of her.

Nix leaned her gently against the wall next to the row of sinks as her eyes closed the rest of the way. He retrieved the pistol from the floor and slipped it back into her holster.

"It won't last long," he said, glancing back at me.

I knelt down and picked up the slug, still warm between my fingers, and looked up at Nix. "What just happened?"

"I am wearing an inertial dampener."

"A what?"

"A type of force shield. We should go before she recovers." He reached down with one delicate hand and helped me to my feet.

"What the hell did you do to her?"

"She is a surrogate. I used the brain band to place her in a pliable state," he said.

I looked at the guard. Her face was sheened with sweat, and her lips had turned full and dark.

"Pliable state, huh?"

"It won't last long," he said. "We should go."

He stepped toward me and when he did, a stray signal tingled at my forehead. I felt my nipples start to harden as the tingle began to wander down south of the border.

"Hey," I said, waving one hand. "Dial it back."

"Sorry."

The heat from him eased off somewhat, and left me feeling dizzy. He took my arm and guided me away from the guard as I ran my fingers through my sweat-dampened hair.

"Are you following me?"

"We should—"

"Answer my question first. Are you following me?"

"No," he said. "I was following Sillith. She was following you."

"Who's Sillith?"

"The haan female who attacked you back at the hotel."

"Wait, you know her?"

"She is the current haan female." He paused, and the glow on his voice module shifted as his tone became softer. "I was wrong this morning."

"I wasn't at my best either. Just forget it."

"I didn't realize how much the haan child meant to you," he said.

"Look . . . I don't want to talk about that."

"No individual is ever lost to us. I knew you were different, but I didn't realize that to you the loss of an individual was final. I didn't understand."

I didn't know what he meant by that, but at the moment I didn't care. I didn't want to talk about my surrogate.

"It's okay," I told him.

"I do now."

"I said it's okay."

"And I'd like to help you, if I can."

I looked at the guard, with her head still lolled to one side. A soft snore came through her nose, but her eyes had opened a little.

"All right," I said. "Come on. Let's beat it before she gets up."

"Beat it where?" he asked.

"I've got somewhere I've got to be. If you really think you can help, you have to come with me."

I crossed back to the guard and pulled the badge from her clip. Leaning over her, I noticed the four-pack of smokes in her shirt pocket and grabbed it. While I crossed back to the security boot she'd put on the door, I shook one out and stuck the thin black cigarillo's end into the corner of my mouth, tasting sweet anise on the side of my tongue.

"You're going to steal from her?" Nix asked.

"Bitch owes me these."

I ran the badge through the boot's reader, and the light flipped from red to green. Digging into my pocket, I dredged up my lighter and flipped the cap open, sparking the flame and then holding the end to it. I puffed clouds of blue-black smoke, then took a big hit, holding it for a few seconds before blowing it out my nose. Chems tickled into my bloodstream, appetite suppressants, stimulant, and something else . . . a narcotic undertone that played well with the double cross. I smiled and flicked the badge back toward the sleeping woman. It cut through the air, spinning in an arc before pegging her in the side of the head with one corner and bouncing away.

When I turned, I felt the same nostalgic pang from

him that I'd felt the first time I met him back in the hotel, only stronger. It startled me, and I looked up into his eyes.

"There it is again," I said.

"What?"

"Nix, do we know each other?"

The three pupils in each of Nix's eyes bloomed like sunspots as he radiated uncertainty. He wanted to say something, but for some reason he couldn't.

"We do now," he said instead.

I sighed, and he took my arm.

"I can help you, if you'll let me."

Vamp, I sent. *When you see me, I'll be with a haan. Don't freak out.*

I logged off before Vamp could respond, then gestured for Nix to come along with me. "Come on. I know a place."

"Then you trust me?"

"I don't know, but I need someone to weigh in on this, and you're the best I've got."

"Weigh in on what?"

I tugged Dragan's wet drive from my 3i port, and it dangled from the end of the lanyard as I handed it to him. "Can you access this?"

"I can."

"Then do it on the way."

"What's on it?"

The guard stirred on the floor again, and I gestured toward the door. "You tell me."

Chapter Nine

After two jumps and a half hour's walking, the GPS flashed to let me know we were close. It had been a long time since I'd spent any time on the row, and being back, I couldn't decide if I'd just forgotten how bad it had been, or if it had gotten worse. It made me think of one of those sags in old blacktop, a cracked pocket filled with road grit and cigarette butts that no one ever picked up. Hangfei's flash had faded, its neon glitz replaced by rusted signs, graffiti, and smog-stained glass. The steamy hot air smelled of asphalt, and everyone walking the street looked like trouble.

"Okay," I told Nix, "keep your eyes peeled for the name Wei. It's somewhere on this street."

"What is this place?" he asked, his electronic voice rising over the hum of traffic.

"My old stomping ground."

I kept my voice calm and easy, but the truth was that I barely recognized the area anymore, and I'd begun to wonder if this had been such a great idea after all. Trash bins were practically buried under heaps of garbage, and the people who sat crowded together on the stoops of vacant shops looked mean and hungry. Eyes glinted in the shadows from hairy, unwashed faces. They followed

us as we passed, while slurred conversations petered out
and grew hushed.

"Why here?"

"Nobody will look for us here. Just watch yourself."

"We have attracted the interest of several humans,"
Nix pointed out.

"We'll be fine."

"The inertial dampener will stop high-velocity im-
pacts but won't stop—"

"We'll be fine," I said, not completely confident that
was true. "I used to live here."

The wind blew and sent streamers flapping overhead,
where two festival ghoul puppets swung by their necks
from a power line. The street up ahead was splattered
with red festival paint. At least, I hoped it was paint. No
one down that way looked too festive.

"Why?" He scanned the crowd and the mass inside
his head made an anxious twitch, silhouetted against the
neon sign that shone through from behind him.

"It wasn't exactly by choice, Nix."

"Your parents lived here."

"No. We lived in Baishan Park. They rented crash
tubes by the week there."

"Why didn't you stay with them?"

"Mom died when I was eight."

"And your father?"

Ditched me.

"He . . . ran into some trouble."

I was pretty sure my dad killed my mom. Not on purpose; I think he just flipped his lid and went too far.
Either way, he was long gone before even a token cop
ever showed up.

"Doesn't the city provide care for orphans?"

"Orphan," I snorted. "Those homes are worse than
the street."

His questions had begun to grate on me. Anxiety

pricked in my brain as he poked at nerves I didn't want poked. I wanted one of the smokes I'd taken at the metro, hoping it would calm me down, but didn't want to take them out in plain view.

"Worse than here?"

"I'll help you. . . ."

I shook my head, waving him off. At the time I thought I'd do anything to stay out of one of those homes, but the truth was I'd questioned that choice a million times since.

The image of an ugly, balding man in a suit seeped up like gas from a sewer grate. Humid air ruffled his coat-tails as he handed me a squashed ration. I'd been so tired, and so weak, that he used his other hand to steady me. I reached for the ration, but it was gone, pulled away, just out of reach as he drew me closer.

"I'll help you," he said. His voice shuddered, and he sounded out of breath. *"I'll help you, but first you have to help me. . . ."*

I shook my head again, a nervous twitch. "Look, I managed, okay?"

"I was only—"

"I don't care. I don't want to talk about it, so get off it!"

My voice had risen without my meaning it to, and my hands had curled into fists. People were looking over at us, some pointing. I tried to calm down, but when I relaxed my hands I felt them shake.

"Sorry," I told him. "I'm sorry, I didn't mean to snap. Just . . . things didn't always go so well back then. I don't like talking about it."

He didn't answer.

"I guess you probably think we're pretty sick some-times, huh?" I asked him.

"Sick? No."

"Yeah, well . . . I do."

"Actually, I find you quite beautiful at times."

"Yeah, right."

"It's true. Not all haan would agree, especially those not born here, but your world is impressive in its own right, and as a people you have a resilience that can be very moving. We were like you, once. One day, you will be like us."

"Everyone wants what you got, I'll give you that."

"It's more than that. We are better for having met you, even if not everyone sees it."

We walked in silence for another few moments.

"So . . . is your planet anything like this?" I asked him. One eye rolled toward me.

"No." He paused, and then corrected himself. "It was quite similar in makeup. Our societies were very different."

"What is it like? Where you come from? You guys never talk about that. Are you not allowed?"

He was quiet for a minute, and from the vibe I picked up from him I thought that he wasn't supposed to say anything. I sensed loss, and a need to communicate it mingled with frustration.

"I'm sorry," I said. "I forget you were born here."

"Through genetic memory I've experienced it," he said finally.

"Genetic memory?"

"None of us is ever lost. When one of us is returned to the vats, his memories are added to our genetic sequence. All subsequent haan gain access to the memories as their brains develop."

"For real?"

"Yes."

"What about the haan who are already born?"

"The genetic sequence is distributed and written into active memory."

"Distributed? How?"

"Genetic information is disseminated through scale-flies."

I grabbed his sleeve, stopping him for a minute. "Wait, what?"

"Scaleflies are more than a stowaway pest as is generally implied. They have been engineered over the centuries to pass complex genetic information and material between haan, mainly retroviruses capable of writing memories or other information into the brain."

"That's why they're always hanging around you?" I asked. "I just figured it was the smell or something."

"Smell?"

"After feeding, your breath can be a little stinky." I thought about what he'd said for a minute. "So, wait, how often do they do that?"

"They constantly ferry new information. If redundant information is received, it is ignored. Otherwise it is stored."

"And other genetic material, stuff besides memories? Something dangerous?"

He hesitated, but didn't answer. I wasn't sure if he'd seen the wet drive recording yet.

"It's how I know my world," he said instead, "even though I've never been there, and will never see it."

"And what's it like?"

"It was perfect."

"Perfect, huh?"

"We had mastered the physical world," he said, and the tide of emotion intensified over the brain band. I felt his painful longing, a deep ache, and also his pride. "We were the architects of our environment, and our physical selves. We had transcended evolution, and achieved the pinnacle of conscious development. We were perfect creatures, who created a perfect world."

"Why do you keep talking about it in the past tense?"

That snapped him out of it a little. The flow of signal ebbed, then stopped altogether as he retreated. He didn't answer the question.

"Well, for what it's worth, I'm glad you're here," I told him. "It's the same with us. Not everyone thinks so, but I do."

"Thank you."

"You know," I said, "after Dragan found me, after he got me away from the meat farm, but before he took me in, I got tied up in the system for a few weeks. Since I didn't have a home or a job or legal guardians, I got spayed."

"You can't have children."

"Yeah, it's why I wanted to stay out of the system as a kid, why I ran from Baishan Park. I knew it was the first thing they'd do." I threw up one hand. "Then they just did it anyway."

"I'm sorry."

"So, when I thought I'd lose the surrogate program too, I—"

"You have been reinstated."

"I know."

"And I'm glad."

"Thanks."

I picked up a faint pulse, as a decision he'd been weighing back and forth tipped in one direction. He reached into his jacket, then handed me Dragan's wet drive back.

"The facility is of haan design," he said.

"Yeah, I recognized the characters." I took the drive back and stuck it in my pocket. "This isn't good, is it?"

"No."

"What are they doing down there? Could you tell?"

"They are experimenting on humans," he said.

"To create the bioweapon."

"The evidence suggests the weapon, in its current

form, is complete and has been deployed. It also suggests that this experimentation is ongoing in spite of that fact."

"Why?"

"I don't know, but the information on this drive is very dangerous."

"Dragan says I should get it to Governor Hwong."

"Do you plan to?"

"Aren't you afraid of what he'll do to you if he sees it? I mean, do you think he could trigger the failsafe over it?"

"Do you?"

I wasn't sure. It had been nagging at me. We were in bed pretty deep with the haan by now, but if the evidence encoded on the drive really backed up what Dragan said, that a haan engineered something that horrible for whatever reason . . . all haan might pay for that, whether they had anything to do with it or not.

"I saw her down there . . . ," I said to myself.

"You were there?"

"No, it was like a dream or something. She was knocked out and it started bleeding over the surrogate cluster. She was there. I just don't understand why. I mean, the Pan-Slavs are our problem. Why would she do something like this and risk so much?"

"Her fertility cycle is ending. She will be replaced soon, but until then she is very influential . . . she may be hoping to effect some kind of change before she is sent back to the vats."

"Hey," a voice called from behind. Nix started to look back, but I stopped him.

"Don't. Just keep walking. What kind of change?"

"I don't know," Nix said, his voice uncertain. "She's been responsible for, among other things, routing offspring through the surrogate program for imprinting. Since all surrogate activities go through military channels, this might explain where she forged her contacts."

A bottle whipped past between us and bounced off the sidewalk before spinning away.

"Hey!"

Nix leaned closer and lowered his voice. "Sam . . ."

"Just take it easy," I told him, but I eased one hand down into my pocket and curled my fingers around the stun gun's grip. Still walking, I turned back to look over my shoulder.

"What's your prob—"

He was right behind us, a scrawny, shirtless old tattooed man with a scraggly, graying beard and bad teeth. Before I could do anything he reached out and grabbed my arm, spinning me around. I kept my hand on the stun gun as I jerked my elbow free from his grip.

"Let go!"

The man slipped a knife out of his back pocket and flicked out the blade. "Humans only, sister."

"What?"

"Take the maggot and go back the way you came."

Anger surged, but even with the shocker I didn't like the look of the knife. I glanced back behind the guy and saw a couple of his buddies hanging back, watching us.

"It's a free country," I said.

"Take the maggot," he said again, "and go back the way you came."

"Sam, it's okay," Nix said. "Don't—"

"Look, we're just passing through," I said to the guy. "What are you going to do? Knife us for walking down the sidewalk?"

He swung his fist, lightning fast. I cringed in surprise, but before I could react Nix had moved one arm out between us. The man's forearm clashed with his, causing a faint flash of blue and a bony thud. The inertial dampening field, or whatever Nix had called it, lit up in a hexagon grid pattern before fading.

"Nix, don't!"

The guy recoiled, pain twisting his face, but it didn't slow him down long. Even as the others started to head toward us from behind him, he reached out and grabbed Nix's wrist. His fingers eased through the field, and I felt a stab of pain through the mites as he pulled Nix off balance.

"Piece of shit. . . ."

I pulled the stun gun out of my pocket, but I was too late. The guy jerked Nix forward and he fell onto his knees. Once he was down, the man grabbed Nix's elbow with his other hand and put his forearm down across his knee.

"Don't!" I yelled.

I heard the break, and received a bolt of pain over the surrogate link that made me stagger for a second. It intensified, until my eyes teared up.

"Let go of him!" I squeezed the shocker's trigger, and electricity arced across the prongs.

The man stood and hauled Nix back up onto his feet. He still had Nix's wrist and had started to twist it back when another guy came from out of nowhere behind us. He swung and caught the man in the jaw with his fist.

The man let go, blood filling the space between his lips as he staggered back. The other guy kept on him, and I saw it was Vamp. We must have been close enough to the hotel that he'd spotted us.

The man raised his knife, but he was still off balance. Vamp hit him again, right in the face, and blood began to run from both nostrils into his beard. Vamp shoved him down onto the sidewalk and then stomped on his wrist. The knife slipped out of his fingers, and Vamp snatched it up.

He held it, glaring down the street at the other men, who hung back, not quite as confident as they'd been a minute ago. They glared back, but then seemed to decide that even though there were two of them they weren't in a hurry to tangle with the much younger and stronger Vamp.

"Take your friend and beat it," Vamp said. "Unless you want jail time for assault on a haan."

They didn't. One of them helped his injured friend up, who then shoved him away. There was death in the bloodied man's eyes, but the three stalked off.

Vamp stepped back toward us, where I still held out the stun gun and Nix was holding his injured arm to his chest. "You guys okay?"

"Yeah," I said. "Shit, Vamp, you're like a badass."

"What about him?" He gestured at Nix.

"I will be fine," he said. "Thank you."

"Vamp."

"Thank you, Vamp."

"No problem." He looked back at me. "Come on, we'd better get him off the street."

"Where is it?" I asked him.

He pointed back down the street. "Right down there."

The place had really gone south. It took me a minute to find the entrance to the old building. The pool hall was gone, but the sign for Wei's was still there, hanging above a set of worn concrete steps that led down from the sidewalk to a heavily spray-painted metal door. A four-pack of whiskey soda sat on one step where Vamp had abandoned it to help us.

"Okay," I said. "Nix, are you okay? For real?"

"Yes. Vamp is right. We should get inside."

Through the mites I could sense his concern, and his fear stirred in with a good dose of haan shame and guilt. He stood up straight, and we crossed the street. Vamp's muscles were tense and his expression was set, warning away anyone else who might get the idea to mess with us as he picked the four-pack back up. Another breeze made the puppets sway on their lines, and sent paper trash skittering across the blacktop.

I pulled the door open and wiped my hand on my shirt as I stepped through into the cramped hallway on the other side. It seemed a little smaller, these days. The walls were plastered with copied advertisements for bars, nudie shows, and illegal rations.

Two stringy men in white tank tops came around the corner. They stared openly at us as they passed, and then I heard them snicker behind us.

"What is a three-way?" Nix asked.

"I'll explain it later."

Around the corner was what Wei called the Foyer, a closet with a chair, a computer, and a piece particleboard adorned with hanging key cards. The bulletproof glass with the honeycomb wire sandwiched between that covered the front of it had been reinforced by a haan force shield that shimmered faint blue in the dim light. Behind the shield sat Wei, looking much older and bonier than I remembered. The monitor was streaming footage of the bombing and he watched, a fat cigar smoldering idly in one stained corner of his lips. His cheeks were hollow, and the skin stretched over them looked thin as paper.

He glanced up when he heard us approach, his watery brown eyes watching us from over the top of the screen. I was ready to explain to him who I was, but as it turned out I didn't have to.

"Niu-niu," he rasped. He broke into a smile that showed his yellowed teeth.

"Hey, Wei."

"I never thought I'd see you here again."

"Me neither."

"You guys know each other?" Vamp asked, sounding a little skeptical.

"Know her?" Wei said. "Little shit used to work for me in exchange for a room. Good times."

I rolled my eyes at him. "Yeah, cleaning up puke and plunging condoms out of toilets. Good times."

"Hey, that was a good deal," he said. The corners of his lips furrowed deeper into the wrinkles of his face as he peered closer. "What the hell happened to your face?"

I saw my own reflection in the glass between us, and the scratches that crisscrossed my cheeks and forehead. "It got introduced to a window."

"Looks like they didn't get along." He chuckled, and pointed at the TV screen. "Hwong's men already caught the fuckers set that bomb off."

"Really?" That was pretty fast, even for Hwong.

"The execution's tonight."

I shrugged. "Great."

"Hey, you used to like executions." He chuckled again, but then slowly his smile began to fade. "You know, Dragan told me if he ever saw me around you again, I was a dead man."

"He doesn't know I'm here."

His smile faded completely. I thought I actually saw a little shimmer in the old man's eyes. "He blamed me for what happened. He thought those meat farmers were getting their marks from the hotel . . . that I sold you to them."

"I know you didn't."

"I—"

"I knew better than to go there at night, alone," I said. "It was my own fault." He nodded, but not like he agreed.

"Well, for what it's worth, I'm glad you're okay," he said.

"Thanks."

His eyes finally moved to Vamp, and then Nix. "It can't stay here, though."

"We just need a place to lie low for tonight. Maybe tomorrow. Then we disappear."

Wei sighed, adjusting the cigar in his mouth.

"You and your boyfriend can stay," he said. "Not the zhameng."

"All three," I insisted, ignoring the insult. He shook his head. "Please. For old times' sake."

"Why here?" he asked.

"Because he's injured," I said. "And because I'm in trouble."

He frowned, but I felt him relent, just a little.

"You know," he said, turning to the others, "when I found her digging in my trash way back then, I took her for a boy. I almost used the stunner on her."

"You did use the stunner on me."

His eyes twinkled a little, and his lips formed a faint smile. "I was going to turn her over to security, but she was so pathetic I couldn't do it."

My earlobes got so hot they started to itch a little. I was hugely aware of Vamp standing right next to me, hearing all this. "Look, this has been a great trip down memory—"

"I liked having you around, kid," he said. "When you left . . . I figured you forgot about me."

"I'll never forget you. . . . I just couldn't come back here."

He frowned, and then shook his head.

"Please, Wei."

He sighed, smoke drifting out from his nests of nose hair. "Is there going to be trouble?"

"Only if they find me. No one knows we're here."

He sighed again. "The zhameng stays inside, until you leave."

"Thanks, Wei."

"Yeah, yeah."

He pushed a key card across the counter toward me, not bothering to include the electronic payment tablet.

"Water still costs," he said. I gave his old bony hand a

squeeze before handing the key card off to Vamp. He nodded, then turned and patted Nix on the shoulder.

"Come on, spaceman."

Nix followed him around the corner. When they were out of sight, I leaned a little closer to the glass.

"Something else, Niu-niu?" he asked.

"You still deal in weapons?"

He raised his bushy eyebrows. "Weapons?"

"Guns."

"What are you going to do with a gun?"

"Hopefully nothing," I said, "but I'm in trouble, Wei, and Dragan needs my help."

"And you think you're going to need a gun?"

"I hope not."

"Guns are trouble," he said.

"Then why do you deal them?"

"That's not the same thing. Come on, you're better than that."

"Please. It's an emergency."

He frowned, but he didn't say no.

"Guns cost money," he said instead.

"I know."

"You don't have any money."

I looked up and down the hall, then nodded at the door to the foyer. "Let me in."

He reached down and buzzed me in, the bolt in the door snapping open. I opened it and slipped into the cramped space. The smoke made my eyes water and my nose burn.

"Look, I can do you a favor," he said, "but the people I deal with don't deal in favors, you know?"

"I know," I said. I pushed an ashtray full of butts away to clear a spot on the desk between us, and put the stun gun down there. "You can use this to trade."

He looked it over.

"Not bad," he said, "but it won't get you a real piece."

I dug out the ration sheet and tore a strip off, then two of the three doses of blue crystal I'd found in the safe back home. One by one I put them on the pile between us.

"The stunner," I said, "plus three ration punches, plus two doses of blue shard. This is all government-issue stuff."

Wei looked it over, nodding.

"What kind of gun you looking for?" he asked.

"Something small and light," I said. "I don't need some hand cannon I can't even lift."

"I still say it's a mistake," he said, "but if you say you need it, I'll get a good gun for you. When do you need it by?"

"I'll try and be out of your hair tomorrow morning. Can you do it that fast?"

"I'll make some calls."

"Thanks, Wei." I leaned forward and hugged him. He kind of stiffened up for a second, but then he relaxed and patted my back.

"Okay," he said.

I gave him one last squeeze, then broke away. "You're the best."

"Not hardly," he muttered.

I caught him smiling, though, just a little, when I slipped out and shut the door behind me.

Chapter Ten

16:11:21 BC

I headed back to the room and was about to knock when I heard Vamp's voice on the other side.

". . . your deal anyway?"

"Deal?" Nix asked.

"Why are you here?"

"Sam arrived in Shangzho last night to return her surrogate, and claimed to have been attacked by a haan pretending to be human. I was sent to follow up with her."

"Why are you still sticking around? She's in enough trouble as it is without looking after you."

"Because I believe I can help."

"Yeah, you've been a big help so far."

"My species stands to lose more than yours."

"If what's on that recording is true, you guys plan to wipe out millions of us—"

"There is no 'we' in this case. One haan made a deal with your species to wipe out your enemies," Nix said, "and as terrible as Sillith's plan is, I am facing the extinction of my entire race. So yes, my species stands to lose more than yours. No haan in their right mind would sanction what's on that recording. I am here because I think I can help stop this."

Vamp made a contemptuous snort, but when he spoke

again his voice was a little calmer. "If the stuff on that wet drive gets out, you guys are pretty much screwed."

"Yes."

"Still, I'm telling you straight up—if it comes to it, I'll hand that recording over. If we don't find that kid and fast, I'll hand it over."

"I understand."

"I'm sorry, but there's too much at stake here."

"The recording doesn't indicate where the boy is now."

"No, but it will let our people know what's going on. Even if the burn starts, if they know how it's spreading they might be able to stop it."

"I understand, and I won't try and stop you."

Vamp didn't believe him. I couldn't see him, but I could picture the look on his face.

It got quiet again, and I was about to knock when Nix suddenly spoke again.

"Do you plan to mate with her?"

"Who? Sam?" Vamp asked. He laughed a little, and I felt my face flush.

"Yes."

Vamp's laughter petered out, and I waited, leaning against the wall with my forehead on the door.

"I wouldn't, you know, put it that way," he said, "but yeah. I mean, I want to."

"Why?"

"I don't know," Vamp said. "Why are you asking me?"

"I'm just curious. I sense your arousal when she is near. You seem determined to hide this from her. I just wondered why."

Vamp didn't say anything for a while. I waited, feeling guilty for eavesdropping, but not guilty enough to stop. When we first became friends he didn't have any interest in me physically at all—zero. It was why we worked because at the time I couldn't handle being touched, not by anybody. I wondered what it was, what I did, or said, that changed his mind.

"It's complicated," Vamp said. When he said it, his voice was soft, distant, thoughtful ... all of the things that he wasn't. "We've been friends a long time. I didn't mean for it to happen, just ... something changed. I don't know if she—"

My hand jerked toward the door like it had a life of its own, and rapped on it three times. The voices stopped.

Vamp opened the door and I saw Nix standing near the basement window where flickering electric light trickled in. The room was a cramped box of water-stained drywall and yellowed paint. There was a single bunk, a musty, flat mattress laid over a wire spring mesh with only a sheet to cover it up. Across from it a tiny TV sat chained to a stand of peeling fake wood, and to its left a plastic curtain hid the chemical toilet. It hadn't changed a bit.

"You two getting along okay?" I asked them.

"Yes," Nix said. "I was just asking if—"

"So, you were a housekeeper?" Vamp blurted, tossing me a bottle. I caught it, then twisted the cap off and flicked it back at him. It bounced off his shoulder and skittered across the floor.

"Hey, watch it," he said. "I'll have management send you in here to pick that up."

We laughed a little. Not long, but it felt good.

"Nix, let me see your arm," I said.

"It will be fine."

"Let me see it."

He held out the arm and ran one spindly finger down the seam of his sleeve. In response, it split and peeled away like the petals of a flower to expose his forearm. Against the light of the table lamp, I could make out the bones inside. Two of them were broken, splinters lodged in the meat around them.

"Shit, Nix," I said, holding the arm carefully and leaning closer.

"It will heal," he said. He angled the arm closer to the light so I could see better, and when I peered through the skin I could see that already little tendrils had begun to form across the break.

"How long?" I asked him.

"By morning."

He moved his arm away and touched his sleeve again. It closed back up, hiding the injury.

"I talked to my folks about getting out of Hangfei," Vamp said. "You know, just in case."

"Yeah?" He nodded.

"I didn't say anything about the recording, but I convinced them the feed rumors are true. They're making arrangements, and you're in, if you want in."

"Dragan comes with us," I said, taking a swig from the bottle. It was fizzy, and burned going down.

"If we can find him."

"His message came from Shiliuyuán Station," I said. "I don't know how that's possible, but that's got to be where he is now."

Vamp shrugged. "Parts of it could still be there," he said. "Since the Impact, no one's been in there to see for sure, and that other name on the recording, Deepwell, fits. I did some digging and Deepwell was the name they gave the site after the station got locked down."

I remembered the story, or the sanitized schoolroom version anyway. Everyone knew the story of the husband and wife who parted at the station, and how she threw him an apple to eat on the train. It stuck in midair, spinning like a tiny planet. Video of it went viral, and people came from all over to see it, but by summer the site was secured. The entire station was enclosed, and the only people ever to see the inside were killed in the Impact.

"Could it have survived it somehow?" I asked Nix.

"I wasn't aware of it," he said, "though the recording indicates it has, at least in part. That would explain how Sillith has been able to operate in secret, away from both Hangfei and the ship."

"Then he's in the Impact zone," I said to myself. "Past the rim."

"Right."

I felt hope dwindle away. I tried to hold on to it, but this was a major obstacle. No human had ever gotten through the force field, and to even try you'd have to cross the rim to get to it. The ruins were buried in toxic ash, and the few places you could get to were taken over by drug labs and meat farms.

"Nix, is there even any way to get through the dome?" I asked.

"No."

"None? How do you get through?"

"The only way in or out is through jump space," he said. "The routes are carefully controlled. No human has access to them."

"Do you?"

"No."

"Great," I muttered.

"However," Nix said, "on the video, your parent clearly traversed a gate."

"So?"

"Whatever Sillith is doing, she's acting in secret. It stands to reason that her jump-space routes are not part of our existing network. If she is moving between Shili-uyuán Station and the rest of Hangfei, she must have a twistkey that allows her to use the existing gate network as access points."

"Search him. Find the twistkey."

"He doesn't have it."

"They were looking for it," I said. "Sillith and the others. It's the blue key, the one he had in the video."

"Keep it safe for me. I'm going to take you someplace safe...."

"He left it with the kid. If we find him, we find the twistkey.... I can get to Dragan, and we turn the kid over and stop the attack too." I thought about it for a minute. "Shit, he contacted me. I had him on the damned line."

"Who?"

"The kid, the little Pan-Slav shit from the video. Dragan's wet drive synced him to my contact list when I plugged it in. He must have seen my name pop up at some point, and he messaged me."

"Where is he?"

"He didn't say, but it means he's still alive, right?"

"What did the location tag say?"

"It said 'Out of range.'"

Vamp pursed his lips. "Out of range," he said to himself. "That can mean any location the chat network doesn't have in its database. It doesn't necessarily mean out of range."

"But he's got to be in Hangfei somewhere. How can it not be in the database? Can you track him?"

Vamp looked a little leery. "Through the 3i chat client? Not easily, if at all."

"Then if eyebot doesn't come through, we'll have to hope he comes back online and see if I can get it out of him. Either way we grab the key, tip security, and while they're busy moving in on him, we'll grab Dragan."

Vamp looked uneasy. "That means going down there."

"Right."

"To the same place where that woman got squashed into oblivion."

"What do you want to do, then? Leave him down there?"

"Let Hwong go in and—"

"And what? Execute him for treason? If we can get

him to Duongroi with us, we'll be out of Hwong's reach until we can get it sorted out."

"Sam, you saw that recording. You know what's down there."

"If you have a better idea, then let's have it."

"I'm just saying you don't even know for sure if he's there."

"It's the best lead I've got," I snapped, holding out my hands and slopping whiskey fizz onto the floor.

"And what are you going to do when you get there?"

"I'm not leaving him there!" I barked.

Vamp just sighed and crossed his arms. "Look," he said. "There's more to this."

He sent over a message that popped up on the 3i screen. Two stamp-sized holodisplays, each of a man's face with contact info underneath it, appeared in front of me.

"I don't get it. Who are they?"

"Two of the soldiers who raided your apartment."

I looked back at the pictures, heat rising into my cheeks. "Where are they?"

"Dead," he said. "Their remains were found earlier today, in different parts of the city."

"Dead? How?"

"They were found in their homes. Their arms and legs were pulled off, Sam."

"Cut off?" I grimaced.

"Not cut off, pulled off. Twisted off. The coroner report says they were alive when it happened. That's not some weird coincidence. I was able to isolate three of the four soldiers who took Dragan in from the eyebot data, and at least two of them are dead. I'm working on tracking down the other male soldier, but nothing at all so far on the woman."

I looked at the images, the men who'd help take Dragan from me. They were dead. In my mind I'd wished suffering on the people responsible for his abduction, but the thought of being quartered alive left me queasy.

"She's killing them," I said. I imagined the whine of combat armor as joints were pulled free from their sockets. "They know the weapon is here, so she's killing them. She doesn't want it tied back to her."

"Sam, be realistic," Vamp said. "Your face is plastered across every channel now. They're calling you a cannibal and a dissident, and they're offering a reward for your capture. If you stay in the city you're going to get arrested. How do you know you can trust that old man at the desk? He could be collecting on you right now."

"He's not." I let out a long, fumy breath. "Look, I know it's bad. I wouldn't blame you if you took off. So if you want out of this, you'd better go now."

He paused, and for a second I was afraid, really afraid that he was going to take me up on that and walk out the door.

"Hey, I—"

"Dragan's my problem, not yours. I don't need your help, so if you want to go, then—"

"Hey," he snapped. "If I wasn't in, believe me, I'd already be gone."

I chewed my lip. My face burned.

"And you do need help," Vamp said, "no matter what you say."

I shrugged.

"I care about you, okay?" he said, lowering his voice. "I don't want you to get killed."

"I know."

Nix had been watching off to the side, like he wasn't sure what exactly he'd just witnessed. Vamp rubbed the bridge of his nose, and sighed.

"I might have something," he said. "I've been grinding on the eyebot data. I've got a few more leads for you."

"If he's behind a gate, though—"

"He had to stash those kids somewhere. Find the kid, and find the twistkey, right?"

I nodded. "So you're going to help me?"

"It's going to take more than us to get Dragan out of there," he said, "but I'm with you, Sam."

I hugged him, and kissed his neck when he wrapped his arms around me.

"So, which one do you want to hit first?" I asked him, bringing up the eyebot images. The original trails he'd come up with had grown, but one had also branched and there was a lot of blank space between them.

"It's still not real clear," Vamp said. "But it's got to be somewhere around there. I've got a script trying to close the gap. Give it a little more time."

"It has to be one of them. We should—"

"We can't just go bouncing around Hangfei half-cocked. We have to have some idea where we're going."

I followed the two ends of the trail, noting the parts of town he'd passed through. There were no gate hubs near the points where they went cold, so I didn't think he jumped, but nothing in the area stood out, at least, no place you'd leave a couple of kids. There was no way to even know at what points he had the kids with him and when he was alone.

"We can't just stay here."

"Security is crazy out there right now. You're not going to be any good to Dragan in a detention center."

"How long will your thing take?"

"By tonight I'll have a better idea where the missing pieces are, and it'll be easier to move too."

I didn't like the idea of leaving Dragan hanging, just stewing in a hotel room waiting while he could be in trouble. For all we knew, the burn of Hangfei had already started, but Vamp was right. I wasn't leaving without Dragan one way or the other, and right now all I had was a stab in the dark, if that. Either lead would be over an hour away on foot, with blocks full of strangers by the thousands. He'd been branded a dissident, so I couldn't just advertise I was looking for him, or someone would ID me and I'd get picked up for sure. Running off wouldn't get me anything but arrested.

"Okay," I said. "Fine."

"Okay?"

"I said okay."

I looked at the trails on the map, willing them, needing them to lead somewhere I recognized, somewhere that made sense.

Hours passed, though. The nervous conversation dried up until I couldn't even respond to Vamp's reassurances while I stared at the screen ready to jump out of my skin. The whiskey was long gone and I was on my third cigarillo, but even the alcohol and the Zen-oil-infused tobacco combined couldn't calm my jitters. Vamp finally took to chatting with Nix in a low voice, hovering near the door, guarding it so I wouldn't run off into the night. I tried not to resent him for it, but I couldn't help it as I climbed into the creaky bed and tried my best to sleep.

Chapter Eleven

"No!" a voice shrieked, the terrorized alto of a little boy. I never learned his name, but I came to know his screams like the sound of my own voice. "No! No!"

I opened my eyes to see that two men had entered the holding pit. Between them, a scrawny little figure thrashed while they held his twiggy wrists. They dragged him away toward the blood trough while a third man lifted the rendering vat cover and released a billowing cloud of steam. I breathed in through my nose, and smelled cooking meat.

"No!"

I managed to turn my head, rolling it against the concrete wall behind me until I could see the old man. He leaned back against the wall, his eyes closed and his hands over his ears.

"Please! Do—"

A loud bang of electricity cut the boy off, and I looked back in time to see him crumple onto the damp concrete floor. One of the men grabbed his leg and dragged him over to the winch. Then he looped the cable in a figure eight around both ankles and secured the hook.

The first man pushed the button of a control box that hung from the ceiling. A motor whined as the cable lifted the boy up off the floor, and they guided him over until his wet hair dangled down over the trough.

I watched. I couldn't look away, even though I knew I should. I watched as one of the men yanked the machete from out of the stained butcher block and then swung it.

It wasn't dramatic, like in the movies. The boy's head didn't fly off or anything. It didn't even look like he hit him that hard, just a little whack to the side of the neck that made the body wobble at the end of the cable, but it was enough. Blood began to glug out of the black, eye-shaped hole that appeared, until a thick stream splattered down into the trough. One little tap was the difference between being alive and being dead.

When it was done, the man thumped the machete back into the block and lit a cigarillo so he could smoke while he waited for the blood to drain out. He offered one to the other man, who took it.

Then they talked about some game they'd seen on TV, bonding like two schoolboys while the tiny figure turned slowly at the end of the cable.

He froze midspin, like someone hit pause or something. The two butchers froze too, one with a cloud of smoke hanging motionless in front of him where he'd exhaled it.

"... *what you are experiencing is not a dream,*" the heavily accented voice said. "*You will find this difficult to accept, but you are receiving an allied transmission from outside the—*"

Static whined, and the voice cut out. The frozen figures flickered in front of me.

"... *hidden inside several native transmissions where we hope it will not be detected by your authorities, who we believe have been compromised . . . in an attempt to get the truth to you. . . .*"

The cloud of smoke billowed and the men's voices continued while the little boy's face turned slowly back around.

"... *the world is in grave danger. You have to . . .*"

The boy's face turned toward me, his eyes wide and staring through the lines of red that bled down into his hair, and I screamed.

I jerked awake with a gasp and felt a big arm around me. I panicked, and began to thrash.

"Sam," a voice said huskily in my ear. "Hey . . ."

A man lay behind me, holding me fast against him with one arm. I tried to kick the sheet away, to get free of the guy who had me, but I was stuck.

"Sam," the voice said again. "Take it easy."

I flipped around, and pushed against a muscular chest. I was staring directly into a man's face, and a spike of adrenaline shot through me even as I realized it was Vamp. He'd pulled his hand away, holding it up where I could see it. He looked stunned.

"Sam, it's me. It's just me."

I let out a pent-up breath, feeling the drool-damp pillow against my face. The air smelled like boozy sweat and bad breath, along with a strong-smelling musk that made my nose wrinkle. A soft green light did a mellow strobe against the wall as Vamp's phone flashed on the nightstand.

"Vamp," I whispered.

"Yeah," he said. "It's me."

"Shit." My heart was still going a mile a minute.

"Are you okay?"

I wiped my face. It was slick with sweat.

"Yeah," I said. "Yeah . . . I'm fine."

"You don't look fine."

I shook my head.

"I'm out of meds," I mumbled. "I'm fine. It happens all the time."

"You sure?"

"Yeah. Just . . . a bad dream."

"What about?"

I tried to focus on the phone's flashing light, but it kept reeling away, then snapping back in an infinite loop. I took a deep breath, trying to calm down, when a second jolt hit me.

"Shit, I fell asleep!" I hissed.

"Sam, it's okay—"

"It's not okay. . . . Damn it, I have to—"

"Calm down," he said quietly. "You've been in overdrive since yesterday. You were ready to hit the floor."

"I don't care!"

Vamp glanced over at Nix, but he didn't shush me. I could feel my anxiety start to spike when a flicker on the 3i tray made it fizzle. A notification flashed there.

"What?" Vamp asked.

I flicked it into the foreground and saw little lines of Pan-Slav.

"It's him," I said.

"Who?"

"The shit, the Pan-Slav shit." I checked his icon. It was pink. "He's still on."

I sat up, running his chat window through the translator and going down the lines of text.

I need help.

Help me, please. I'm scared. I want to go home.

I don't know where I am.

"He doesn't know where he is," I said, leaning back onto the pillow. The chat window floated between me and Vamp as he leaned over me.

Alexei, are you there?

I sent the message through the translator, hoping it would turn it into something that made sense to the kid. His little pink heart pulsed, ticking off the seconds.

"What's he saying?" Vamp asked.

"Shh."

Are you Sam?

I smiled. *Yes.*

Is Dragan with you?

No, but I'm going to help you. Tell me where you are.

I don't know.

"Sam, what's he saying?"

"He doesn't know where he is. Hang on."

Tell me about where you are. Are you inside?

Yes. I'm in a small box. Like a closet.

Can you get out? Is the door locked?

No door.

There has to be a door. Is it dark? Can you see?

I can see. Four walls. No door.

I curled my fist in frustration. That didn't make any sense.

Maybe it's hidden. Try—

Metal walls and floor. No windows. No doors.

What else is there?

A lamp. Water. A metal tank. No more rations.

What else?

Nothing else.

"He says he's in a metal box," I whispered. "He's got a light, rations, water, and maybe an air tank or something."

Are you alone? Is a girl with you?

She was, but he only put me in here.

Who? Who put you there?

Dragan.

I struggled to think it through. Dragan stashed him somewhere, hid him so no one would find him, then . . . what?

"*. . . I have to take care of a few things, but I'll be back for you. I will find help for you. I promise I'll be back for you—*"

Dragan meant to go back for him, but he never got the chance.

"Why keep him in a place like that?" I wondered out loud. Why lock him up in a box like that? Why him, and not the girl?

"A place like what?" Vamp asked.

"It sounds like he's in some kind of cage or some-thing." I checked the message info again, hoping to get lucky.

Out of Range.

Can you remember anything you saw before he put you in the room? I asked. *Any street names? Signs?*

I can't read them.

"Damn it."

Did you see anything that might—

Dragons. Paper monsters.

Festival stuff. He could have seen that anywhere.

Don't let them burn my country.

The words hung there.

Please, he said.

I started to answer, but I didn't know what to say. I wanted to tell him I wouldn't, but I wasn't sure I could do anything about it. If the weapon was still in Hangfei, which it probably was, I probably wouldn't even be able to do anything to save myself.

We don't hate you, he said. *Please. My family is there. My friends. My school.*

Alexei—

I don't want them to die. Please. We don't hate you. Please don't burn us.

I couldn't think of anything to tell him. I just lay there and stared at the words while Vamp leaned over me to grab his flashing phone. Before I could come up with anything, a new message popped up.

It's happening again. They're coming.

Who?

He didn't answer.

Alexei, who's coming?

His icon went gray.

"He signed off," I said, rubbing my eyes. Vamp leaned back into bed with me. "What's up with your phone?" I asked him.

"Eyebot's done," he said, squinting at the little screen. "Anything?"

"I'm not sure. What about the kid, he have anything useful?"

"Not really," I said. "He can't read anything, and Hang-fei must have seemed like a maze to him. I don't think he knows where the hell he is. He's just stuck in some metal box somewhere with nothing but water and . . ."

Vamp looked up from his phone. "What?"

"Rations," I whispered.

"Didn't they pay you a new ration sheet?"

"It's gone."

"What?"

"It's gone. . . ."

Vamp nudged me. "You okay?"

"After an assignment, Dragan always comes home with a fresh ration sheet," I said.

Dragan didn't come back alone this time, though; he came back with two mouths to feed, and he had to ditch them somewhere. Wherever that was, they had to eat. He'd cashed in the ration sheet.

"Give me your phone."

He handed it over and I flipped it around so I could see the screen. My head throbbed with each heartbeat as I traced the route Dragan had taken but when I saw it, I smiled.

"There," I said, snapping my fingers. "Render's Strip."

"Where the bomb went off?"

"Yeah." Along with the government centers, all the private ration distributers worked out of there. That's where Dragan had gone. It was after hours, and locked down because of the bombing, but he was a soldier and could get through.

I pointed to the screen. "That's where he took them. The place is called Fang's Café."

"Maybe . . ."

"It is, I'm sure of it."

"No place was open to—"

"He knows the guy who runs it. They fought together. They're tight. If it was an emergency, he'd help him no matter what time it was." I tapped the screen again. "It's him. I know it is. What time is it?"

I checked the phone.

"The redemption centers will start opening in a few hours," I said. "We can head out in two and be there before the rush."

"Sam—"

"I'm going," I said. "Are you coming with me?"

"Yeah. I'm in. I'll go, Sam. Just don't get too—"

I kissed him. I didn't think about it; I was just so happy that I kissed him full on the mouth. When I broke away, he looked a little surprised. I hadn't meant to do it exactly; I was just so excited. For the first time since the whole thing started, I felt like I had a lead, a plan, something I could do to set everything straight again.

"I'm glad you're here," I whispered.

"Yeah?"

"Yeah."

I took a deep breath and let it out, one hand still on his chest. He paused for a second, and then put his arm around me. I felt the warmth of his palm on my back as he pulled me in a little closer.

"I'll always be here, Sam. You know that, right?"

I moved my hand up his chest and over his collarbone. He tensed as I ran my fingers along his neck, then nestled them into his hair.

"I know."

The air under the sheet had turned to soup and I was going to kick the blanket off when Vamp moved his hand from my back and over my ribs to my chest. He ran one thumb over my left nipple deliberately and lingered on the point of it.

Blood rushed to my face as I put my hand on his and held it. He squeezed back and laced our sweaty fingers together as I felt a faint pulse down between my legs.

I don't know if it was the moment, or my excitement over the lead I'd just gotten, but I pulled him closer until I felt his breath on my face. In the neon light that flashed through the window, I could make out the tattoo on his banded shoulder, and the glint on his sweat-slick skin. The air that huffed up between us from under the sheet was so thick and hot it was hard to breathe as his stubble brushed my forehead. His lips pressed there.

The heat had me dizzy, and I reached down to push the sheet away. I felt my fingertips run over the buckle of his belt, and then brush the significant bulge that pressed against the seam beneath it. When I did, I felt him tense and the pulse below my waist turned more insistent.

Don't, a voice in my head said. *Don't do this.*

No, no, another voice said. *Definitely do this.*

He kissed my forehead again, then my cheek. His nose brushed mine, and then our lips were almost touching. Thoughts zipped through my brain so fast I couldn't focus on any one. The world could end tomorrow, but all I could think about was that if I kissed him again I'd cross a line I couldn't step back over. He was waiting, wanting me to cross it, but he didn't know everything.

"Vamp," I whispered.

"It's okay."

"I've done things."

He touched his forehead to mine. "I don't care."

I struggled to say more, but nothing would come out. He said he didn't care, but that's because he didn't know. He didn't know what he would be getting, not really, and if he found out after it was too late, and he hated me, I'd never be able to undo it.

"Whatever it is," he said, "I don't care."

Vamp held me gently, but he was coiled like a spring

ready to snap, and I could feel the want coming off him like a flood of radiation. One kiss, one touch was all it would take to break the dam, I could tell. He'd take me, never mind Nix. He'd take me, and I'd let him expend all that pent-up energy, and all that love he thought he'd kept such a careful secret, until—

"... but first, you have to help me."

The voice nagged in the back of my brain, pricking through even as I tried to push it out. My heart, which beat under Vamp's hand so hard I thought I'd lose control any second, stuttered as I remembered the old man's whiskey breath in my ear.

"Touch me. . . ."

I remembered the sound of my hard-soled shoes, heels scraping as I tried to pull away, but—

"I have to pee," I blurted. I could barely think. I was afraid Vamp might get mad, but instead he laughed once through his nose into my hair. He ran his thumb across my nipple one last time, then relaxed his embrace to let me pull away. I opened my mouth to say I was sorry, but then thought I'd better just leave it alone. I had to get out of there before I did anything even stupider than I already had done.

Instead I touched the side of his face, letting the five o'clock shadow scratch my palm as I stroked it once, and then got out of the bed with the soft squeak of springs. Vamp sighed, but he was drunk. We both were. With me gone, the combination of chems and booze won out. When I draped the damp sheet back down over him, he bunched the pillow against his face and began to drift off again.

I snuck between the two sleeping figures and slipped through the bathroom curtain, pulling it closed again before I switched on the light. When the overhead clinked on, I squinted in the sudden brightness and found a stray coin in one pocket to feed to the sink. Once it had clattered down into the slot, a green LED circle around the faucet flickered on and began to quickly disappear, like a fuse burning out. I turned it all the way to cold and held my hands under the weak, warm stream.

Cupping as much as I could, I drank it, and as I swallowed, it soothed my dry, sore throat somewhat. I cupped another double handful and dumped it down over my head, letting it trickle through my hair and down the back of my neck. I managed one more before the last of the green circle petered out and the valve thumped shut again.

I pulled down my pants and sat down on the toilet with my elbows on my knees and my chin resting in my hands as the stream began to dribble.

He wants me, I thought. *Shit, he wants me bad.*

I picked my phone back up off the sink and turned it over in my hands. A new message had come through while I was asleep, and it was marked urgent. I brought it up and saw it was from Kang.

Sam, we need to talk.

I looked up his status and saw he was online. I brought up the keypad and replied.

About what?

He didn't answer for almost a full minute, and I was wondering if he was really around or not when his answer came back.

Can we meet?

I checked the time. It was after three in the morning. I was beat, but meeting him felt like doing something. I needed to feel like I was doing something.

Where?

Where are you now?

I'll come to you.

He paused again. *The Rukou. I'm sending the address.*

I checked the map. It was across town. I'd need to use the gates if I was going to get there and back in time to hit Render's Strip early. I was hesitant to give him any kind of a lead, anything that might give him or anyone else who might be listening a search radius, but I was pretty much broke.

I'll need some credit.

No problem.

I fished out my card and slipped it into the reader. The transfer application popped up and Kang dumped some cash in. It was more than enough to get me where I needed to go.

Thanks, I said. *On my way.*

He signed off.

I snuck back out into the room and stood there for a minute watching the two guys sleep. I thought about waking them up and letting them know where I was going, but Vamp would insist on going for sure and I didn't want him getting involved with Kang. Kang might cut me some slack, but he wouldn't cut Vamp any.

Neither of them stirred as I slipped out into the hall and heard the door latch behind me. Down the hall, Wei's cubby behind the glass was empty. No one else was around.

I padded down to the front door and headed back out into the night.

Chapter Twelve

10:36:44 BC

My gas tank was getting close to empty, but the dream and the incident with Vamp had left me wired. My legs were restless and the walk felt good as the post-chem surge carried me deep back into the heart of Tùzi-wō. It felt good to get out in the open too, away from the sweat-heavy air of the hotel room. It had been getting hard to breathe in there, and getting back in that bed might have stirred things up again with Vamp.

Gonzo, I almost jumped him. I still wasn't sure how I felt about that.

Kang's credit had bought me two jumps there and two back, but I decided to take one there and hoof it the rest of the way just in case he tried to do the math and track my distance from him. When I stepped through to the other side across town, the light flashed green with no yellow warning shade.

The main drag was hopping, and through the gaps in the crowd I saw floodlights shining up ahead. A crew was doing night work, and the shop fronts across the street from them danced with the shadows of men moving along scaffolding. When I got closer, past the end of the block, I saw a crowd of people clustered at a chain-link fence that had been set up around an empty lot where a giant festival air float was being put together.

The float's base was a platform about the size of two tractor trailers side by side, and the metal framework mounted on it was a story tall. Wire mesh had been wrapped around the frame in the shape of a giant face, and shirtless workers moved along the scaffolding applying the plastic skin around two giant, googly eyes that stared down over a grinning, toothy mouth. Huge plastic streamers along the edge of the face were tied down, but a few had come loose to wave lazily over the street in the hot summer breeze. I watched them for a moment and sighed.

I just want to go to the festival with Dragan, I thought. *That's all I want.*

I didn't want to care about secret haan gates, pre-Impact conspiracy theories, or bomb-toting nut jobs. I didn't want to care about refugees or gonzos or SIPS. I just wanted to live with Dragan, earn enough to pay my way, get enough to eat, and have enough left over to stay in smokes, shine, and double cross. Was that too much to ask?

The streamers waved, like long ghostly tentacles that reached out over the crowd. Apparently, this year anyway, it was.

"Jiangshi," a voice said. I turned and saw kid with a wooden pole slung over one bony shoulder. Festival masks hung from the pole by their string ties.

"No, thanks," I said, but before he even got his mouth open to haggle me down, I changed my mind. "Actually you know what, that's perfect."

He beamed as I picked the closest one, and then he held out the credit reader. I wiped my card over it, letting Kang pick up the tab.

"Thanks," I said. He made a cute little bow and scampered off into the crowd until all I could see was the pole, jutting up over their heads and tracing his path like a wobbly paper periscope.

I slipped the mask on, hiding my face, and tied it snugly in place. The GPS pointed left, down a narrow side street, and I squeezed through the flow of foot traffic to pass in front of a set of headlights. The guy in the two-seater honked its anemic horn and muttered something at me through the glass as I made my way down the uneven sidewalk where grit and flakes of scrap plastic from the float construction had accumulated. Up ahead was the sign for the Rukou Bar, blazing red neon against the drab concrete.

Something crept along a power line overhead as I wove through a crowd that lingered outside along the street, drinking and smoking. No one was manning the door, so I pushed it open and went inside.

The bar was packed way over capacity, four to each table along the wall to my right and a row of sweaty backs all the way down the bar to my left. I made my way between them, squinting through the thin haze of smoke. Over the drunken babble around me, I heard someone call out from the direction of the bar and saw a tall man back there with a do-rag plastered over his brown, bald head. He pointed at me, scowling, but stopped when someone whistled. Kang was sitting a few tables down, the only one by himself. He signaled to the bartender, who nodded and went back to what he was doing.

Kang had a fogged glass in front of him where whiskey formed a moat around a big ball of nitrogen-chilled crystal, and the ashtray was filled with ash. In front of the empty chair across from him was a shot of something clear sitting on a wrinkled cocktail napkin. I hopped up on the empty stool and he gave me a faint smile.

"Nice mask."

"It's my cover," I said, pulling it back so that it sat on top of my head. The hanging streamers still covered most of my face like thick white hair. Kang nodded at the shot.

"Take it," he said. "You'll need it."

I drank it. Whatever it was, it went down like drain cleaner. "Gonzo, Kang. You trying to kill me?"

"Quit kidding around," he said. "This is serious."

"Yeah, I got thrown out a window, Kang. Believe me, I get it," I said. Kang sighed and shook a black cigarette out of a squashed pack. He offered me one, and I took it. "So, what do you need to talk to me about?"

"Dragan's not in any of the detention centers," he said, lighting his smoke, then holding out the lighter to me. He watched my face as I puffed mine alight. "You don't look surprised."

"I thought you might lie," I said, sucking in smoke.

"I wish I was lying."

"So where is he?" I asked, watching his face.

He looked nervous. "Not anywhere easy to get to."

"Shiliuyuán Station?" I asked, and I saw his eyes widen, just for a second.

"There is no more Shiliuyuán Station."

"The haan have him, don't they?" I asked.

He wiped sweat from his forehead and drained his glass. His hand shook a little as he put it back down and took another drag off his cigarette. "All I know is after she took him at the apartment, she—"

"How did you know it was a she?" I asked, but even before the look in his eye changed, I'd already put it together.

"I'm sorry," his wife had told me when I called. *"Jake is out on assignment."*

"Is he on the security sweep?"

"No, I don't think he is. . . ."

"You were there," I said.

He looked down into his empty glass for a minute, and I noticed then how tired and red his eyes were. He watched fog drift around the stone, and nodded.

"Yeah," he said. "I was there."

"You were the third soldier."

He nodded again, and I slapped him across the face so hard it knocked the cigarette out of his mouth in a cloud of embers. The people around us turned to look. Some of them laughed.

"It wasn't supposed to happen like that," he said evenly.

"How was it supposed to happen, Kang? Huh? How was it supposed to happen?"

"It was just supposed to be an arrest," he said, and his eyes looked haunted right then. He ran one hand over the stubble on his face. "He wasn't supposed to get hurt, and I never thought she'd . . ."

He trailed off.

"When I saw you go through the window . . . ," he said, and shook his head. "I knew you only had a few seconds. She provided us with free-floating gate tech for the duration of the mission . . . so while she was busy with Dragan I went to the balcony and managed to catch you with the graviton field, then drop you through to our exit point. It was the best I could do."

"That was the best you could do?"

"Hey, I saved your life."

"You fucking sold us out, Kang!"

"I know that," he hissed. "Do you think I don't know that? I had to!"

"You had to?"

"Yes." He waved his hand, and I could see he was pretty drunk. "There's . . . too much at stake."

"Your wife drafted the adoption papers. . . . How could you do it?"

He didn't have a good answer for that, and there was only so much satisfaction I could take from watching him squirm.

"Does she know?" I asked him.

"Look," he said. "You might think you have some idea of what's going on, but you don't."

"He's not a goddamned—"

"I know."

"It's the kid, isn't it? He's got the weapon."

He nodded. "Yeah, it's the Drugov kid."

"Why?"

He raised his eyebrows raised a little, surprised, even while the crazy fear still brewed in his drunken eyes.

"Why? Why would she—"

"I don't know what she's getting out of it, and I don't want to," Kang said. "All I know is there are people who want the Pan-Slavs out of the picture for good and she delivered. After she rigged him and let him go home, he was supposed to stay there and burn the PSE, eighty-seven percent of the landmass pushing east from an ignition point inside Kostroma."

"Eighty-seven percent?"

He stared, gritting his teeth and not speaking for a moment.

"A pandemic," he said finally. He looked scared now. "An accident. Nobody's fault. The haan would step in and fix things, like they always said they would."

I couldn't believe what I was hearing. I mean, if I was to be honest, I'd thought it before, especially lately, but thinking about it was one thing. Doing it was something totally different.

"But why risk it?" I asked. "Why would she want to destroy them so bad?"

"She doesn't," Kang spat. "She doesn't give any more of a shit about the PSE than she does us."

"Then why?"

"Deals are made, kid. We see new tech appear, new benefits, better standards of living, but behind closed doors, deals are made."

"What kinds of deals?"

"I don't know!" he snapped. "I don't know who approached her first, but whatever she was promised, she went for it. If this gets out, it will be bad for everybody, but if we can just set things right, set things back on course, it will be okay. No one has to know."

"But all those people . . ."

"Sam, look around. You know how this is going to end. How easy was it for you to imagine they'd launched this biological attack against us? Even though it was Dragan, didn't you wonder, just for a minute?"

I gritted my teeth, not wanting to admit I had.

"The way things are going, how long do you really think it will be before they do something like it, or worse? We can't just sit back and hope it won't happen—"

"But all those people, Kang. That's kids, babies . . ."

"I know." He leaned close, looking about ready to crack. "That's why we have to get that kid back. Do you get it now? None of that matters anymore. We can't stop it. It's happening. Now it's just us or them. That's the only choice we've got left."

"And what about Dragan?"

"He saw everything, Sam. He's not coming back."

"Then I'm going to get him."

"This is bigger than him. I know how much he means to you, but he's just one guy. He'd tell you the same if he were here."

"I'm going to get him."

"You'll never get in there, Sam, and you'd never get out alive if you did."

"I'll find the kid, and trade him."

"There's not going to be any trade. You have to give it up."

"No! I want Dragan back, and I want my life back!"

I yelled that last part loud enough that people looked over again.

Kang slammed his fist down on the table, causing butts and ash to jump out of the ashtray.

"I'm through playing games," he snapped. "I'm a dead

man, do you hear me? Sillith doesn't think we can stop it, so she's going to make damned sure no one finds out what she did before it blows up right in the middle of Hangfei, but I'm not going to let that happen, goddamn it.... I sacrificed everything to save this country, and this is all I've got left. Forget about Dragan. He's gone, but you can still do the right thing. Where the hell is that Pan-Slav brat?"

There was desperation in his red eyes and I realized then that this was why he'd called me out there. This was why he'd made contact again. Dragan either wouldn't or still couldn't talk, and they didn't have any way to find the boy. Sillith had given up on finding him and was trying to distance the haan, but Kang hadn't given up. Not yet.

"I don't know where he is."

"Bullshit! Tell me where he is!"

"I don't know!"

"Please," he said, changing his tone suddenly. "Do you know where he is? If you do, tell me, please."

"I don't—" Kang reached across the table and grabbed a fistful of my tank top, dragging me halfway over.

"Hey!" the bartender snapped finally. "Easy, over there!" Kang didn't let go.

"Get off," I said, tugging loose. I pushed away from him, but he held on to my wrist. "Let go of me, asshole!"

"He's dead already, Sam," he pleaded. "I thought I could get him back, but I can't. I can't even save myself. You can't let this happen.... The burn will start the night of the festival.... Our country will be left in ruins! We're the only hope left for this damned world and we'll be wiped out! We deserve to live, more than them. You have to—"

I jerked my arm away and started back toward the door, Kang knocking his stool over as he got to his feet and followed after me.

"Sam," he said. "I swear if you walk out that door you're dead. You can still do the right thing and walk away from this. Let me help you."

"Screw you, Kang," I muttered. There was a lump in my throat as I pushed open the bar door and stepped back out onto the sidewalk.

He was right behind me, swinging the door a little too hard in his drunkenness. He grabbed my arm and pulled.

"Hey!"

Before I could stop him he'd hauled me right up off the ground and pulled me into the narrow alley next to the bar. He slammed me up against the rough brick face, and held me there.

"Let me go!"

I kicked his shin, and stomped one heel down on his foot, but he held me fast, leaning against me and pressing his stubbly chin into my neck as he spoke in my ear.

"I don't give a shit about them, you hear me?" he said. "Those barbarians deserve to die. All they contribute to this planet is violence. They suck up food, water, and air that other people, better people could be using. The world would be better off without them. Then the haan would have enough. Don't you get it? They wouldn't have to take so much from us. We could eat again. We could breathe again, and they'd be in our debt. The world would be better off without the PSE. You know it's true."

"I never said—"

"Just take me to wherever you're hiding and give me what you've got. We'll take it from there. You don't have to ever know the details. Lijuan is on her way to Duongroi already, and I'll make sure you get over the border in the morning, just in case. I—"

I blasted him with my knee. He twisted his leg at the last second, but I clipped his groin hard enough to make him let go. He staggered back, trying to stand up straight as I grabbed his suit jacket and pulled it down back over his shoulders until his elbows were pinned. While he was off balance, I shoved him forward as hard as I could and he went face-first into the wall.

"Goddamn it!" he grunted. He wasn't carrying his gun, but there was a stunner clipped to his belt. I snatched it and squeezed the grip as he tried to push away, jamming the business end into his ribs. His eyes bugged out as the prongs made a rapid-fire popping sound, and then he pitched over on his side and went limp. Breathing hard, I tossed the stun gun down on the blacktop next to him where his cigarette pack had fallen from his shirt pocket. I took it and backed out of the alley. The people up and down the street were still boozing it up, laughing, and talking. None of them even looked over.

"Sorry, Kang."

I stuffed the smokes into my pocket and headed back out to the street. A bottle rocket whistled high into the air and then popped as I pulled the mask back down and sprinted back to where they were working on the parade float.

Overhead, the silhouette of an aircar drifted past as I approached the gate, a cone of light shining down and sweeping the sidewalk back behind me on the lookout for trouble it had just missed.

Chapter Thirteen

By the time I got back to Wei's, dawn had begun to peter down through the neon haze, and the streets had thinned out as much as they ever did. Most of the derelicts from the night before had abandoned their spots on the old stoops and left behind bottles, butts, and crumpled paper bags. The sign for Wei's buzzed, casting a feeble red glow onto the grungy landing as I climbed down to the heavy door.

Just as I grabbed the handle, the door flew open and some big dude knocked me back as he barged through. I went down on the concrete steps but he just blew right past, not even looking back as he hustled down the sidewalk.

"Excuse you, asshole!" I yelled after him.

I got back up and brushed off, then pulled open the door and headed inside. The lobby was empty, but I could hear voices down the hall, anxious voices that put me on edge. Something was up, a fight maybe. I wondered if the guy I'd just passed hadn't just robbed the place or something.

When I got to the corner, a woman in a miniskirt and heavy lipstick came scooting around to squeeze past me. Her eyes were streaked with mascara, and she carried her heels in one hand.

"Hey," I called. "What's going on?" She didn't answer. She shoved open the door and took off.

Something was up. No cops yet, but they probably weren't far off. We were going to have to make ourselves scarce before they got here or else ...

I rounded the corner and saw Wei's foyer. The force field was down and the window on the other side had been blown in, the heavy glass splintered around a fist-sized hole. The metal mesh sandwiched between the layers had been pushed through the crater, and wire bristles ringed the hole.

I rushed over to Wei's door, which hung open, the jamb splintered. Wei lay inside on his back next to a toppled stool.

"Wei!"

I kicked through the trash that had spilled from a waste bin and knelt down next to him, pushing the jiangshi mask back to hang behind my head. His right leg was snapped at the shin, and his nose was smashed flat. Blood had run down his neck and stained the collar of his shirt.

"Wei," I whispered, leaning close to him. One of his eyes was swollen shut, but the other opened a slit and I caught a gleam there. He was still breathing. The cords in his neck twitched as he swallowed.

"I didn't ... ," he rasped.

"Wei, what happened?"

He looked confused, like he wasn't sure where he was. His eyes swam for second, then focused on me.

"When they ... took you ... ," he wheezed.

"Took me?"

"When they took ... you ... I ..."

I realized then that he was talking about the meat farmers, all those years ago.

"I know, Wei," I said. "I know. Just tell me what happened."

"I looked ... for you ... for days ..."

"Never mind all that," I said in his ear. "Who did this?"

"Soldier . . ."

"A soldier attacked you?"

He managed a nod.

"She's gunning . . . for you," he whispered.

I glanced back through the open doorway and saw someone scoot past, headed for the front door. More voices shouted from somewhere down the hall, and then something crashed.

"Get out," Wei said. "Quick."

Damn it. I couldn't tell if any of the voices belonged to Vamp or Nix.

"I can't," I told him. "Just don't move. Stay still."

He pawed with one hand, and I saw that his fingers had been broken. With his swollen, knobby index finger he pointed at the safe under his desk. The door was open a crack.

I pulled it open. Inside were stacks of documents, some paper money, and on the top shelf, sitting on top of a couple of ration sheets, was a small, snub-nosed pistol. I grabbed it. It felt light in my hand, but solid. The surface was worn and dull, like it was old. When I squeezed the grip, the holostamp that flickered into the air next to it showed twenty-two rounds.

"Go," he said. "Get out of here."

"I can't, Wei."

"She'll kill you," he said. "Don't go back there."

He coughed, spritzing blood as he tried to say something else, but I stopped him.

"Just lie still," I told him. "Take it easy."

"Wait," he moaned.

Gun at the ready, I slipped back out through the door and sprinted down the hall. A guy sporting a bloody gash on his forehead ran past me headed the other way, and up ahead the body of a bald man lay facedown in a pool of blood. His soaked left sleeve hung to the floor, and a long red spatter led across the tiles to a severed, tattooed arm that lay amid overlapping sneaker tracks. Just past that, the door to our room hung open.

"She won't come back," I heard Vamp say from inside. "I told you, I already warned her. She's long gone."

"She isn't," a woman's voice said. It was Sillith. I crept up and crouched next to the doorway, listening.

"She doesn't know anything," Vamp said. "Why don't you just leave her alone?"

Don't antagonize her, I pleaded silently. Vamp didn't know what he was dealing with.

"She knows," Sillith said.

I risked a quick peek and saw her standing with her back to the door. Vamp sat on the bed, the sheets still wadded up next to him, and Nix stood in the spot where he'd been sleeping when I left.

The combat armor would stop a handgun round. If I could put a shot into the dispersion mask, I should hit her in the face, which was probably unprotected, but that was a shot I wasn't sure I could pull off.

"I know you're there," Sillith purred. "If you don't come out, I will kill your male."

I stood up and stepped into the doorway. Through the mite cluster, I felt satisfaction course just underneath her excitement over the promise of more violence.

"You really get a charge out of this, huh?" I asked her.

"Step into the room."

I took a step forward, and as I did I saw Vamp slink off the bed and move in behind her. I opened my mouth to stop him, but it was too late. She turned, and Vamp threw a punch directly into the face of the dispersion mask.

"Vamp, don't!"

His fist disappeared into the field, but I heard the thud and Sillith stumbled back a step as he threw a follow-up that caught her right in the face again, and she reeled.

She didn't go down. The armor hummed as she swung the back of her fist at him. Vamp ducked as it swooped over his head, and he nailed her in the face again with a solid, meaty thud.

Even a human would have been thrown for a loop by a hit like that, but it should have been devastating to a haan. The armor, maybe combined with something like Nix's inertial dampening field, might protect her body, but his fist connected hard. I felt the burst of signal, her surprise and pain, through the cluster. A strike like that should have shattered those delicate bones, but what I felt from her was more surprise than pain, fast turning to fury.

"Vamp!"

Nix moved toward her while her back was turned to him, and I saw something in his hand. It was the electronic wand he'd used to take his sample with the morning he showed up in my hotel room, only now he held it like a weapon. He swung it around, ready to stab her with it, but something, some invisible force, stopped his arm cold before he could land the blow. The needle-like prongs quivered an arm's length away from her as the two struggled, and then Nix's hand sprang open and the wand fell to the floor.

Without stepping away from Vamp, Sillith made a violent shrugging motion and something struck Nix. For just a second I swore I saw a hand, a haan hand whose long fingers were curled into claws as it thumped into the middle of his chest, but then it flickered and was gone.

What the ...

Nix's feet came up off the floor as he was hurled back toward me. His shoulder crashed into the lamp and sent pieces spinning across the floor after him. His body flew through the air and bashed into the wall next to the doorway so hard it broke the jamb. A slat of fake wood spun away as he caromed off and went down like a rag doll onto the floor.

Vamp was about to throw another punch when she turned back to him.

"Vamp, no! Get away from her!" I screamed.

He looked, and ducked down low when he saw me raise the pistol. Sillith reached down to grab him, and I squeezed the trigger.

I expected a single shot that I hoped would hit Sillith square in the head. Instead the gun let out three loud, overlapping bangs as it bucked in my hand. The first shot punched through the wall in front of her, but the next two got her, one in the shoulder and the other in the side of the neck. The armor absorbed the rounds, but they hurt her, I could feel it, and she stepped back from Vamp to face me instead.

I raised the gun again, ready for the recoil this time, when a sudden, crippling pain jabbed into my gut like the blade of a long knife. I gasped and doubled over, the gun's barrel drifting off target.

Not now. . . .

My vision blurred as the pain came again, and the strength went out of my legs. I couldn't breathe, and as I fell to my knees the gun slipped from my hand. It thumped onto the floor, and when I screwed my eyes up to look I saw Sillith's armored boots clomping toward me.

Something boomed from behind and for a moment all I could hear was a low ring in my ears. A smoking plastic shell bounced off the toppled dresser next to me, and then a second, muted boom sounded.

Covering my head, I looked back to see Wei leaned against the doorway. He supported himself on one leg, holding up the broken one as he stared down the barrel of a shotgun.

Before he could fire again, the gun leapt out of his hands, torn away by something I didn't see. He stared, confused, and then something grabbed him and jerked him forward off his feet.

One of his shoes clipped my ear as he flew past and came down hard in front of Sillith. Vamp tried to get to his feet and was slammed back down onto the floor, pinned there by something invisible, with his face turned away. She reached down and picked up Nix's wand, aiming the needles down toward Wei's neck. The door slammed behind me and I heard the bolt lock, but when I turned, no one was there.

"Look!" Sillith snapped. I stared at the door, still trying to figure out what had happened.

"Look!"

I turned back toward her. She held Wei by the hair, craning his neck back so that his chin pointed up at the ceiling. The needles were an inch from the pit between his collarbones.

"Tell me where that boy is."

"I don't know," I said. I kept the gun pointed away from her, but didn't drop it.

"I don't believe you."

"It's true," I told her. "I don't know. We're looking for him, but we haven't found him."

"I'm a dead man anyway," Wei wheezed. "Just run—" His voice choked off as she pulled back harder on his hair.

"The man Shao stole a twistkey," she said. "He used it to bring a boy and a girl back here with him, and while he was there he made a recording. I want the boy, the girl, the key, and his wet drive."

"Is he alive?" I asked her.

"If you don't—"

"Just tell me, is he alive?"

She punched the needles deep into Wei's chest.

His eyes bugged out as an electric whine rose in pitch, and the veins in his neck and face bulged. They popped up under his skin like squiggling worms, until they looked ready to burst.

"Stop!" I yelled. "Wait!"

With a loud snap, Wei's entire body erupted. I jumped back, cringing as sheets of warm rain splashed down over me. In the second before I shut my eyes, I saw a wrinkled, empty blob of skin shrink down through the collar of his shirt.

It slopped down onto the floor between us like a big, wet towel. I kept my head turned away, paralyzed, as fat drops dripped down from my hair. The front of my shirt was soaked, but it wasn't blood like I'd first thought. It was water. Warm, salty water. I wiped it from my face as my mind reeled back to Nix's first visit, when those needles were pointed at me.

"What's that?"

"It will take the sample I need."

"Is this going to hurt?"

"Turn around," Sillith said.

I remembered Nix's anxiety, his uncertainty as he'd moved the needles closer.

". . . no, it won't hurt."

"Turn around," she said again.

I turned to see Vamp, soaked and struggling, as she reached down into the wet pile of Wei's empty clothes. From inside she pulled what looked like a big blood-colored amoeba, fat tentacles slithering out from the sleeves and pant legs while Vamp stared in shock from a few feet away.

She touched the needles to the blob, and water squeezed out of it like a sponge as it shriveled further. She held up the little mass left behind so I could see.

"What did you do—" I had started to ask when she fed the fist-sized jelly through her mask's dispersion field.

I heard a long slurp, followed by the gurgle of a sink draining. At the same time, through the mite cluster, I felt the familiar rush I felt whenever I gave a bottle to

one of my surrogates. It was pleasure, and the relief of
hunger being satisfied, if only for a while. Sillith had just
eaten Wei.

"This is what you are," she said, displaying her empty
hand. "This is your place."

Vamp was jerked up off the floor, then slammed back
down in front of her. His knees splatted down onto the
wet floor, and his arms were pulled back taut behind him
as if bound by invisible ropes. His head craned back and
Sillith leaned in to point the needles down at his exposed
throat.

I couldn't speak. It was hard to even breathe. All I
could think at that moment was that I didn't have an
answer for her. I didn't know where Alexei was, not for
sure, and I didn't have the twistkey she wanted either.
Even if I wanted to tell her, and if it would stop her from
sticking Vamp with those needles, then I would have. I
couldn't, because I didn't know. I couldn't even think of
a lie.

"Last chance," she said.

"I have the wet drive," I told her. "It's all I have. I'll
give it to you."

"Not good enough."

Vamp looked over at me from the corner of his eye,
his breath coming fast as the needles moved closer.

"Run, Sam," he managed. "Don't watch this, just—"

Out of nowhere, Nix flew across the room and planted
one heel in the middle of Sillith's chest. The force threw
her into the wall, and caused her to let go of Vamp, who
pitched down onto the floor. The wand spun in the air
and then clattered down next to him as Nix leapt between the two. Sillith sprang back to her feet, every inch
of her bristling as she glared back at him.

Nix closed the distance between them and I heard a
chirp as he punched through the spot underneath her
chest plate.

His fist went straight through, and splintered the latticework bones underneath. I expected to feel agony from her, but it didn't come. Even when he wrenched his fist free and I saw he had dragged something out with it, I sensed no pain. Instead, she looked down at the wormy mass that pulsed between his fingers and I felt fury from her, and something else ... betrayal maybe.

"You—" she started, when all at once the air around her warped and shimmered like water. The ripples grew, and then she vanished.

I jumped as air rushed into the vacuum left behind with a loud bang, and then everything was quiet. Nix turned from the empty space where Sillith had been, his eyes leaving pink trails in the air as he looked down at me.

"Are you okay?" he asked. I nodded, staring at the thing in his hand. The air around it had already begun to ripple when he tossed it away. Before it could hit the floor, it popped out of existence.

"Where did she go?"

"When a haan dies, the body and anything else caught in the warp bubble is gated back to the ship for processing. I tricked the mechanism into believing she was dead."

"So ... she's not?"

"No."

I looked at the hand he'd punched her with. It was clean, and dry, with no evidence of what he'd done. I could almost have imagined it.

"What did you do to her?" I asked him.

"We need to leave," he said.

"No, answer me."

She'd hit him hard—hard enough to kill him, easy. Some stupid street dreg broke his arm in two without even trying, but even though he'd hit the wall hard enough to break through, there he stood like it never happened.

Vamp backed away from the wet clothing and wiped his face, flicking the salty water away.

"What the hell was that?" he asked. "What did she do to him?"

"Organic nutrient condensation," Nix said. "It's food processing technology. Part of the Phase Seven package, though it isn't meant to be used on living creatures."

"You okay?" Vamp asked. He put his hands on my shoulders, but I was still staring at Nix. "Sam, what's up?"

"I know what I saw," I told Nix.

"The inertial dampener was able to—"

"That wasn't the dampener. . . ."

My voice faded as he approached me on a wave of signal that drilled straight into my brain. I felt the confusion and the fear drift away.

"It was the inertial dampener," he said again. "We have to go."

"So she's on the ship?" Vamp asked.

"Not for long," Nix said. "She's already on her way back, I guarantee. The trick won't work a second time."

I looked at the crack in the wall where Nix had struck it, still unsure.

"What is it?" Vamp asked.

I looked from the splintered wood back to Nix. *He's lying. Again, he's lying.*

"Nothing," I said. "He's right. We have to get to Render's Strip. If Dragan did cash in his ration sheet there, Fang might know something."

I picked the pistol up off the floor and stuck it in my pocket, then gave Vamp a hug. We were both still wet.

"Thanks for trying to cover for me," I told him, "but she's dangerous, Vamp. Don't mess with her, okay?"

"Where did you go?" he asked.

"I had to check something out. I didn't want to get you guys involved."

"I woke up and you were gone."

"I'm sorry."

I looked back down at Wei's wet clothes and saw the needles lying on the floor next to them. When I reached down to pick them up, though, Nix intercepted and snatched it away.

"Vamp, wait for me outside," I said.

He looked from me to Nix, wary, but he did as I asked. When I heard him moving down the hall, I moved closer to Nix and lowered my voice.

"I want to know what's going on," I said.

"I've told you everything I can."

I sighed, and I think he knew what was coming next. I could sense his unspoken protest, his dismay, in a way that reminded me unpleasantly of Tānchi.

"Nix, thanks for all your help, but I think I'll take it from here."

"You are sending me away." Again, the thought of Tānchi jabbed at me, that look he gave me as he looked back from the hopper.

"Yeah. I guess I am. No offense, Nix, but I've got enough going on right now without having to watch my back."

"But I—"

"Tell me," I snapped. "Give me a straight answer. If you can't give me one straight answer, then leave. I mean it."

He was quiet for a minute, and I sensed him as he struggled with something. Then he raised his arm, the injured one, and ran his finger along the seam of his sleeve. When it peeled apart, I could see his arm was fine. No break. It was as if it never even happened.

"I wasn't sent to help you," he said. "I was sent to kill you."

It was the truth. I could tell. This time, it was the truth.

"Why?" I asked.

"You knew a haan had murdered, or attempted to murder, several humans. Our leaders were afraid of retaliation by your government. The ones who sent me reasoned that you were thought to be dead already, and loss of one life would be better than the loss of many."

"So why didn't you do it?"

"Because I couldn't."

"You couldn't?"

"No."

"Why not?"

He took my wrist, his long fingers closing around it with a firm but gentle pressure. I had opened my mouth to say something when he reached out through the surrogate bond and I froze.

His presence surged through like an icicle pushing into my forehead. It was more intense than anything I'd ever felt before. Even the dream images that had bled over from Sillith were nothing compared to the way he poured into my mind and filled it.

The hotel room disappeared, and I was somewhere else as suddenly as if I'd been gated there. I knew at once that I wasn't seeing through my own eyes, that this was something Nix was showing me, a memory he had plugged directly into my consciousness somehow. Ghost images flashed throughout the room, towering bars, and a large figure that loomed next to me. It was a giant human skeleton, the gray bones surrounded by the cottony blur of transparent soft tissue. Large, translucent orbs rolled in the empty, saucer sockets of the skull face as it looked down at me. Tiny points of light, electrical impulses, flashed through the wrinkles of the giant's brain, flowing up and down the spinal column and coursing along the vast network of nerves that branched from it.

It's not a giant, I realized. *It's not big. Nix is small. This is an old memory.*

Pulses of light flashed through household wires, inside appliances, and even through the air where drifting particles carried scents and pheromones. The amount of information pouring in was overwhelming, like a flood that threatened to carry me away.

This is how he sees the world, I thought. *How the haan see our world.*

It was more than that, though. I sensed that flow as it was processed, packaged, and stored. A scalefly flitted down and I felt it scurry through a pore in my side, felt it inside me somewhere, then a faint tickle as that information, the sum of everything he observed, was transferred for distribution.

They're watching us.

A pang of hunger gripped me, urgent and frightening. More ghost objects came flickered into focus, images of other figures, humans, walking and sitting and lying down in the distance, behind the walls that contained the world beyond the bars.

The giant leaned closer and I saw the compact squiggles of a brain appear inside the skull. Bright dots flitted inside, like spastic insects. They flashed up and down the dark shadow of the spine, sparking through muscle tissue as the giant lifted an object into view. It was a bottle. It was a surrogate formula ration whose stamp, in haan, evoked an image of a female who I recognized as Sillith. Not the Sillith I'd encountered, but an icon, an idol who had served, and been loved, for a long, long time.

The giant cracked the seal on the surrogate bottle and pulled the tube out. Its skeletal hand lowered it down into the cage from above. Nix had been a surrogate, of course. He was showing me a memory from when he was an infant of his surrogate mother.

She leaned closer still, and I felt the bottle's tube squelch its way into an opening near my throat where complex muscles drew it deep down into my body. I felt air vent from other pores in my skin where more scaleflies burrowed and crawled. Then the gel was flooding into me, blanketing the hunger, dousing it, and spreading out through my entire being. Shriveled cells were saturated and grew fat as nerve clusters reconnected, making me whole again. It was like coming back from the verge of death.

The whole time I felt an alien sense of thanks, warmth, and a child's worship of the only mother it knew. He wanted to touch the giant, to connect with it, and as I stared over the surface of the bottle, I saw the pigment beneath the layer of cottony skin. It was formed in an artful band around the biceps, where complex characters I immediately understood spelled out the syllables of a name.

DRAGAN.

As suddenly as the world had changed, it changed back. I was back in the wrecked hotel, stinking of Wei's shed water. Nix released my arm.

"You," I whispered, staring at him. He hadn't just been a surrogate; he had been my surrogate.

"You cared for me," he said.

"I remember you." He'd been my second surrogate. I'd gotten that tattoo just a week before I picked him up. "You're Xiǎiogu. My little demon."

"Nix now."

"I called you that because you kept throwing your bottle."

"I remember."

I hadn't realized they grew that fast, but after what I'd just experienced I didn't question it. His eyes blazed pink, the pupils like coals nestled within.

"I could never hurt you," he said.

He took out the little tablet he carried and swiped the screen with one finger. When the gate opened, he placed the wand inside.

"When I didn't do as they asked, I was pruned from the axial hive. When I return I will be sent back to the vats and my memories will not be preserved. I have no other purpose now but to help you."

He handed me his tablet, and I took it.

"And I want to help you," he said.

I looked over the tablet. The spot where the field opened was solid, glossy silver.

"Okay. Fine. You win."

I turned the tablet over in my hand once, then handed it back.

"Little demon," I said.

"Thank you."

"Can you gate us to Render's Strip?"

"No. I can only gate to and from places I have previously stored the location of, or places close enough so that the device's scanner can set a dynamic access point. We will need to use the street network."

"How long do we have?"

"She'll use a twistkey to give her a direct route," he said. "Even so, it's a long distance, but I'd say less than an hour."

I looked around at the mess, and wiped my face. The water that had steeped into my clothes smelled like sweat.

"Come on, then," I said. "That's not much time."

Chapter Fourteen

The sun had just started to blaze by the time we reached Render's Strip, and already the crowded streets were beginning to brew in the heat and humidity. A nearby sign flashed a temperature of 104 as scaleflies bounced off the marquee.

I'd put the festival mask back on but pulled it to the top of my head so I could breathe. With the festival that night, the restaurant district was filling up fast with people looking to load up on chems and other illicit buys in spite of the added security. The underground food market especially thrived around festival time, and behind the backs of uniformed guards paper money changed hands all around us. I noticed splotches of red festival dye on the pavement, and on people's clothes. By tonight, the place would be covered.

"Sam, come on," Vamp urged. People streamed around us, some of their eyes lingering on Nix as they passed. I held up one hand, pressing my phone to one ear with the other, as someone finally picked up.

"Fang's Café, what do you want?"

"Mr. Fang?"

"What do you want?"

"I want to talk to you about Dragan Shao—"

The line cut. I looked back at Vamp and held up the phone. "He hung up."

"Never mind, it's in here somewhere."

Down the main drag of the strip, a cordon was still in place around the shattered remains of the government ration reclamation center. The one solid, shiny structure that used to stand tall among the hundreds of bookend storefronts surrounding it had been reduced to blackened rubble. The half-burned remains that littered the site, toppled counters, and twisted electronics and safety glass melted to slag were the only indications of what used to go on inside. The bodies had all been removed, but the pavement under the boots of the guards who stood at the perimeter was still stained with dried trickles and spatters of rust brown.

I turned away from the guards and wiped sweat from my forehead as I scanned the crowded rows of little signs. Each one hung over a narrow door that led into a sliver of restaurant space, flashing bright, happy neon over old buildings covered with a lifetime of sweat, smoke, and grime.

Ninety percent of the restaurants there were basically holes in the wall where you could redeem ration punches, and tiny tables to sit and eat them at if that was your bag. The only thing that made one different from the other was what was on the TV, whether or not they had AC, and what kind of little side rackets they had going on. Signs with white tags meant they sold booze. Red tags meant they sold pills. Blue tags meant clean water, orange tags meant smokes, and pink tags meant "live entertainment." Two pink tags meant they had girls to get you off in the back. A yellow smiley face on a black background meant street meat. A black smiley face on yellow meant scrapcake.

It was a complete mess, but I'd grown up sneaking

through those streets looking for marks, and I knew where all the side streets and alleys were. The GPS marker put Fang's Café two blocks up on the right, underneath rippling plastic tarps that had been stretched across the street from building to building two stories up.

"This way."

There were more haan wandering Render's Strip than I expected to see, standing a head or so above most people as they moved carefully through the flow of pedestrians, motor scooters, and bicycles. I saw a woman bump into one, and watched her apologize up and down as the haan assured her he was okay. He was fine, I realized now. There was no chance at all he'd been hurt, but his reaction seemed so genuine he still could almost convince me. The surrogate cluster even picked up a slight internal wince, a small pain he felt but kept from the woman so as not to worry her. If it was an act, it went layers deep. I watched him make an elegant bow, and the woman smiled as she watched him walk away.

Fang's Café was tucked in a dense row of shops, each front about two doors wide. His sat between one that traded ration tickets for booze, and one with a double pink tag. Through the tall front window of the double pink, a woman stood naked, leaning against a pole and smoking a cigar butt. Her body was bonier than mine even, with all of her ribs sticking out and a little patch of bush at the base of her jutting pubic bone. She was completely covered in sweat from being in the glass case, and looked bored, stoned, or about to keel over. Maybe all three. She just stood there while a small group watched from a few feet away. I wondered how much she got paid to stand there naked.

I hopped the single step and pushed open the narrow door under Fang's sign. It had a white and an orange tab. According to the scrawl underneath, he sat fifteen at five-minute intervals and took all ration sheet colors except gold. I could see he was over capacity when I went in, with each of five tiny round tables surrounded and more standing. Smoke had collected up under the high ceiling where a three-bladed fan pushed hot air around. A short length of counter stood nestled in one corner, and behind it sat a scrawny older guy with a big gap between his front teeth who stared at something on the screen of his phone. There was a glass jar packed tightly with thin brown cigarettes next to him, and a shelf with empty bottles behind him showing the five different kinds of booze he carried. As I made my way over, a red light flashed from under the counter and he raised his eyebrows a little but didn't look over.

"No weapons in here," he said.

"Mr. Fang?" I asked.

"I said no weapons in here. You deaf?"

"Are you Mr. Fang?"

He looked up from his phone then and squinted at me through the smoke.

"What do you want?" he asked.

"I want to talk to you."

"I'm at capacity," he said. "Beat it. Take your friends with you."

I took three of the cigarettes out of the jar and put them down on the counter along with my cash card. Fang hesitated, then grabbed a paper fan off the counter next to him. He fanned himself with it a little as he picked up the card.

"Now I'm a customer," I said. "The three cigs, plus five minutes."

He ran my card through a plastic scanner that was plugged into his phone. He tapped at the screen for a minute and then pushed the card and the smokes back toward me.

"You a cop?" he asked.

"Do I look like a cop?"

"You look like shit."

I felt my face flush.

"Watch it," Vamp warned, but Fang just smiled.

"What happened? His wife come home early?"

"Ha, ha. I need to ask you about a man named Dragan Shao."

As soon as he heard the name, his expression changed. At first I thought he was going to clam up, or throw me out, but he didn't do either.

"Oh," he said, relieved. "That was you on the phone. I thought it was security or something."

"Why would security be calling you about Dragan?"

"You know why." He held up a hand to cut off my response. "We go way back. I know it's bullshit, but when they get that scent they stick their noses in deep. I don't want any trouble."

"No trouble," I told him. "I just want to know where he is, that's all."

"Why? What's it to . . ." He trailed off, then smiled and pointed his finger at me. "Wait a minute. You're Sam."

"Yeah," I said. "Yeah, that's me. How do you know me?"

"Like I said, Dragan's an old friend. I've seen your picture."

"Dragan showed you my picture?"

"He showed everybody your picture. The day he adopted you he bought smokes from that jar and handed them out," he laughed. "Bōlí."

"He never told me."

"War's ugly. Makes people do ugly things. He likes to keep the bad old days from you, I think."

"He thinks I can't take it?"

He laughed. "You ask me, the lady boy's worried what you might think. He likes being a father."

In the back of my mind I'd wondered why he never took me along to Fang's. In my worst moments I thought he was embarrassed about me. I hadn't expected this. I had plenty of things I didn't want to admit to anyone, not to Dragan, or even Vamp. It never occurred to me Dragan might carry around the same stuff.

"Was he in here the other day?"

Fang's smile faded, and he nodded. He looked down at the counter. "Yeah. He was here."

"With two kids?"

"Yeah. One girl, one boy. He needed to cash out a full ration sheet, and he wanted it kept quiet. He also needed someone to deliver them. Someone he could trust."

"Where? Where did he take them?"

"He said he was going back for you next."

"Fang, where did he take the two kids?"

"The Pot," he said. "I dropped the rations off there for him."

"The old Zun-zhe Housing Project? You have an address?"

He nodded. "Yeah. Another old war hound. Name's Chen."

He took a business card out from somewhere behind the counter and wrote it down in small, neat handwriting before sliding it over.

"The Pot's close," Vamp said.

It was. The project was at the far end of Render's Strip, a low-income dumping ground for about a quarter million old people. It was only a few blocks from the end of the district. Things were looking up.

"When did you make the delivery?" I asked Fang.

"First drop was the morning after he got back," he said. "Next is in two days."

"I need to find them, Fang."

"Why?"

"The boy has something I need."

"What?"

"Never mind that," I said. "Look, you don't want any

trouble, right? It's better if you don't know. Just give me the rations, I'll drop them, and you won't have to worry about it again. Okay?"

He paused for a second and then waved for me to come closer, back behind the counter. I did, but he stopped Nix and Vamp when they tried to follow.

"Not you two," he said. "You wait here. Better yet, wait outside."

He grabbed a rope knot from the floor and pulled, lifting up a trapdoor next to his chair that revealed a narrow set of concrete stairs leading down into the dark. He reached under the counter and pushed a button that activated a force field to keep customers away from the inventory and till.

"Come on," he said.

"Just wait here, guys," I said. "It's okay."

Vamp didn't look too sure, but he nodded. I climbed down as Fang turned on a light at the bottom of the stairs, closing the trapdoor above me. I followed him into a small basement that had been painted in warm pastel orange and yellows, and fitted with overhead lights. A TV was mounted in one corner, and a desk with a pretty impressive computer rig was set up against one wall. In the far corner was a futon that had a little nightstand next to it. An open doorway with a bead curtain led into a closet with a sit-down toilet. Another doorway on the other side of the room led to another closet stacked with trunks that I guessed contained his inventory.

On the walls, he'd taped up neat arrangements of news printouts and photos. The closest one was a picture of a monorail platform, with a sign reading SHILIUYUÁN STATION in the foreground.

"Shiliuyuán," I said to myself.

Fang looked over. "Before your time."

I followed the line of them, and saw that in each picture there were more and more security walking the platform, all decked out in black uniforms and helmets. A makeshift construction wall became a boxed-in structure, which grew until in the last picture the place was barely recognizable.

"Isn't this stuff classified?"

"Isn't everything?"

"Do you know what went on inside?"

He moved to stand next to me, looking at the pictures over my shoulder.

"No," he said. "My mother took these, over fifty years ago. She didn't even know."

"Who does?"

"The place was locked down. Whatever they were doing in there got wiped out along with them. Maybe no one knows."

He left me to go get the rations.

"Did Dragan say what was going on? Why he needed your help so late at night?"

"No, and I didn't ask."

"When we came in, you said no weapons . . . you have a scanner, then?"

"Of course."

"Did the boy have anything on him?"

"The boy? No, he was just a little kid."

"Do you have the footage?"

"Sure, hang on."

He parted a bead curtain to expose a small cubby where he had two big glass terrariums stacked. The one on bottom had five big rats in it, sectioned off into separate compartments. The one on top had a grow light shining down onto a little bed of green sprouts.

"Holy shit," I said, approaching them. One of the rats sat up, putting its feet on the glass while its pink nose sniffed curiously. "Where did you get these?"

"Trade secret."

The others inside squirmed around while the first

tried to sniff my fingertip through the glass. Its feet looked like tiny human hands with a knobby thumb and claws. I'd never seen a rodent up close like that. They were cute.

"Can I hold one?"

"No," he said, waving his hand. "They're sneaky little fuckers." He came over and pointed to one of the partitions inside the cage where paper scraps had been piled over a little clutch of tiny pink bodies.

"Street meat?" I asked.

He nodded. "People pay real money for real meat. Especially around festival time."

"How do you feed them?"

He grinned, holding his index finger and thumb very close together and squinting a little.

"I scrape a tiny bit off the sides of every ration. Then I rewrap them," he said. "It adds up."

"What are the plants?"

"Soybean hybrid. They don't need much water and fruit in the small space and shitty soil."

"Still illegal, though."

"Everything's illegal."

Rats were disease carriers and even after processing could, in theory, still pass prion sickness on. He'd get jail time for raising and selling unscreened meat. The water the plants needed would put him over his allotment easy, so he had to be siphoning it from somewhere in order to grow them. He'd lose his business if anyone ever got a look down there.

"Here you go," he said, lifting a box out from behind them. It was a quarter sheet's worth of government-issue rations, a krill and scalefly mix. He handed it to me, and I took it.

"Come on," he said. "Over here."

He gestured for me to come over to his desk, where he tapped the keyboard and brought the system out of sleep mode. I stood next to him while he accessed something on the screen.

"Dragan's not coming back, is he?" he said.

"He's alive. I'm going to find him."

"Well, good luck."

"I am. I'm going to get him back."

"They got to him," Fang said. "He's not coming back for those kids."

"He would if he could," I snapped, "and when I find him and get this straightened out, he will. You don't know shit about Dragan."

"I know Dragan better than you do."

"He risked his ass for me. He—"

"He went into a scrapcake processing plant, inside the rim," he said. "When he realized there were still some survivors, he went in even though the order hadn't been given yet. I know all about it. He was doing his job. He didn't even know who you were yet."

"He didn't have to do what he did," I shot back, "and he didn't have to take me in after. That wasn't part of his job. If he said he's coming back for them, then he is, one way or the other."

"Look," Fang said, putting his hands up, "I'm not bad-mouthing him. Dragan's a stand-up guy, but they got him. You know what happens next."

What happened next was they executed him. Bars, and places like Fang's, often streamed executions.

"So, fine," I said, pushing the thought out of my mind. "I'm here in his place. I'll get them."

"Well, like I said, good luck." He fiddled with the computer console, and images from his security camera went flicking by. He swept one finger across the screen, and images scrolled past until he spotted what he was looking for.

"There," he said, pointing.

The camera was aimed at the front door to his shop,

where Dragan stood with a little boy and a little girl. When I saw him, I smiled. He looked like shit, and I could see the blood spattered on his uniform, but the sight of him still made me smile.

Fang tapped at the console, and the image changed, color draining away to leave a sharp contrast grayscale. The three figures became ghosts, their bones standing out in faint, blurry black. Dragan's gun was clearly visible, along with the rest of his gear. I could see the twistkey looped around the boy's arm, but other than that, neither the boy nor the girl had anything on at all.

Fang tapped the image of the twistkey.

"That what you're after?"

"Yeah."

I was confused, though. Everything pointed to the boy's having carried the weapon over. Maybe there was something behind his back the scanner didn't pick up?

I looked at the girl, straining my eyes. She didn't have anything either, although there was a strange blob of distortion just under her rib cage.

"What is that?" I asked, pointing.

"I noticed that too," he said, leaning closer. "Just a glitch."

"Did you notice anything weird about her?"

"Hell, the whole thing was weird," he said. "That girl, she was sick, though. I mean, Dragan was freaked out, and the boy was just disconnected, but that girl was like the walking dead. She was sick with something. Dark circles under her eyes. Like you."

I stared at the image a moment longer, but I couldn't find anything that looked like it could be a bomb, or a vial or something. There was no weapon, at least none that I could see. Had the kid already ditched it? If he did, that would be it. We'd never find it in time.

"Thanks, Fang."

"Does it help?"

"Yeah."

The image could be a mistake, or just not clear. I decided the first thing to do was to find the kid. Even if he didn't have the weapon, he had the key, and that meant I could get to Dragan. With a little luck I could even do it far enough ahead of the festival that we'd at least be far away from Hangfei if the sky started falling. All we had to do was get to the Pot, which was no more than a half hour away on foot.

"Come on," Fang said, standing. "I need to get back up there before I get looted."

"Okay."

Fang headed over and pulled down the stairs again, the steps creaking as he started up. I stopped on the way back to take a picture of his photographs with my phone, then another quick shot of the squirming pink things in the terrarium.

"Hey, come on," Fang called down.

I hoofed it up the stairs after him. "Sorry. I was looking at the rats."

"Say it louder."

"Sorry. You really are the best."

"Yeah, yeah," he said. "Get out of here."

"Thanks again."

As I moved out from behind the counter, he tossed me a free smoke and I caught it. I stuck it in the corner of my mouth and blew him a kiss.

"If you do find him," he called, "like I said, he likes being a father. Let him be that."

I nodded. "Come on, guys."

Nix and Vamp exchanged glances, and then followed behind me as I stepped back out into the square.

"You got the rations?" Vamp asked as the door closed behind us.

"I got them," I said. "If we hustle we can be there in thirty."

"Are we actually going to pull this off?" Vamp asked. I checked the time.

"We'll make it," I said, and wished I was as sure as I sounded.

Chapter Fifteen

At the far end of Render's Strip, the dispensaries and eateries trickled out into a shantytown built on the remains of the Pot's old construction site. The temporary housing structures used by the crews fifty years prior were abandoned when the money ran out and eventually taken over by squatters. Old one-room homes, storage shacks, and even portable bathrooms had all grown into a massive commune over the years, glued together by new units of varying quality that sprouted up in the empty spaces. Tarps covered leaky roofs, tied down over clusters of shacks and spanning the winding makeshift paths between structures that served as streets.

Hanging out in the packed patches of dirt that served as yards to some of the homes were groups of filthy, scrawny people dressed in Dumpster clothes. Some sat in salvaged lawn furniture, while others just sat on the ground sharing smokes and playing cards. A lot of them didn't seem to be doing much else other than sitting back to watch the tide go out near the edge of the flats beyond, and the distant hulks of foreign ships that loomed on the horizon.

Vamp was crowding me, walking with a confident, aggressive strut that said *Don't come near us*, while Nix stuck close behind. The crowds of squatters were interested in us, but unlike the Row punks, none of them seemed aggressive so far. They seemed more fascinated by Nix than anything. I doubted haan ever came into their territory.

"This place is a shit-hole," Vamp muttered, and an old woman glared at us as we passed by. She and a man I imagined was her husband sat on folding chairs in front of a little TV. A cable trailed from the back of its cracked, yellow shell and off into the maze of shacks.

"Then get the fuck out, shit-head," the woman said.

"He's sorry," I told her.

"Never mind them." The man yawned.

"You're on the wrong side of town, assholes," she muttered.

"You're from the ship, huh?" a new voice asked. I looked down to see a filthy little girl tugging on the tail of Nix's jacket. He looked down at her, and when the triad of pupils in each eye revolved in a slow circle, the girl smiled.

"No," Nix said. She narrowed her eyes, still grinning as she put her hands on her narrow hips.

"Yes, you are," she said. She pointed back over the roofs of the shantytown where off in the distance you could see the main tower of the ship looming up above the rest of the skyline. "You're one of them."

"I am," Nix said, his voice box flashing, "but I live in the settlement of Shangzho, not the ship."

"Why?"

"So I can be closer to your kind."

"Why?"

"It will help us learn to live together."

The girl scrunched her brow.

"If you want to live together, then why don't you just take down the force field?" she asked.

"Yeah, Nix," I said. "Why don't you just take down the force field?"

"Yeah, just take it down," the girl said, holding out her hands.

"Because my people are afraid to," Nix said.

"But the failsafe can zap through it anyway."

"True," Nix said, "but your people would have to be very, very angry to do something like that."

He knelt down and placed his hand on her nest of dirty hair, stroking it gently before resting his fingers along the back of her scrawny little neck.

"We will take it down one day," he said.

"When?"

"Someday."

She nodded, then abruptly changed the subject.

"My grandmother said you promised to fix everything," she said. "Before you came out of the ship, you promised."

"That's true."

"Are you really going to save the world like she said?" she asked.

"No."

"No?"

"You are," he said, "but we will help you."

A woman stepped out of the crowd and grabbed the girl by the arm. She jerked her away from Nix so violently that the poor thing fell back into the dirt, half dangling from one arm as she was dragged away.

"Get away from it," the woman hissed. Her face was pinched, and pockmarked from chronic chem use.

"Hey," I called after her. "Take it easy."

"Fuck you," she spat. The girl had recovered her footing and, apparently used to the treatment, followed along after the woman without so much as a complaint. She looked back over her shoulder as they went, and waved at Nix.

"Let's go," Vamp said, pointing down the row of shacks. "The sooner we're out of here, the better."

"Hang on."

I backed out of the GPS and tried the phone number I'd dug up for the address again, letting it ring while I plugged one ear. Up ahead was the big gate that led into the project. It looked like it might have been impressive at one time, but now it was rain rusted and corroded from exposure to sea air and scalefly spray. It still stood tall, though, with a weathered sign over the arch: ZUN-ZHE.

The skyline shot up steeply past the gate where the housing project began. Dragan said the whole thing was some effort from back before the haan to resection the city and ease congestion. According to him, all it did, though, was mass everyone whose income level forced them to take the deal into one of the most overpopulated spots in the city, while everyone who could afford not to live there got "an extra inch of space."

"Still no answer," I said.

"How are we going to find anything in there?" Vamp mumbled.

"We have an address," I said, looking past the gate and into the tightly packed urban sprawl. I was a little unsure myself. "No sweat."

The streets through the Pot were narrow with no shoulders and rows of buildings that practically scraped up against each other lined the sides. Stoops at the front entrance of each stepped right off the curb and into the street. In the cramped alleyways I saw the odd motorbike or bicycle along with scattered trash. Small windows crowded each building face, and overhead a bedsheet flapped from one of them, unable to dry in the humid air. It made Tùzi-wō look roomy.

Ten minutes later, I thought I'd located the right building. It wasn't marked, but the one to its left was. Three stories up a plastic tarp had been stretched between several of the windows on opposite sides of the street, maybe to create shade or to catch rain from the gutter there. No one mingled on the sidewalks, and the whole area was strangely quiet. I checked the address again.

"This should be it," I said.

There was no lock on the front entrance, and it opened into a dimly lit cubby whose walls were lined with little mailbox doors. Each one required a key and a few hung open. Through a doorway up ahead, a feeble light shone over the landing of a narrow stairway leading up. Two elevator doors on the wall across from it were plastered with faded recruitment posters. Pasted over those was a strip of plastic tape that read OUT OF ORDER.

After nine flights, I thought I might keel over. When I finally pushed through the stairwell door, I had to stop and lean back against the wall to catch my breath.

"Gonzo," I muttered. I looked over at Nix, who, obnoxiously, didn't seem fazed at all by the climb. Even more obnoxiously, Vamp didn't either.

"Aw, you tired?" he asked.

"I'd hate to be an old person and have to make this climb every day."

"You are not an old person," Nix pointed out.

"I didn't say I was."

"Your body is substandard because you smoke and take too many chems," he added.

Vamp laughed suddenly through his nose.

"Shut up," I said, wiping sweat from my brow with my equally sweaty wrist. "Haan have better stamina. . . . That's just, like, physics."

"Biology."

"Whatever."

I shrugged him away and stomped down the hallway. The apartment doors were crowded together almost like lockers and as we passed by each, I could hear activity in some of them, TVs, radios, snoring, and talking. Number

9112 was down near the end of the hall on the right, a TV blaring behind it.

I knocked on the door. No one answered. I knocked again, harder this time. When still no one answered, I tried the knob, but it was locked.

Nix stepped closer to the door, moving me gently to one side, and put one hand on its surface beneath the spy hole. He moved his face close to it.

"Someone is inside," he said.

His chest expanded, his suit ruffling as he drew air in and then vented it with his quiet rattle. The mites delivered an anxious tingle.

"Someone has died," he said.

"Move, I'll kick it in," Vamp said.

"You're not going to be able to kick it in, Vamp," I said. "We'll get the super, just—"

The door unlatched, and then opened. Standing in the doorway was a little girl, the same girl from the wet drive recording. She was wearing slightly oversized pajamas, like they had belonged to someone else once. She looked up at us, her eyes wide, as she held the door open.

"Hey," I said. I tried to sound soothing, but she was looking at the scrapes on my face and shoulders with unease. "Hi there."

She didn't say anything. Over the TV I heard the buzzing of flies. I looked past her and saw a small cloud of them swarming around a sofa that faced a small TV set, perched on a wooden crate in front of a small window. It was showing some news program, the announcer yakking on about the festival while cameras showed different floats being built. There was a door inside on the left, and two on the right, one closed and the other an open doorway.

"Can we come in?" I asked the girl. She looked to Nix, then back at me and nodded.

I moved past her and stepped into the living room. Inside, a faint stink lingered in the air and I waved the air in front of my face as I looked over the back of the sofa. Blankets were piled over it as if someone had been sleeping there, and what looked like dried blood had spotted the edge of one. I tapped the TV's contact and switched it off.

"Are you alone here?" I asked her. She glanced toward the closed door on the right and I heard a low, raspy moan come from behind it. She shook her head.

Just then a signal trickled in through the surrogate cluster. It was strained, like its source was trying to pinch it off, but it was haan for sure.

"There's a haan nearby," I said.

Vamp tensed, looking back toward the front door. "Sillith?"

"No." I felt pulses of apprehension, fear, and hunger. It wasn't Sillith, or Nix. "Nix, are you picking that up?"

"Yes," he said. "A surrogate maybe?"

I found it hard to believe anyone who lived in a place like this would be part of the program, but if there was one here, it could be in big trouble.

"Was a haan here?" I asked the girl. She didn't seem to understand, so I pointed at Nix. "A haan, like him?"

She shook her head. It was strange. There was a current of fear in the signal, but there was a weird vibe to it. A surrogate who'd been left alone would want to be found, but this was the opposite. The haan was hiding. It was scared that it might be found.

"Vamp, Nix, look around for—" The signal winked out and was gone. Had it moved out of range? Nix moved closer and spoke in a low voice.

"The boy," he prompted.

"Over here," Vamp said, leaning to look through the doorway to the right.

I headed over and flipped on the light. It was a bedroom, with a single twin bed jammed into one corner. A squat dresser took up a chunk of the precious free space near the head of the bed.

"Nix, keep an eye on the girl," I called.

Lying on the bed under a sheet was an old man with white, wispy hair and deep hollows in his cheeks and eyes. His papery skin was ashen and sheened with sweat. When I approached, he opened his eyes a little.

"Dragan?" he whispered.

The walls were covered in pictures, almost every inch of them. Each one had been printed and put in a plastic frame. Most of them were close-ups of men and women in uniform; some were groups of uniformed soldiers or photographs of ships or planes. One of the pictures was of a man I recognized, a young Dragan.

It was weird to see him so young. He'd been handsome, and rugged-looking, with a cocksure expression on his face. I spotted him in some of the other photos, with men I'd never met. It bothered me a little, that familiarity. These were old friends, comrades. I didn't know who any of them were.

"Dragan?" the old man wheezed again.

I knelt next to the bed and felt his forehead.

"He's burning up," I said.

Vamp had followed me in while Nix stood in the doorway, holding the girl's hand.

"How long has he been like this?" I asked her. She just shook her head, holding up both hands.

"She doesn't understand you," Vamp said.

The girl pointed at the man. "*On bolen.*"

I brought up the 3i translator as she kept going.

"*On ochen' bolen. On budet normal'no?*"

He's very sick. He will be okay?

"Where is the boy? The one you came here with?" I asked. I pantomimed, indicating a tall person and two little ones. "Do you know where Alexei is?"

She perked up at the name a little, but the old man waved his hand.

"*Ne govorite im,*" he croaked.

Don't tell them. The girl looked at him, then back at me. She didn't say anything else.

"He is severely dehydrated," Nix said, gesturing at the old man. "I'll get him some water."

Nix patted the girl on the head as he moved back into the apartment. She looked up at me, tears brimming in her eyes, and I knelt in front of her.

"It's okay." I smoothed her hair behind her ears and smiled as best I could. "Don't worry, we're going to get you all out of here."

"*Ne govorite im,*" the man whispered.

I glanced back at him. "Help is coming, just hold on."

Nix came back carrying a wet facecloth. He handed it to me.

"Careful," I said to the old man, holding the cloth over his mouth. I squeezed until just a trickle went in. He let out a weak cough, but managed to swallow it. He took me by the wrist, and his hand was so frail that it broke my heart. He pulled for more water, and I squeezed again before letting him suck on the corner.

"Did Dragan come here?" I asked him. "Dragan Shao?"

He nodded.

"It's okay," I said, stroking the old man's hair. "We'll get you help. You'll be okay. Was there a boy with him too? Did he bring a boy here?"

The man shook his head.

"I know he's here," I said. "Why won't you tell me?"

He just shook his head again, and fear flashed in his eyes as he glanced at the top of his dresser. I looked back, but couldn't tell what he'd been looking for. "What? What is it?"

He turned away. I squeezed some more water for him from the rag, but it just dribbled from the corner of his mouth.

"Please," I said. "Where is he?" His eyes rolled.

"He needs help," Vamp said. "Call the hospital."

I fumbled out my phone and made the call.

"First Response Medical," a voice on the phone said. I had opened my mouth to speak when she continued in the same breath. "Please hold."

"Damn it," I muttered.

The old man choked, a subtle, almost inaudible sound, and then his eyelids drooped.

"Mister?" I said, giving him a little shake.

"I think he gave it up," Vamp said.

The old man lay limp in the bed, the rag still hanging from his mouth, which had curled into a faint smile. His eyes were unfocused, and his chest wasn't rising and falling anymore.

"Hey," I said. I gave him a gentle shake, but he didn't move. When I checked his pulse, I didn't feel anything.

The phone clicked as the hold music stopped and someone picked up.

"Sam?" a voice asked over the phone.

"Yes," I said. "Yes, I need help."

"Your estimated hold time is twelve minutes," the voice said. "You may as well spend it learning about a cheap, noninvasive procedure that can change your life."

"I don't need to talk to some A.I. salesbot," I snapped. "I need help!"

"I can help you," the A.I. said. "Believe me, substandard breast size is something a lot of young women live with, but the good news is that you don't have to."

"Damn it, I —"

"Sam, he's dead," Vamp said.

I hung up.

He put a hand on my shoulder. "There's no other kid here, Sam."

"He's got to be."

"This place has four rooms. He's not in any of them. He's got to be somewhere else."

"He brought him here."

"Sam—"

I pushed past him and moved to the dresser. The top was covered with little pictures in frames, printed article snippets, and loose change. Lying on top of a cash card was a little remote with a single button on it. I picked it up.

"What's that?" Vamp asked.

I pushed the button. Nothing happened. I pushed it again, but I didn't hear or see anything respond to it.

"That could be to anything," Vamp said. "We can't stay here."

Right then, Alexei's 3i icon lit up pink.

Sam?

"Hold up, he's back on," I said.

I'm here. I'm at the place they took you. Where are you?

Metal room.

I thought for a minute, and then pushed the button on the remote again.

Did something happen just then? I asked.

Bell went off.

I smiled. *What does the bell mean?*

They're coming. Move away from the wall.

"He's here," I said. "He said the remote rings a bell, to signal they're coming. He's got to be somewhere close."

Alexei, when they moved you to the room where you are now, how did you get there?

Kitchen door.

I headed back out into the living room and crossed past the sofa where the flies were still swarming over the blanket. The girl was standing next to it, and I took her hand as I headed into the tiny kitchen to look around. There was a cupboard under the sink, and inside I could hear a buzzing sound.

The girl cringed as I opened it, and immediately caught a blast of rot stink that made me gag. There was a big plastic trash bucket under the sink, lines of blackish red drying to the sides. Inside was what looked like a big, wrinkled mess of skin and blood that was covered in scaleflies. Some kind of papery material with a dangling, blood-soaked tie hung from the bucket's edge.

With my face turned away, I kicked the door shut.

"It's okay," I told her. "Never mind that."

Nix guided her away from the cupboard and I crossed the kitchen to a closet door next to the little half fridge. I pulled it open, but it was empty except for a big cardboard box on the floor.

Alexei, can you hear me?

No.

I banged on the inside walls of the closet with my fist.

Can you hear that?

No.

"Damn it."

The box inside the closet was empty. I picked it up and tossed it behind me onto the floor but saw nothing else in there except wood backing and floor. No secret door or hatch.

"Where could he be?" I hissed. There was nowhere else in the room he could have gone. There wasn't even a window, just . . .

With the box out of the way, I noticed something hanging just on the inside wall from a thin loop of wire. It was a black twistkey.

"Here."

I knelt down, snatching the key off the hook and then feeling around inside the pantry. The rear of it had a square metal frame, big enough to crawl through. It was just a frame, butted against the back wall, but there was a socket fixed to the bottom right corner of it.

I slotted the twistkey into the socket and turned it. A hum sounded, and my hair began to stand on end as a white point of light appeared in the middle of the frame, then expanded to fill it. The back wall of the pantry disappeared, and I was looking into another room with a metal floor and metal walls. Alexei hadn't heard us because he wasn't in the apartment. He was somewhere else, somewhere even the GPS couldn't zero in on, completely isolated in some kind of storage tank.

"A black hole," Vamp said, looking down over my shoulder.

"Huh?"

"Smugglers use them to hide contraband. The actual location is masked, usually somewhere outside the government's jurisdiction, just in case."

The room was lit, and I could see an air canister leaned against one corner next to an electric lantern. The floor was littered with ration wrappers and empty water bottles. In the other corner was a bucket, the inside stained with brown specks.

"Kid?" I called.

I poked my head in and saw him off to my left, huddled in the corner of the metal cube. His wide, teary eyes stared back at me from through thick, greasy black hair. It was definitely him, the kid from the recording. Why would Dragan put him in a place like this?

"Alexei?" I called. The kid just stared. "That's your name, right? Alexei?"

He couldn't understand me, I don't think, but he heard his name and nodded, quick, jerky movements. He sat with his knees hugged to his chest. Looped around his left arm was an elastic band, and hanging from it was a metallic blue twistkey.

"It's okay," I told him, holding out one hand. "You're okay. You're safe."

He glanced at my hand, then back up at me. He scratched at a raw red patch on one forearm where tiny beads of blood had formed.

"You can't understand me," I whispered. "That's okay. You're okay. Come on out."

"Just grab him," Vamp said from behind me.

"Shut it," I snapped back over my shoulder. Alexei cringed a little, and it took me a minute for him to calm down again.

"You know Dragan?" I asked him. That got a response. His face changed, and he nodded.

"Dragan?" he asked, scratching at his arm again. I pointed to my face with my index finger.

"Sam," I said.

He paused, and then nodded again.

"Good. Okay." I pointed at the twistkey around his arm. "Can I see that?"

He glanced down at the key, then back at me.

Can I see that? I sent over the 3i.

"Careful," Vamp said, "he could still have the weapon."

Alexei, where is the weapon? I asked.

He shook his head, confused. *What weapon?*

They gave you something, something dangerous.

He shook his head again.

"He says he doesn't have it."

"Maybe he swallowed it," Vamp said. "Or they implanted it, and he doesn't know."

"Maybe," I said. That would explain why Dragan had put the kid himself in there, and not just the weapon. "Nix, your tablet, where does it lead to?"

"The storage area is inside a sealed cell located inside the ship's—"

"So behind the force field?"

"Yes."

"If we could drop the weapon in, would that contain it? The flies can't hurt you guys and they couldn't get out, right?"

He thought for a minute. "Yes."

"Okay," I said to the kid. "Okay, come on out. Can I have the key?" I pointed at it again.

"*Dragan govorit chtoby ne poterjat' ego,*" he said.

Please? I sent over the 3i.

Dragan said don't lose it.

I won't lose it. I just want to see.

I reached out toward him slowly. He hesitated, glancing over my shoulder at Vamp.

It was a smart move giving it to you, I sent. *Thanks for keeping it safe. Dragan said you should give it to me now.*

He looked unsure, but he held the key out and placed it in my hand. When I curled my fingers around it, he let it go.

"Bingo," I said over my shoulder.

"Should I call security?" Vamp asked.

"No, let's search him first. Besides, I want to wait until we're the hell out of here. I don't want them tracking us."

They killed her, he sent.

When I looked back to him, he suddenly looked so lost, so pathetic, that I couldn't help feeling sorry for him. Whoever the kid was, he wasn't some terrorist come to attack us, or anyone else. He was just some kid they grabbed off the street, a patsy who was supposed to go home and never know it was him who wiped out all of his people.

I know.

He didn't cry, but I could see that was because he was cried out. I remembered the footage on Dragan's wet drive, how the woman's head had sprayed across the floor, and remembered that was the boy's mother.

I know. I'm sorry. I sighed. *Look, I'm sorry it has to play out like this, okay? I know this isn't your fault.*

Don't kill us, he said. His eyes looked hollow, and way too old to belong to such a little boy. *Please. Don't burn us.*

No one is going to kill you. It's okay.

I heard them. The invaders are going to make you attack us, to kill us all. Please don't. Please.

I rubbed my eyes. "Goddamn it."

They were the ones attacking us. Where did this kid get off laying this on me? All those threats, all the troop buildups and suicide bombers. They attacked us, all the time. They were the ones that started this whole thing.

Please. Please don't.

The kid was maybe eight, though, ten tops. He didn't know about any of that. None of it was his fault.

We want to help you, he said.

Help us?

Everyone just wants to help you. Please don't kill my family, don't kill my friends, please don't, please.

I chewed my lip. *They won't hurt you. Look, just give me the weapon. We'll get rid of it and nobody gets burned, okay? They won't hurt you.*

He shook his head. *I don't have it.*

It could be small. You might not know you have it.

He shook his head again. Could it be he didn't have it at all? That Dragan got him out of Shiliuyuán Station before it was ever planted on him? It was tempting to believe, but I wasn't feeling that lucky.

"Come on," I said, gesturing for him to come out of the room. "Come on out. Let's have a look at you."

He still looked unsure, but he moved, a little. When I reached for him again, he didn't back away.

"You can trust me," I said. "Come on out."

He crept out through the gate and into the light of the kitchenette where I could see more raw patches on his arms. He began digging at one of the spots again, smearing blood.

"Stop that," I said, taking his wrist. "Come on, stop."

"Sam, you've got the key," Vamp said. "What are you doing?"

"I just want to see if he has it."

Nix moved closer to him and held out his tablet. The field was closed, and the silvery front panel had changed to a view screen. When he passed the tablet in front of

Alexei, I could see his skeleton on the screen along with buttons, zippers . . . and that was it. Nix moved the tablet slowly, scanning him top to bottom. There was nothing in any of his pockets.

"He might have ditched it," Vamp said.

I shook my head. "No, Dragan put him in there to isolate him. He must have it on him. Nix, check his stomach."

He did, but there was nothing there. It wasn't until he moved the tablet past one of his arms that I caught a flash, and grabbed Nix's wrist to stop him.

"Wait," I said. "There."

Nix zoomed in on one of the raw patches of skin where a series of dark spots were scattered like buckshot. They were all down the boy's arms and covered his back. Nix focused the view on one of them and zoomed in even closer.

"Nix . . ."

The dark spots were flies. Scalefly larva. They were buried under his skin. The weapon wasn't on him; it was in him.

"They will emerge soon," Nix said, peering closer.

"How long?"

"In a matter of hours."

I looked at the specks. There were thousands of them. "Can we . . . pick them out?"

"Not all of them. Not in time."

"Can we kill them?"

"They are very hard to kill. Anything that would do so would kill the boy as well."

"Shit. Shit!"

"Sam," Vamp urged.

"I'm thinking," I said.

He leaned close, to whisper in my ear, "We might not have a choice."

I shrugged him off.

"Put him back in the hole," Vamp said. When I glared at him, he held up his hands. "Just until we can figure out what to—"

"Nix, what about if we bring him behind the force field?"

"They'll never let a human through."

"This is an emergency, though."

"We may not have time to convince them, and even if we do there's no guarantee we won't deliver him right to Sillith."

"Damn it. . . ."

Just hand him over, a voice said in the back of my mind. *Just hand him over to the authorities, and let them do whatever they're going to do. It can't happen here. No matter what else, it can't happen here and with their gate connections they could have him back to his original drop point in minutes. . . .*

Or you could just seal him back in the hole and close the gate forever.

I looked back at him. His eyes were wide and frightened. He couldn't understand us, but he knew enough to know that his fate was being decided. I could see the defeat in his eyes, a helpless resignation. Any fight that had been in him was gone.

"He's coming with us," I said.

Vamp's eyebrows jumped. "What?"

"We'll take him to Shiliuyuán Station," I said. "We've got the key. It's behind the force field, and we won't need permission to—"

I stopped as Nix's tablet moved past me, and something on the scanner screen caught my eye.

"Nix, wait," I said, grabbing his wrist. He let me take the tablet from his hand, and I angled it down the front of me, to my own belly.

My mouth dropped open. Perched on my belly was a huge ticklike construct, its abdomen sticking out like a giant egg. Its spindly legs gripped me, and I could see a tube had snaked through into my stomach where a squiggly ball had formed.

"Sam, what's wrong?" Vamp asked.

"Take the kid over there," I said, pointing.

"Why?"

"Do it!"

He looked peeved, but he guided Alexei away from us as I grabbed Nix's sleeve.

"Nix," I said, staring. "What the hell is that?"

I looked around the side of the tablet, down to my belly. There was nothing there, but when I looked back to the screen, there it was again. I began to feel woozy, and when I spoke again my voice cracked.

"Nix, what the hell is that thing? Is it real?"

He moved closer to look at the screen. "It's real."

"What is it?" I whispered. I glanced back at Vamp, who looked away.

"It's . . . an umbilicus," Nix said.

"A what?"

"An umbilicus," he said, moving the screen for a better look. "It's sending nutrients to the mass behind it."

"Why can't I see it?"

"It is in jump space," he said, "except for the point of contact inside you. You can't interact with it directly."

I looked at the shadowy ball of tissue the tube fed into. "What is it doing? Why is it there?"

The shape moved, just a little. It reminded me of a haan brain.

"It's Sillith's weapon," he said quietly.

"But—"

"Not the one she fashioned for your people, the one she has continued to develop in secret." He leaned closer to my belly, until I could feel the heat of his face against it.

"Get it off me," I said. I swept at the spot, like I was

trying to flick away a spider. I wanted to crawl out of my own skin. "I have to get it off me right now. I can't . . ."

He put one hand on my shoulder, and I felt a calm come over me as he eased through the mite cluster. Part of me was still freaking out, but it helped, a little.

"I can't," he said.

Out of the jumble of my thoughts, the image from Fang's security footage jumped out. Dragan had been there with Alexei, and the girl. There had been a small distortion near her belly. . . .

I took the tablet and pointed it back toward her. There was nothing there.

"Sam, what are you doing?" Vamp called.

I moved the tablet across the room, sweeping past the sofa until something jumped out. There, lying on its side next to the TV stand, was one of the ticklike objects. It looked dead. When I moved the tablet away, it disappeared.

"Nix, what the hell is going on?"

"I'm not sure, but the genetic material is definitely haan, and it is consuming tissue around it to fuel growth. When Sillith realized this, she must have fitted you with the umbilicus to keep it from feeding on you."

"But she wants me dead. Why would she—"

"So you can lead her to the boy."

My ears pricked as a door outside down the hall banged open, and Alexei cringed back farther into the cubby.

"She knows we're here," he said.

Several people had just entered the hallway outside the apartment and were heading in our direction.

Chapter Sixteen

"Sam . . . ," Vamp warned.

"I hear them."

Heavy footsteps tromped toward us from down the hall outside. Not just two or three people, but a group.

"Down here!" a voice barked, followed by chatter over a radio.

"Sam, we have to leave now," Vamp said.

"How the hell did they track us?"

The footsteps came to a stop outside the apartment's front door, and I heard them take up positions there.

"Here," a voice said. "She's in there."

I pressed my fists to my temples. "Shit!"

Alexei backed away and darted back through the closet door.

"Alexei, wait!" I took a step toward him and he slammed it shut.

"Cordon is secure," a voice said. The sound of the airship outside was getting louder. "Move on my mark."

We weren't going to make it. They were coming in.

"Nix," I called, snapping my fingers at him. "Your tablet. Hurry up."

He hurried over and took it from inside his coat, swiping his finger across the screen to activate it.

I grabbed the tablet from his hands and waved my

hand over the field. The honeycomb scrolled past, and I caught glimpses of his things as they went by, including the double-needled wand. I dropped the twistkey into the empty cell next to it.

"The pattern you trace with your finger," I said. "Is that the pass code?"

"Yes."

"Can you change it? So we can both get into it?"

He reached over my shoulder and tapped at the virtual keys until a prompt appeared.

"Ready!" a voice outside said.

"Trace a new pattern with your finger," Nix said.

"Vamp, watch."

I traced the hanzi for "apple" in the middle of the screen. With a crackle, the field solidified again into the shiny metal plate.

"Got it?" I asked.

"Yes," Nix said. Vamp nodded.

I headed back to the living room and they followed. I stood next to the little girl and squeezed her shoulder.

"It'll be okay," I told her.

"Clear!" a voice outside barked. Nix took back the tablet and quickly stowed it in his coat as the door crashed open.

Two soldiers stormed in, but they weren't in full combat gear. They were street-variety soldiers kitted out in basic patrol gear. When they entered, Vamp's app started painting their faces and calling out transponder IDs. Names and ranks appeared as the app began recording their actions onto my wet drive.

"Freeze!" one of them yelled, his rifle pointed at my chest. The girl threw her hands up over her head as two more men crowded in after them, scanning the room through their scopes. One kicked open the bathroom door and pointed his weapon inside.

"Clear!" he said over his shoulder. One of them stood

over the couch and pointed down at the blankets while
another approached the bedroom door.

"Blood," he said.

One of the men stepped forward with his eyes locked
on to the screen of some sort of scanner he was holding.
He moved it around the room and then settled on me.
He moved in close, until it was almost touching me.

"This is her," he said over his shoulder.

"Good," a voice said back.

I looked, and my eyes widened as a woman in uniform stepped into the apartment. She was an older
woman, pretty but severe looking, with jet-black hair in
a short bob. I recognized her immediately from TV. It
was Lieutenant Pei Ligong, Governor Hwong's right
hand.

"We've got one human male, one haan male with
her," she said into a wrist radio. "What do you want to do
with them?"

There was a pause on the other end.

"Hold them for now."

"Understood."

"Lieutenant Ligong," I stammered. She glanced at
me. "Lieutenant Ligong, I can explain all of this."

"Shut your mouth and get down on the floor."

"Please listen to me," I said. "I can explain—"

She drew her pistol and pointed it at me. "Now! All of
you, down!"

My hands shot up and I knelt down alongside the girl,
who cowered with her hands in front of her face. Nix
knelt down next to me, but Vamp stayed standing.

"Wait," he said. "You don't understand."

I gaped, trying to grasp the fact that Vamp was still
standing when she'd told him to get down. Ligong sometimes carried out the televised executions herself.

Her eyes hardened as she glared at him like he was
some kind of bug. "On your knees."

"Vamp, do it!" I hissed, pulling his shirt. I turned to address Ligong, to move her attention away from Vamp. "He'll do it. It's okay. He'll do it."

Vamp's face wavered, but he stepped back and got down onto his knees next to Nix while soldiers filed through the apartment and into the bedroom. He put his hands behind his head and laced his fingers.

Ligong stepped toward me, crouching long enough to pull Wei's little pistol out of my pocket. She tucked it in her belt.

In the bedroom one of the men shined a light down on the old man while the little girl watched from the foot of the bed. The other one leaned in to check his vitals.

"He dead?" Ligong called. The man had turned to say something when a loud, wet snap made them all jump. He whirled back to the bed, but I couldn't see what made the sound.

Ligong furrowed her brow. "Is he dead or not?"

Her eyes narrowed, and she cocked her head all of a sudden just as I noticed the signal myself. It was another haan, maybe the same one from before. The signal was hesitant, like the first one. Like it was trying to stay quiet.

She has a surrogate cluster, I thought, watching Ligong. There was no way she was a surrogate, though. She used it to keep track of the haan.

"I just picked up an unidentified—"

The signal disappeared. Ligong paused a minute longer, then signaled to one of the soldiers nearby.

"There's another haan around here somewhere. Find it," she said in a low voice. He nodded, and signaled to another to join him as he left the apartment.

Ligong turned back to the bedroom, where, to my surprise, the old man sat up, peeling the sweat-soaked blanket off and dropping it onto the bed beside him. He looked up at the soldier.

"Are you okay, sir?" the soldier asked. He still looked

a little confused. The old man nodded. He looked to the little girl, who managed a weak smile.

I met Vamp's eye and he shook his head, not sure what to make of it either. I'd sworn he was dead.

"Get him dressed," she called in. "Take both of them back to central."

The soldier nodded. He swatted a scalefly on his neck and approached the bed as the old man fussed with something underneath it.

"What's happening?" I asked again as they helped the old man to his feet. "Are we being arrested?"

A shadow passed over the window, and the whistle of an airship got louder as the curtains flapped at either side of the TV screen beneath the sill.

The lead soldier took out a scanner and aimed it down at Vamp. He swept it up and down him, then did me and Nix, frowning at the display. As one of the men helped the old man out into the hallway, he clipped the reader back on his belt.

"Okay," he said to me, "we know you know where the kid is. Talk."

Realization set in, and I frowned. "Kang."

Sillith hadn't sent these guys; Kang had. She was tailing us too, and might even be nearby watching, but if she was she couldn't move now. Ligong pushed past the soldier and looked me square in the eye.

"Tell us where—"

"How'd he do it?" I forgot myself, and interrupted her. Anger flashed in her eyes, but she kept her voice even as she spoke.

"He spiked your drink with a tracker isotope," she said. I shook my head, my face burning.

"Son of a bitch . . ."

"He might have just saved our entire country," she said. "Show some respect. Now, where's the kid?"

"Listen, please, there's more to the story," I said. "A

group of soldiers were conspiring with a haan. My father, Specialist Shao . . . he's loyal. He tried to blow the whistle on them and so they pinned that charge on him. Please, I need to—"

"We got him!" a voice boomed from the kitchen. "It's the kid!"

"What in the hell is that smell?" another voice said in an aside to the first.

Ligong peered through the kitchen doorway to get a look at Alexei, who was still cowered in the closet. "Get him out here with the rest!"

She spoke into her wrist radio again.

"We've got him," she said.

"Ow!" the voice grunted from the kitchen. "He fucking bit me!"

"Soldier, secure that kid and get him in here now!"

There was a struggle, and then Alexei began babbling in Pan-Slav as the soldier hauled him back into the living room by one wrist.

"Alexei Drugov?" Ligong asked. Alexei nodded, his face pale.

"Shit," a soldier spat from back through the doorway. He coughed, and flies buzzed.

"What is it?" Ligong asked.

The soldier stepped back into the living room, his face twisted into a grimace. What looked like a bloody towel hung from the barrel of his rifle, and I realized it was the remains I'd seen in the trash bin under the sink. I caught a glimpse of what looked like limp, rubbery skin and matted hair before I turned away from it. The little girl looked over at the old man, who looked back.

"What the hell is that?" Ligong asked. She crossed past us, and the other soldiers followed. For a moment, they stood around whatever he'd found, their backs to us, and Alexei, forgotten for a moment, off to one side. I looked at him, and our eyes met.

"Damn it!" one of the soldiers spat, slapping his neck to swat a scalefly.

They were as distracted as they were going to get. I crooked my head, hearts scrolling across the 3i display until I saw the one for Nix and grabbed it.

Nix, can you gate us back to the ship?

He turned, looking back at me. *Yes, but they'll send us straight back when they—*

We'll have to take our chances.

"Vamp, change of plans," I whispered.

"Sam, what the—"

You take the girl, I sent over the 3i.

I grabbed Alexei by the wrist and dragged him along after me as I bolted toward the window. Vamp, a beat later, scooped the girl up in his arms and started after me.

"Stop them!" Ligong barked. She raised her weapon toward me and fired just as Nix rose to his feet, fanning his suit out in front of us. I heard the round hit it, then two more as she fired again.

The slugs clattered to the floor as I hauled Alexei out the window with me, Vamp hot on my heels. I scrambled down the stairs toward the next floor as Nix came through the window after us and put the girl down on the landing. Through the grate, I could see that the street below was full of security vehicles, and armed soldiers that were clustered around them.

A shot from above glanced off the building face next to me, pelting me with brick powder. Back on the landing, Nix covered Vamp as the two headed down after me.

"Nix, do it now! Open it!"

An airship glided out from behind the building and descended above the street to our level. A pattern of red lasers blinked flashed on the wall overhead and began to glide toward us as the wind sent my clothes flapping around my body. The lasers drifted down past me and I saw a turret follow them to take aim at the stairwell and landing below. I stopped short, causing Nix, Vamp, and the girl to pile up behind me.

The gun spun up and began to fire, bullets sparking off the fire escape and thumping into the brick face where it was mounted. We couldn't go down the stairs without walking right into the line of fire. I looked up and saw Ligong climbing out the window after us. Over the rail was a several-story drop.

"Stop where you are," a voice boomed from the airship's bullhorn.

"Nix!"

The turret was winding up again, and the spinning barrel angled toward us. Down through the grate I saw soldiers assembling, ready to either come up after us or secure the mess when it fell. We weren't going to make it.

The turret open fired as Ligong closed in from above. Nix reached into his coat for something as the fire escape below us broke loose and dropped a few feet before catching again as glass and rubble showered down onto the sidewalk below.

Nix manipulated something in his hand and a bright white point appeared in the air above the street, just over the metal railing.

"He's opening a gate!" Ligong shouted.

The point of light got brighter and brighter until it suddenly expanded into a hexagonal opening with a thin white edge that floated a half story down. On the other side, I could make out dim light and a black surface.

"Jump!" Nix called.

Several shots went off and I saw Nix's head jerk, a honeycomb pattern flashing brightly as a round glanced off the inertial dampener. He was trying to move away when suddenly he staggered, clamping one hand down on the railing for support.

I looked back and saw Ligong was headed down the

steps toward us, a graviton gun trained on Nix. She adjusted the field, and he crashed down onto his knees.

"That dampening field won't stop the turrets!" she yelled. "I'd rather have you alive, but you're not using that gate! Close it now!"

The airship banked around, and I squinted as the red laser flashed in my eyes. They'd realized what we were going to do, and were targeting us for real. Nix struggled to pull free of the graviton beam but could barely lift his head.

"They can contain it!" I called back. "On the ship, they can contain it!"

Ligong kept the pistol trained on Nix as she drew a stun gun from behind her back and fired.

"They can—"

I felt a jab in my neck, slapping one hand over a metal prong that trailed a thin wire.

"Sam!" Vamp shouted. He moved toward me, reaching for the needle as the wire went hot and the lights went out.

Chapter Seventeen

06:39:41 BC

"... *message will repeat indefinitely as long as we can maintain the signal,*" a voice said in the dark. It was faint, and tinny, like it was bleeding over the 3i's audio tap.

My head pounded, throbbing in time with the 3i contact hearts, which had begun to fade back into view.

"... *have somehow managed to alter your—*"

The voice cut out as I snapped fully awake. I was lying on something soft, something plush and cool. My ears were filled with the rush of air and the low thrum of a graviton engine, and I reached out and felt smooth plastic as a chat window popped up in the dark.

Sam, are you okay? Vamp.

Yeah. You?

Yeah.

I opened my eyes and saw I was in the backseat of a posh aircar. The inside was beautiful, with a big crescent-shaped seat that was soft and smelled great. There was a table in front of me, and on the other side of it was another seat where Pei Ligong sat, looking idly out the window. Next to her was ...

I sat up suddenly, and the two turned to look at me. The man sitting next to Ligong was Military Governor Jianguo Hwong himself. I'd seen his face on TV and on billboards enough to know it in my sleep. Hell, there was a statue of him in Ginzho Square. He was bigger in person than I had expected, an older guy with cropped gray hair and a leathery, lined face, but his shoulders were broad and his chest was thick. He wore a silver machine pistol on his belt, and his colored medal bars stood out against his dark gray shirt, laser-thin gold trim glinting in the sun that streamed through the window.

"Welcome back," he said.

I looked to my left and saw Nix slumped in the seat next to me, a shock pin sticking out of the back of his neck. Only a very faint glow flickered in his eyes as he stared down at the tabletop.

"Where's Vamp?" I asked.

"Your friend? He's up front," Hwong said, pointing toward the closed divider.

A shadow passed over the vehicle as we cruised underneath a massive skyway, and then I saw our vehicle reflected in a mirrored building face as we began to rocket upward. In that reflection, the Pot sprawled off into the distance, the smaller building spires falling away as we went up and up.

"What about the others?" I asked.

"The old man and the girl will be debriefed. Then he will go home and she will be held until we decide if she should be deported or not."

"And the kid? Alexei?"

"He is being seen to." He leaned back in his seat. "You know, a disaster was narrowly averted today. You caused us quite a bit of trouble."

"But they didn't ..."

I trailed off as Ligong turned from the window to look at me. There was a cold, dangerous look in her eyes.

"Didn't what?" Hwong asked. "Didn't do anything?"

"Please," I said, "sir, we didn't do anything wrong—this whole thing is a misunderstanding."

Hwong smiled faintly, and he raised one hand to quiet Ligong, who was about to interrupt me.

"I want to hear what she has to say," he told her. He turned back to me. "Go ahead."

"My father . . . I mean Specialist Shao . . . was just on assignment working border security at Camp Juanhai."

"Where he met a Pan-Slav terrorist named Innuya Drugov, and her son, Alexei."

"That's just it, it's a mistake. She wasn't a terrorist. She was just one of the refugees."

"Our intelligence confirmed she had terrorist ties," Hwong said. "I understand this is hard to accept, and I don't blame you, but Alexei Drugov is not the legitimate son of Innuya Drugov, and they are not from the border territory of Lobnya. A terrorist cell embedded them there, where Innuya began looking for a foreign soldier she could ply. She found one in Specialist Shao, who has blood ties to the PSE."

"Dragan is not a—"

"He is. I'm truly sorry, but he is. I don't know if he became a true sympathizer or if he just believed her lies and was trying to do the right thing, but her purpose was to deliver Alexei to this country as part of the biggest biological attack this world has ever seen. If we hadn't recovered him, do you know what would have happened?"

"You're wrong," I said. He raised his eyebrows, and I quickly added, "Sir."

"And how do you figure that?"

"I'm sorry. I don't mean any disrespect, but please listen. There's more to the story you don't know. I've got inside information you need to hear."

Hwong's face was stony, and I thought he might shut me down before he finally waved one hand at me to continue.

"The intelligence was faked," I told him.

"Faked? Why?"

"To cover up a mistake. Some of your guys, your soldiers, are working with a haan," I told him.

His eyes narrowed a little. "Go on."

"A female. The haan female. She was there the night they picked up Dragan," I said. "You've got guys working for her in secret, behind your back."

"To what end?" Hwong asked.

"The Pan-Slavs weren't going to attack us. It's the other way around," I said. "These guys set up some kind of secret deal with the haan to get rid of the PSE. . . . We were going to attack them. Dragan didn't bring the kid here as part of an attack. He was trying to quarantine him, and it got out of control. He meant to turn the evidence of all this over to you. He just never got a chance."

Ligong glanced at Hwong.

"You're saying the haan are behind this?" Hwong asked.

"Just one. She's killed all but one of the guys who helped her, but the one guy left, Kang, told me he and some of your guys made a secret deal with Sillith. I'm telling you it's true. If he's still alive you can ask him yourself."

"Even assuming there is a conspiracy to destroy the PSE, why would the haan be involved?" Hwong asked. "What would they stand to gain from it?"

"I'm not sure, but she was promised . . ."

I felt an anxious spike through the mite cluster and stopped myself from saying any more. Nix was awake, and growing more and more anxious as Hwong's eyes turned bright, and predatory. I remembered what Kang had told me, back in the bar:

"Deals are made, kid. We see new tech appear, new benefits, better standards of living, but behind closed doors, deals are made."

"Promised what?"

"I don't know," I said, "but I swear it's all true—"

Hwong nodded at Ligong, who leaned across the table and gave me a hard push away from Nix.

"Move over," she said.

"Why?"

She grabbed a fistful of my shirt and pulled it until my tit poked out the armhole. She shoved me away, into the corner of the backseat opposite from Nix. "I said move it."

"Hey," I spat, pulling my shirt back into place. "Just wait—"

Ligong pulled a small controller from out of her jacket and pushed the button. When she did, an electric crackle sounded that was so loud that I jumped in my seat. Nix's body went rigid.

"Hey!" I shouted. One of Nix's legs had kicked out into the table between them, and sparks flashed from the shock pin in his neck. The strobe lit up the car interior as the angry snapping sound grew louder and a horrible burned smell filled the cab. Ligong's face never changed as she cranked up the juice until I could see muted red light flashing inside Nix's chest. His heart clenched behind his rib cage, and the shape beneath his skull had begun to twitch rapidly.

"Stop!" I screamed. Ligong balled her free hand into a fist, and, still holding the controller's button with her other hand, she hammered it down at me as I cringed back into the seat.

The blow caught me in the forehead, and my head snapped back against the window. I began to slide down the seat toward the floor and caught myself, grabbing the door handle for support. Warm blood dribbled down over my lips and chin, and when I shook my head to clear it I spattered the tabletop with red drops.

"Stop shocking him!" I screamed, my voice breaking.

I lunged for her arm, but she stopped me with her hand and held me back until she finally released the button.

The snapping sound stopped and the flickering light went out. Nix's body collapsed back into the seat as a thin curl of black smoke drifted up from the base of his skull. I tried to squirm free from Ligong's grip.

"Get off!" I grabbed one of her fingers and tried to peel it off as she reared back to hit me again.

"Enough," Hwong said. Ligong pulled her hand away and leaned back, glaring at me. She put the zapper back inside her coat and straightened it out as I scooted back over to Nix.

"Nix?" I whispered. "Hey, Nix?"

He didn't move, but his eyes, which had rolled back into his head, slowly reappeared from the bottom as if they had done a complete revolution. The pink glow returned like two rising suns.

"Nix, are you okay?"

I touched his chest, thin smoke drifting out from between my fingers. The spot was still warm, but the heart hadn't stopped.

"What Sillith was promised," Hwong said, his voice calm, "was a small portion of what will become the occupied PSE—an autonomous haan state bordered by our new territory."

I turned to stare at him, and it finally sank in. The deal that was made, it wasn't just made by a small group of rogue soldiers. It went higher than that, a lot higher.

"This was your idea," I said under my breath.

"Specialist Shao didn't just bring back the boy, and a recording," Hwong said. "He brought back something else. A twistkey."

I looked from Hwong to Ligong.

"Twistkey?" I asked.

"Don't play dumb," Hwong said. "That key is the only

way to access the labs in Shiliuyuán Station, and you know it."

"But—"

"My men scanned you all, and no one seems to have it," he said. "So where is it?"

We were in trouble. I'd made a huge mistake, and we were all in big, big trouble. Hwong was in on this from the start, and now all three of us knew way too much for him to just let us go. I realized then that the only thing that might be keeping us alive was the fact that he wasn't sure where the information he wanted was, and he thought one of us might know.

"Look," I said, "I just want my father back. That's all. If I give you the key—"

"That's not how things work," he said. "Decide which one of you has what I want before we get where we're going. Otherwise I will find out myself, one way or the other. Do you understand?"

"I got it," I said. Nix groped with one hand, putting it on mine. He urged me with his eyes not to provoke them any further.

"I understand," I added.

"Good. Just sit tight. We'll be there soon."

A window popped up on the 3i, floating between me and Nix as he messaged me. The letters came slowly, and erratically, crawling across the chat window like the trail of a dying insect.

Don't do it.

Nix...

Don't let them into Shiliuyuán Station. If you do, and they see she what she's done, then one individual's actions will be the end of all of us.

Nix, I don't know if I can stop them.

You can. Bring the boy there, like you planned. Stop the burn. Sillith will be gone soon. Her cycle is at an end.

It will be over. No one has to know what she tried to do. Please.

He closed his eyes, and the little beating-heart icon next to his name went still and gray as he dropped off-line. I looked back to Hwong, who was now gazing out the window, calm, and almost bored.

The weight of millions of impending deaths did not register in his eyes at all.

Chapter Eighteen

The ride took us high over Tùzi-wō proper, and I was surprised to see the blue dome of the haan force field growing larger in the windshield.

"Are we going to the ship?" I asked, peering out the window. We were getting so close that I could make out the hexagonal light formations through the blue haze. Behind them, the ship towered above all else, a spired behemoth that loomed over the surrounding skyline. Pinprick lights twinkled from within seams along the hull.

"Not even I can get in there," Hwong said.

The buildings beneath the aircar began to thin as we approached the dome, and the radio crackled up front as the wall surrounding the skirts appeared up ahead. I watched out the window as the shadow of our car passed over the spherical outer hull of one of the giant lenses, arcing down toward its jutting array of emitters. Turrets sat hunkered along the rim like huge mechanical gargoyles, aimed inward toward the ship and any criminals lurking in the wasteland between who might try and run the gantlet.

"Approaching vehicle," a voice crackled, "transmit your transponder code."

"Stand by," the driver said, reaching forward to fiddle

with something on the dash controls. A moment later the voice came back.

"Thank you. You are cleared."

"We're coming in," the driver said over his shoulder.

Nix stirred next to me as the wall passed beneath us and we began to descend down over the skirts. As bad as they looked from a distance, they looked a million times worse up close. Between the wall and the translucent electric blue of the dome force field was a fifty-year-old graveyard, a ring of toxic, unusable trash neither we nor the haan wanted. Stumps of buildings were still recognizable, sections of wall and steel framework poking up out of several stories of dust and ash that covered everything, but any trace of life was long gone. There were no lights, no fires, nothing.

In the rearview mirror I could see the dust cloud billowing behind us and blotting out the city skyline. When I looked down at the blanket of soot and sludge that streaked past below the aircar's belly, it made me uneasy. If for any reason we crashed down there, we'd be buried with no way to get out.

A jagged section of wall huffed past on our right, fog streaming through the rows of empty window holes. The skewed slope of one of the floors sheared down from one side and into the soot below. People had lived there. They'd been sitting at tables eating, or lying in their beds sleeping, when it happened. Everyone knew the story, but it was spooky to see it up close like this. Black bits of ash streaked through the aircar's headlamps as they blinked on, and off in the distance I spotted a faint electric red light that would be invisible from the outer rim through all the debris and dust.

"What is that?"

The driver throttled the emitters back and we dropped lower. Hard charred bits peppered the windshield as we passed through a cloud, then down a pow-

dery slope to where a deep, dark pocket had been dug
out up ahead.

The red light flashed three times, went out, and then
flashed three times again before coming back on. The
driver closed in on the spot and hovered, making a lazy
circle around the pit below. They'd blown out the dust
and ash, then dug out the underlying layers of packed
dirt, concrete powder, and soot to expose a big section of
tiled floor about twenty feet down that they were using
as a landing platform. An old twisted section of fire escape was half embedded in the wall of debris on one side
to form a makeshift signal tower, the red electric lamp
trailing cables down to a generator below.

There were four other airbikes lined up down there,
and we landed in an open space near one wall that still
had an exposed doorway on it, though the other side was
packed solid with dirt and debris. Across the old tiled
floor on the other side was another piece of wall that had
buckled a little under pressure from above. A metal
doorframe in the middle had held its ground, and the
chipped blue door had a red LED shining over a mag-
netic lock. Through the car's sunroof I saw smoke and
dust moaning over the pit's mouth in billowy gray
streams, the bright point of Fangwenzhe bleeding
through like a tiny second sun. The car settled down, and
floating grit suddenly dropped back down to the ground
as the emitters deactivated.

"Now what?" Vamp asked from up front. Fear flashed
in his eyes as he looked out the window.

"Let's go," Ligong said.

The doors opened and we piled out, Vamp with his
hands still pinned behind his back and Nix a little unsteady on his feet as we were escorted across the buckled
floor. It was at least twenty degrees cooler there, and the
air had a bittersweet chemical smell. When we reached
the door at the far end, the LED turned from red to

green, and I heard the bolt pop over the rush of wind. The door opened, and a man stepped out. He was tall and sinewy, with waxy skin and an ugly pockmarked face. He was dressed in uniform, but had a black rubber butcher's apron on over it, and a cigar butt glowed in the corner of his wide, thick lips.

"You," Hwong said to Vamp, "go with him."

Vamp bristled, glancing back over his shoulder toward the car.

"There's nothing back there," Hwong said. "Go with him."

"Wait," I said. "Just hold on."

"Alive or dead," Hwong said, his voice hardening. "Your choice."

Vamp took an unsteady step toward the man in the apron, who just watched, not smiling. Ligong shoved him then, causing him to stumble forward.

"You too," Hwong said to Nix. "Go with them."

Nix didn't argue. He approached the uniformed man in the apron, and waited with Vamp as the man took a scanner from his belt and aimed it at him. When he switched it on, a holoscreen appeared in the air above it, displaying a vague outline of interference where Nix would be.

"He's got an Escher Field," the man said. "The destination's scrambled and it won't respond with an inventory."

"Let's have it," Ligong said, holding out one hand.

I watched as Nix gave up the tablet and she held it up to the light. She angled it back and forth, but the screen appeared as nothing more than a seamless silver plate. She handed it to Hwong.

"Take them in," Hwong said to the man. The guy nodded, then put the scanner away and gestured for Nix and Vamp to follow. Vamp looked back over his shoulder as he went, making eye contact with me.

"Where are you taking them?" I asked.

"You'll see," he said. "Lieutenant, go with them." She nodded, following along behind. They disappeared down the corridor branch ahead, and Hwong took us down the broken hallway in the other direction, to a heavy metal door. He held it open and signaled for me to go inside.

The hallway of whatever building had been buried all those years ago had a floor and walls that had shifted and cracked, but it was still mostly intact. They'd strung up a tangled length of holiday lights all the way down on both sides, held in place with carpenter staples. There were other doors on the walls along the way, but they looked like they were jammed shut and I saw rubble poking out of a gap in one of them. Up ahead the corridor opened into what might once have been an old office.

When I stepped through the doorway, my foot splashed into a black puddle of water and creosote, but beyond that it was dry. A desk had been set up in one corner, and there was computer equipment set up there, shielded wires trailing off through another open doorway on the far side of the room where a cracked glass window looked out into what might have been an auditorium at some point.

"What is this place?" I asked him.

"The important thing for you to know," he said, "is that with all the interference it's impossible for even our scanners to effectively sweep here. Anything that goes on here is invisible to the outside world. I am authority out there, but I am God in here. Do you understand?"

I stepped closer to the cracked glass window, and through it I could make out rows of shipping containers that had been fashioned into makeshift holding cells. There were people inside them, men and women in dirty prison grays who looked like they'd been there for a long time. Some were young men, tough-looking types, but most were older . . . balding men with glasses, and women who could be mothers or office workers. They didn't look like criminals.

"This place is illegal," I said.

"This place doesn't exist."

He leaned back against the desk, and it creaked a little under his weight. He held up Nix's tablet in one hand.

"Since this is haan tech," he said, "I have no hope of getting it open without the pass code. Do you know how to open it?"

"No."

"Does the haan?"

"No."

"So you're telling me he is in possession of a device that neither he nor anyone with him is able to access?"

I didn't say anything.

"You're lying," Hwong said. "I know he knows how to access it, but I don't think he'll tell me."

"I don't know how to get into it. I—"

"Back in the Pot, the soldier's scanner recorded you manipulating the device and then handing it back to the haan shortly before they entered," he said. "I think you do know how to access it."

"Why do you care? What does it matter to you what he keeps in there anyway?"

"Because I suspect the twistkey I'm looking for is inside it," he said.

I'd grown up watching Governor Hwong on the news. He wasn't a guy you messed with. He was going to kill all three of us. The only thing stopping him was that he knew he'd never get the tablet open on his own. He had to satisfy himself that what he wanted wasn't stuck in there where he couldn't get to it.

"Once you have it, you'll just kill us," I said.

Hwong grinned, slowly. He was still smiling when he pulled a gun out of his jacket and pointed the barrel directly between my eyes. My next words fizzled in my mouth and I took a step back, bumping into the table behind me and knocking over a phone headset that clattered to the floor.

"I could kill you right now," he said calmly.

"You're afraid it's still inside," I said, keeping still, not looking at the gun.

"The haan will open it, eventually."

"No, he won't," I said. "He'll die first. You know he will."

The huge black eye of the gun barrel was staring down at me, and when he cocked the hammer back deliberately with his thumb, my legs went watery.

"Then you open it."

"I can't."

"You're lying."

"I can't because I need it," I said. He narrowed his eyes. "I need the twistkey."

"Why?"

"My father's down there. She's got him."

Hwong hesitated. After a few more seconds he released the hammer slowly and moved the gun away from my face.

"If Sillith has Specialist Shao," he said, "then he's gone. You can't bargain with her."

I didn't say anything.

"I mean it. I hold a gun at her race's head and she still plans to betray me. She'll eat you alive." He half smiled, with no real humor. "Maybe literally."

"Why make a deal with her, then?" I asked.

"Because she's about to become obsolete, and she knows it."

"Her fertility cycle is ending," I said. He seemed surprised.

"Yes," he said. "She understands that right now she holds great power, and that she's about to lose it all. If she wants to effect any change, this will be her last opportunity to do it."

"So?"

"So we both want something. She wants the haan to have their own state after she's gone, and I want that rogue country burned off the map."

"Is that what this is about?"

"It takes people with real will to effect real change," he said. "In that respect she and I are alike. This will change the world, as we know it, for the better. We need the haan, but we can't keep accommodating them. They need more room, more resources . . . more food than we can give them. Thirteen settlements will turn into thirteen hundred, eventually. Right now they consume over eighty percent of our food just to stay alive. Projections put it at over three hundred percent over the next twenty years."

"But the haan have a plan to fix all that."

"In the long term," Hwong said. "So they say. In the short term, things are going to get worse than you could imagine."

"But . . . killing all of them?"

"The world is buckling," he said. "We pretend we are isolated from that, but everyone knows it. The truth is that not even everyone in this country is going to survive the years to come, even with the haan's help. Others will fare far worse and there will be only us to feed on. They're going to keep attacking us, keep gathering their forces until one day—"

"The haan defense shield will stop them," I said. "Once it's up they'll—"

"And when will that be?" he asked. "The PSE, the Americans, the EU . . . they all have arsenals that would make your blood run cold. You think a few bombings are bad? There are nuclear, chemical, and biological weapons spread all over that fractured state of theirs, and they're building those forces, getting ready to come in—"

"But to just wipe all of them out like that . . . please, think about it. Just have the haan undo whatever they did to him, or keep him behind the force field so he doesn't—"

"It will appear to be a natural pandemic. Once they fall, we can go in and secure their weapons, including their WMDs. The world will be a safer place, believe me."

He was serious. He was completely serious. It didn't matter that the Americans and the EU would never just stand by and let that happen. He had to know that. If I thought of it, he had to know it, but when I looked in his eyes I saw he had every intention of going ahead regardless.

He stepped closer, and leaned in close. His voice was calm and reasonable.

"In the end, when it's all over and the dust has settled, the entire world will benefit. Everyone will see. The Americans, the EU, even our own leaders. I may not survive what follows, but my legacy will."

I could see by the look in his eyes that he'd come to terms with what he'd decided he had to do. There was even doubt there, just a little, a small glint in his eyes as he spoke that worried at the cost of the path he'd chosen, but he was going ahead anyway. He wasn't going to be talked out of it, not now. Not by me.

"If you have Alexei, and you've seen the recording," I said, "then why do you need the twistkey?"

"Because once this is over," he said, "I'm taking a team in there to kill her, and to burn any evidence that Shiliuyuán Station was still intact off the map."

"You're going to double-cross her?"

"They'll have their state," he said, "but I happen to know something few others do. The haan share memories. They are stored and disseminated after death as some kind of virtual construct any of them can access. She has to go before that can happen."

"But there's people down there," I said.

"What happened there can't ever come to light, I'm sorry."

"But my father is down there!"

"I'll do what I can about Specialist Shao."

"You're lying."

"I'm not lying. Hand over the key and I'll do what I can."

"No."

"No?" He stepped closer, until he loomed over me.

"It's in the tablet," I said quickly. "If you kill me you'll never get it."

"The haan—"

"Won't tell you. You know he won't. Everyone knows the story about the school in Shangzho. You can beat a haan to death and he won't retaliate."

My heart pounded. I was losing control of the situation, and I could see in this man's eyes that violence would come next. Some men could do things like that and some couldn't. This man could, and he would. He closed in and grabbed my wrist with his big hand, pulling me toward him. I struggled to break free, but his grip was too strong. He headed back toward the desk, dragging me along behind him.

"Be still," he snapped. I stopped struggling, breath coming fast through my nose, and I held the tablet in a death grip against my chest.

Dragan needs me. He needs me. This is my one chance to get him back. If I lose it, I'll never see him again. No matter what this man does, I can't—

He stabbed at the console, and a holographic screen appeared on the far wall, six feet on a side. An image appeared there, a live feed from a small room with a concrete floor and cinder block walls. The soldier who'd met us at the door was there along with two others, all in uniform, and all wearing black rubber aprons. The man who'd first met us held a big electric concrete saw in his hands. In the room with them were Vamp and Nix, both zip-tied to a chair with a big, heavy chopping block set between them. Each chair rested against a metal support pole, and their arms were bound behind them. They were both awake, and I could see Vamp's chest rising and falling rapid-fire as he kept his eyes fixed on the saw.

Hwong leaned in toward the microphone. "Are you ready?" The man with the saw nodded.

"What are you going to do?" I asked, staring. Nix sat, staring down at the floor in front of him, while the men circled.

"That depends," he said. "Are you going to open the tablet?"

"I can't," I said. "I need—"

Hwong spoke into the microphone again. "Start with the haan."

The man with the saw pressed his thumb to the contact on the side and it roared to life. The circular blade spun into a blur underneath the guard as the soldier hefted it into position. One of the other men pointed a remote at Nix and triggered it, causing light to flash from the shock pin in his neck. He went rigid for a few seconds, then slumped as the man let go of the button.

"Don't!"

While he was dazed, one of the guards unshackled Nix's left arm and slammed it down onto the block next to him. He held the wrist and leaned back, pulling the arm taut.

"No! Wait!"

The man with the saw lowered the whining blade down onto the meat of Nix's arm, which burst into a spray of blood and sinew.

The horror and pain that drilled through the surrogate cluster paralyzed me. It wasn't just the empathic flood of agony that bored deep into the flesh and bone of my own arm, but the terror that followed it. Rapid flashes of desperate denial arced over the sickening knowledge of what would come next.

That isn't faked, I thought. *What I'm feeling couldn't be faked. Could it?*

The saw's whine lowered in pitch as it dug deeper, shattering bones and spraying mists of blood until it cleaved straight through at the elbow and the meat separated.

I scrambled for the monitor, pushing against Hwong's hand, clawing at him as he held me back. Nix stared at the arm in shock while Vamp, his eyes wide with terror, struggled to free himself from the chair.

"Stop!" I shouted, but my voice broke. "Stop it!"

The guy holding the severed arm stumbled back when it came loose and dropped it. When he did, the limb seemed to go rubbery for a second, writhing in the air as it fell. When it hit the floor, it seemed to shatter almost, or split apart. I didn't get a good look at what happened exactly, but the next thing I knew there was not one but three severed arms lying on the floor next to the table. They were all identical, right down to the suit sleeve and cuff.

"Incredible," Hwong whispered. For a second, even I just stared.

The guard nudged one of the severed arms with the toe of his boot, and I saw the look on his face had changed. He looked a little scared now. A few seconds later, the air around the arm warped and it vanished with a bang that made him jump back. The other two limbs on the floor popped out of existence right behind it.

The guard looked back at the camera as if to ask Hwong what to do next. Behind him, I could see that somehow Nix's arm was still on his body, hanging by his side, as his eyes began to open again.

"Well," Hwong said quietly. "This just got interesting."

"Wait," I said. "Just wait."

On the monitor, the guy with the saw had hefted it back, blood dripping steadily off the circular blade as he got ready to cut again.

"Stop it!"

"If you want them to stop, then open the tablet."

"I . . ."

I gripped the tablet in my hands, frozen. They were going to kill him. That man was going to cut Nix into pieces right in front of me, and Nix knew it too. When they were done, they'd do the same to Vamp.

Hwong turned back to the microphone. "Again."

"Wait!"

The man lowered the saw, bringing it down on Nix's knee this time.

"Wait!"

He angled the saw and the blade's shriek lowered to an angry, gurgling buzz as he pushed it in farther. I covered my eyes with my hands and tried to back away, but Hwong had me. He pulled my hands away from my face and held me as the saw came down again. As I squeezed my eyes closed, Nix's heart icon turned pink and began to beat. The 3i window appeared, floating in the darkness behind my eyelids as the blade ground down again.

Don't do it.

Nix, I have to.

None of us are ever lost. Don't.

Vamp was screaming. The man with the saw stared stonily as he worked, lifting the blade away from the severed leg and then pushing it into Nix's rib cage with no trace of emotion whatsoever. My stomach rolled and I gagged, coughing spit through my teeth.

"I'm going to puke," I groaned. "Let me go. I'm going to puke."

Hwong shoved me toward the desk and I fell down on

my knees next to it. Through a blur of tears I found the wastebasket and dragged it in front of me as I wretched, watching the precious nutrients splatter into the plastic liner.

"Stop," I moaned when I could speak again. Cold sweat rolled down my forehead as I spit into the mess.

"Hold it," Hwong said into the microphone. I lifted my head and saw the guy raise the saw back up, spitting red as the blade wound down. Blood gushed down onto the floor around the chair where Nix hung limp in his restraints, not moving. When I looked back to the 3i window, his heart had turned gray again.

"Please stop," I said.

"Will you open the tablet?" Hwong asked. "Or do I have him start on the boy?"

"No," I rasped. "Please. Stop. I'll do it."

He stared at me for a long minute, and his face didn't seem human. The acts that had reduced me to jelly in less than a minute didn't affect him at all, not even a little, and I realized they never would. I held one shaking finger over the tablet's screen, and felt a warm tear run down my cheek.

"Let him go," I said.

"Open the tablet."

Sitting back on my heels, I swiped at the screen using the hanzi for "apple." On the third try the metallic surface dissolved away. I reached in and grabbed the twist-key in fingers that felt numb.

"What about me?" I asked him.

"You can return home."

"They can come with me?"

"Yes."

"I don't believe you," I said, but still I removed the key and held it out to him in one shaking hand. He grabbed it, and I watched the only chance I had to get Dragan back move away, out of reach. On the monitor, I saw the guy with the saw hoist it up onto his shoulder, dripping blood down the back of his apron.

"Turn it off," I said. "Please."

Hwong flipped off the display, and I struggled back onto my feet. A wave of dizziness came over me like a dark cloud as the blood rushed back into my legs, and I stood still for a minute with one hand on the back of his chair until it passed.

Hwong turned the twistkey over in his hands, and then squeezed it in one fist. He moved around the desk and began to walk toward the office door, his back turned to me.

My fingers moved to the buckle of my belt, and threaded the cloth band back through as I raised one leg. My foot came down on the edge of the desktop and I hoisted myself up, taking a single running step down the too-short runway before launching myself off the opposite edge and springing into the air toward him.

He heard me too late, only just starting to turn as I came down hard onto his shoulders. My crotch pressed onto the back of his neck as I locked my legs under his arms and whipped my belt free from my pant loops.

He grunted, trying to reach into his coat for his gun, but my legs were strong and I kept his arms pinned back as I wrapped the belt around his neck and pulled. The room spun around me as he thrashed like a mechanical bull, trying to shake me off as I tightened the noose. The belt dug into the flesh of his neck just below his jawline, and when I looked down at him from above I saw his big eyes bugging out of his blood-filled face like veiny marbles. His mouth worked, unhinging as his tongue formed a purple peak.

His legs gave out and he dropped, stumbling back and then crashing sideways into the desk. My ribs struck the edge hard enough to knock me off his shoulders, but I held on to the belt, rolling and twisting my body around to form a tourniquet with it. His big hands groped, managing to get a hold of the band around his throat, but he was weakening. He gave up, and one hand drifted down over his chest to reach for the gun whose grip was sticking out from a shoulder holster, but he never made it. His fingers pawed once at the metal butt, then went still.

I let go. I had no idea if I'd killed him or not, but there wasn't time to find out. Someone could have heard the racket and be on their way. I untwisted the belt and threaded it back through my belt loops as I stood up, then hiked my pants and tightened it. I scanned the floor until I found the twistkey lying partway under the desk and snatched it up.

In the quiet, I listened and heard voices somewhere down the long hall, along with Vamp's high-pitched panting. I started across the room back toward the exit. On my way past, I delivered a hard kick to Hwong's ribs, then grabbed my pistol back and ran out the door, back down the hallway the way we'd come.

I had no idea what I was going to do next; all I knew was that there was no way in hell Hwong was going to let any of us out of there alive. The others must have heard the struggle, because footsteps were hurrying down the hall from somewhere up ahead. I ducked into an old metal door that had bowed back into a wall of debris, and squatted down in the shadows as the clamor got louder. Holding my breath, I pressed myself against the door as the soldiers tromped past on their way back to the office with Ligong leading the charge. When they turned the corner, I darted out and sprinted into the darkness toward a dim light that came from around a corner up ahead.

Vamp's panting grew louder as I closed in on the light, ducking under a hanging length of rusted sprinkler pipe when I rounded the corner. Ahead, I could see the open doorway and the blood-splattered floor on the other side. The concrete saw lay there, lying on one side in a pool of red. I barreled through and almost slipped in the mess, not wanting to look but having to. Nix was slumped in the chair, not moving.

Vamp's eyes stared wildly as I approached him.

"Come on," he hissed. "Come on, cut me loose."

I ran to him, flicking out my pocketknife and slashing through the zip ties that held his wrists behind the support pole. When his arms were free, I bent down and freed his ankles from the chair.

"Okay," he said. "Okay, good, let's go, let's go. . . ."

I went to Nix and yanked the shock pin out of his neck, but as soon as I cut him loose he slid off the chair and collapsed onto the floor.

"Come on," I said. "Nix, get up."

"Go," Nix said. The voice box flicker was faint, like his connection to it was waning. The pool of blood around him grew, slow but steady.

"We can't just leave you here," I said in his ear. "Come on, you have to get up."

"No," he said. He reached up with his one free hand and touched my face.

"Nix, come on. . . ."

"Sam, we gotta go," Vamp whispered. Footsteps were headed back in our direction.

"Stop her," Nix said again. His body went slack, and the air around him warped suddenly, rippling like waves of heat.

He's dying, I thought. *His body is going to gate back to the ship. . . .*

"Stop right there!"

I looked up to see Ligong storm through the doorway, the others right behind her. She held a pistol in one hand.

"Drop that fucking key," she growled, aiming the gun at me. "Do it now!"

The air around Nix warped again, and before she could do anything else I put the twistkey in Nix's free hand, curling his long fingers around it. Ligong barked from across the room, "I said—"

Nix's body vanished. My gun hand had been resting on his chest, the side of the pistol pressed against him, and my palm tingled as the weapon gated off along with him. Air rushed into the vacuum left behind with a loud crack that I felt in my chest, and the ties that had held his wrists and ankles clattered to the floor in a heap. Nix, the twistkey, and the pistol were gone.

"There," I heaved as Ligong stalked toward me. My head was spinning. "Now nobody—"

She threw a right cross that caught me hard on the cheek and sent me sprawling, unconscious, onto the bloody concrete floor.

Chapter Nineteen

04:11:53 BC

I woke up with my face pressed into some kind of rough material, canvas maybe, while heavy footsteps clomped around me. My whole body was wrapped in it, and I swayed as though in a hammock. Through the cocoon of fabric I heard the clang of machinery in a large open space, and the whistle of escaping steam. Pain throbbed at the base of my skull.

"What the hell . . . ?" I mumbled. I tried to reach out, but my arms were pinned.

"She's awake," a man's voice said. It came from somewhere behind me.

I'm in a bag, I realized. I was facedown in a canvas bag, hanging between two men who carried me like so much deadweight.

"Doesn't matter," another voice answered.

Up ahead, a third someone pushed a door open and then the footsteps around me changed as we entered a room.

"The second dissident," a voice said. "Female."

"Get it on the scale," a fourth voice said.

The guy carrying the foot end of the bag dropped it and my hip crashed down hard on the floor. The other guy up front dumped me out like a load of laundry or trash, jerking the bag away once my head was clear.

The hard, tiled floor felt cold under my bare ass, and I realized I was completely naked. Four men stood around me in a big white room that was lit by work lights that hung from hooks. The floor was covered with a gritty film, and stained with green-black mold that also spotted the walls. A row of lockers were set up along one wall, and one hung open so I could see a set of work coveralls that hung inside. There was an old, lime-caked dry-scrub station next to that, and an electronic medical scale set up in one corner that looked newer than everything else.

To my left and right were two big shirtless guys, their skin covered with ornate tattoos. One of the men was bald, and the other's hair was gelled back into spikes. Both of them had festival jiangshi masks hanging back behind their heads like they were getting ready to go to the parade. In front of me, a foreign green-eyed man stood holding a stack of papers and in front of him a short, ugly man with a comb-over and dark freckles sat behind a big folding table. He wore a pair of long shorts and a colorful, draping shirt sporting a tropical palm pattern.

"The scale," he said again. One of the men dropped a greasy cardboard box on the table in front of him.

"You heard him," the green-eyed man said.

"Where am I?" I rasped. "What's happening?"

Green-eyes nudged me with his knee and I lost my balance, falling forward onto my hands.

"Where's Vamp?" I asked. "Tell me what's going on."

"Don't talk to it!" the old man snapped. "Get it on the scale!"

The man sighed, like he'd been scolded by his father.

"Get on," he said, pointing toward the scale. I stayed on the floor and shook my head. He raised his voice. "I can weigh you whole or in pieces, but you're getting weighed."

I knew where I was then. I sniffed the air and smelled

cooking meat, along with the metallic tang of blood. I was in a scrapcake factory. The smell came from rendered human flesh.

I stood on shaky legs, my mind clutching at any denial no matter how flimsy, but I knew it was true. The scale seemed far away, like it was at the end of a long tunnel.

"Wait," I said, choking on the word.

"Get on the scale!" he barked, and I raised my hands between us as he took a step toward me.

"Okay, okay," I said, my voice wavering.

The room seemed to tilt as I walked toward the scale, looking around as I went. There was only one way in and out, through a green metal door back behind me. The two guys who'd carried me lingered near it, and could close the gap in a second if I tried to run.

The metal was cold under my bare feet as I climbed up onto the scale. A warm light snapped on over my head, and then a pattern of red laser dots appeared on my chest as the scale numbers flipped around. The scanner traveled down my stomach, flickering on and off before going dark. The old man consulted the screen of his electronic tablet.

"Ninety-two," he said. "Body fat four point three percent. Barely worth the fuel to run the equipment."

"Call the prison back and see if she'll give you a refund," Green-eyes taunted. The old man didn't take the bait.

"Take it out back with the rest and see what we can render out," he said. "Cut it with machine oil if you have to."

An empty pit formed in my stomach. The distant hum that I felt through the floor and the slow whistle of steam were variations on white noise that had been burned into my brain years ago, and never quite forgotten. The smell of cooking meat in the air, the smell that made my mouth water, came from the steam of a rendering vat.

Hwong was selling prisoners, people he needed to disappear, to meat farmers.

"You're cannibals," I whispered.

The others ignored me, but not Green-eyes. His brow lowered and before I could react he lashed out and slapped me in the face with one big palm so hard I almost fell off the scale.

"Hey, you're fucking up the scan," the old man complained. Green-eyes shoved his index finger in my face.

"I'm no goddamned cannibal," he said, "and even if I was, it's better than being a terrorist."

"I'm not a terrorist," I said. I tasted blood in my mouth.

"I know," he mocked. "The government's evil, and all you dissidents are just misunderstood."

"Don't talk to it!" the old man barked.

Green-eye's face grew darker, and his body was wound like a spring. The hand he'd slapped me with curled into a fist.

"Some are going to eat, and some are going to starve," he said. "The only thing on this sorry planet we got a surplus of is idiots, drug addicts, and separatist assholes. We solve two problems at once here."

"I'm a human being," I said, looking around the room at the faces there. "My name is Xiao-Xing Shao. My father is—"

"Damn it, shut your mouth!" the old man snapped at Green-eyes. "I said don't talk to it! Don't talk to it means don't talk to it, not keep talking to it!"

Perched on the scale, I looked from face to face but didn't find anything like compassion in any of them. The old man and Green-eyes were angry, righteous. One of the other two looked amused. The last one looked bored. None of them were going to help me.

I scanned the room for something, anything that might get me out of there. On the folding table was a cardboard box, and through a gap in the top of it I could see the buckle of my belt shining under the overhead work light. They'd thrown my clothes in the box and brought it in to pick through. My knife might still be in my pants pocket. It wasn't much, but it was sharp, and better than nothing.

"Hold it," the old man said. His tone changed suddenly as he frowned down at a screen that faced away from me. The red laser dots had stopped their sweep and were doing a slow circle around my belly button.

"What's that?" Green-eyes asked.

"I don't know," the old man said.

Green-eyes crossed to join him and squinted down at the screen while the old man tapped it with his finger. "Something wrong with the scanner?"

"No," the old man said. "It's localized right there. A dispersion field or something."

"What . . . in there?"

"Something's implanted in there," the old man said. He sounded a little nervous now. Green-eyes just looked annoyed.

"Like what?" he asked.

"They're fucking fanatics," the old man hissed, glancing over at me. "It could be a goddamned suicide bomber for all we know!"

Some of the annoyance melted away from Green-eyes' face, and his eyes turned calculating as he looked back at me. I looked at the other two men, who no longer appeared amused, or bored.

"Take it outside and shoot it," the old man said. "If nothing happens, bring the body back and—"

I jumped off the scale and lunged for the table. The two guys by the door had expected me to go that way and stepped in to block me, while the old man seemed surprised and actually backed away. Green-eyes had my number, though, and took a swing at me. The only reason it missed was that my ankle gave when I hit the floor and I dropped under his passing fist. I felt it graze the hair on top of my head as I pitched forward and fell headlong into the table. The legs on the far side of it collapsed and folded back in, causing the whole end to crash down onto the floor.

My hips slammed into the edge of the table and I flipped forward face-first onto the sloped tabletop. The momentum threw my bare ass up over my head and I landed on the edge of the box, crumpling it underneath me.

"Grab it!" the old man shouted, backing away into the wall behind him like I was some kind of wild animal that'd just gotten loose. One of the guys by the exit threw open a locker door and grabbed a machete from inside.

I rolled off the box and pulled it open as someone got a fistful of my hair. He yanked back, but it was too short for him to get a grip on and I was able to slip through his fingers. As soon as I did, the heel of a boot came down hard on one of my shoulder blades, bowling me over and sending the contents of the box spilling out across the grimy floor. My sneakers rolled away as my pink tank top and cargo pants flopped out after them. I hauled myself up onto my hands and knees and made a mad crawl forward, grabbing my belt as the boot stomped me in the ass from behind.

The force of it hurled me forward into the lockers, and my forehead collided with one of the metal doors hard enough to make it spring open. For a second I saw stars as equipment from inside fell out and crashed down around me. The point of a machete thumped into the tile next to my hand, and then it clattered down onto the floor as a box hit me in the back of the head. It popped open, spraying plastic zip ties across the floor as I spun around and pulled my pants toward me.

"Hold it!"

I looked up and saw Green-eyes as he towered over me, glaring down out from beneath the shadow of his heavy brow. He raised his foot, ready to stamp me out like a cockroach, and I kicked away, my back slamming into the lockers behind me. I scrambled to find the pockets of my pants, but they'd turned into a tangle of material and my brain had begun to short-circuit. I slid to one side, rust and metal scratching my bare back, as the boot crashed into the locker door next to me and made the whole row shake. One of the guards was coming up on my other side while the last one blocked the door.

There was nowhere to run. My hand found one of my pockets and reached in. I felt my pocketknife in there and I when I pulled it out the sheet of blue crystal I'd taken from Dragan's safe flipped out onto the floor after it, along with a tube of lipstick. I flicked the blade out and jabbed it into the first piece of skin I saw. Someone swore and jerked back out of range with the knife still stuck in his forearm.

Before anyone else could grab me, I snatched the lipstick up off the floor and popped the cap off. I squashed my thumb down over the protruding red end of the stick, then held my fist out in front of me like the tube was a cross to ward off vampires.

"Anyone moves and I'll detonate the bomb!" I screamed.

The two guards backed off and then bolted through the door, leaving me alone with Green-eyes and the old man. The old man was backed up against the wall like he was about ready to piss in his tropical shorts. Green-eyes didn't look so sure. He was wary, but a dangerous gleam still lingered in his eyes.

"I mean it," I said. "Back off."

"I don't believe that's a detonator," he said.

"Go ahead and try me, then."

I crouched down and grabbed the pill sheet, still holding the lipstick up as I edged toward the door. Blood had run down my forehead into the corner of one eye, and I wiped it with the back of my hand.

He took a step toward me, causing the old man to shout in a high-pitched voice, "Just let it go! Wait until it gets outside, then shoot it there!"

I bolted for the exit. My shoulder struck the green door's lever hard and I slipped through as it opened. A hand brushed my back as I ran, stumbling down onto the skewed tile floor before I managed to get back on my feet.

"She's bluffing!" Green-eyes yelled from behind me. "Stop her, goddamn it!"

The hallway ahead ended at a corner and I banked, pushing off the wall. I headed down another hall that had been fractured halfway down its length. The floor rose toward the break and then sloped down on the other side, where the air grew hotter and more humid. Up ahead I could see light flickering through a big open doorway. With every step I took toward it, the hiss of steam grew louder and the smell of meat grew stronger. A few steps later I heard what sounded like a child's scream, the high voice cutting through the rumble of machines.

Cooler air gripped my skin as I passed by a corridor branch. My body, seeming to act on its own, jerked to a stop so suddenly that I almost twisted my ankle.

That's the way out.

I looked back and saw the men were hot on my heels. Down the branch to my right, I could hear the moan of wind and feel the current of cool air that was free from smoke, steam, and sweat. There was no time to think it through. It was either right, toward possible freedom, or straight on toward the sound of sizzling and screaming.

It was the thought of Vamp that made me move again. He'd be in with the rest, and I knew I couldn't leave him

no matter how scared I was. I took a step toward what I
hoped would be him. My brain screamed not to do it, but
if he was there and I left him, then I knew what would
happen. He'd watch the other captives get slaughtered
and cut up, until it was finally his turn. I took another
step and picked up speed as I moved toward the light.

The air turned so thick it got hard to breathe, and the
miasma of it covered my bare skin. In my mind, I heard
the rattling of a chain and collar, my collar, as I dug at it
with raw, bloody fingers with the little strength I had left.
I remembered how fear had turned to terror, then terror
into near disconnect as I had seen the others who arrived there before me hauled away to be strung up. Next
would come the high-pitched shriek and gurgle. No matter how big the man was, it came out sounding like a girl
until it stopped and the chopping began.

I couldn't breathe. My legs were pumping on automatic pilot now, threatening to seize at each step.

You can do this. I said it to myself over and over, trying to make it be heard over the sound of the jingling
chain and gurgling screams. My mind seemed to separate
from my body, until I felt like I was floating forward.

You can do this. What if Dragan had left you?

I'd have been dead for sure. My number had finally
come up when he stormed in. I remembered how strong
he looked, how fearless as he marched across the factory
floor. He'd looked over and seen me just before the men
entered. He looked right in my eyes and then turned on
them.

By the time he was done, the concrete floor was slick
with blood. No arrests, no trials, only just deserts. I had
lain back against the concrete wall, the collar's chain digging into one cheek, while I listened to the shots, regular,
rhythmic, and final.

Dragan . . .

I felt the impact at the same time I heard the pop. It

slammed into my right shoulder blade and sent me pitching forward as pain drilled down my spine.

My momentum carried me, and when I came down on my left heel, it slipped out from under me. I felt a brief, weightless sensation as I flew through the doorway, and then an abrupt, bone-rattling impact as I crashed down onto the rusted metal deck.

Chapter Twenty

"Sam, get up!"

The voice came from somewhere up above me. I was facedown on a filthy, damp floor, surrounded by the sounds of bubbling hot liquid and churning machinery. Pain throbbed from my skinned palms, and I felt a tight knot in the muscle behind my right shoulder. I reached back, my muscles stiff and sluggish, and felt something sticking out there.

"I got her!" a voice echoed through the halls. "She's down!"

I winced as I pulled the object loose and it clattered onto the floor. It was some kind of little black dart, with a tuft of red fluff at the back end.

"Sam! Get up! Quick!"

My head felt like it was full of wet concrete as I lifted it up off the deck. A little ways away I saw the lipstick tube, the end squished flat, and the crumpled sheet of blue crystal. A few meters past them, a naked boy stared at me from behind the mesh of a wire cage, tears streaked down his soot-covered face.

There were more cages on either side of his, some empty and some occupied by other kids or teenagers. Some lay on their sides with their backs to me; others were awake now and staring at me.

I looked up and saw more cages stacked on top of each other, eight layers high. They went all the way up to the factory ceiling, where foam tiles had broken loose and exposed a maze of ductwork. A set of scaffolding had been built in front of the wall of cages, two stories connected by ramps to allow access to the upper levels. It all looked like it had been there a long time.

"Up here!"

The tower of cages swayed above me. At least, I thought they did. I couldn't focus, and pins and needles pricked at my fingers and toes as I squinted to find the source of the voice. Way up, on the second-level platform, I saw fingers laced through one of the cage doors. They shook it as a familiar face looked down at me.

"Vamp?" The word squeaked out. I didn't think he heard me.

"They're coming. Move it!" he called down.

I looked back at the little dart. They'd drugged me, and it had really started to kick in. I didn't have long before I'd be out, and then it would be all over.

I lunged and grabbed the pill sheet, then rolled over onto my back. Using my legs, I pushed myself back behind a big piece of machinery just as the men entered the room.

"Where the fuck did she go?" one of them asked.

It wouldn't take them long to figure it out. I moved the pill sheet close to my face. Black spots bloomed in front of my eyes, and my fingers felt cold as I pushed the blue pill into my bloody palm. I popped it into my mouth and crunched down on it until the intense bitterness filled my nose and throat.

"Back here!" someone shouted.

The shard kicked in fast. In seconds the drug cut through the haze, and the approaching black cloud scattered. Energy pulsed through me, and as I sprang back to my feet I saw little white sparks flash in the air in front of me.

I had no idea how long it would last, but I knew I had to make it count. I bolted for the ramp that led to the first platform just as two figures emerged from the steam from that direction, and shoved the closest one away as I passed.

"There!" a voice shouted.

I skidded to a stop. When I turned back the other way, I saw another guy heading in my direction. They'd flanked me, and were closing in. I wasn't going to make it to the ramp, and I couldn't go back.

I put my foot on top of the nearest cage and heaved myself up. The woman inside stared as I grabbed the wire mesh above me and began to climb.

"She's going up!"

"Load another dart, you stupid asshole!"

The crystal kicked in for real. The sweat that covered my body turned cold and sent a sick feeling into the pit of my stomach as every muscle came alive with a flood of pure chemical energy. My pulse revved as one foot slipped on the cage beneath it and I dropped, hanging from my hands for a second until I got my footing again.

A pop came from below, and something banged off the face of the cage next to me.

"Shit!"

The tower of cages swayed under my weight, but held as I scaled my way up past the first platform, toward the second, where Vamp was being held.

A gunshot boomed through the air, and a hole punched through the platform above me to my right. The people in the cages around me pushed themselves back, trying to get out of range, as I scurried past. The scaffolding shook now as the men below began to storm up the ramp, but to reach the second level they needed to traverse the whole platform first. I could get much higher, much quicker than they could as long as the crystal didn't burn out first.

"Sam!"

Vamp had his back to the rear of his cage and was pushing against the door with his feet. The wire bowed outward, biting into his heels and drawing blood, but the latch wouldn't give. My foot slipped again, a J-clip slashing my shin as I hauled myself up to the second platform where I pitched over the rail and rolled onto the wooden planks.

Looking down over the edge of the scaffolding, I saw a huge rendering vat through the haze of steam. It was a giant metal pit, embraced by slick, snaking pipes that kept its temperature constant. The inside was filled with a deep layer of bubbling ochre liquid littered with red-brown specks. Dark, glistening chunks were jumbled together on the surface, and among them I could make out bobbing hands and feet. Crisped skin puffed at the edges of cured, fried meat where the jutting ends of broken bones stuck out, white around a center of blackened marrow.

I pulled myself back up onto my feet as another shot went off, this time blowing a hole through the platform six inches from my foot. Two of the men had reached the base of the second ramp and were heading up to my level.

I bolted toward Vamp's cage, reaching it just as Green-eyes appeared at the top of the ramp. Before I knew it he was on top of me, the barrel of his pistol an inch from my face.

"Sam!"

I swatted his wrist, knocking the gun aside in the same second it went off. Heat flashed against my cheek as the boom all but deafened my left ear and the smell of burned powder went up my nose. There was no time to think. It felt like electricity was coursing through my entire body, making me feel fast, powerful, and invincible, but when I kicked him in the ribs I got almost no reaction at all. I ducked under his arm and kicked him again, but he was heavy, and solid, and he didn't even seem to care. It wasn't like the movies. He didn't go down. I couldn't even move him.

I ducked down out of the way as he made another lunge for me, scooting behind him as he pitched forward. Still off balance, he tried to turn and bring the gun around behind him.

"You slippery little bitch!"

I rammed him with one shoulder before he could shoot, and he stepped backward, not realizing the ramp was so close. His ankle twisted, and he barked as it gave out underneath him. He fell back, his other foot slipping off the side of the ramp. He started to fall back, over the edge, and his gun clunked down onto the floor as he grabbed the scaffolding at the last second.

He started hauling himself back and I barreled into him with my shoulder. His hand slipped and he pitched back, grabbing at me as he fell. His fingers brushed my arm as I hooked one elbow around a metal support and he dropped down, crashing onto his back on the platform below.

"Sam!"

Vamp was in the cage just behind me. I felt along the top of the doorframe until I found the latch, then pulled the bolt free just as two more men topped the ramp.

The door crashed open and Vamp sprang out, going for one of the men without a second's hesitation. He threw a punch and creamed him right in the eye, following up with a left hook even as the guy began to fall. He went down and Vamp turned to the other one, the one with the spiked hair, just as he raised his shotgun. Vamp saw it, took a step back.

"Vamp!"

Green-eyes' pistol still lay on the platform where he'd dropped it. As the shotgun barrel zeroed in on Vamp's face, I scooped it up and aimed down the sight.

It bucked in my hand as it let out an earsplitting bang. At first I thought I missed. The guy didn't fly back or spray blood or do anything like what I thought might happen. He just kind of jerked once, like the sound of the shot had surprised him, and a little hole appeared in the middle of his chest. He stood, kind of frozen, with the shotgun still pointed at Vamp but not pulling the trigger.

The barrel listed to one side, and a big blob of blood grew from out of the hole before running down over his stomach in a dark trickle. He took a step back, and his eyelids drooped as the shotgun slipped from his hands and fell to the floor. A second later he fell down after it, crashing down onto the wooden planks.

Vamp stared as I stood there, the gun still held out in front of me. The barrel of the pistol shook as I looked down at the man's body. Vamp stepped over it and approached me carefully.

"Sam . . ."

I couldn't take my eyes away from the body.

"I killed him," I said.

"Sam, come on," Vamp said. "There's more of them coming."

I could hear them. They sounded far away, but down below I could see more men headed for the scaffolding. The captives were screaming to be let out, shaking the cages.

"Sam!" Vamp snapped. He grabbed the shotgun from the floor and shook my shoulder. The man he'd kicked had recovered, and was back on his feet. He reached back and pulled a pistol from where he'd tucked it in the waistband of his pants as several more armed men appeared at the base of the ramp behind him.

The air next to us warped suddenly, and the cage doors buckled. A point of white light appeared inside a ball of distortion and then expanded out into a hexagon-shaped portal as a figure stepped through it with his back to us. The gate collapsed, and the figure rose. I saw a length of spine running down under the smoke gray skin of his neck, and the two slowly shifting brains beneath his skull. The figure's head turned, and I caught a flash of sunset pink.

Nix . . .

Vamp shook me again as something flickered in front of my face.

Sam, forgive me. I couldn't let them do it. The message popped up on the 3i display, reeling across the air in front of me.

"Dragan," I whispered.

Nix moved suddenly, darting out between us. Over his shoulder I saw the other two men reach the top platform, but that's as far as they got. They both stopped short suddenly, like they'd hit an invisible barrier. My heart thumped rapid fire until the pistol, still stuck out in front of me, began to drift toward the floor as Dragan's words continued to scroll past.

I know that you—

His connection dropped as one of the two men halted and grabbed his own throat. His feet came up off the platform, his toes dangling, as his cohort fell to his knees. He jerked, then with a meaty crackling sound his head twisted around completely. A second later his arms did the same.

"Sam," Vamp said. He was looking at me and hadn't seen. His voice sounded low, and thick, like he was talking in slow motion. "Sam, are you okay?"

Everything began to sound like it was coming from far away. Nix stood before the men, his arms held out by his sides with his palms turned upward. He never touched them, but somehow a tattooed arm, then a leg went spinning through the air behind Vamp in slow motion. My ears began to ring, drowning out the mayhem as a chunk of meat with jutting rib bones flipped in the air. It sprayed blood as it tumbled back down the ramp to the first platform, and warm drops spattered down onto my face.

"Sam!" Vamp cried.

I turned my eyes back to him, my stomach bunched into a rock-hard knot as my heartbeat turned to one continuous rumble. The fear in Vamp's eyes was like nothing I'd ever seen in them before. He reached for me like he wanted to grab me but was afraid to.

"Dragan," I croaked.

He shook his head, eyes wide. "What?"

"Dragan . . ."

"Sam, what's wrong?" he asked. As my head began to bob, I followed the flat muscular ridges of his abs down to his crotch, then pointed with one shaking finger.

"What?" he asked. "What is it?"

"You're circumcised."

Then all at once the machine-gun beat of my heart stopped.

I choked as pain pulsed up my neck and down both arms. The factory reeled around me, and I fell back with the wind rushing in my ears. I barely felt the floor when I hit, and Vamp's shadow crouched down over me.

"Sam!" he screamed. His voice sounded very distant, and soft. "Sam!"

He was still screaming when his voice faded, with the light.

Chapter Twenty-one

03:53:55 BC

Darkness surrounded me, seeping into every crease and crevice like cold, thick mud that pushed me deeper and deeper into nothing. The warmth of life fell away, until it was no more than a fading star I had no hope of reaching.

Is this death?

Was I was crossing from the realm of the living and into the realm of the dead like in one of Ling's stories? Some distant part of me hoped I hadn't let everyone down . . . Dragan, Vamp, the little Pan-Slav kids, and even Nix. What would they all do with me dead? Would they still try and stop the burn?

It doesn't matter. You did everything you could.

The worry faded as I fell. The burn, even the world itself, seemed far away by now. It would continue to turn after I was gone, and without my help. I wondered if I wouldn't arrive on the other side to find Dragan waiting for me there, and I decided that if he was, then that would be okay.

Yes, it's okay. You can let go. . . .

It was more of an idea than a voice, an unspoken urge to give up what little fight I had left in me, and let the inevitable come.

Just let go. . . .

Maybe my mother would be there too. Maybe we could hang out, she, Dragan, and I. Would any haan be there? Would they get to cross over too?

Just—

Something slithered in the dark, a cold, fat worm that snaked under my right arm and down my bare side. I wanted to cringe as whatever it was crept up over my belly, but I couldn't move. I couldn't even breathe.

It coiled around my waist as a second worm slipped down over my shoulder, its tip branching into two wandering feelers that crept down over my chest. Gentle pressure built around my waist and I was being moved, dragged as the things touching me were joined by another, and another, and another.

I began to panic, but my body wouldn't respond even as the feelers pulled me back into an enveloping mass and squirming cilia engulfed me. They drew me in deeper until the shapeless cold gave way to a hot inner core that warmed my back and sent a shudder through my whole body. They were on my face now, writhing, and though I felt a scream build up in my chest, I couldn't take a breath to release it.

A faint hum broke the quiet, an anxious buzzing noise. I felt a tickle on my lips and realized it was a fly. Not just one, but a swarm of them. More and more began to crawl across my face and down my neck, arms, and legs. All I could think of was the jiangshi, the folklore festival ghouls, mass victims of the Impact's burial who were left to rot away in the rim.

A louder sound, a low rasp that rumbled over rhythmic insect clicks, vibrated deep in my chest as one of the slithering worms found the middle of my chest. It coiled there and split into a squirming mass that grew warmer as it branched out down my rib cage and over my bare breasts. The center of the mass turned hot, and a tingle at my breastbone turned to a sharp, painful jolt. . . .

My eyes opened, and faint light seeped through. In the shadows I saw glistening, ropy strands that entangled me. Shiny black shells, the backs of scaleflies, scurried in rows down the length of them, crawling in and out of the dark pits that covered each one.

They slithered as one, squeezing me tighter. I opened my mouth, nearly gagging on a fly whose buzz echoed inside before it spiraled away above me, then was finally able to suck in a breath and scream.

Chapter Twenty-two

My scream echoed into nothing as my back arched against damp concrete. A light flickered somewhere high overhead, casting shadows from the scaffolding's metal skeleton and wire cages across the wall. Something nearby made a low clicking sound and I smelled cooked meat.

"Holy shit," I heard Vamp say over the rapid-fire tick of cooling metal.

I opened my eyes and saw him kneeling next to me shirtless, his tattoos as recognizable as his face. He'd found his pants and shoes and put them back on.

"Hey, Vamp."

He broke into a wide smile, and his eyes turned shiny.

"You're back," he said.

I squinted up at him, trying to focus. I felt like I'd been asleep for days.

"Where are we?" I asked. "Are we—"

I broke off as all at once it came back to me. I jerked up into a sitting position, almost knocking heads with Vamp before he put his hands on my shoulders to steady me.

"Easy," he said.

I darted my eyes around the room, telling myself that if Vamp said I was safe, then I was. Pain and sickness lingered in my mind, but they seemed distant now. Almost forgotten.

From our perch on the platform, I could see the rendering vat down below, where steam still rose in a faint, slow-moving cloud from the surface. The engines had been shut down, and the fat was cooling.

I looked back at Vamp, and his eyes were bright like he might cry. "What happened? What's wrong with you?"

"They darted you," he said. "Before you dropped, you took a dose of blue shard. Do you remember that?"

I had faint memories of Vamp leaping from the cage. There was a fight, and then . . .

"The crystal stopped your heart," he said. "You OD'd. Your body couldn't take it."

"No," I said, still fuzzy. "No, I'm okay, I just . . ."

"You died in my arms." One tear started to roll down his cheek, just one before he wiped it away. "I felt you go."

"Vamp . . ."

I put my arms around his neck and squeezed as he held me. His hands were warm on my back, and for the first time in a long while I didn't feel that tension I'd felt in the months gone by. That awkwardness that started when his feelings changed and any contact between us turned into something complicated. It was gone, at least for now, and he just held me like he used to when I needed to be held and he was just my friend.

"I'm here now," I said in his ear. I put my hand on the back of his head and ran my fingers through his thick hair.

"Yeah."

When I broke the hug, he didn't try and hang on. I leaned back, my fingers still laced behind his neck.

"Nix?"

"He told me he would take care of you," he said. "After . . . he told me to go get my clothes, and that he would take care of you."

"Where did he go?"

"We let the others out of their cages," he said. "Then he took them away from here, to wait until help comes."

I got onto my feet and realized that, in my sleep, either Vamp or Nix had dressed me. I bent over and laced my shoes back up.

"Hey," Vamp said, "take it easy. You're still pretty beat up."

"I know, but we don't have time. We could already be too late."

Nix, I'm coming down, I said on the 3i. *Where are you?*

The room, where they keep their lockers. Go down—

They took me there when they brought me in. I know where it is, thanks.

I headed down the ramp, feeling more energetic. It wasn't until I saw the body with the bullet hole that I remembered firing the gun, and the way the life had faded out of the man's eyes. He was still lying on the ramp, his eyes open and a fat red trickle drying on his belly.

Skirting around him, I headed quickly down the ramp. The cage doors all hung open, and the captives were gone. Sprawled on the second platform below were two twisted, broken arms trailing ragged skin from their stumps. The planks were covered with dark, tacky blood and I hopped over a trail of discarded guts whose squiggly end trailed off to the floor below.

Nix had done that. I'd always been so sure I'd known better than most what the haan were, and what they were all about, but not anymore. If I'd been asked the day before, I'd have said the haan didn't even understand the concept of violence. That even if they did, they lacked the capacity for it, at least in our world. Now I'd seen with my own eyes that they weren't only capable of it, but good at it. The haan had hidden a strength from us that allowed them to pick apart a human being as easily as a child picked the wings off a fly.

He did it to defend me, I told myself. *No other reason. To defend me, and because they deserved it. It's no different from what Dragan did when he rescued us from men like these.*

But I couldn't look at their remains, and it was different.

When I got to the bottom of the second ramp, back down onto the concrete floor, I headed back the way I'd come in, crossing past the spent tranquilizer dart and the crumpled foil pill sheet that still lay a few feet away from it. In the hallway outside the rendering chamber, I passed the corridor branch where the pocket of cool air had collected, and heard the rush of wind in the distance. Some of the captives had gathered there, sitting and standing along the walls in varying states of dress depending on what they'd been able to recover. They couldn't just go out into the rim or they'd get lost in the sea of debris and dust. If they didn't choke outright, then the toxins they breathed in would kill them long before they ever found the wall. They waited, frightened eyes following, as I passed by them on my way toward the locker room.

"Nix!"

When I pushed open the door, he was standing in front of the lockers. The contents had been arranged neatly on top of the folding table which he'd set back up, along with my pocketknife.

"How do you feel?" he asked.

"For a dead girl? Pretty good."

"I'm glad."

I approached him, and cut in front of him as he tried to dig around in the locker some more.

"You messed those guys up pretty bad."

He nodded. "I acted rashly."

"I don't blame you, Nix. Nobody would."

"I do."

"But how? How did you . . .?"

"I am stronger than I appear," he said, and would say no more on the topic. "Do you remember anything after your collapse?" he asked instead.

"Not really," I said, but he wasn't convinced.

"What do you remember?"

"Nothing," I said. "Just . . . a hallucination or something. Like a near-death experience, I guess."

"What did you see?"

"Nothing," I said again. "For a second I felt like I was being dragged down into the dark by something horrible. I thought I might have been going down, instead of up."

"Down?"

"To hell."

I felt vague amusement from him.

"Your neural pathways had begun to shut down," he said. "What you experienced was a by-product of that, nothing more."

I shrugged, not certain I believed that. "Sure, if you say."

"Your brain activity ceased," he said, "but I was able to pass you through jump space and slow your functions long enough to revive you."

"You brought me back to life?"

"I revived you using technology you will receive in Phase Seven. I don't have the ability to bring the dead back to life."

"That'll probably be in Phase Eight."

I sensed confusion from him for a minute before it clicked.

"A joke," he said.

"A bad one. Thanks, Nix. Either way, you saved my life."

"I told you once that none of us is ever permanently gone," he said, the mass in his head shifting uncomfortably. "When I first met you, I knew that it was different for you, but I didn't really understand it. You were the first human who ever cared for me, but it was more than that. I found the longer I stayed with you, the more attached to you I grew."

"You must be a glutton for punishment."

"No," he said. "Your death has permanence. It's why you weren't able to let them take the boy back with them, even though it was the easy thing to do, even though it would have helped you. Your feelings for your father, for your friend . . . even for a boy, a girl, and an old man you'd never met . . . even for me, the thing that makes them so compelling comes from the fact that you could lose them, forever, at any time. I . . ."

His voice box flickered out. He went quiet for a minute.

"I realized that what holds true for you would also be true for me, since you are human. If you were to die, it wouldn't be like a haan who I would still maintain a connection to. You would be gone forever, even to me."

I leaned over and planted a kiss on the cheek of his smooth, glasslike face.

"Well, that's the nicest thing any haan ever said to me," I told him. "Bizarre, but nice."

I touched his arm, and winced then as I remembered the concrete saw. The arm felt fine, and completely undamaged, as I ran my fingers down the length of it.

"Things aren't always as they appear," he said, holding up both arms to show me.

"Like one arm turning into three?"

"I will be fine," he said. "The gate activated as an emergency measure, but I will heal."

"Don't duck the question."

"Things aren't always as they appear."

He wasn't going to answer me. I decided that, for the time being, it could wait.

"So, wait, while you were . . . reviving me, did you remove that . . . ?" I pointed down toward my belly, where the invisible umbilicus was perched.

"No," he said. "The fact that it is helping to maintain your systems is one of the only reasons you're still alive. Even if it weren't, it will need to be removed under controlled conditions."

I looked down at the spot, pulling up my shirt to probe the spot above my belly button. "What's going to happen to me?"

"I don't know, but we need to extract the foreign tissue before it begins to grow again. Ideally, I would like to keep it intact for study."

"How long do I have?"

"The umbilicus is nearly empty."

"Then we'd better get going," I said.

He gestured at the table, where six airbike keys lay in a row.

"We need to leave this place," he said. "Quickly. A radio signal was transmitted from this location, and we have to assume Hwong knows something has gone wrong here. There are several vehicles in the lot outside we can use."

"What about the others?" I asked. "The other captives?"

"They should leave as well."

I looked over the keys on the table. Six keys meant six airbikes in the lot. In addition, Nix had recovered three phones, two covered in blood that was still sticky, three pistols, a tranquilizer gun, and a stack of five rations, three krill and two scalefly.

I grabbed the phones and the rations, plus two sets of keys.

"We're going to have to double up," I said. "Those things won't seat three, so we'll need two."

"What about the others? There are thirteen of them total."

"Some of them are kids," I said. "A bike will probably lift one adult and two kids. We'll take two of them."

"That's still not—"

"They're going to have to sort it out," I said, grabbing two sets of keys. "We have to go. Tell me you still have the twistkey."

He reached into his jacket and removed the blue metallic key, holding it up under the light.

I took it. "We saddle up, cross the wall, and meet at the closest public gate. The parade's started by now, so it's going to be a complete cluster out there. Follow my lead. We'll land and be through before they know even know we're there."

"That is a very risky plan. You could turn the key over to Ava, and let us take care of it."

"No," I said. "Not to her or anyone else. Let's go."

"She might be better equipped to help than we are."

"And she might decide Sillith had the right idea, or that the people down there are expendable, or that she doesn't want the truth about that place getting out," I said. "I watched her throw a baby into a meat grinder, right in front of me, like it was nothing. I'm going. Me. Not your shipmates. Not the soldiers. Me."

"But you'll fail."

"We'll see."

"You've seen what Sillith is capable of," he said, more softly this time. "You'll die for this man."

"Yeah, Nix. I would. I would die for him. So what?"

"Would he want that?"

No. He wouldn't. I knew it too.

I tossed him Dragan's wet drive, and he caught it.

"He's just going to have to understand," I said.

Chapter Twenty-three

The captives were huddled in the corridor that led to the factory exit, but most of them were still pretty jangled. They watched, anxious, as we approached, and some backed away. I noticed that the strangers had already formed loose groups. The kids, three scrawny boys and four girls, were bunched together in a small section of room exposed by a partial collapse. Two women and one of the men lingered near them while others stood by the metal door that led out into the rim.

One of the men, a middle-aged guy with graying hair, seemed to have taken the leader role. A woman stood near him, shaking in spite of the heat. Her long hair was plastered to her neck and shoulders, and she stared through the tangles as we approached them.

The man stepped forward to meet us and held out his hand. When I shook it, I could feel plenty of strength left in his bony fingers.

"I'm Jin," he said. "You saved our lives. Thank you. All of you." He nodded at Nix, and Vamp behind me.

"No problem," I said, not quite sure how to react to that. I looked to the others, and then back to him. "You don't really look like a criminal."

"Depends on who you ask," he said. "I'm an astronomer. Or I was before they threw me in here."

"What did they arrest you for?"

"Telling the truth." He shook his head. "Never mind. You got us out. We're in your debt."

Before he could say anything else, I handed the cardboard box full of stuff to him.

"There's some food here," I told him. "Not much. Cell phones too. You can call for help."

He rooted down and found one of the phones, holding it up and making sure it worked.

"There's also keys for four of the vehicles outside," I said. "We need two. We can take one, maybe two of the kids with us when we go."

Jin shook his head.

"They've got an airtruck in the other lot," he said. "I saw it when they brought me in, and I've seen it come and go through the window. We can get the kids out using that, but I'll call this in and get us some help first. I've got some contacts who can move under the radar."

"Don't wait too long. We think the soldiers who brought us here are on their way back."

He nodded.

"Maybe, but trying to cross the wall is suicide," he said. "They'll gun you down for sure. Wait for help."

"I can't."

"Well, if you're determined, then don't keep in a straight line. Speed won't save you. It takes those turrets a second or two to adjust their aim. Best bet is to let them lock on, then change course. Don't let them lead you."

"Thanks."

"I had a front-row seat back there," he said. "That was gutsy, what you did."

"Thanks," I said, "but—"

The woman stepped forward then and before I knew it her arms were around me. She crossed them over my back and pulled me close, pressing her lips to the side of my neck.

I wasn't sure what to do. I rubbed her back like Dragan used to do to me, even though she was much older than I was, while she trembled. Then she pulled away, turned, and retreated.

"Good luck," Jin said. I watched the woman chew on her thumbnail, not looking back at me.

"You too."

Vamp pushed open the door and I squinted into the wind that rushed through, stinging me with ash and grit. The door whipped out of his hand and clanged against the outside wall as the shredded remains of a tarp snapped overhead.

"Does this mean you're in?" I asked him.

He nodded. "I'm in."

"I'll take one bike," I called over the wind. "You guys double up. They might be able to still track me, so probably best if no one's right with me."

"Where are we headed?" Vamp called back.

"The parade must be going by now," I said. "With all the air and road traffic, it'll be a complete mess. If we can lose ourselves in there, we'll have a better chance. Is eyebot running?"

Vamp nodded. I brought up the 3i app and saw that a map of the soldiers' movements had already begun to emerge. From the look of it, security was grouped in clusters at key points and then staggered in between. There were gaps, though—probably by this point they were watching for us, but most of them had been deployed for general crowd control. They weren't guarding the gate hubs.

"There," I said, pointing. "The hub at the intersection of thirty-six and 103rd. It's a pretty straight shot from the edge of the wall."

"Okay," Vamp said. He took a deep breath.

I hugged him, squeezing him hard around the neck as he squeezed back. I tucked my chin into the crook of his neck as we were pelted with rim grit.

After a minute, I broke away, keeping one hand on his chest. I took the twistkey from my pocket and pressed it into his hand.

"If they shoot me down or grab me," I said, "you get him out, okay?" He nodded.

"Promise me."

"I promise."

I stepped out into the howling wind, shielding my face to look back. Vamp was moving toward one of the bikes, and I spotted Nix's eyes shining like embers through the smoke as he followed.

I gave them one last wave, then sprinted back toward the row of airbikes. As I approached, I triggered the key that disengaged the emitter locks and zeroed in on the one that chirped in response. It was a slick-looking black and chrome deal, and when I jumped on the seat, I saw the rearview mirror was adorned with hanging tassels. Each strand was threaded through a row of human teeth. I jerked it free and threw it away as I fired up the bike.

"Thirty-six and 103rd!" I called. Vamp straddled the bike a few spots down, and signaled back.

I opened the emitters, and my stomach dropped as I rocketed up through the stream of wind and ash howling over the top of the lot. Black grit and soot chaff stung my arms, raining against the side of the bike until I cleared the worst of it and was out into the open air where twilight had fallen. The city blazed with light past the wall in the distance.

Off to my right, I saw Vamp and Nix appear in a plume of gray ash. Behind them, the force field glowed faint blue in front of the great wall of the ship's north face.

I didn't know how long it would take for security at the wall to detect us, but I guessed not long. I brought the bike around and locked on to the gate hub's location with the GPS.

Please let this work. . . .

I leaned forward and held on tight as I gave the bike everything she had. Below me, the sea of ruins and rubble became a blur of gray and black.

Less than a minute later, something flashed up ahead. I shielded my face with one forearm, squinting into the light as one of the floodlights found me. A red warning message appeared on the windscreen's heads-up display.

Stop your approach and wait for security to escort you back to the wall.

There wasn't time to worry about what Vamp and Nix were doing. The message flashed as I cut the wheel and the bike spun around 180 degrees in the air. The wave of dust and ash kicked up in the wake blotted out the worst of the blinding light, but the engine sputtered and when I tried to breathe in I choked on it.

I opened up the emitters, and the nose of the bike lurched upward. Hard flecks of rim sediment rained over me as I rocketed up out of the cloud and into the clear night air above. The bike threatened to go over, but I locked my feet in the metal stirrups and held fast as I tried to aim the nose back down.

The floodlight swept back in my direction and found me again as I cranked the throttle, but when I tried to turn, the bike hesitated. Rim dust had clogged up the cooling vents, causing one side to drag. As I dove, I went into a spin.

The skyline streaked by in front of me, and I caught a flash of Vamp and Nix's bike as a warning shot boomed through the night air. I began to slip off the edge of the seat, and struggled to right myself while more warning messages flashed on the windshield's holoscreen: *Stop the bike or you will be fired on.*

I wrestled the spin into a wide spiral. I'd intended to head back down on the other side of the cloud before they could find me again, but I was still way too high and totally exposed.

Don't shoot, I broadcast. I had no idea if they were listening or not. *Don't shoot. We escaped from—*

You are wanted by Hangfei security. Stop your approach to the wall and await a military escort.

I can't, I—

This is your last warning.

I pushed back my heel on the right pedal, killing the emitter that had lost its partner. The bike steadied about ninety feet in the air and below I could see the big, lazy swirl of dust beginning to lean in the night breeze. A shower of grit streaked diagonally through the beam of the floodlight as it zeroed back in on me.

A bright light began to flash from somewhere ahead, and something whipped by on my left like a stream of giant, angry hornets. A beat later I heard the low, rhythmic thumping of automatic gunfire.

Last chance. Stop the bike—

I cut the channel and pegged the forward throttle. As I picked up speed and the wind began to roar in my ears, the turret opened up again. Tracer rounds spat through the darkness below as they struggled to adjust the angle.

There was a break in the shooting and I killed all the emitters at once. The inertia carried me forward, and then my stomach fluttered as the bike began to fall like a thrown stone. I began a free fall down toward the wall where a turret spat out an arc of shell casings. Rounds whistled over my head as I dipped below the line of fire.

Almost there. . . .

Red emergency lights lit up all along the wall, and a klaxon began to sound, echoing off into the night as the wall of buildings ahead rushed forward to meet me.

Another turret opened up as I turned the emitters back on, stopping the bike fast enough to make my tailbone bang onto the seat cushion. More rounds whined past and now I could actually see the guards stationed along the wall below, one pointing up in my direction as two more fought to reposition the turret. One soldier pulled out a handgun and aimed it toward me as I closed in.

I heard the pops as the row of red lights flashed past beneath me, the klaxon so loud now that it hurt my ears. A bullet punched through the windscreen, leaving a single hole in the middle of a web of cracks. Two more rounds hit the bike's underbelly as I cleared the wall and then plunged in between two buildings on the other side.

The street below was filled with a cheering, waving mass of people. As I rocketed past a building face, I saw rows of parade-goers lined up on the fire escape there, shouting as I passed. Masked faces turned upward to follow me as I came in way too fast, and the crowd surged as people scrambled to get out of the way. Up ahead, a set of blue lights flashed and a siren chirped, changing in pitch as I streaked past.

In the rearview display I could make out a sliver of the rim wall between the towering buildings. Red lights still flashed there, but I couldn't see the other bike. The klaxon was still going, but they'd stopped firing.

I sailed over the sea of bodies, whipping out of the side street and into an explosion of colored neon lights, flashing signs, and dancing, singing, screaming people.

The main strip was alive, all four lanes filled with a parade of multistoried floats, marching soldiers, dancers, stilt walkers, and fire-breathers, all moving through a polyethylene blizzard of confetti. Above the procession, enormous balloons depicting the different forms of jiangshi lumbered between the buildings, staring down at the crowd with their huge iridescent eyes.

I banged a left, and my turn went wide as I veered toward the parade line. I banked, just clearing the side of a massive balloon being towed down the street below by a large utility vehicle. Trailing streamers that made up the jiangshi's seaweed hair slapped against the bike's windscreen as I tried to peel away, thumping along the balloon's outer skin. The bike bucked underneath me as I pushed through, cracks from the bullet hole splitting along the length of the windshield until it finally snapped. Half of it broke loose and hit me in the shoulder as it spun off into the air behind me. I bumped the balloon again, then pushed off it with one foot and dove down over the heads of the cheering crowd.

Up ahead, the parade trailed off like a giant, electric caterpillar, the floats and balloons crawling forward down the length of the strip. Floodlights crisscrossed through the sky above while bottle rockets and bags of red dye jumped up out of the blanket of parade-goers like bubbles popping over the top of a soda glass. Designs of sparkling light paint covered the surfaces of the behemoths as they lumbered, venting waves of streamers and confetti in their wakes.

The thumping beat of music swelled as I closed in, so loud that it managed to drown out a crowd that covered every inch of sidewalk below as far as the eye could see. Masks of monsters grinned up from the blanket of bodies, while fists pumped in time with the music. As I passed, costumed dancers writhed and stomped on the tiers of a gaudy float temple, shaking the grave markers above them. Another siren whooped briefly before the techno beat snuffed it out. Blue and red flashing lights were piling up down the street behind us, angry strobes against the frantic light show.

I slipped around the street corner between the face of the building and the temple float next to it. On my left, people were hanging out of the windows hooting and hollering, while on the right a row of skull-masked dancers at window level were writhing, shaking tasseled bronze pasties at guys who leered and whistled across from the building next to them.

The bike's main emitter sputtered out with a series of

loud, electric snaps. Dropping down past two more rows of dancers, I leaned on the horn as the crowd tried to make a hole below.

When the last guy was clear, I killed the engine. The bike dropped the last six feet and crashed down onto the sidewalk.

Chapter Twenty-four

A packet of dye struck my chest and exploded in a cloud of red powder. Another came right behind it as the crowd surged back in around the crashed bike.

I tried to see through the sea of flailing bodies, but between the costume streamers and the shower of plastic bits, it was hard to see much of anything. I stood up on the airbike's seat and squinted into the bright parade lights that shone down from the massive balloons above, cocking my head to bring up the 3i display.

Vamp, where are you?

Here.

The underbelly of another bike veered out over the street above while people cursed at it from the windows. It banked back around to the corner about thirty meters away, and I caught a glimpse of Vamp riding on top, Nix tucked in behind him, as he signaled down at me. He brought the bike down, buzzing the crowd in a tight, descending circle to try and clear them out of the way so he could land. As he dropped down toward the street, he pointed back behind us.

Behind you.

I turned and looked up in time to see a security vehicle coming in fast from above. Its lights were going full tilt, and in seconds the siren wail rose over the cacoph-

ony of music, fireworks, and screaming. The car dove
down at a sharp angle, and the crowd around us back-
pedaled into one another, trying to scatter as the aircar
closed in.

When I turned back, Vamp had the bike down. I could
make out the headlamp shining through the crowd
across the street. He and Nix were struggling to reach me
while a second security vehicle zipped out from over a
side street and disappeared behind the giant parade balloon that filled the sky above us. Its enormous, leering
face gazed down over the procession of floats below it,
light paint flashing in brilliant patterns down the sides of
its serpentine body. Long feathery fins trailed from both
sides, rippling in the wind as it swam through the air.

People scrambled as the sirens grew louder, shoving
each other to try and get out of the way. The ship's floodlight snapped on and a cone of bright white light shone
down over the parade-goers. Bits of paper and other as-
sorted road trash were caught in the gravity field and
formed a cresting wave in the air before sprinkling back
down over the crowd below.

"Coming through!" I yelled, pushing my way through
the crowd toward Vamp. All I could see was a wall of
sweaty chests and armpits. "Move!"

*This is a madhouse. We'll never even make it to the
gate.*

I chanced a look back and was able to spot the vehicle's flashing lights through the crowd. A uniformed man
stood up on the side of my abandoned airbike, pointing
in our direction.

Pushing on, I managed to reach Vamp and Nix and
signaled toward the opposite side of the street. Vamp
signaled back to me as he tapped the side of his head.

Check eyebot.

I brought up the 3i map and saw that the security
team that had just landed back behind me was now vis-

ible as a cluster of red markers on the map, and there were two more growing at each of the block's street corners.

A path between them was clear, at least for now. I pointed again, then squeezed through the crowd and ducked under the street barrier as a group of stilt-walking ghouls approached through the falling plastic flakes. Firecrackers popped overhead as I dashed out across the street, Nix and Vamp hot on my heels. A forest of rhythmically swaying stilts began to close in, towering in front of a pair of giant, glowing, googly eyes that stared out of a monster face behind them. I darted between the moving stick legs and made for the sidewalk as one of them lurched to try and avoid me. The crowd oohed as the guy perched up on top almost lost his balance.

"Halt!" an amplified voice boomed from back behind us.

A shot boomed over the racket, and the crowd around us cringed, ducking their heads as one. A big shirtless guy clipped me and I pitched forward and went down into a forest of legs and stomping feet.

"Vamp!" I screamed. "Nix!"

I tried to get up and got knocked down again. I couldn't see anything, and as I turned, a knee thudded into my forehead.

"Vamp!"

I was woozy but forced myself to stand, grabbing the belt of the guy next to me and hauling myself up. I spun around but didn't see Vamp or Nix anywhere. I'd lost them.

Another shot banged through the air, and a man standing next to me stumbled back. A plastic bag slipped from his hand and hit the ground with a glass pop as blood began to bloom through his T-shirt along his left side. He stared, confused, as the blood began to burble down his side to stain the hip of his shorts red. His eyelids fluttered and he fell back onto his butt.

Through the crowd, I spotted Ligong aiming down the sights of a pistol while people scrambled to get out of the line of fire. I tried to push through, but the crowd had squished together to form a tight knot.

Vamp, where are you?

Sam, look out.

Red laser light flashed in the corner of my eye. I had turned to look for the source when I saw a glowing dot drift down to my chest.

Someone grabbed my wrist. I turned and caught a flash of pink and the ruffle of a suit jacket as Nix scooped me up in one arm just as the shot went off.

I heard the bullet slam into him as his arm tightened around me, and one hand slipped down to cup me under the butt.

Hold on.

The next thing I knew, we were in the air. His leap took us up over the heads of the people piled up around us, and through the snapping tails of his jacket I saw some of them follow our arc, pointing and staring. Festival-goers on the other side of the mob scattered, one pitching off the curb and down between two parked cars, as Nix landed nimbly on his feet and skidded forward, grinding across a patch of street sand to where Vamp was waiting. He held me to his chest and I looked back through the crowd to see Ligong appear through a break in the crowd, her gun aimed in front of her.

The crowd panicked. All of them tried to run at once, spilling into the streets in a hail of honking car horns. I heard the shriek of tires followed by the crunch of plastic and fiberglass as the towering float next to us stopped too quickly and was struck from behind. The tiers of the float teetered, and something snapped inside its frame. A platform above gave way and several dancers fell, gold tassels trailing as they went down into the rows of costumed marchers below. Ahead, people dove to get out of the way of the renegade haan who was barreling toward them with a human girl in his arms.

Up ahead, Vamp waved us forward. Nix dropped me onto my feet as Vamp whipped his arm around and threw something back behind me that caused a thump and a collective groan from the people there. When I turned I saw people spattered with bright red festival dye, some wiping at their faces. Ligong was there, her face looking like it had been covered in a mask of red war paint as she blinked, trying to clear her eyes. She forced one eyelid open and stared right at me as she took aim with the pistol.

Everyone ducked as the gun went off and the slug pounded into the wall next to me. I crouched low and scanned the side street ahead, thinking that if we could disappear into the sprawl we could lose her. At least long enough to get to the gate where, without the twistkey, she wouldn't be able to follow.

I checked the map. Red pixels had begun to appear sprinkled up and down the parade route. Even with the incomplete data I could already see they were forming a net to close in on us with.

Where was the gate? I zeroed in on the GPS marker, and my heart dropped. I'd lost the bike too soon. The hub was three whole blocks from where we were.

"Damn it! Come on!"

Vamp and Nix followed as I bolted, into the alley, sprinting through the blanket of confetti that had accumulated between the buildings there. I darted between the alley shop fronts where shoppers were clustered under flapping canvas signs, then around the side of a metal trash bin where a second narrow alley branched farther into the maze of buildings.

The way opened up into a little blacktop cubby nestled between several buildings where three guys and two girls were hanging out zoning under a string of paper festival lamps. Two of the guys and one of the girls were leaning back against the graffiti-covered brick face passing around a hand-rolled cigarette, while the other girl stood bent over in front of a shirtless guy with her hands on her knees. Her skirt was hiked up and the little bit of rear-end padding she had rippled each time he thrust into her. They both looked bored until the moment a girl, a guy, and a haan all clomped to a stop in the middle of the group. The girl getting pounded went to stand up suddenly and cracked her head on the U-clamp of a rain gutter. She staggered and fell forward onto the pavement as the dude behind her stood there with his dick pointing due north.

A shot went off and I spun around to see that Ligong had entered from the alley behind us. The gang snapped out of it long enough to scatter, leaving the girl on the ground with her bare ass still sticking up.

"Wait," I said, holding out my hands. Ligong stalked closer while two more soldiers marched in behind her. "Just . . . wait!"

Before she could pull the trigger, a gust of wind blew down hard from above, and the lights from an aircar filled the cubby. Everyone looked up as a siren chirped, echoing through the small space as a military police car dropped down toward us.

One of Ligong's soldiers took aim with a Gauss rifle, but before he could get a shot off, heavy gunfire erupted from underneath the descending vehicle. His body jerked, and the front of his armor flashed hot red as the rounds bored through the plating there. His chest exploded in a shower of blood, muscle, and bone while his arm, carried by the weight of the weapon, slid right out of the armor's sleeve. It tumbled across the pavement, his body thumping down after it. The girl had regained consciousness and was back on her feet, staring in horror as she pulled her skirt back into place.

I looked up, shielding my eyes, and saw a face I recognized through the car window.

Kang.

The back door opened, hydraulics hissing over the sound of the engine as the car floated over the cracked pavement.

"Come on!" Kang shouted. Ligong was signaling toward the vehicle while the girl turned tail and disappeared down the alley.

Kang had already screwed me once, and I didn't like the look of the back of that car. There were no interior handles to open the doors again, and a metal grate separated it from the cab. It would be stepping into a cage, but right now the alternative was worse. I climbed in, the other two hot on my heels.

"Stop!" Ligong barked over an amplifier.

Bullets thudded against the outer plating of the aircar as she fired at us, her aim following as we rose past the second floor of the buildings on either side. Pressed in the corner next to Vamp and Nix, I cringed as a round thumped into the safety glass right next to Kang's head.

He leaned back and slid open a small window in the grate that separated us so he could look back.

"You okay?" he called back.

"Just go!"

Kang looked down over the dome of his armored shoulder pad and spotted Ligong below as she gave up on the pistol and picked the heavy Gauss rifle up from the ground, shaking the severed arm away from it. I saw her aim it up toward us and squint through the scope.

Kang turned the stick and the aircar yawed just as the shot went off. A thin trail of smoke flashed past the window and I saw the round punch through the brick face of the building that appeared in front of us. His hand moved to the console, gloved fingers dancing across the array of controls there while he kept one eye down on the street. A heads-up display flickered onto the windshield in front of him where a camera's reticule locked on to Ligong below and then zoomed in. A motor grumbled under the seat somewhere and I saw a gun turret's long black barrel move into view as Ligong adjusted her aim.

"Go!" I yelled. "Up! Up!"

The rail slug popped through the vehicle's thick glass, and in a flash, Kang's head exploded into a shower of gristle that painted the cab's interior red.

The vehicle shuddered, threatening to stall, as his body slumped over in the seat. One lifeless hand slipped off the control stick, then flopped down as we began to list toward the building face to our left.

"Shit!" Vamp spat. "Goddamn it!"

"Hang on!" I said.

I slipped my arms and head through the opening in the grate, almost getting stuck at the shoulders. I managed to grab the control stick and then wriggle the rest of my body through as another hole popped through the glass inches from my nose.

"Sam!"

I shoved Kang's body out of the way as best I could and reached one foot down to the pedals underneath. When I found the emitter control, I stomped on it and cranked the stick.

We spun, veering toward the building until I saw myself reflected in the glass there, looking very small behind the wheel of the big vehicle. We hit, crunching against the glass until it exploded and crashed down over us.

"Turn!" Vamp yelled from behind me.

"I'm doing it!"

The racket drowned both of us out as we scraped along the building side, plate glass buckling, then shattering as we went, until I managed to pull the nose around. I veered, and pointed us down the alley in the direction of the gate.

Something hit the undercarriage with a heavy thud, and red lights began to pop up on the dash.

I shoved the stick forward, and the buildings sheared past on either side as we accelerated back toward the main drag.

Chapter Twenty-five

The car was going down. In the rearview mirror I saw red fluid spraying through a trail of black smoke, and even with the emitters cranked we were losing altitude fast. Two more vehicles had picked us up and were pursuing, but we were close. The intersection, and the gate hub, were just up ahead.

"Hold on!" I called back.

There wasn't any time to be delicate about it. I took us in, siren wailing the whole way as people scattered. We crashed onto the pavement right in the middle of the intersection, sparks spitting as we dug a short trench through the blacktop.

The car lurched to a stop, the tail coming up off the ground and threatening to take us end over end before it slammed back down again. As soon as we stopped moving, I found the door control and slammed my palm down on it. All four doors sprang open.

"Move!" I barked. "Go, go!"

The people queued up at the gate hub were looking at the vehicle now, pointing and taking pictures with their phones as the other two aircars closed in from over the street behind us.

"Out of the way!" Vamp barked. "Move!"

"Halt!" a voice boomed from above. "Stop where you are!"

The crowd backed away as the shit storm closed in, and we ran for the gate. Through the portal, I could see a street somewhere across town, and through the buildings there I saw the distant lights and fanfare of the parade going on only three blocks behind me.

"Vamp, the twistkey!"

He dug in his pocket and pulled it out, handing it to me. I found the socket, guided the key in, and turned it.

The air crackled as the view through the gate faded away to nothing. In its place, a dark, interior view appeared where I could make out a grimy floor and stained, pitted concrete walls.

"Freeze!"

I turned and saw that our pursuers had landed, and Ligong was heading toward us as more soldiers piled up behind her.

"Now!" I said, pulling Vamp's arm. "Come on!"

I stepped through just as the first shot went off behind us.

The sound waves of the shot caught up the second I plowed through the gate, and then the waveform flattened into silence. Out of the corner of my eye, for just a second, I could see a bullet suspended there and then we stumbled out the other side.

The room was dimly lit by the glow of battery-powered lamps, mounted on mold-stained cinder block walls. Two bullets struck the wall ahead, one exploding in a small shower of concrete and the other knocking out one of the lights with a loud pop. I turned around in time to see Vamp come through, and there, through the gate behind him, was Ligong, making a run for it.

Sam, forgive me.

The message from Dragan popped up from the 3i tray just as we came through. I went to stick the twistkey back in, to collapse the gate before Ligong could reach it, but there was no socket.

"Change it back!" Vamp snapped.

"I can't!" I turned to Nix. "She's coming. Shut it off!"

"The gates are on a centralized grid," he said. "I can't just shut one down. It will revert to its original point of exit once the timer expires, but not before then."

Sam, forgive me, I— Another shot zinged through the air and struck the wall as we scrambled back, away from the doorway. Ligong was closing in fast with her group of soldiers. They were going to make it with time to spare.

"Back," I said, waving down the corridor behind us. "Go!"

I darted back between them, patting Vamp on the ass as I went. They followed as I bolted down the broken corridor, following the string of lights and trying to keep my footing on the uneven floor. My toe banged into something and I nearly tripped as I passed through a rusted metal hatchway. A heavy door was pinned there under the buckled ceiling above. Farther up ahead, the hall opened up into a dimly lit room.

"That way!" Ligong's voice echoed down the corridor behind us. I risked a glance back. She'd put a lock on the gate, holding it open, and more soldiers were moving through.

Nix stopped suddenly, skidding along the floor and then reversing course.

"Nix, what are you doing?" I shouted, slowing as Vamp stopped between us.

"Keep going," Nix called back.

Flashlight beams appeared down at the far end of the corridor as Nix grabbed the edge of the thick metal hatch and braced himself as he began to pull.

"It's stuck!" Vamp called. "You'll never—"

Plaster and concrete rained down from the ceiling as

with a low groan, the door began to move. When he'd managed to pull it away from the wall, he repositioned and jammed one shoulder against it. Vamp sprinted back and joined him, putting his back to the door and pushing against the wall with his feet. The hatch caught as the footsteps approached from the other side, but then came free as more rubble sifted down from overhead.

A shot struck Nix, the slug bouncing off the material of his jacket as two more rounds sparked off the metal hatch. The door moved a little farther, coming within a hand's width of being shut before sticking again, this time for good.

"That's it," Nix said. "Go."

A body slammed against the other side of the hatch and I heard a grunt as one of the soldiers tried to move it but couldn't. The beam of a flashlight shone through the gap as footsteps pounded on the other side, piling up in front.

"Out of the way!" I heard Ligong snap. Her face appeared in the gap, and when she spotted us she tried to sneak through but couldn't.

"Go!"

I turned and made for the end of the hallway, Ligong screaming a string of threats after us that got lost in the racket and echo. I darted through the doorway with Vamp right behind me, then Nix. I slammed the door behind him.

"Get this thing open!" I heard Ligong bellow back in the distance. "Now!"

Sam.

"He's here," I said, pulling up the chat.

"That hatch isn't going to hold them long," Vamp said.

I waved him away. "Shut up, he's here. Hang on."

Dragan? Dragan, it's me. Where are you?

I couldn't let them do it.

"Damn it," I muttered.

"Where is he?" Vamp asked.

"I don't know. I don't think he's picking me up. He's just firing off text, like in a loop."

"He may still be comatose," Nix said, "or semiconscious."

"Okay," I said. "Okay, then, let's find him fast."

"How are we getting out of here once we get him?"

"Nix, can you gate us?" I asked.

"I can form a freestanding gate, with end points at three points in Hangfei."

"What about the ship?"

"One on the ship."

"Okay," I said. "Let's find them and then let's get out of here."

I stepped forward into the shadows, and my foot came down on something that crunched. When I looked down, I saw the floor was covered in black powder that had sifted down into the cracks around old, buckled linoleum tiles. Lying sprawled there facedown was a skeleton with the rotted remains of a lab coat tented over the bones. I'd stepped on the bones of the forearm, snapping them under my heel.

I jerked my foot away. There was a second body next to the first one, also facedown, and a few feet from where they were I spotted a clipboard partially buried in the black powder.

I shined the flashlight beam through the room. It had been some kind of office at some point, but the walls had crumbled to blackened framework, exposing the surrounding rooms. As I passed the beam through the empty spaces, I saw rows of desks piled with mold-covered computer equipment, wires trailing underneath layers of dust and ash. Some of the desks still had figures slumped over them, mummified bodies fused to their swivel chairs and claw hands still at their keyboards. Pens rattled in a dusty coffee mug as the low vibration hummed through the air.

The 3i tray wobbled at the corner of my eye, the display warping as my hair suddenly stood on end. Particles of dust rose from the floor and hung suspended in the flashlight beam for a few seconds before drifting back down.

"I'm getting major interference," Vamp muttered.

"It was on the wet drive footage too," I said. "Nix, what is that?"

"Our power grid extends into the colonies, but it all converges here. The field generators must be above us."

"Is it safe?"

"It should be."

I shined the flashlight back down at the floor, casting the shadows of old toppled equipment as the beam drifted past. Fresh footprints were tracked through the soot there, shoe and boot tracks overlapping along a path that led through the room.

"Dragan came through here," I said. "It was on the recording."

even for you. I know that you will

Dragan's looped message stopped short as the vibrations swelled, rattling in my chest and causing dust to drift down from the bowed ceiling. It drowned out the sounds from behind us, the hissing of the torch and the sounds of the soldiers, before fading back to a steady hum. The chat window warped, and the connection dropped.

I chewed my lip. "He's close."

Dust rose around my feet as I pointed the flashlight and followed the footsteps into the gloom.

Chapter Twenty-six

Scaleflies flitted past as we moved deeper into the ruins, forming a small swarm that buzzed toward a set of heavy metal doors up ahead of us. They'd clustered over the jagged bits of glass poking from an empty window frame on the right-hand door, while trails of them buzzed in and out. A swath had been cut through the dust and grease at the base of each door as if they'd recently been opened, and the footprints stopped in front of them.

Vamp moved ahead and pulled one of the doors open, waving away the cloud of disturbed flies so I could shine my light through. The way looked clear.

The chamber on the other side had been sheared in half, the floor coming to an abrupt stop off to our left in a wall of packed dirt and stone. The ragged ends of three huge pipes jutted out there up near the ceiling, torn free from their joints during the collapse. Lime had caked around their rims where brown water condensed and dripped under the slow escape of steam.

"Sam—"

Another surge in the vibrations drowned out Vamp's voice. They got so intense that the 3i cut out and stemmed off Dragan's text messages, which I was kind of glad for. The pipes shook, and something above us creaked, low and ominous. I pointed the flashlight up toward the ceiling and saw spindly haan constructs creep through the exposed wiring and ductwork. Snaked in and around the old electrical system were shiny coils of filaments like I'd seen in Shangzho. Nestled in and among them were unfamiliar devices that hung like flies in a spider's web.

The room, or what was left of it, seemed to have once been some kind of control center. The hunkered shapes of computer consoles and equipment, long dormant and speckled with mold, sat in the gloom with stools and swivel chairs at the helms. Wires hung from the damaged ceiling, while power and data cables ran from the workstations, through the grime to disappear into the rubble. The far wall of the hub was dominated by three huge rectangular windows that looked on into blackness, huge fractures marring safety glass that must have been a meter thick. I shined the flashlight around, until it swept across a soot-streaked sign mounted on one crumbling wall.

DEEPWELL BIOTECH LAB: AUTHORIZED PERSONNEL ONLY.

"Deepwell," I whispered.

The echo of the humans who'd run the place lingered here—coats draped over chairs, personal photographs, and wrinkled, overlapping newspaper printouts whose edges had warped were taped up here and there—but like Shangzho it now carried that distinct haan fingerprint. Graviton plates covered a section of wall, disappearing through a dark hole in the ceiling, and black, shiny scales had formed over the floor in clusters. Scaleflies crawled over the abandoned equipment and swarmed through the air, carrying their messages to and from haan who no doubt lurked somewhere nearby.

A row of glass domes, some kind of specimen jars, covered a work surface that ran the length of the room's far side, and I could see clouds of flies bouncing around inside. The jars were fixed to bases where pinprick indicator lights flashed, and slimy tubes trailed to a bank of haan equipment behind them.

I moved farther into the room, sweeping the flashlight over the news clippings. I peeled one of the stained photos off a soot-covered console and wiped it on my shirt. It showed an apple, floating in midair. I held it up so Vamp and Nix could see.

The apple floated in the middle of a makeshift wooden shack that had been surrounded by a sandbag enclosure where armed soldiers stood guard. Across the other side of the sandbags, people had gathered near a row of sawhorses, and through the wooden shack's open doorway a hanging plastic tent was visible. Hazy figures stood inside.

SECURITY ERECTED AROUND "FORBIDDEN FRUIT," the headline read. I tossed it down onto the desk and looked at the next, which showed a picture of Fangwenzhe, shining brightly above the Hangfei skyline.

NEW STAR APPEARS IN NIGHT SKY.

"New star ..." The date on the article put it fifty years or so ago. I blew dust from the paper, trying to make out the writing underneath.

> ... no explanation for the sudden appearance of a previously uncharted star closer than any recorded ... astronomers are unable to explain ..."

"This doesn't make any sense," I said. I looked at Vamp, the paper still dangling from my fingers.

Fangwenzhe had always been there. Stars didn't just come and go. They didn't just appear from out of nowhere. It wasn't possible. Even if it somehow had, people would know. Astronomers . . .

"What are you in here for?"

"Telling the truth."

"Sam, we've got to move."

"He knew," I said. "That guy, Jin, back in the prison. It's why he was there."

Vamp tried to take the paper and I snatched it away. I folded it and slipped it into my pocket.

"Sam, which way?"

I looked around the room, trying to think back to the images on the video recording. They'd had to climb before they arrived in this room. They'd scrambled up a collapsed section of floor. . . .

"There." I pointed toward the corner where the tiles sank, sloping down to a big fracture that had opened up into a large open space below. Electric light flickered down there, casting jerky shadows.

Vamp leaned over the edge and peered down. "Are you sure?"

"I think so."

When I turned back to him, the flashlight swept back around and passed through a large, open section of wall to his right, where a human face stared back at me from the shadows.

"Shit!" I yelped, nearly dropping the light. Vamp and Nix both turned as I steadied the beam.

The face belonged to a Pan-Slav man. He looked like he might be dead, but he wasn't shriveled like the other bodies. His skin looked fresh, if ashen. He sat with his knees up by his chin and wrapped in some kind of black membrane that had him stuck to the wall. His eyes stared back at me, blind and unfocused, while his mouth hung open.

He wasn't alone. As I moved the light through the room, I saw there were more in there like him, men and women all wrapped in the same kind of wet, leathery cocoon.

"Holy shit," Vamp said under his breath.

I looked over and followed his light to a series of jagged, broken tiles along the edge of a giant sinkhole. Beyond the edge a great, yawning pit in the floor dropped down out of sight, but from where we stood I could make out what looked like spines, or huge, thick bristles ringing the interior. The ceiling had a similar hole directly above it.

"She has them in stasis," Nix said. "Storing them for later use."

Through the crumbled wall next to it, electric lights flashed from an array of equipment and live monitors that displayed crowded columns of haan text. The room had been some kind of laboratory, with a big metal work surface surrounded by broken-down equipment. A light shone down onto the metal tray that trailed clusters of disconnected tubes and wires.

Mounted on the wall behind the equipment were Haan holoscreens that displayed a dizzying amount of information. The rows of alien characters overlapped one another several layers deep, in varying brightness and color, including blank areas that I suspected I just couldn't see. I couldn't read any of it, but popping from the clouds of haan text were images of human body parts ... arms, legs, heads, various organs, then tissue, cells, all the way down to the DNA. They formed the jigsaw pieces of a broken-out human figure.

The worktables and trays were filled with equipment that included scalpels, bone saws, and hacksaws.... Some were shiny and new, but some were old, like the rest of this place.

"There's something behind them," Vamp said, pointing at the haan displays.

I looked, and saw that there was an image behind

them. A large diagram had been on the wall, now covered by the haan monitors. I stared at the fractured image, but there wasn't enough showing to get a full picture, just disconnected glimpses of what appeared to be thick black strands, and what looked like bundles of worms. I couldn't piece them together to form any kind of whole that made sense. Every edge I followed showed something unfamiliar, something that had no human correlation. Panic scratched at the back of my mind as I tried to connect the dots and couldn't.

"Nix . . ."

He'd crept up behind me.

"You shouldn't be here," he said in my ear. "You don't want to see this."

"What is that?" I asked. He didn't answer.

I looked back to the surgical equipment, the blades caked with black tarry blood and spotted now with fuzzy blossoms of mold. A row of metal coolers ran along the far wall in the gloom behind them, marked 1 through 13-A, and 1 through 13-B. Spots of mildew had grown across the walls, finding purchase on the microscopic remains of something that had once been spattered there, and then later scrubbed away.

"This is from before the Impact," I said.

"Yes."

"You were here before the Impact."

"Yes."

"But how? You crashed. . . ."

I looked down at the muck-stained metal tray. There were metal bands still rusting in there, restraint straps that were twisted and bent, but not broken. There were dozens of them.

"What did they do?" I asked.

"They didn't know what he was," Nix said. "They couldn't have."

"So, what did they—"

"The same thing Sillith is now doing here with your people," he said. "They studied him."

I shook my head, not wanting to believe it in spite of what I saw in front of me. No human could see something as sophisticated as a haan and then just strap it down and dissect it. Men like Hwong maybe, but even then for a reason, however twisted. Not just out of curiosity.

"Our young don't recognize you as thinking creatures," Nix said quietly. "Not at first. It's why the surrogate program is so important. This was the same. You cannot form empathy for something you can't recognize or understand. When our envoy stepped through the gate—"

"But you look so much like us."

Something banged from back down the corridor behind us, and I jumped, knocking into one of the trays and sending surgical tools clattering down onto the floor.

"They're in," Vamp said. Something clanged farther in the facility, echoing through the empty hallways. "We've got to go now."

"There!" I heard Ligong bark, her voice echoing through the halls. "It came from there! Move!"

"Sam, snap out of it!"

I was still staring at the crisscrossing streaks of black blood when Vamp grabbed my wrist and pulled, dragging me along through the doorway.

The haan couldn't have been here before the Impact, I thought as I followed him. *They didn't come here on purpose. Everyone says so. All the official records, everything on TV, and in school, and on the feed says so. They didn't come here on purpose.*

Did they?

How could they not have? a tiny voice whispered,

struggling to be heard from some deep place in the back of my mind. *What would the chances be that they would accidentally come across us in a universe so vast?*

Vamp tugged my arm again, and I looked back at the row of metal coolers one last time as I stumbled away after him with no good answer.

Chapter Twenty-seven

I slid down the slick, soot-covered slope with Vamp and Nix close behind me. Vamp looked unsure about heading down into that hole, but he looked even less sure about the sounds coming from back down the corridor. There was no way they could have cut through the hatch so quickly, but they must have found another way around because the sounds were getting close. When I glanced back through the gap in the broken floor above, I saw a flashlight beam sweep past.

The tiles ended abruptly in front of me, splintered support struts jutting from underneath along with the broken ends of rusted pipe-work. There was a drop of maybe five feet down to the corridor below where hot, wet air billowed up like the breath of some giant creature. Vamp joined me at the edge, peering down.

"I'll go first," he said. "I'm taller. I'll help you down."

Back behind us, a burst of radio chatter echoed through the hallways, rising over the constant low rumble of machinery. Heavy footsteps, the unmistakable tromping of many boots, grew louder as they approached.

"This is crazy," I muttered, looking back down into the darkness.

"I know," Vamp said.

I glanced back at Nix. "Is she down there?"

Nix drew in a long, deep breath, then slowly released it. I felt it vent against the side of my neck, until it petered out into that soft bone rattle.

"Yes."

"How close?"

"Close."

He dropped from the edge, down into the shadows, and I watched him touch down on the floor below, where his eyes cast a mellow glow in the darkness.

"You ready?" I asked Vamp. He nodded, and I put one hand on his chest. "I'm sorry I dragged you into th—"

He touched my cheek, then leaned forward suddenly and kissed me on the mouth. His lips were full, and soft, and I felt his fingers move through my hair, cradling the back of my head. Before I knew it I felt the rough stubble of his face under my palms, and I was kissing him back. He let it linger just long enough, and then broke.

"Just in case," he said, and jumped down to join Nix. I hesitated on the edge, my cheeks hot. Vamp was a good kisser.

I dropped down after him as a flashlight beam floated past the hole above. Two more joined it, casting through the room.

"Here," a woman's voice said. One of the beams stopped at the top of the slope, shining on the tracks we'd left behind.

"This way," Nix whispered.

We followed him down a corridor that was nearly pitch-black until the dim light in the distance took on the shape of a doorway. Something slammed back behind us, and I heard the sound of voices accompanied by the jingle and clatter of equipment. I picked up the pace as we approached the light, and I was able to make out a white cinder block wall somewhere on the other side of the doorway there.

"Jesus," Vamp muttered.

In the glow cast through the doorway ahead, I saw an empty set of clothing that was plastered to the floor. A pair of shoes lay empty in front of a pair of blood-drenched pants and shirt. A few scaleflies scurried over the sticky pile, and had formed a crawling mass above the empty neckline. Where the head would have been, the floor was painted with a slick of red-black, littered with bits of white and gray.

"It's her," I whispered, putting my arm in front of my nose and mouth to try and block out the stench. "Innuya, the woman from the recording. We're getting close."

In the face of it, the jealousy I'd felt when I'd first learned about her seemed stupid. Dragan had cared for her. He cared for her son, who had to watch her die in such a horrible way. He'd tried to save them, the way he'd saved me.

I stepped over the remains and through the doorway, squinting through salty sweat as we entered a large, open space where hanging lamps glowed from the bowed ductwork exposed high above. It looked like it might have been a storage warehouse at one point, broken boxes piled between rows of metal shelving and a grimy forklift lying on its side. Ahead, a space had been cleared and I could make out flashing lights and their reflections that shimmered on the ceiling above.

As we crept down the row, toward the source of the light, I saw the movement of little haan constructs, hundreds of them skittering along the shelves and the cracked concrete floor.

"Look," Vamp breathed.

Rows of shelving had been cleared and in their place six large, circular vats formed from thick plastic sat arranged in a hexagon. Each vat contained a single haan female, steeping in some kind of chemical stew while tubes dangled down around them from a cluster of electronics above. Their faces were all identical, saucer eyes glowing coal red and ringed with blue coronas. They floated there, just beneath the liquid whose surface rippled with the underground vibrations. They looked dead at first, but as I pointed the flashlight beam and moved closer, I could see their hearts pulsing slowly and a nervous jittering inside each skull.

"Nix, what is this?" I whispered. "Who are they?"

"They are clones of Sillith."

"What are they doing?"

"She is using them to develop and grow genetic samples."

Vamp stepped closer, shining his light into the face of one. The clone didn't seem to notice him as he moved the beam down into the liquid where what looked like little worms were wriggling around.

"This goes far beyond a simulated pandemic," Nix said in my ear. "Whatever she is attempting to create, you carry a prototype inside you. This place has to be destroyed before—"

He broke off, cocking his head, and a moment later I felt her. The mites jumped alive and sent a jolt of signal into my brain. The force of it made me stumble a little, and I grabbed on to Nix for support.

"Sam, what's wrong?" Vamp asked. He stepped in to get an arm around me, but I got my footing back and squirmed away. Sillith had tapped into the mites and I could feel her in there, worming into my mind. Her voice whispered from inside my head.

You shouldn't have come here.

"She's here," I said.

A lithe figure dropped into view from somewhere up above, seeming to pour down onto the floor, where she landed on the balls of her feet without a sound.

The hatred she felt bored into my mind, and the sheer intensity of it made me feel physically sick. Acid crept up my throat as she stepped closer, her molten red eyes staring through coronas of blue flame. She'd dropped the masquerade of the combat armor, and appeared as a nude haan female, an exact duplicate of the six in the vats. Her face was severe but beautiful in its haan way, an oversized, flawless mask with a stiff expression, and the two coiled shapes beneath her translucent skull flexed, causing the network of tissue around it to ripple in response. She had a long, slender neck and strong square shoulders, her chest sloping down to a pair of breasts that hung above her rib cage. Inside each I could make out a network of squiggling veins branching from the nipple and ending in a series of shadowy nodes behind them. Something was moving inside her belly, and a smaller, more subtle movement slithered beneath the skin above her crotch.

"You're too late," she said.

"Sillith," Nix said, stepping forward. "Reconsider this."

I felt another surge of anger and contempt as the smaller brain fluttered beneath the mass of the larger.

"Reconsider?" she asked. She took a few slow steps toward him.

"It's their world," he said.

"They had their chance. This planet has already been pushed past the point of sustainability. That wasn't my doing."

"It doesn't have to—"

"Here!" a voice barked from behind us, and I felt a vague skip through the mites, anticipation interrupted by annoyance and then anger as she looked over my shoulder. The pupils in each did a slow revolution, as anger grew into fury.

I turned and saw soldiers streaming in through the doorway, armed with assault rifles. They immediately dispersed, breaking into formations and taking aim at

Sillith as Ligong moved in behind them, carrying a Gauss rifle in one hand. Translucent red beams flickered pencil-thin through the fog, their points clustering over the throbbing mass inside Sillith's chest.

"Clear!" Ligong snapped back through the doorway, and unhurried footsteps rapped sharply in the sudden silence as Governor Jianguo Hwong came through the doorway.

A low, almost inaudible purr or growl began to emanate from deep in Sillith's chest as she watched the soldiers part for him. He marched between them, and as he moved past the metal drums, he glanced back and forth at the clones there like he was performing a military inspection.

"Go back with the others," he said without looking at me. "All three of you. Now."

His neck was still bruised from where I'd choked him, and the tone of his voice didn't do anything to suggest he was there to help us, but none of us were about to get between him and Sillith. I followed Vamp and Nix back, past Ligong, whose eyes promised death, until we reached the formation of soldiers and moved behind them.

"Didn't expect to see me here, did you?" Hwong taunted, facing Sillith. He stood tall, fearless, as he addressed her like one of his lowest grunts. Without the surrogate mites he couldn't directly experience her intent, but I could, and I felt all of her anger and all of her hatred as it focused on him like a laser.

"Yes," she said, her voice low and smooth. "I did."

Hwong drew a heavy rail pistol from his holster and pointed it at the nearest clone's head. I heard it charge, and then emit a flat boom. There was a brief flash of light as a sizzling hole appeared in the side of the clone's skull. Fluid began to jet from holes in either side of the vat; then a shock wave thumped under the liquid's surface as the skull shattered like an eggshell around a murky cloud of black blood and brains.

"If you so much as twitch," Hwong said, jabbing his index finger at her, "my men will open fire on you and we'll just see what's left when the dust settles."

That actually made her pause. Her eyes moved from Hwong to the soldiers, scanning slowly down the length of the formation. When she spoke again, her voice had changed. It became more subservient, and softer. A husky, even sexy quality had crept in, but through our connection I could tell it was a lie. Ligong picked up on it too.

"I have honored my part of the deal," she said.

"This wasn't part of the deal," Hwong countered. "I saw Specialist Shao's wet drive footage. Whatever you were planning ends right now. Hand over the boy."

"And then what?"

"My men will destroy him and bury him along with everything else down here under a ton of rubble."

She hesitated. "Your enemies will eventually—"

"Maybe so, Sillith, but our deal is off. Hand him over."

A surge of hostility flooded from Sillith, and her posture changed subtly as she took two steps toward him.

"And if I don't?" she asked. The voice that issued through her voice box had grown dangerous, rising in pitch and taking on a piercing, dissonant tone. Hwong almost took a step back but held his ground.

"We are the only chance you have," she said. "Your race is pathetic. You look down your nose at the rest of this world, ready to scrape them off rather than deal with them but this city, and this country you are so proud of is pathetic. Your whole race deserves the slow death it has fostered—"

"Is that some kind of threat?" Hwong asked. "Because one word from me will trigger the failsafe and wipe what's left of your race off the surface of our planet."

"This is not your planet!" She took three more quick steps toward him, and every movement in her body implied a threat. The shape inside her skull bristled as her muscles flexed and coiled around the bone underneath. Even the alien movement inside her guts seemed to have focused on Hwong as she stopped with only ten yards separating them, her hands flexed into claws. It was clear Hwong still believed her to be as breakable as she seemed, though, and despite the display he still stood his ground.

"You won't detonate those weapons because you wouldn't dare," she said, glaring at him. "Your leaders want the defense shield we can provide, and the promise of more power to come, and they wouldn't allow it."

"They aren't here, Sillith. I am. I am empowered to give the order."

"You only think you have power because we let you believe it. We stay in your settlements and let you stand guard outside so that you will feel superior, but you aren't. This isn't your world."

"This is our world!"

"This was never your world!"

"It was always ours!" Hwong snapped, barking his words out suddenly in a spray of spit. "Our world! Our planet! You are refugees at best! Any benefits you get, any privileges you get are all at my discretion. Do you understand me? You continue to exist at all here because I let you! Me! No one else! Do you understand me, Sillith?"

"I am warning you," she said, lowering her voice. "If you attempt to go back on our deal—"

Hwong glanced back and signaled Ligong. "Kill her."

The gunfire that erupted was immediate, and pounded through my ears even as I plugged them with my fingers.

I could feel the rapid-fire reports rattle through my chest as shell casings spat through the air all around me, and I crouched to try and stay out of the line of fire.

Vamp and Nix hit the deck next to me, Vamp shielding me uselessly with one arm as bullets sparked off the shelving in front of us. Sillith had disappeared from the spot where she'd stood, but my eyes caught a flash from the shadows above and I looked up to see a pair of flame red eyes where her body hung at the peak of its leap.

"There!" a voice boomed. Lasers traced conflicting paths through the hazy air as the soldiers attempted to retarget her. Nix slithered an arm around my waist, and I was jerked away from the soldiers with Vamp in tow as Sillith plummeted down through a cloud of steam.

She landed so hard I felt it through the floor, and when I looked back I saw the soldier between us jerk in surprise as his rifle flew from his hands. The weapon went soaring through the air, end over end, as she lashed out toward him. His body seized, and he let out a scream as his arm came free in a spray of blood. Before I could see what happened, he was falling to the floor in three big pieces as, at the same second, the two soldiers next to him had their weapons ripped away from them.

From the ceiling above, constructs were being shaken loose and dropping down like pedaling, squirming rain. I turned away, swatting a small, crawling machine from off my shoulder where it landed as I bolted through the fray. Soldiers were regrouping, adjusting to account for Sillith's sudden new location. Bullets whizzed by over our heads as we approached a cluster of crouched soldiers who had begun firing a heavy volley at something behind us.

Lights like hot coals appeared in the murk of the vats, and I realized they were eyes. One of the clones broke the surface in a shower of fluid and grabbed the soldier standing nearby. He screamed, but before he could even turn around, something struck his back and his chest exploded outward. The remaining four clones erupted from their vats as his body fell to the floor, clambering over the sides as the soldiers fired.

The curtains of wire filaments that extended up toward the ceiling high above us were undulating now, rippling, as more and more movement began to fill the room. Nix led us past one of the shelves as a burst of gunfire managed to punch through the neck and face of one of the clones. There was another doorway on the far side of the room, and Nix was signaling, pointing toward it.

A torso, trailing ragged shirttails in the place of legs, went arcing over our heads and crashed into the shelves farther down. As we made a run for it, I glanced back to see Hwong faced off against Sillith. He took aim with the rail pistol, but before he could fire, it was torn out of his hand. Sillith slammed one palm into his chest and he staggered back, nearly falling to the floor before righting himself. He sucked in air with obvious effort, his face dark and his normally cool expression twisted in pain. The fibers of his light combat armor flexed as he unsheathed a wicked-looking knife from his belt and angled it toward her.

She went for him and he ducked, whipping around in a circle and slamming the point of the knife into her side. Before she could grab him, he'd pulled it free and spun around behind her. He lunged again and buried the blade deep into her opposite side.

He was clearly expecting her to be crippled if not dead, but Sillith didn't appear fazed at all. Hwong wrenched the knife free and skated back, preparing to strike again, when suddenly his body seized as if he'd been grabbed by invisible hands. The armor plating creaked, and his eyes bugged out.

"Shoot the fucking thi—" he grunted through his teeth.

His arms shot out by his sides to form a cross. Then the armor plates cracked and sprang away as they both rolled suddenly, hands spinning 360 degrees and the shoulders twisting out of their sockets. Under the suit the material of his shirt tore away along with rubbery strips of skin until the two limbs were pulled free. They hung in midair for a second, and then thumped down onto the floor next to him.

Before he could even scream his feet launched up off the floor. Armor cracked apart like an insect's shell as his legs were splayed, splitting him down the center. I turned away at the last second, covering my mouth as I heard the guts splash down onto the floor.

The mites tingled with sadistic delight as Sillith took a moment to admire what she had just done. I felt her satisfaction drum down into the pleasure centers of my brain not only for squashing a human but also for silencing Hwong, who she hated even more intensely than most.

Why does she hate us so much? I'd felt arrogance, annoyance, and frustration from the haan . . . even contempt at times, but never hatred and never anything approaching this level. Something deep inside Sillith made her hate us and everything we stood for in a way that I couldn't even begin to understand.

She was still soothing that hatred, letting the sight of Hwong's mutilated body slake it even if it was only for a minute, when Ligong took aim with her rail gun from across the room and fired.

She almost got her too, but Sillith spotted her at the last second and the shot went wide. She never got a second shot off. Sillith lashed out, and the fog between them was disturbed by something I couldn't see. The gun leapt from Ligong's hands and spun away, punching through the curtain of filaments like a rock through a spider's web before clattering across the concrete to strike the wall next to the doorway ahead. Ligong flew forward, across the room to Sillith's waiting hand, which clamped down on the chest plate of her combat armor.

The armor whined as Ligong attempted to wrestle free, but before she could the collar of the suit broke free with a crunch and one half spun across the floor. The chest plate was peeled free then by some invisible hand as she was forced to her knees, and Sillith's right fist reared back behind her.

"Screw you, you fuck—" Ligong spat as Sillith let her fist fly.

It punched straight through Ligong's breastbone, forming a deep pocket in the middle of her chest. The life went out of her face, one eyelid drooping as her struggles stopped cold, and her arms fell by her sides like hanging lead sashes.

Sillith shoved her away like a piece of garbage, and the body tumbled back into the fray still going on around them. Then, without warning, she turned and ran. Steam swirled in a wake behind her as she darted through the doorway on the other side of the room.

"Shit," I said. "Go, go now."

"Where the hell is she going?" Vamp asked.

"She's going to get the kid," I said. "She's going to take him through herself before it's too late. Come on!"

"Sam—"

I shoved past a soldier, his uniform spattered with blood, and ran as fast as I could after Sillith.

Chapter Twenty-eight

03:10:41 BC

I snatched up Ligong's rail gun from the floor next to the doorway, hefting the heavy weapon as I stormed through. As soon as I did I stopped short and skated across the slick floor a few feet before regaining my balance.

The far side of the room was littered with piles upon piles of human bodies. Some were so badly eaten from the inside out that they were little more than empty skins, torn open and slopped down. Others had empty guts, empty rib cages, or were missing limbs. Sillith's failed experiments covered the floor, stacked four high and even higher in the corners, hundreds and hundreds of bodies, decaying and oozing together into a swamp of bones and jellied flesh.

Vamp coughed, holding one arm in front of his nose and mouth, as he clomped to a stop next to me and Nix moved in behind him.

Sam.

The 3i chat came back, flickering on in the air in front of me.

"Dragan's back on," I said. "He's close."

"Where did she go?" Vamp asked.

I turned, clamping a hand over my nose and mouth to keep from gagging. Across the warehouse floor the concrete had been broken away to form a huge, jagged sinkhole in the floor. Trickles of water wandered through the creeping green-black lines that covered every surface, and a haze of steam boiled up under the ceiling.

Old hospital bunks with their bedding removed were stacked along the walls, while trays of equipment that looked new were positioned at the mouth of the pit. Wires snaked down the walls in thick bundles, then wandered across the floor and down over the edge of the hole.

As I gazed down over the side, I saw the pit plummeted down into darkness. Arranged in a ring about six feet down from the top were a series of metal framed bunks, their heads fixed to metal supports that left the length of each hanging out into the open air. There were maybe twenty total, and beneath them, a few feet down, was another ring, and below them another. I counted eight levels before they were lost in the shadows below. Glassy, hexagonal plates interlocked to form paths between the beds, starting at the sinkhole's lip and then following the wall down into blackness.

"There," I said, pointing.

The plates were graviton emitters. Sillith was marching down the wall, dragging Alexei behind her as she passed under rows of beds that fanned out over them like archways.

I crept to the edge of the pit and looked down. Lying in each bed was a person, the eyes covered with a slick rubber mask and tubes sprouting from the nostrils. Warm, wet air rose from down below, creating a low moan as it passed through the bed frames and ruffled the sheets. Some of them were stained with blood, and some were more red than white as the hot air inflated them like sails and then subsided, letting them settle back down over the bodies underneath. When the blanket of one of the closest beds stirred, I saw exposed ribs underneath, and a dark, glistening gap where the man's insides had been. Somehow he was still alive, his eyeballs moving back and forth behind the thin rubber mask.

"Sillith, wait!" I shouted.

More gunfire erupted from back the way we'd come as I edged closer to the mouth of the sinkhole. I squatted down, and when I touched the surface of the nearest hexagonal plate with one palm, it seemed to almost stick there.

Forgive me, I couldn't—

"Vamp, come with me," I said. He hustled over as I put the sole of one shoe down on the pathway, then the other. They seemed to be drawn toward it. Not stuck like glue, just a gentle but insistent pull.

"What are you doing?" he asked, grabbing one of my arms. I squirmed loose.

"It's okay," I said. "They'll—"

The words stuck in my throat as my butt came up off the floor and in a flash the whole world flipped around me. I heard Vamp bark something and his hand clamped down on my wrist in a death grip as I stumbled but didn't fall.

I was standing on a smooth metal walkway at the base of a circular tunnel that extended forward into darkness, where Sillith was dragging Alexei. To my left and right, the edges of metal bunks extended upward, each at a slight inward angle. A few feet forward, another set of bunks were propped behind them, each with a man lying on it completely upside down. The bedding and the men on them seemed stuck to the bunks, the sheets hanging toward the far end of the tunnel like they were stuck in a perpetual strong breeze.

Looking up, I saw the bunks ringed the entire tunnel. All of their occupants' feet pointed in toward the middle.

"Sam!"

I turned back around and saw the tunnel ended abruptly in that direction into what appeared to be the middle of a big open space with no floor or ceiling. Across the chasm were metal rafters, with light fixtures that were pointed toward me.

Vamp was standing on the wall just at the bottom edge of the tunnel as if he lay on an invisible platform.

"Come on," I said, gesturing for him to follow. "I'm going after her!"

He shook his head, but before I turned I saw him sit down and put his feet on the plating. Ahead, Sillith got snagged on one of the bedsheets and tore it away. Not sure which way to fall, it did a weird tumble in the air as it tried to zero in on any one of the eight walkways that lined the tunnel at regular intervals. When it couldn't decide, it fluttered down the tunnel in front of her like some kind of festival ghost, rippling away until it disappeared into the shadows.

"Shoot her," Vamp called from behind.

"I can't. I might hit—"

I stopped, staring as a rush of hot air stirred the sheets around me.

"What?" Vamp asked, closer now.

"There." I pointed up ahead. "There!"

I could only make out his hair, but it was all I needed. The salt-and-pepper sweep had become so familiar I'd have recognized it anywhere, and when I did my mind seized on it.

"Sam, hold on!"

I sprinted down the walkway to the bunk and stopped short, grabbing fistfuls of the sheet. As I pulled it away, a lump rose in my throat, and my eyes filled with tears until his face blurred in front of me. It was him. It was Dragan.

His broad chest rose and fell slowly as the air current disturbed the black and gray mat of hair there. The tattoos were his, indelible markers that labeled him mine, and nobody else's. The military tat on his shoulder, the dragon coiled across his chest . . . they belonged to Dragan—no one else. It was him, and he was alive.

Sam, forgive me, I couldn't let them do it. I know—

I moved onto the edge of the bed, and as my second foot left the walkway, the world flipped again and I fell down into the bed next to him. Over the edge of the bunk, the pit went down into oblivion, Vamp staring back up at me from where he stood on the wall at a ninety-degree angle.

"Dragan!" I yelled, pulling the sheet away. He didn't move. I saw the more recent tattoo that ringed his right forearm, braided patterns bordering the name Xiao-Xing, and my voice broke as I shook him again. "Dragan, wake up! Wake—"

I choked as pain stabbed deep into my guts and I doubled over.

I couldn't let them do it. I know how it looks, but I couldn't.

"Sam!"

Vamp came to me as I slid off the bed and tumbled back onto the graviton plating, my stomach lurching as the world spun around me. I went down on my knees, curling over until my forehead touched the metal plate. Something was moving in there, growing. I felt his hand touch the back of my neck, his thumb stroking the knobs of my spine as he leaned close to whisper in my ear.

"Sam, can you move?"

"It hurts."

"I know, but it's got to be now—"

He let out a grunt as something whipped past me and hit him in the chest. He staggered back on his heels, his mouth gaping, and then fell onto his back.

"Vamp!" I screamed, but he didn't respond. He didn't move.

. . . but I couldn't let them all die, not even for you.

I made myself uncurl. It felt like there were pins in

there, and a bad stitch stopped me for a second, but I was able to sit up and rest back on my heels. My breath was coming fast and shallow.

"Sillith, wait!"

She stopped, and I could see there was something in her free hand. She activated it with her thumb, and a point of bright, white light appeared in front of her like a tiny sun.

"Oh, no."

The point expanded into a large hexagon with blazing white edges. Through it, I could see brick face and peeling paint on the side of a metal trash bin. Graffiti was scrawled next to it in sloppy Pan-Slav characters.

Alexei struggled a minute more and then his body slumped. Sillith grabbed him by his neck and hurled him through the gate.

I glanced back toward Vamp, who still lay sprawled on the tunnel floor next to Dragan's bed, but there wasn't time. I hobbled toward Sillith as back behind me—or above me, I suppose—something exploded with enough force to shake the bed frames mounted to the tunnel walls.

She turned, the gate control in her hand, and I knew she was about to close it. If she did, Alexei would be stuck on the other side and that would be the end of it.

I knelt, propping the butt of the rail gun against one hip and raising the barrel. The scope's laser wandered as I tried to steady it, but there wasn't any time left. As soon as I saw the red dot drift over her midsection, I pulled the trigger.

Despite the weapon's size and how heavy it was, it had almost zero kick. It just made a low chuff sound. For a second, I had thought it hadn't gone off at all when a tunnel appeared through the haze of fog followed by a loud boom. At the same instant, Sillith looked down at a neat hole that had formed in her belly.

The slug bored straight through, then punched into the tunnel wall next to the gate. When the shock wave erupted inside her, she jumped as if she'd been electrocuted. An explosion of blood blew out from in front and behind, some of the mess splashing down onto the graviton plates and the rest raining down the tunnel behind her. A wobbly ring of beaded blood formed in the air behind her as the drops circled the tunnel's gravity field, then broke apart a moment later.

She went down on one knee. One hand reached forward to stop her fall, coming down in the muck as an aftermath of bits splashed down around her. The pieces seemed to squiggle and morph as they hit, some forming half-glimpsed shapes of hands, limbs, or feet before one by one they warped away and disappeared in a series of firecracker bangs. The air around her distorted, and it looked for a second like she was going to go too, but she didn't. Instead she raised her head, and her molten eyes glared down the tunnel at me.

I adjusted my aim, the laser beam cutting through the mist as it homed in on her, but before I could fire again, something clamped down on the barrel. It was a hand, Sillith's hand, somehow, flickering like a hologram or a ghost.

I held on, trying to steer the laser against her grip, when another huge explosion went off, and with a shower of sparks from somewhere behind me, the power went out and engulfed the tunnel in darkness.

Chapter Twenty-nine

03:03:03 BC

Debris rained through the tunnel, peppering my back and shoulders as some went up and some went down. Then the last of the graviton plating's charge left it, and I felt the tunnel swivel beneath my feet as my center of gravity changed. All at once the tunnel ahead became a straight drop and I pitched forward, legs pedaling in the air, while Sillith stared up from below. I flailed with my free arm and managed to grab on to one of the sheets of the bed mounted next to me, pulling it free and dragging it down to the next frame below me, where I managed to land just as Vamp flew past.

"No!"

I leaned over the side in time to see him jerk to a stop, as if he'd been impaled on an invisible spike. Something had him, and turned him over like a spider spinning a fly in its web.

The soldiers shouted in the darkness, and I could make out the winding down of machines as I struggled to keep hold of the rifle. By the light of the gate's outline, I could make out Sillith's plated fist still curled around the rifle's barrel, but as I was dragged toward the edge of the bed frame, the hand began to flicker. It warped, going out of focus, and then coming back, while in the darkness below Sillith's smoldering eyes left trails of bloodred light.

How is she doing it? How . . .

Sillith's hand turned from delicate smoked crystal to tar black. Her skin turned rubbery, pocked with huge open pores as the fingers merged together to form a coiled, wormlike tentacle. A scalefly crawled out of one of the pores and onto my hand as I followed the tentacle down the length of the tunnel where the rest of her body shuddered, uncoiling into a writhing mass. Her blazing red eyes dimmed, the light fading as they collapsed into a cluster of glossy black marbles.

"Things aren't always as they seem. . . ." Nix's words came back to me as I stared, unable to look away. I couldn't see her clearly in the darkness, but I saw enough. It wasn't a hallucination. As impossible as it seemed, part of me recognized that a veil had begun to break down, allowing me to see, for the first time, the truth.

More wormlike cilia slithered from the mass and wrapped around the rifle, tearing it from my hands, and I saw a long, ropy arm whip away as she smashed the weapon to pieces against the tunnel wall.

My hand shook as I groped for my flashlight, unclipping it from my belt and switching it on. I could hear her coming, a heavy, dragging sound, and I cast the jittering beam toward her as she rose a full head taller than she had been.

The light passed over Vamp, who hung suspended by several more of the black ropes, then reached her, and the strength began to go out of me. I saw a shadowy mass, a squirming ball in a nest of tangled arms and legs. The delicate, almost beautiful latticework of bones had been replaced with some kind of wiry webbing that formed a flexible mesh surrounding the organs. I caught a glimpse of those two familiar brains lurking under a murky blister filled with cloudy, amber soup, and her heart, pulsing near the center where damaged tissue dangled around the gaping hole left behind by the rail gun's slug.

All of it was crawling with flies. So many flies scurried over, in, and out of the creeping silhouette that her skin looked alive. My mind struggled to find a familiar shape—any familiar shape—but between her movements and the shadows I couldn't.

I understood then how she could reach so far and to so many places. How Nix's severed arm could become three. The thing below me wasn't just Sillith, but all of them. Something, some haan technology, forced us to see what they wanted. We saw something harmless, something symmetrical and familiar. We saw something delicate, and even beautiful, but it was a lie. It was an illusion, and for whatever reason that illusion had just broken down, if only for a moment.

Her body sprang apart, strands bursting free from the mound, forming groups, and then parting again as they carried her body with an ease and grace that reminded me of a machine. She lunged for me, and the flashlight fell, spinning end over end before plunging through the gate. I scrambled back to get away from her as the tunnel filled with a low, eerie rasp, overlapping whispers that hissed over a mechanical clicking sound. Light flickered from above then, and shadows moved across the bedding in front of me as electronics began to power back up. The graviton plating hummed back to life, and I rolled off the bed to land in a crouch as the tunnel wall became the floor again.

"... I will eat him," Sillith said, her voice burbling up out of the fading clicks and rasps, "and I will make you watch."

"Sam, move away from her," a second voice called. It was Nix.

A shadow moved across the tunnel wall as he came toward us, a creeping, undulating mass that was already beginning to change. In seconds, the wriggling mound condensed into a form that was recognizable, understandable, and comforting. By the time I turned, the drapes of Nix's suit were flowing behind him like a cape, and his face looked the way it had always, handsome and familiar.

I know what haan look like, I thought desperately. *I know what they look like, and feel like. I know—*

"Sam, move away," he called again.

Something whipped around my ankle and jerked my leg out from under me so that I fell hard on my back. The grip around my ankle squeezed like a steel band, and I cried out as I was dragged down the tunnel toward Sillith. I skidded across the floor, groping for something to grab on to. My fingers closed around the edge of one of the bed frames, but were wrenched loose just as fast as Sillith hauled me down the tunnel, where I crashed onto my chest.

I pushed myself up, standing, as Sillith limped toward me, one arm hanging at her side like deadweight and the other dragging Vamp. The dead arm flickered and two were displayed there for a second, merging again as she closed the distance between us. Blood flowed freely from somewhere I couldn't see, and left a wet crimson trail behind her as she came.

She hurled Vamp aside, then lunged and I ducked as her fist struck the tunnel wall, sending shards of shattered plating over my head. I stumbled away, back toward Nix, and her hand clamped down on one of the bed frames as I ducked behind it. Metal groaned as she wrenched the frame free from the wall and hurled it away.

My heel struck a ridge in the fractured plating and I fell back onto the floor. I looked up just in time to see Sillith's balled fist bearing down on me like a piston, and I rolled. She struck the floor as I pushed myself up and stumbled away, out of her reach.

"Sillith," I said, backing away, "wait...."

Nix removed his tablet from inside his jacket as he sped past me, but before he could reach her she grabbed him by the throat and bore down on him. The tablet fell from his hand, spinning across the floor, as she slammed him down in a spray of shattered tiles. Blood spattered from the spot where his head struck, and the wound cast a pattern of dots across the wall as she hurled him back the way he'd come. He rolled to a stop in a heap and didn't move.

"Nix!"

The mites lit up and I staggered, as if she'd somehow found the strings that made me move and had taken control of them. She was dying, delirious. The room around me flickered as the incoming signals found their way into my visual cortex, and I fell back, the tunnel dissolving away under a flood of alien images.

I saw cities, great cities, greater than anything we'd ever even dreamed of. They were so huge, so vast, and yet so perfect and clean that they made Hangfei look like nothing but campfires scattered in the dark, and above them, in a sea of scattered stars, hung the bright, shining ball of Fangwenzhe.

I understood then. The star hadn't always been there. It had never been there. The others might look the same, but no matter what we were told, Fangwenzhe hadn't been a star in our sky. Not until the haan came.

"Where are we?" I asked her. I sensed Sillith move closer, until she loomed over me.

"You cry about the Impact," she croaked, "but you don't know what pain is. All of our history and all of our accomplishments were wiped away in an instant, and replaced with this."

She said it with disgust, but the signals she radiated were of despair. For a moment all I could feel was her fatigue, and suffering, and as strange as it was I found myself feeling sorry for her.

"How?"

"We never left our planet," she said. "We were look-ing for another habitable world, a way to sustain multi-ple instances of our planet in dynamically created universes, unoccupied but habitable, when we found you."

"You didn't crash. . . ."

"No," she said. "The opportunity to meet another race was too tempting. We tried to travel to your world, but the gate imploded. Our dimensions overlapped, and then merged, collapsing your universe."

"Our universe . . . ?"

"Was destroyed."

I stared, struggling to grasp what she was saying.

"After the collapse the field surrounding our world broke down, and in your universe's last moments, your planet's instance was pulled through to replace ours. It began at the opposite side of the planet and circled the globe in hours. In our last minutes we managed to estab-lish a field around the facility, to stop the collapse there, but by then it was too late. All that was left is what you call Shiliuyuán, the facility where the experiment took place."

"Our universe . . . ?"

"Your universe is gone," she said. "It died with my world." Her voice was a little softer, and I could feel that she meant it, but then the moment passed, and the de-spair shifted back toward resolve. Anger. Violence.

"Wait," I said. She swung again and I just managed to launch off one leg to leap out of the way. My hip struck the floor as her heel came down on the spot where I'd been, fracturing the concrete there with a heavy thud.

"I'm sorry," she said, "but it doesn't matter why. My species is perfected. It deserves to survive. There is a moral imperative to ensure that it survives, even at the expense of yours."

She went for me, and I ducked, but she got hold of my arm and when I tried to twist loose, her grip closed and pain shot up all the way to my shoulder. She forced me down and my back slammed onto the floor of the tunnel, knocking the wind out of me.

I looked for something, anything to knock her off with, but it was no use. She was too big, too heavy, and too strong. Even after the hit she took from the rail gun, she could still squash me like a bug and there wasn't anything I could do to stop her. A few more gunshots went off as my reaching fingers found the edge of something hard.

Looking over, I saw Nix's tablet. Straining as hard as I could, I managed to hook my nails over the edge and pull it just close enough to grab. My other hand was still free. If I could just . . .

I managed to get the tablet in front of me and place the finger of my other hand on the screen. Carefully, I traced the hanzi strokes. The screen dissolved, and the honeycomb storage cells appeared under the gate. There were items sitting in the different pockets that I didn't recognize, but none of them were what I was looking for. I swiped the field, and the cells began to scroll past.

When the shape jumped out at me, I plunged my hand through the field, feeling the icy air on the other side chill the sweat that covered it. I curled my fingers around the grip of the electronic wand with its coiled needles and pulled it out of the Escher Field just as Sillith swatted the tablet away.

She reared back, but before she could strike again I jammed the needles into her side and squeezed the grip.

I had no idea if I'd done it right, or if it would work. She slammed my wrist into the floor, and the wand fell free, clattering away. She squeezed, and I screamed.

The bones were going to break. I could feel them start to go, but then suddenly the strength seemed to go out of her. Her fist went slack, and her whole body shuddered.

I sensed confusion, then pain, and then finally fear as the reality of what had just happened sank in. She looked down at the site where I'd stuck her, clutching at it with one hand as she hauled herself back up onto her feet.

With a loud snap, Sillith's entire body erupted at once into a huge blob of water. Her skin snapped away like a wrinkled, broken water balloon as the payload of water flew apart and came crashing down in a huge splash.

I closed my eyes, covering my face with one arm as the warm flood gushed over me, followed by a rain of cooler drops and mist.

Wiping my face, I opened my eyes in time to see Sillith's head go thumping down the tunnel. Swaths of her skin lay quivering on the graviton plates between me and the gate that was just starting to collapse. They had begun to flicker, the air around them rippling.

I looked down at my chest and saw what looked like a giant black amoeba lying there, its network of slick tentacles plastered across the floor like veins on either side of me. I sat up and shoved it away, kicking it into a pile as it rolled down onto the wet floor.

I hauled myself to my feet, facing the gate, where I could still see Alexei as he lay in a heap on the other side. It would be closed in a matter of seconds.

Sam, forgive me. I couldn't let them do it. I know how it looks, but I couldn't let them all die, not even for you. I'm sorry to leave you. I know what that means to you, but I'm just one man and you're strong enough to make it on your own now.

The soldiers were going to destroy this place, and everything in it. I only had one shot. I wasn't sure if it would work, but it was the only shot I had.

One shot. Save my father, my friends, or save them.

I couldn't let them all die.

Don't worry, I sent. *They won't.*

I sprinted for the gate, grabbing one of the flickering sheets of skin as I passed. It peeled up off the floor, trailing sticky threads, a sickening, still-warm streamer that tickled against my palm like millions of tiny, squirming worms.

The gate shrank, closing like an iris to choke off the alley on the other side as I ran. When I reached the edge, the world around me skipped, turning dark before flashing back again.

It's going to go, I thought, pulling the skin to my chest. *It's going to take me with it.*

I jumped through the gate, an electric jolt shooting down my back as my head brushed the glowing white edge. Everything slowed down for a beat, and then I came out the other side.

Freezing cold braced my skin, chilling the sweat that covered my body as I fell and rolled to a stop on the gritty pavement. Alexei was there, stirring now.

"Don't move," I called, my breath pluming in front of me. He looked down at his arms and hands in horror as small back bodies began to worm their way up from beneath the skin. I could see their wings pulling free, and their hooklike legs pawing at the air as they struggled.

"*Jej!*" a Pan-Slav voice barked from the alley mouth. "*To chto proishodit tam?*"

I caught a glimpse of a man dressed in a long wool coat and carrying a machine gun as I ran to Alexei.

"Don't move!"

One of the flies wriggled free and extended its wings. I swatted it down onto the ground and stomped on it, dropping to my knees in front of Alexei and throwing the skin around both of us.

Please let this work. Please—

"*Ostanovit'!*" the guard yelled, raising his weapon as he marched toward us.

I looked back through the collapsing gate and saw Nix, his pink eyes staring back at me. He stood in the tunnel next to a second gate he'd opened, while a cloud of flame erupted behind him. Vamp was with him, conscious now and struggling to run after me as Nix held him back. Slumped in Nix's other arm was Dragan.

Nix pushed Dragan through and forced Vamp in after him. He had turned then to grab a woman from the bed behind him when another explosion went off, and a column of flame roared down the tunnel.

"Nix!" I shouted.

In the second before the fire took him, he closed his gate. I saw him, a dark shape engulfed in the brilliant blaze, and then Sillith's portal winked out.

"*Ostanovit'!*" the guard yelled again. He stepped in front of us, pointing his rifle.

Sillith's remains quivered one last time. The world hitched again, the walls of the alley warping in front of me, and then flashed away.

Chapter Thirty

2:59:29 BC

I awoke to darkness, phantom tickles from Sillith's slimy skin still playing on my neck and shoulders. My body felt weightless, suspended in warm, thick fluid, and when I reached in front of me I couldn't find the surface.

"Don't panic," a voice said. It came from the 3i's audio plug, tinny and faint. I flailed, struggling to swim toward what I thought was up, but it was like trying to move through oil, and if anything, I sank deeper.

"Don't panic," the voice said again.

I pulled the 3i display up, my jerky movements sending windows and pages spinning every which way. The air burned in my chest.

"Breathe," the voice said. I shook my head.

"Yes, you can."

I struggled again, panic welling up inside me.

"Trust me. Calm down, and breathe."

I didn't trust the voice, and even if I did my brain wouldn't cooperate. It wasn't until I began to suffocate that my body gave in and out of desperation sucked in the breath that I knew would kill me.

It didn't. I sucked warm liquid in through my mouth and nose, and it gushed down my throat into my lungs. The sensation was horrible, but instead of choking, relief flooded through me. It felt as if I'd taken a big breath of clean, crisp air.

"See?"

I nodded.

"Good. Breathe."

I relaxed, and let myself get used to breathing the heavy stuff. A contact request appeared on the 3i, the pink heart pulsing in time with my own. I accepted it.

Nix?

"No. You know me as Ava."

Right. The new haan female. The one who I first approached, and who sent Nix to kill me.

Where am I?

"You are on what you call the ship," she said. "You are safe."

Why can't I see?

"There is nothing wrong with your eyes. There is no light for you to see by, that's all."

An image of Sillith flashed through the fog, the real Sillith, and panic spiked. I jerked again, sloshing in the darkness.

Dragan.

"He is alive."

I shook my head. *He was—*

"He is alive. Your friend Vamp is with him. They are both okay."

My body relaxed, a little. *The kid?*

"Also alive. The engineered larva have been removed and destroyed. He will no longer be a danger when he leaves."

And Shiliuyuán?

She paused, just a beat, before responding, "Destroyed."

What happened to the people down there?

Again, the pause.

"Gone."

I felt her presence, then, a tentative approach through the surrogate cluster.

"We were able to heal your father," she said. "He is still weak, but he will survive. You will all be returned to Hangfei shortly."

What do you—I cut the message short. I wanted to know how much of what I'd seen was real, and what else the haan might be hiding from us. I wanted to know what the haan's real intentions were, what the exact nature of the deal they'd made with our government was. I wanted to know if the men who made that deal had any idea of what they were really dealing with when they made it.

I wanted to know all that and more, but it occurred to me that with Sillith dead, along with every human who had planned the burn, there might be no one left who knew how much I'd learned. It was possible that, for all Ava and the rest of her kind knew, I was still unaware of their secret.

"What do you wish to know?" Ava prompted.

I was wondering if you knew anything about Nix.

"Nix has not returned."

Is he dead?

"He has not returned."

I wasn't sure how I felt about that. We'd been through a lot, he and I. I'd raised him, and he'd helped me now, a lot. If I was honest, I knew I wouldn't have succeeded without his help, but I couldn't get the images out of my mind. I told myself it was the lie, the deception, and not the way they looked, the way they were, but I don't know. I think it was both.

I want to go home.

"Shortly."

Thank you.

"You have done us, and your people, a great service, Sam," she said. "It will not be forgotten. Had you and

your father not intervened, it might have meant the end
of both our species."

Both?

"As we need you, you need us. If we don't help you
ascend, you will not survive. Remember this."

Her presence lingered just for a moment, like a hand
on my shoulder that was reluctant to move away. I had
started to ask what she meant when there was a tingle
inside my head, and I felt sleep come. It rushed in, sending me into blackness so fast I barely had time to think.

"Don't judge us based on the actions of one individual." Her voice had grown very faint.

My body felt weightless, like I was adrift in space, as
the 3i began to fade. The pink borders flickered, and began to disappear.

"We care about you . . ."

The 3i went dark, and the blackness closed in.

". . . and as promised, we will save you."

Chapter Thirty-one

336:42:03 AC

The elevator squeaked as it made its way up, and I adjusted my gear's strap on my sunburned shoulder. It had been a long, hot day, and the cold air dribbling down from the overhead vent felt like heaven. I closed my eyes and looked up, letting it cool the sweat on my face.

"Sam?" a voice asked. I opened my eyes a slit and saw that the ad box screen had lit up gray.

"Don't start," I warned.

"You could always take the stairs," the A.I. pointed out, and I sighed, still looking up into the vent.

"Go ahead."

The screen flickered, and an image of a man in uniform appeared. He was handsome, square-jawed, and had perfect features. His uniform was clean, crisp, and sharp. He stared out of the screen at me, not smiling, and his piercing eyes met mine. I didn't know if he was an actor, a virtual construct, or a real soldier, but his eyes were dead-on. They had that same intense, confident, powerful look that Dragan's had.

He didn't speak. No music played. No logo or crawling text appeared. A few seconds later his image faded and was replaced with mine, a shot taken when I'd first stepped into the car. I looked sunbaked and sweaty, my hair greasy and wind-mussed. My eyes looked glazed and tired.

I got a good look at myself, wondering if the A.I. had tweaked it or if I really looked that ragged, when the image faded again. In its place appeared a combination of the soldier and me. My face and body, in a smartly tailored version of his uniform. The sweat was gone from my face. My hair was impeccably groomed, styled even shorter than it already was and not a one out of place. The tired look left my eyes and was replaced with that same look of stony, confident power.

The image stayed there for a minute. Then the logo for the United Defense Force appeared, with block letters underneath: BE MORE.

The words, and the image, faded. I smiled, laughing once through my nose.

"That's a good one," I said.

"Yeah, that one gives me chills," the A.I. said.

"I figured it would be butt implants or something."

"I do have several ads in that category."

"Maybe next time."

The elevator stopped, and as the doors squealed open I stepped out into the elevator lobby.

Our new building was nicer than our last one, and in a nicer part of town. Not posh by any stretch, but nice. After a month it was starting to feel like home finally, and things were beginning to approach normal again.

As I headed down the hall, I noticed a sticker on someone's door. The logo had been popping up in the subway, and on everything from bumper stickers to T-shirts. It showed a silhouette of the PSE, with three nukes about to strike it.

Hwong's death was a big deal. Pretty much every media outlet covered the terrible news nonstop for weeks, telling the story of how he was killed by Pan-Slav bombers during a visit to the border zone. The whole city was in mourning at the loss of a hero, and their hatred for the Pan-Slavs and everyone who lived there had all but boiled over. Chat rooms and netcasts were glutted with cries to fry them into a giant field of slag.

A month earlier, I would have been chanting right along with them, but a lot had happened since then. I'd never been able to get the image of that soldier with the concrete saw out of my head. He'd acted on Hwong's orders and Hwong, not one to be content with stickers and online venting, had actually tried to do what the anonymous masses were calling for. He had done a lot for us, and I couldn't ignore all that, but I couldn't be sad that he was gone either.

I rounded the corner and crooked my neck, lighting up the 3i and bringing the holographic window to the front. I did a quick spin through the social taps, sending out an update that I was off work and back home. A message immediately dropped into the tray from Vamp.

Check this out. There was a video attachment.

I set it aside, and as I headed down the hall I sent back a response.

I will. It's my last night here. Talk to you tomorrow.

When I got to the front door, I tapped my badge to the scanner and waited for the snap of the bolt. I went in and put my gear down next to the wall on my right as the door swung shut behind me.

"Hello?" I called. A light was on in the kitchen, but it was quiet. I expected to hear Pan-Slav chatter, something I still seemed to hear all the time in spite of Dragan's efforts to wean the kid off it, but there was no conversation, no TV, no music, just the hum of the air conditioner.

I crossed the room toward the kitchen and found Dragan sitting at the table there. There was an expensive bottle of anise liquor in front of him, and two shot glasses, one in front of him and the other in front of the empty chair across from him. An ashtray sat between the glasses, along with a fresh pack of cigarillos whose tips had been dipped in Zen oil.

He smiled when he saw me, but I could see something else behind the look. His eyes were thoughtful, and serious.

"What's all this?" I asked him.

"I figured we'd spend your last night here hanging out, just you and me. Like old times."

I hadn't expected it. When I first told him I was moving out, it seemed to make him mad, but he was so relieved I was alive that he didn't harp on it. Afterward, as the day got closer, he kind of clammed up more and more. I'd been waiting for a fight, or something.

"You know it's not because of you, right?"

"I know. You're twenty, Sam. It's time."

"I'm not going far."

"I know," he said. "I'm still going to miss you, though."

I crossed around the table and leaned down to hug him. He put his arms around me and squeezed, holding me the way he used to when I was little, the way that always made me feel safe. We stayed like that for a while, until he patted my back. Then I kissed his cheek and stepped away.

"I'll never be far," I said.

"Same here."

"So, where's the brat?" I asked, moving to the free chair and sitting down.

"Ling's got him for the night."

"Lucky her."

He cracked the bottle and poured out two shots. He held his up, and I clinked it with mine before we knocked them back. The liquor was sweet, and smooth going down.

I looked at the pack of smokes and the ashtray. "You gonna let me smoke in the apartment?"

He shrugged. "You do it all the time anyway."

"When you're not here."

"Go ahead."

I reached for the pack and peeled the foil off, then opened it and held the smokes under my nose. They smelled good. I drew one out and pinched off the tip containing the Zen oil, dropping it in the ashtray. Dragan grinned.

"Sorry," I said, sticking the cigarillo in the corner of my mouth while I fished out my lighter.

"Don't be. You're better off."

"Yeah, well, you don't have to look so happy about it."

"How long has it been?" he asked.

I shrugged, lighting the smoke. "A while." It had been exactly thirteen days.

"What changed your mind?"

"Got tired of being fuzzy, I guess."

Dragan's grin turned to a smile, a real smile that made crow's-feet spread from the corners of his eyes. He nodded, and the smile faded as his look turned serious.

"About what happened," he said, putting the shot glass down, "at Shiliuyuán Station."

We hadn't talked about it since that day, not really. We'd talked about everything that led up to it, and how we both managed to get out, but we'd never talked about the main thing, the big thing.

I nodded, and felt my throat begin to burn. I guess I didn't think I'd make it out without him saying something, but I was afraid, terrified of what he would say.

"I left you," I said.

"You did the right thing, Sam."

I shook my head. "I ran, and left you both there to—"

"You didn't run," he said.

"I did, though."

"You made a tough call," he said, leaning forward to rest his elbows on the table. "You put your own needs aside and made a very tough call. You could have lost people who are important to you, and I know what that means to you, believe me. You knew that, but you chose to save them. That was the right thing to do. The life of one forty-something-year-old man isn't worth the lives of millions."

"It is to me."

"And still, you made the call. I'm proud of you."

I swallowed, feeling relieved and sad at the same time. "I thought you might feel like I betrayed you or something."

"Is that what this is about? Why you're leaving?"

I shook my head. "No, not that. It's just . . ."

"Time."

"Something like that."

He poured out two more shots and I sucked in smoke and held it while took the second shot, blowing it away while gazing out the window. The sun had just dipped below the skyline's staircase row of the Bojo Towers, and off in the distance, beyond the rust brown, one swatch in the sky had turned a particular shade of pink.

"You ever hear from your haan friend?" Dragan asked.

I shook my head and rubbed my latest tattoo. I made sure to have it inked on my left arm and not my right, but I think Dragan still wasn't sure what to make of it. I turned it up and looked it over, the redness around the edges of the band still visible in the fading light.

NIX.

"He's not my friend," I said.

"Then why the tattoo?"

"We're bonded. And I owe him."

"But he's not your friend?"

I wondered where he was now. I thought about going to Shangzho, to try and find him, but I couldn't bring myself to go there. I couldn't bring myself to be surrounded by them, to put myself in their hands like that. Maybe he was okay, and like us he was just kind of lying low, and keeping the boat from rocking too much, but every time I checked his chat icon on the 3i, the little heart was gray.

"He's not my friend."

"Is that why you withdrew from the surrogate program?" he asked.

I shrugged. He didn't say anything for a minute, but when he did, his voice was low, and serious.

"Sam, what did you see down there?"

I hadn't told him. I hadn't told anyone, not even Vamp.

"Nothing," I said.

The haan's deception bothered me, but I could, in a way, understand it. If that's how they really looked, they were right to think people would freak out because I still shivered when I thought of it. What really bothered me was Fangwenzhe. There wasn't an astronomer in the country who would say it hadn't been there forever, and yet it had only appeared in the sky less than fifty years before. Anyone who contradicted that disappeared, like that man Jin, who escaped the meat farm with us. The haan might cloud our minds, but that lie wasn't just theirs; it was our own. Fifty years of isolation, propaganda, and information control had made an entire population believe something the rest of the world had to know wasn't true. They'd worked together on that, and who knew what else?

Why?

The foreigners, the people in the ships massed up around us, they'd been trying to tell us. They still were, through the signal Hwong had labeled a cyberattack. Outside the range of the haan's influence, what else did they know? What were they trying so hard to warn us of?

A fat scalefly buzzed around the overhead light before lighting down on the tabletop, drawn in by the sweetness of the liquor. It sat there, its single compound eye staring up at me as it rubbed its hooked legs together.

"I know how important the program was to you," Dragan said. "You love taking care of them."

"I just need a break from it, I think."

He knew me well enough to know there had to be more to it than that, but he didn't press. The truth was that I missed having one around. I really missed it, but I couldn't look at the haan in the same way anymore. I wasn't sure I would ever be able to again.

Another message from Vamp popped up about the 3i tray, and began to flash an urgent orange.

You need to see this. I looked back to Dragan, and saw concern in his eyes. He had begun to suspect something was wrong.

"You know," he said, "if you had seen something, something you weren't sure you could talk about, you could tell me. You know that, right?"

"Yeah, Dad, I know."

I hadn't meant to use the word. It just popped out, but as soon as it did I could see that it meant something. His expression only changed a little, so little that someone else might have missed it, but it was enough. I smiled, and squeezed his hand.

"Mind if I put some music on?" I asked.

"Go ahead."

I headed into the next room and took the opportunity to check out what it was that Vamp thought was so important. The video file was small, just a clip of something. I dropped it into the media player and moved it to the foreground as I pulled up the music tuner on the TV.

As soon as the recording began to play, I could see it was part of an eyebot log. It was video recorded from the app after it tagged a couple of security guys. A few seconds in, I saw one of the soldiers was Pei Ligong.

This was in the Pot, I realized. *This was taken in the old man's apartment, from my feed.*

The view turned back to the kitchen doorway as one of the soldiers stepped through. The little girl stood nearby as he approached the others, holding up the sheet of bloody remains he'd found in the trash. Part of a matted hospital gown was plastered to it, and a circle appeared around it with a message.

The girl wore this.

It was true. The gown was just like the one the girl had been wearing in Dragan's wet drive recording.

The soldier passed the girl, and behind him she and the old man, the one I was sure had died, looked right at each other. The looks in their eyes didn't quite fit, somehow, like something was passing between them.

Vamp, what am I looking at?

The video highlighted the open bedroom door, and another circle appeared over the mattress, which had a big bloodstain on it. The old man knelt in front of the bed while soldiers milled around outside. The video zoomed in on him.

I hadn't been paying attention to what he was doing. On the recording, though, it was clear that he pulled something out from under the bed, something wet and rubbery. It was only visible for a second, but long enough for me to make out fingers and even part of a face.

It was skin. It was the old man's skin.

Didn't you sense a haan in that apartment? Vamp messaged.

I nodded. *Yes. Two.* I'd noticed the first when we first entered, and the second appeared just as the old man, who we were both convinced had died, sat back up.

On the recording, the old man bundled the skin up and hid it in the dresser.

Vamp, where are they now?

No one knows.

The man stepped back through the bedroom door and for a second, just a second, his shadow on the wall seemed wrong. The shape of it didn't line up. Almost, but not quite. Then it resolved, as the soldiers joined him.

The video zoomed in on the girl as a scalefly landed on the back of her hand. She raised it up, close to her face as it vibrated its iridescent wings, and stepped closer to one of the soldiers.

"Sam, everything okay?" Dragan called. My hand felt numb as I tuned into one of the feed stations. As mellow music began to pipe through, Nix's words from just before we entered the Pot came back to me.

"We were like you once. . . ."

The little girl blew out a breath, and sent the fly buzzing toward the soldier's neck as if blowing him a kiss.

"One day, you will be like us."

About the Author

James K. Decker was born in New Hampshire in 1970, and has lived in the New England area since that time. He developed a love of reading and writing early on, participating in young-author competitions as early as grade school, but the later discovery of works by Frank Herbert and Issac Asimov turned that love to an obsession.

He wrote continuously through high school, college and beyond, eventually breaking into the field under the name James Knapp, with the publication of the Revivors trilogy (*State of Decay*, *The Silent Army*, and *Element Zero*). *State of Decay* was a Philip K. Dick award nominee, and won the 2010 Compton Crook Award. *The Burn Zone* is his debut novel under the name James K. Decker.

He now lives in Massachusetts with his wife, Kim.

3 2953 01162094 7